MW01671186

Havana, Cuba. December 1958. Two brothers find themselves on opposite sides of Castro's revolution. One dark night, after rescuing of a leader of the revolt under house arrest, one brother finds himself hunted. The other, an influential attorney, must make a choice. Help his brother, placing the whole family at risk, or let Batista's forces capture him. His decision will haunt them both for the rest of their lives. How far will we go to protect those we love? Based on a true story, Incident at San Miguel takes us there.

Praise for Incident at San Miguel

"In this riveting tale of heartbreak, loss, and forgiveness, we see the Cuban Revolution in an entirely new light as several generations of a Jewish Cuban family grapple with the dreams and disillusionments of a historical moment that continues to unfold today. A wonderful collaboration between author A.J. Sidransky and storyteller Miriam Bradman Abrahams which I hope will inspire others to come forth with their Jewish-Cuban stories."
—Ruth Behar, author of *Letters from Cuba* and *An Island Called Home: Returning to Jewish Cuba*

"Alan Sidransky's new historical thriller, *Incident at San Miguel*, explores the limits of family love and loyalty during Fidel Castro's Cuban Revolution and its aftermath. He movingly describes Cuba's Jewish community whose members built lives in this island paradise, and now find themselves facing political terror. It's a place and time where their very success might lead to their destruction. Through its portrayal of a fascinating and politically opposite pair of brothers, the novel is one you'll find hard to put down."—Victoria Weisfeld, author of *Architect of Courage*

"A twisty tale of intertwined family and politics set in a time that will soon disappear from living memory. Grab it now."—Albert Tucher author of *Blood Like Rain: A Big Island Mystery* and *The Diana Andrews Mysteries*

"Sidransky transports his readers to 1959 Cuba where we meet the Cohan brothers, Aarón and Moises. They share a name and a Jewish heritage, but little else. Aarón is a lawyer and an official in Batista's government. Moises is a communist rebel and supporter of Castro. And yet, they are brothers. It takes them a lifetime to discover what that means. *Incident at San Miguel* is a compelling family saga. I highly recommend it."—Jeffrey Markowitz, author of *Hit or Miss*.

OTHER WORKS BY A J SIDRANSKY

Forgiving Máximo Rothman
Forgiving Stephen Redmond
Forgiving Mariela Camacho
Stealing a Summer's Afternoon
The Interpreter

Incident at San Miguel

By

A.J. Sidransky

A Black Opal Books Publication

GENRE: HISTORICAL/CUBAN REVOLUTION/CUBAN JEWS/ REFUGEES/BROTHERS

INCIDENT AT SAN MIGUEL

Cover Design by Transformational Concepts

Print ISBN: 978-1-953434-96-8

First Publication: MAY 2023

Published by Black Opal Books **http://www.blackopalbooks.com**

DEDICATION

For Juan and Pola Bradman

Thank you for your bravery

Foreword

Growing up in 1960s Brooklyn, the Cuban-born daughter of Cuban-Jewish refugees, my parents' experiences shaped my identity. To begin, as a native Spanish speaker, I felt quite different from my classmates, mostly children of Yiddish speaking Holocaust survivors and second generation Americans. My dad sounded charmingly like Ricky Ricardo.

Brooklyn's public schools were not the best back then. My parents valued education above all else. They chose to enroll my sister and me in Jewish day school. How I think, speak, and react today; what I cook and eat; how I communicate with my parents, my husband, grown kids, and community are a direct result of being tri-lingual and tri-cultural.

My grandparents were exiled from their own parents' cold, dangerous, shtetl life in Poland and Belarus in the 1920s and 1930s to a tropical island that welcomed them. They began with nothing but hope and a desire to survive and succeed. That success required a new language and way of living life, while retaining their heritage and customs as best as possible. With few resources they nonetheless succeeded, raising and providing for their children. Their children, my parents, knew only Cuba.

My grandparents owned their own businesses. My father and his brother attended university. My mother and her sister were raised in the Jewish community but worked in the larger society. They imagined their futures in Cuba. Little was spoken about the old country, about the epic loss of loved ones due to poverty and war, or about the intense pain of separation. My parents knew close to nothing about their grandparents' lives and fates. They've told me that like the fourth child in the Passover seder, they didn't even know how or what to ask. They deeply regret their lack of knowledge about their own personal histories. My mother had only a hint of what happened to her father's family when a letter arrived from overseas and he retreated to another room to read and weep.

In the late 1950s, when signs of intense political change and growing fears about their future in Cuba seeped into their daily lives, my parents, then in their twenties, were faced with making serious decisions. Those decisions mirrored the ones their own parents made in their youth. They would leave behind all they knew for another climate, language, and culture. They could barely imagine the enormity of what faced them. This leaving and arriving, setting down roots and then suddenly having to pull them up to survive, has been part of Jewish DNA for millennia. It is the biblical story of Abraham, Noah, Joseph, and Moses.

From my great love of reading historical fiction, I've always known that each person, each family, has a unique story to tell. It's a story from which their children and grandchildren may glean something useful. An emotion, a lesson, a way to move forward. My parents ingrained their own stories in my memory, thus creating a strong desire for me to see for myself where I was born, a place I left at the age of one, long before I could form my own memories. I imagined the world where they lived, laughed and dreamed as young people. The tropical colors and rhythms of this island unknown to me only ninety miles away from the southernmost tip of Florida. More importantly, I wanted to meet my uncle and his family on their own turf, to see the flip side of what I'd been told and what my life might have been like.

My father refused to return to Cuba. He had deep-seated

fear about his safety and by extension mine in the communist system he escaped. He insisted there was nothing for him there and it wasn't worth the risks. My aunt's stories about her wonderful first visit to Cuba when it reopened to Americans, and then reading Ruth Behar's first book about her journey to explore her own roots further ignited my desire.

After some years of coaxing, explaining that I would go anyway but preferred the option of seeing it with the nostalgia of a parent at my side, my mother's sense of curiosity won out. She generously financed my dream trip, and finally, through the advice of June Safran, a Cuba mission leader, my mom, sister, and I joined a Jewish humanitarian mission to Cuba during Chanukah, December 2008. At the time, group travel was the only legal entry for us. It required a sheaf of intricate forms, substantial fees, and plenty of red tape. The trip was led by Miri Saul, an expat who, like me, also left as a child. My father implored us not to mention his name or talk openly about our opinions.

Our family was separated by distance and politics for forty years. I treasured black and white photos of my first birthday in Havana in January 1962, taken days before my parents and I secretly fled to the United States. I didn't know much about my three first cousins, except that one had a chronic illness. The same was true of my uncle. I knew only that he was a communist idealist, had chosen to stay, and had been married twice.

In 1998, my parents relayed the nearly unbelievable news from my uncle that my first cousin—a computer programmer in Havana as I was in New York—had access to an email address at work. While he now had email, he, like most Cubans, had no outside internet news sources. I excitedly jumped on this opportunity and slowly he and I go to know each other.

I was very cautious in my questions. Anyone could be reading our correspondence. U.S.-Cuban relations were fraught with suspicion and possible danger for my cousin. He asked me to tell him about our grandparents whom he'd never met as he was born after they left Cuba, never to return.

Eduardo and his brother, Osvaldo, soon left Cuba too. Eduardo to Israel, and Osvaldo to Spain with financial support from my parents. After announcing their intent to leave Cuba, life became even more difficult for them. They risked losing their jobs, suffered from a feeling of otherness, and worried about the possibility of endangering those family members who remained.

When the Cuban government opened travel for Cuban citizens to the United States in 2001, my father sponsored his brother Salomon and Salomon's wife to spend a month in Brooklyn. My cousin Eduardo, now living in Israel and engaged to be married, timed a visit to stay with us on Long Island at that same time. My parents, sister, and I, along with my aunt and uncle, celebrated Eduardo's and Haya's civil wedding at the courthouse in downtown New York City. It was an amazing reunion, especially for me. I relished the excitement of rediscovering my long-lost family.

When I met my uncle for the first time I felt a visceral connection to him. He looked exactly like my grandfather, though way taller, and just like he did in the photo I had of him holding me as an infant in Havana, only a little older. Though we spoke little of substance, I basked in the togetherness. I knew that he felt connected to me as well. After that, we met in Cuba in 2008, and once in Israel as well.

When my uncle passed away in 2012, I grieved that so much time had been lost. I wrote a personal piece about it for Tablet Magazine. He was buried in the Jewish cemetery in Guanabacoa outside Havana. My husband and kids and I visited his grave with my aunt and cousin in 2016. My aunt, cousins, and I, continue to strengthen our connection with each email or WhatsApp. It is truly a miracle that we can do this so easily now. To date, I still don't know much about the forty years our family lived apart in radio silence. My uncle was loathe to speak openly about his experiences. When asked, he gently brushed my questions off. I understood this to be a reaction to his life under communism where one is watched closely.

My cousin Eduardo raised a beautiful family with his wife in Israel. He recently passed away, much too young, after a short difficult battle with cancer. I am grateful for the twenty-one years we shared together. His brother Osvaldo lives in Spain with his wife and children, and we hope to meet up again here or there. My aunt and a few other family members remain in Cuba.

I related my story to author A. J. Sidransky, whose books I reviewed for the Jewish Book Council. As a fluent Spanish speaker with connections to the Dominican Republic and a grandson of refugees himself, I knew he could connect emotionally to my story. As a fiction writer he could fill in the gap of so many missing years with his creative touch. He melded some of the facts of my family's time in Cuba and the difficulty of their emigration with purely fictional events and people. I am grateful for A. J.'s ability to grasp the different personality types and how each was affected by critical decisions made. I provided him with pages of interviews I did with my parents. He then visited and conducted his own detailed interviews at my parents' home and gleaned even more information than

I was able to gather. He also recorded the interviews for posterity.

I am sure that this story will offer insight into the serious hardships experienced by immigrant families and their long-term effects. I am grateful for my father's foresight and decision-making, my mother's courage and adaptability, my sister's everlasting companionship and support, and my husband's and children's love and understanding.

I sincerely hope that no reader will mistake the fictionalized parts as real. Please read the historical notes and author's notes and acknowledgments before you read the book to understand what's real and what's fiction. I ardently hope the reader will sense the fears and hopes, the desire to preserve family and identity, the need to pursue one's truth while maintaining *'shalom bayit'* - peace in one's home and heart that this story, my story, offers.

With deep love and care for my whole family I dedicate this story to my uncle Salomon and my cousin Eduardo.

'Con carino por toda mi familia, le dedidico esto para mi tío Salomon y su hijo, mi primo Eduardo'

Miriam Bradman Abrahams
October 2022
Long Beach, New York

Historical & Author's Notes

When writing historical fiction we authors have a very specific goal in mind: to transport the reader to a time and place and into the mind of a character that they themselves can't go to. The key to the experience of great historical fiction is to feel like you're there. With that in mind, we take some liberties. In the case of this book, Incident at San Miguel, there was no incident at San Miguel del Padron.

Though the inciting incident described in this book is completely fictitious, the Cuban Revolution was not. The historical personages mentioned in this book, Fidel Castro, Raul Castro, Che Guevara, and Fulgencio Batista, were real. The characters of Aaron and Moises Cohan and their wives and families are based on real people and real events, but the remainder of the characters in this book are purely fictitious.

For those who are not familiar with the Cuban Revolution, it occurred in the 1950s and culminated in the defeat of Fulgencio Batista, the dictator of Cuba, on New Year's Eve, December 31, 1958-January 1, 1959. It was led by Fidel Castro and was known as the 26 of July Movement. The beginning of the uprising is generally considered to be the attack on the Moncada Barracks on 26 July 1953.

Fidel and his brother Raul were the leaders of this movement and the government that resulted from the revolution's victory for more than sixty years. Born in Birán, near Santiago de Cuba, they were from a prosperous, land-owning family. Fidel was born in 1926, Raul in 1931.

Che Guevara, the purported architect of the socialist approach to Cuba's post-revolutionary path, was the scion of a wealthy family as well. He was born in Rosario, Argentina in 1928 and was trained as a physician. He led revolutionary movements throughout Latin America, including Bolivia where he died in 1967.

Fulgencio Batista was born in Veguita in 1901. Unlike his revolutionary antagonists, he came from a humble background. He led a revolt against the Cuban government known as the Sergeants' Revolt in 1933. Batista came to power officially in 1940, originally as a reformer. In 1952, running behind in the presidential race, he staged a coup and established himself as Cuba's supreme leader. He remained Cuba's 'President', until he was outed by Castro. He was known for his corruption, cruelty, and his connections to the American Mafia.

I have written extensively about life under fascist regimes in my previous novels. This book is my first foray into life under communist rule. I have to admit that I came into this project with a bias. I am on the left politically and I have long thought that communist regimes are judged unfairly by American observers. These observers focus on the repressive nature of communism, while rarely acknowledging its achievements in areas like education, health care, and housing.

Having traveled extensively in both communist and capitalist societies I noted the differences in how the population lived. The level of poverty I saw in Peru in 1987, for instance, far exceeded what I saw in China the previous year. With that said, during the writing of this book I traveled to Hungary, Czechia, and Slovakia with my son in September 2021 to see where my grandparents were born and to visit with family there. These distant cousins are all that's left of a family that once numbered in the hundreds throughout these countries. My family was a victim of the Nazi Holocaust. To me, fascism was the enemy and danger, not communism. It still is.

While in Budapest we visited an attraction known as the Museum of Terror. In the spirit of transparency, I should note that this museum is the brainchild of Victor Orban, the current prime minister of Hungary, and poster child for modern-day fascism. His view of Hungarian history is tailor-made to promote his view of Hungary's future. In the case of this museum, Hungary holds no responsibility for its fascist history before and during World War II. Instead, he portrays Hungary as the victim of both the Nazis and then the Soviet Union in a continuous occupation from 1944, when the Nazis invaded Hungary, through 1989, when the Soviets left and communism collapsed.

While the Museum's approach to Hungarian history is heavy handed and often over-simplified, I found this visit to be an epiphany. What I learned was that while communism and fascism may have diametrically opposed economic systems, they share identical systems of social control. There is no place within either system for free thought or expression. Individual freedoms are subjugated to the needs and desires of the state.

As in all totalitarian systems, there is always a boogeyman. In the case of the Nazis and the Hungarian Fascists in the 1930s and 1940s that boogeyman was the Jews. In the case of communist systems, including Hungary under Soviet communism and Castro's Cuba, the boogeyman is the entrepreneurial or capitalist class. In the absence of a religious, ethnic, or racial minority to blame for the nation's problems, communism points its finger at an economic class to which it ascribes the suffering of the people and the nation. Sadly, what achievements these systems may have made pale in comparison to the repression they impose on their populations through what can only be described as terror.

A. J. Sidransky
Washington Heights, New York
October 2022

Psalm 137:4

"How shall we sing the Lord's song in a strange land."

Part I
December 1958

Chapter One

The two-hour ride from Havana to Matanzas left Aarón and Beatriz dusty as they stepped off the rickety bus. Beatriz knew the way to their destination. She'd spent many weekends with Aarón's family in the six months since their engagement. Nevertheless, Aarón took her hand and led her onto a nearby street more earthen than paved. The street was cast in golden hues, the tropical sun making its inexorable descent toward the horizon accenting the brilliantly colored bougainvillea that lined it.

A city girl, a *Habanera*, Beatriz was always a little shocked at how primitive Matanzas was, though she knew she shouldn't be. Visiting here was like moving back one hundred years. Burros more typical than cars, bare feet more common than shoes or even *chancletas*, especially for children. There were *barrios* in Havana that were no better. Whole *vecindades* existed on the rooftops of buildings, which were in some ways worse, crowded and decaying.

Esther, Aarón's mother, stood on the porch of their house, a wood structure clearly more durable and more prosperous than the shacks that lined the road. The two story house featured large windows, setting it apart from most of its neighbors. A second-floor terrace over the veranda caught the breeze from the sea nearby, carrying the sweet-citrusy scent of guanabana inside. One could step from the bedrooms directly onto the terrace, a view of the Bahia de Matanzas inviting over the treetops and rooftops. The sound of *son*, tinny through radios, filtered through the air.

"*Mijo*," Esther shouted, waving. "You've brought me a surprise!"

"I told you to tell her I was coming," Beatriz whispered in Aarón's ear, her sense of her own mother's propriety overtaking the easy informality of Cuba. Their parents raised them with the sensibilities of Europe, but both she and Aarón had absorbed the nonchalance of the tropics, easily imbibed and as refreshing as coconut water.

"Nonsense," Aarón replied, pulling her a little bit faster down the road. "She loves you and she loves a surprise. What could be better?"

"I suppose," Beatriz said, smiling.

Esther enveloped Beatriz in her arms. "*Shabbos* is always better with you here," she said.

"I don't want to be a bother."

"You're never a bother. You're part of the family. Come in and sit down. I'm sure the bus was slow and bumpy."

"That it was," said Aarón, stretching his back a bit. He pulled a bouquet of birds-of-paradise from a large paper sack and handed them to his mother, enveloping her in his arms. "It's so good to see you, *mamá*."

"And you too, both." Esther reached for Beatriz's hand again and kissed it quickly and gently. "Come in, freshen up a bit. Dinner is nearly ready."

Aarón followed Beatriz through the screen door. The interior was cool, but then it was December. By August the house would be stupefyingly hot, the air still and thick with humidity. Unlike the second-floor bedrooms, the first floor didn't benefit from the sea breeze.

Aarón's eyes adjusted to the semi-darkness. The lush vegetation that surrounded the house filtered out much of the sunlight. He looked to his right to the dining room, the table set for four. Had his mother suspected he would bring Beatriz? He watched as she added another setting. Aarón looked left into the living room and the small, screened veranda behind it. On the couch sat his brother, Moises. Aarón wondered if his mother knew Moises was coming and had chosen not to tell him. Or had Moises just showed up, as he was wont to do when he needed a good meal and extras to take back with him to Havana? A half smile crept up Aarón's mouth as he imagined his brother's calculations. He didn't begrudge him their parents' generosity but found Moises's need to justify it amusing.

Moises balanced a book on his left thigh, his hand scribbling furiously on a pad balanced on his right. His glasses sat atop his head as he squinted at the pages below. He'd grown a scraggly beard since the last time Aarón saw him. Moises was deep in thought, not even raising an eyebrow to their arrival, or perhaps that was the impression he sought to give. Forever the student, even in the absence of an open university. Or perhaps the forever-student, absorbing, no, devouring, whatever knowledge that volume in his lap had to offer.

Not that Aarón was a stranger to books or to studying. He had completed his law degree some years earlier. Study was a part of his life and his work, yet he never had the compulsion for constant learning that drove Moises. Whatever it was, from the philosophy of economic systems to the mechanics of accounting, Moises approached learning like a Talmudic scholar, always with laser-like intensity. Had Aarón's parents not made the journey from Poland to Cuba that's likely what Moises would have become. Here though, he could scrutinize whatever took his fancy.

"Good *Shabbos*," Aarón called out.

Moises looked up. He smiled. "To you as well. Give me just a few minutes." He pointed at the book on his thigh. "I want to finish this."

Aarón smiled weakly. "Of course," he mumbled. "Take whatever time you need." He recognized the worn volume in Moises's lap. Marx always came first.

The soft, sensual sound of *bolero* drifted into the dining room from the radio in the kitchen. Beatriz and Esther removed the dishes from the table. Esther cooked a spectacular meal, as always. Jewish yet Cuban at the same time. The chicken soup shone with matzah balls spiced with bits of cilantro and green onion. The traditional brisket Esther's mother prepared in Poland was replaced with *ropa vieja*, spicy and succulent with tomato and peppers. This far from Havana the meat wasn't kosher. Rice was substituted for the endless potatoes of Esther's childhood. She carried a tray of *cafecitos* from the kitchen. Beatriz followed with a coconut flan on a hand-painted dish she had bought for Aarón's parents upon their first meeting.

"Would you like some brandy and a cigar?" Rafael Cohan asked his sons.

Aarón glanced at Moises awaiting his response. None came. "I'll take some brandy, *papá*," Aarón replied.

Rafael reached behind him to the mahogany credenza. He slid open its double doors revealing a mirrored bar and slipped out three cut crystal glasses. "Esther, Beatriz," he called out, "Brandy?" A yes and a no came back to him. Rafael took a fourth glass and placed it on the table as the women returned from the kitchen with plates and silverware for dessert. He opened the lid of a cedar humidor on the bottom shelf of the credenza and took out a cigar for himself. He passed it quickly under his nose, the combination of tobacco and cedar both intoxicating and soothing.

Cigars were a habit acquired here in Cuba, a self-confirmation of his success, a salve for choices he'd made despite his reluctance to accept them. He knew his life would have ended in the same ashes into which his cigar would be transformed if he had not left Poland and his parents behind. Rafael poured the brandy. Esther served the flan, passing the plates as Rafael passed the snifters. Moises accepted his without question or comment.

Rafael snipped the tip from his cigar and struck a long match, puffing at the cigar as he lit it, the flame jumping and expanding with each billow. Acrid-sweet smoke filled the space. "*Salud*," he said, raising his glass. "It's a delight to have our family here with us for *Shabbos*."

"Thank you, *papá*," both Aarón and Beatriz replied, sipping at the brandy, and tasting the flan.

"*Mamá*, this is excellent," said Beatriz. "Next time I'll come on Thursday. You can teach me to make it."

Esther touched Beatriz's hand. "Any time you want to come you're welcome. With or without my son."

Aarón laughed. "She's happy to teach you. She wants you to fatten me up a bit."

"You could use to put on a few *libras*," Esther replied.

"You're running?" asked Rafael.

"*Sí*," replied Aarón, "when I can. It's tough with my schedule, with the new job."

"And how goes your job at the cathedral of capitalism," asked Moises, breaking his silence as he finished his flan, washing it down with a long gulp of brandy, reaching for another slice.

"It goes well," Aarón said. "I have a little good news to share." He looked at Beatriz and smiled. She nodded her head. "I've received a small promotion. I'm to be counsel to the director of industrial development loans."

Rafael raised his glass again. "*Mazel Tov*!" he shouted. "We're so proud of you."

"We're ready to set a date for our wedding," said Aarón. "We want to discuss it with you before we make a final decision."

"So many plans," said Esther, taking Beatriz's hand and squeezing it.

Moises smiled. "That sounds like a big promotion. I suppose now you'll move to Miramar?"

Aarón glanced across the table to Beatriz. They both knew what Moises really meant. She told Aarón with her eyes not to respond. He smiled and nodded, almost imperceptibly. "Miramar isn't for us," she replied, placing her hand over Moises's. "We're modest people. Anyway, it's too far from my sister and mother, and from the center. If the university ever reopens I plan to continue my studies."

"No life as a lady of society for you, *hermana*?"

"No."

Moises took Beatriz's hand and kissed it. "I'm glad to hear that." He shifted himself to face Aarón across the table and raised his glass. "I'm truly happy for you. I hope you will do some good for the people in that den of thieves in which you work."

"That's my intention. We're committed to lifting the people. The government has pledged hundreds of millions to create industry, not just tourism, but all types of manufacturing."

"And who will be the vanguard of this revolution?" asked Moises, purposely choosing this term. He knew it would irritate both his father and brother. He considered whether Aarón would go for the bait he had cast with such obvious purpose. It wasn't that he doubted his brother's good intentions or sincerity. He knew Aarón had both. Rather, he believed that no amount of good intentions could overcome the corruption inherent in the current system. These millions of pesos, much of which he was sure came from the Americans through their corporate proxies, would end up lining the pockets of Batista's men. The money would never reach the people. The chance of individual Cubans benefitting, of rising above the poverty that gripped generations, was so small as to be insignificant.

Of course, the government would make a show of it. They would provide the poor relative of some loyal associate of Batista the opportunity to be the front man for a new factory or some such venture—a retail operation selling locally made clothing for example—at a business silently owned by American investors. The press, both Cuban and American, would be all over it, but the poor would remain poor. They would be even poorer when this program faded into obscurity after the money ran out, stolen by those who had the connections to abscond with it.

"The people, of course," said Aarón. "I will be in charge of vetting the applicants and distributing the funds. I intend to keep the process clean. No bribes, no corruption."

"Good luck with that," Moises retorted.

Aarón leaned across the table. "We are a true and honorable people, brother. Look what our father created here out of nothing. We can create a paradise."

"I agree," said Rafael.

"All it takes is one honest man," Aarón said.

"And so said God to Abraham about Sodom and Gomorrah." Moises smiled, scanning the faces around the table, all outwardly unfazed by either his humor or rabbinic response. "Are you that honest man?"

"Yes," replied Aarón. "I believe I am."

Chapter Two

Moises watched Ana Teresa as she fed her plants small sips of water. Her gauzy nightgown fluttered in the gentle breeze. She hummed absentmindedly, offering the plants words of care and encouragement as she nurtured them. Moises loved to watch her, especially when she was unaware of it. She was at her most natural, her most unguarded. At these moments she let herself show her innermost beauty, her softness, her ability to care for the smallest of things. It wasn't that she didn't show how much she cared when she knew others were watching, but rather at those times she presented herself differently, as a leader, as a vanguard of the people.

They met at a political rally. He volunteered to work the crowd, to hand out literature, to encourage the people to join the march to revolution. She was one of the speakers. She entranced him, not only by her beauty but by her commitment. When she spoke, she spoke for all women. She spoke of their futures as equal partners in the new world. No more servitude to men. They would contribute equally to Cuba's future. Cuba would bring freedom to the world. Women would rise up. They, in turn, would bring that freedom to their daughters and their mothers.

The curves of her bare body were revealed through her

thin linen gown. Light shot through it as in a Renaissance painting. The gown shifted upward each time she bent forward to whisper to her plants, to feed them a little bit of encouragement and life-giving water, exposing her buttocks and beyond.

Her body brought him much pleasure. He hoped he brought her the same, or more. She was a little older than him, three years, but her life had been much different than his. She learned to be a woman at an age when he was still a boy in short pants. The sight of her thrilled him as did the softness of her skin and the humanness of her scent.

"*Te quiero, mi amor*," he said, from the bed, his hand under his cheek, propping him up.

She turned her head and smiled, her back still to him, the luscious curves of her body contorting pleasantly. "How long have you been watching me?" she asked, placing the watering can on the sill. She took the few feet to the bed, almost gliding, never for one second self-conscious. She lay down on its edge and caressed Moises's cheek. "I love you, too," she purred into his ear, brushing her lips against his.

Moises marveled at her sensuality. She was a chameleon, as soft and carnal as a summer's night, or as powerful and dangerous as a hurricane. He returned her kiss, harder and more demanding, telling her what he wanted.

She quickly shifted away, her smile still on her lips. "You came in very late last night," she said, pulling her hair back, slipping a kerchief around it.

The prior night flashed through Moises's mind much more quickly than it happened. His father's factory foreman was driving to Havana at midnight. He had business to transact the next day. And he wanted to spend the night with his girlfriend. Rafael had given him the company truck. Moises returned with him. When he crept into their bed, Ana Teresa welcomed him with her body. They fell asleep in each other's arms a little while later, not a word having passed between them.

"I got a ride back. I didn't want to stay. I missed you too much."

She kissed him quickly on the tip of his nose. "And how are your parents?" she teased.

Moises knew what she was really asking. "They're well."

Ana Teresa returned to the window and continued watering her plants, slowly and deliberately. Sunlight crept in through the window now, bright on the walls, reflecting the paint. It cast a turquoise hue through the room. "You still haven't told them about me?"

Moises sighed. "*Verdad, no*."

She kept her back to him. *Danzon* drifted through the window. Havana was rarely without music. "It's because of my politics, isn't it? Your father wouldn't approve." Ana Teresa chuckled.

Moises remained silent. He didn't want to engage in this discussion.

Ana Teresa put down the watering can, turned to face him. Now streaks of sunlight seared through the fabric of her nightgown, rendering it opaque, emphasizing the shape of her breasts. "Yet, he tolerates your socialism."

"You know that's not it. He thinks I'll outgrow it. He believes it's a fad, a pastime. He believes once I finish my apprenticeship and go to work for him, I will leave the struggle behind."

"Then what is it?"

Moises sat on the edge of the bed, his head in his hands. He rubbed his eyes and took in a deep breath. *"Necesito un cafecito, por favor, amor."*

"*Pues*," replied Ana Teresa, "tell me the truth amor, and I will prepare one for you." She struck a pose, smiling. "Or is it that you are just using me? If that's it, you know, it's all right. We both get what we want and need from this relationship. You know, to each according to her needs, from each according to his abilities."

Moises stood. He covered the few steps to the window quickly. He took Ana Teresa in his arms and kissed her softly. "Why do you torture me?"

"I only want the truth."

Moises sighed. He led her by the hand to the far side of their room to the small table. He sat down wrapping his arms around her waist, kissing her stomach. "Please, make me *un cafecito*."

"Por supuesto," she replied, pushing his hands away. She turned and filled the pot with coffee from a small, unadorned, waxed-paper bag.

Moises took a cigarette from Ana Teresa's pack on the tiny table. He lit it quickly with a wooden match he struck against the chair. "I promise, you will meet them. When the time is right."

"When will that be?"

"Before my brother's wedding."

Ana Teresa turned. "They've set a date?"

"Yes. He received a promotion."

Ana Teresa nodded. "How nice for him, and for…what is her name?"

"Beatriz."

"*Sí*, Beatriz."

Ana Teresa placed the tiny demitasse cup in front of Moises. He sipped the warm, thick liquid. She had sweetened it as he liked, the bitterness of the coffee balanced by a little sugar, yet still there.

"Why is this so important to you? I haven't met your

family, either."

Ana Teresa laughed. "No, you haven't."

The room dissolved into silence. "It's your religion," Moises blurted, drowning the last syllable of "religion" with the final gulp of his *cafecito*.

"I have no religion," Ana Teresa said, sitting across from him now. "And neither do you." She leaned forward, her hands clasped in front of her, her breasts nearly tumbling out of her nightgown, the large brown areolas peeking out above the lace stitching at the neckline.

"I know that," Moises replied. He touched the tips of his fingers to hers, then slid his hand over them. "But that's not how they see it. Let me phrase this a different way. You're not Jewish."

Ana Teresa leaned back in the chair. "Is that all?"

Moises entered the darkened room in the basement of an apartment building in La Habana Vieja. The lights were off, but who knew why? Perhaps Students for an Equitable Society hadn't paid their rent. Or perhaps the landlord hadn't paid the electric company. Or perhaps the electric lines had failed again. Regardless, the room was warm and airless, the blades of the various fans scattered about the room idle. The windows were open to the street, nearly five feet above the floor. Candles flickered on the desks providing a weak, eerie illumination.

Marcos Abreu waved from the back of the room. His face was lit from below by the candle in front of him. His scraggly beard caught by the candle's flame made him look like a ghoul in a Hollywood movie. Marcos wanted to look like Fidel, but in fact bore no resemblance to him at all, save the unkempt beard. "*Compañero*," he called out to Moises. "Come here. See what we've done!"

Moises walked through the crowded space slipping between the tightly packed tables, piles of pamphlets, and handbills stacked haphazardly everywhere. Marcos grabbed him by the shoulder, handing him one. It was new, different from the rest. It was in color. Moises grinned, shifting his gaze to a table behind Marcos. On it sat the printing press Moises had salvaged from the pile of industrial refuse behind his Tío Avi's printing business. His father's friend, Abraham Silverstein, the man he had known all his life as Tío Avi, had purchased the latest in American printing presses in anticipation of an exclusive government contract. Tío Avi had the right connections, Moises's father had said. He would make a killing.

It was from Tío Avi that Moises was learning the mysteries of accounting. A hotbed of revolution, the University of Havana had been closed for years. Moises took courses in philosophy, economics, and politics at a private American university. But he needed an education in business, or so his father said.

Rafael, Moises's father, treated his socialism like an elephant in the corner of the room. Moises went along with the charade. His education in business and Tío Avi's practical tutorials gave him additional clarity into the evils of the current system.

When Tío Avi's workmen removed the old printing press, Moises took Marcos and two other *compañeros* in the middle of the night to the rear of Tío Avi's store. They carted away the discarded pieces of the old press and reassembled them in the basement.

Moises was always amazed by these boys from the *campo*. They could fix anything, make anything work, often with odd parts and pieces saved from God knows what.

Next to the press, covered in various colors of ink, stood Esperanza, Marcos's girlfriend. The wavy tresses of her long, lustrous, black hair framed her face, visible even in the semi-darkness. Her smile confirmed their success. "So?" she said. "Who should we thank? Your *tío*? You? Or the boys who put this back together?"

Moises smiled. "All." He examined the handbill. Esperanza had done excellent work. The time, date, and location of the demonstration stood out in jet-black letters in the middle of the page. Underneath was an image of Fidel in red, his beard wild, his fist raised. At the bottom in huge, yellow, block letters rimmed with black, the word, *LEVANTESE*, ARISE! "How many have you printed?" he asked.

"Five hundred," Marcos replied. He pointed to a large, less than orderly pile on the table in the corner. "We will distribute these first. We can print more as we need them." Esperanza stepped next to Marcos. She took his hand, entwining their arms.

"We are prepared then?" said Moises.

"Yes," Esperanza replied. "The police are sure to be there, in force."

"I would expect so."

Marcos smiled. "That will occupy them while we complete our main objective."

Moises nodded. He was entirely comfortable with the objective Marcos referred to but not with the plan. It was critical to break Professor Edgardo Alarcón out of house arrest and spirit him out of the country. His voice was essential to the Movement. It was Alarcón's tutelage that brought Moises to the cause. But, if this was the only way, so be it. "Hopefully, this will be a success. Has a team been chosen?"

Marcos glanced at Esperanza.

"Excuse me," she said, releasing Marcos's hand. She moved quickly away from his gaze, knowing this information wasn't for her ears. Moises's eyes followed her as she walked into the shadows.

"Yes," Marcos replied, Esperanza out of earshot. "Luis will announce it tonight, at our meeting."

"Who do you think he will choose?"

"You."

Moises felt himself blush. He was both flattered and frightened by the prospect. Mostly, he was self-conscious, concerned that Marcos and the others would think Luis showed him preference for Ana Teresa's sake, rather than confidence in him for this mission. In truth, Moises knew he played an important role in the organization, but his skills had more to do with logistics and planning than with executing revolutionary actions. He knew how to fill a need—like finding a printing press—but breaking someone out of heavily guarded house arrest wasn't his forte, though the idea of it thrilled him. "Why would you think that?"

"You've earned it," Marcos said, pointing to the press.

Moises chuckled. "I had inside information."

"Nevertheless, you are to be rewarded. Besides, who knows Professor Alarcón better? You've been to his villa many times. We need that knowledge for this mission to be successful."

Moises smiled. "We shall see." He looked at the clock on the wall behind Marcos. He had a meeting in thirty minutes.

"How is Ana Teresa?" Marcos asked.

"She is well."

"Will we see her tonight?"

Moises thought the question odd as Ana Teresa was the vice-chairman of their group. "Of course."

Marcos smiled. "Good." He handed Moises a pile of leaflets "Perhaps you can dispose of some of these. In places where the police will be sure to see them."

"Happily," Moises said. "To our success."

Moises met Ana Teresa in a tiny park near the grounds of the University of Havana at eight o'clock. They stopped at a food cart nearby. He treated her to dinner, compliments of the money his mother slipped into his pocket when he was leaving. They ate *chicharrones*—fried pork rinds—with *tostones* and *yuca*. His parents had warned him and his brother never to eat food from the street carts for fear of becoming sick. Ana Teresa had introduced him to these foods, and now he loved them.

They drank from huge cups filled with sugarcane juice, *guarapo frio*. The sweet and salty combination of the *chicharrones* and the juice was both satisfying and refreshing. Afterward they walked hand in hand to the meeting in Luis's apartment nearby.

Luis lived on the second floor of an old mansion with his brother and sister, converted to apartments when the rich moved on to newer neighborhoods. Its owners now lived in Miramar. He lived on the second floor, which featured a veranda. Luis often mentioned that the main room was bigger than the shack they had grown up in back in the *campo*. What once was a huge living room overlooking the street and front yard was permanently converted to a meeting hall, chairs lined up in tight rows.

The police kept regular surveillance. While they normally fell asleep in the rear seat of their patrol car parked directly across the street, they paid more diligent attention on nights such as this when Luis held court in front of his revolutionaries. The lights in the room were ablaze, his voice carried into the street below. What the police might have suspected but didn't seem to know was that Luis spoke in code. The information they gleaned from his exhortations to his guerillas was meant specifically for police consumption. The real secrets were passed in whispers in private or were encoded in terms and words the troops understood but were meant to deceive others who might be listening.

Moises and Ana Teresa climbed the formerly elegant stairs to the second floor. The door to the apartment was open. Ana Teresa entered first. Moises loved to watch her transformation as she arrived anywhere. Something about an audience changed her. Her chin lifted like a queen appearing before her subjects. In return, those in the room turned to her and smiled, many calling out to her, "Ana Teresa, *Bienvenidos*! We've been waiting for you."

Moises followed after her as always, receiving greetings as well, but to his ears not with the same enthusiasm. He'd felt like this all his life, something of an afterthought, but with Ana Teresa he didn't mind. He was content to bask in her reflection, to share her, because when they were alone, she was his entirely.

"*Bienvenidos*," Ana Teresa replied, waving back. She crossed the room to the table at the front near the door to the kitchen. Moises took a seat at the end of the third row by the balcony next to Marcos and Esperanza, embracing both. Luis, seated at the table, rose. He kissed Ana Teresa on each cheek and then whispered something in her ear. She laughed and took her seat next to him.

"*Atención*," Luis said, banging the small, chipped, wooden hammer that acted as his gavel on the top of two books protecting the table from its force. He turned to the kitchen and gestured, several others quickly taking their seats. The room was nearly filled. "Our most valued vice chairwoman is here! We can begin."

Ana Teresa feigned celebrity, nodding her head in the regal style and suppressing a laugh. Those assembled responded with mock applause, laughing as well. Moises loved to watch this, to watch her. The light from the crystal chandelier hanging in the exact center of the ceiling—so out of place in the current setting—was stark against the walls and the faces of those assembled.

"Quiet down," Luis called out. "I call this meeting to order," he lowered his voice and himself into the chair next to Ana Teresa. He reached for the pile of papers in front of him and handed her a sheet. "The vice chairwoman will read the manifesto and we will sing our anthem."

Ana Teresa stood and cleared her throat. She read out their creed clearly and loudly, its promise to bring justice to the Cuban people. To free them from the tyranny of the oligarchs. Everyone stood. They sang the proud anthem of their movement. At the end, they shouted in unison, "*pa'lante*," forward.

"I call this meeting to order," Luis shouted, as his gavel landed with a loud bang.

Luis rambled through his agenda. Reports on their various activities. How many people their soup kitchen had served, how many notebooks were donated for poor children, and what measures were taken to force landlords to make the hovels for which they overcharged habitable. He even mentioned, quite loudly, the name of a sympathetic police officer who passed along information on how well their own misinformation was working. The crowd chuckled at this news. The listening cops would leap on this unreliable intelligence. Maintaining charades was hard work. One had to remain attentive to everything said and heard. Some thirty minutes later he called

Esperanza for her report on the upcoming demonstration.

Esperanza walked to the lectern next to the table. She flipped her hair back and revealed a huge smile of perfect, white teeth, gleaming against her full, red lips. A current ran through Moises's body. If he wasn't with Ana Teresa… He glanced at Marcos. No matter the level of his desire, he would never betray a fellow revolutionary, especially over a woman.

"*Compañeros*," Esperanza said, "I am glad to report that we are ready for next Saturday. We must give special thanks to Moises," she gestured, "and to Paolino and Raul."

She didn't need to mention for what. The audience knew who had obtained the color press and who had rebuilt it. The police would speculate on what this recognition was for. They were good at spinning conspiracies and plots. "We shall meet at the central plaza at the University at seven o'clock. We have a special surprise for you. A speaker of international note and a champion of our cause!" While this was met with murmurs from those assembled in the room, Moises knew it was misinformation; meant for the police. "Please take some posters with you as you leave tonight."

Esperanza returned to her seat as Luis returned to the lectern. "Next, I want to announce the formation of a new committee for outreach to organize youth in the *barrios*. We will start in Parque Central." Everyone in the room knew this was the moment they were waiting for. Luis would announce the names of those who would break Professor Alarcón out of house arrest.

"The governing committee has chosen the following six *compañeros* to organize the master committee which will oversee the initial outreach and then extend it to other *barrios*." Luis drew a breath. He smiled and let the first name out slowly. “Our committed vice deputy Ana Teresa Colon.” Luis hesitated a moment before continuing, assessing the crowd. “Marcos Abreu will be her vice deputy. Along with them,” Luis continued, “Rosario Martinez, Clarita Urroa, and Maelo Dos Santos.” Luis hesitated again as the crowd reacted, smiling, whispering, and shaking the hands of those chosen. “And finally,” Luis said, looking directly at Moises, “the most dedicated man among us, Moises Cohan!”

Moises’s stomach knotted. He was dedicated. But was he dedicated enough to carry a gun?

Chapter Three

Aarón settled into his desk chair. His promotion carried with it not only more money and more responsibility but a more elegant office. The office sat in the corner of the fifth floor of the National Bank of Cuba overlooking the street and the plaza beyond. His office, paneled in rich mahogany, gave the impression of both power and wisdom. He questioned how much real power he had, and how much wisdom he had acquired to date.

Along the wall opposite the windows was a bookcase that ran the length of the room. Alma, his secretary, had already moved his books from his old office. Upon returning from lunch, he would buy her some flowers as a thank you. Aarón had fought hard to hire Alma and then to bring her with him to the new position. A woman secretary was rare in this world of men. He noted her intelligence and ability the first time he met her. To sentence her to the life of a salesgirl in one of Havana's department stores fawning over the vacuous wives of the rich and powerful would have been a travesty.

The green leather of the chair behind the massive wood desk was supple and smooth to Aarón's touch. The chairs' previous owner, his mentor Alejandro Martinez, had retired a month earlier. His endorsement and campaign on Aarón's behalf had been critical in winning him the position.

There was plenty of competition for the job. Every one of the bank's directors wanted to place his own man in the chair. The position provided access to capital, the lifeblood, and lubricant of the system. Aarón believed Martinez had gained support for his appointment exactly because he was retiring. The likelihood of graft and abuse was greatly reduced if Aarón was beholden to no one.

Tucked into the fold where the chair's back and seat met was a small envelope. Aarón reached for it. Within was a handwritten note from Martinez congratulating Aarón and assuring him that his mentor would be made proud. Aarón smiled.

Shortly after nine o'clock the phone rang. It was the Deputy Director of National Investments, Diego Pimental. Pimental had pushed his own deputy for the job. In the end he joined with Martinez, an alliance of competing forces. "Congratulations and welcome," came his high, raspy voice through the handset. "I wanted to be the first to welcome you to your new position."

"Thank you, sir," Aarón replied. "I am ready."

"Very well, then. Let's meet this afternoon to begin mapping out our program."

Though not surprised, Aarón was caught a little off guard. This was his first day. He had yet to put his thoughts on paper, let alone a proper proposal, but nonetheless, this was how the game was played. "Of course," he replied. Putting Pimental off would give the wrong impression. "Your office?"

Pimental hesitated. "No, I'll come to yours. Four o'clock?"

Aarón swallowed. "Of course." The line clicked off

before Aarón could say goodbye. “Alma,” he called out. A moment later Alma’s slight, thin frame appeared from behind the opaque glass panel in the heavy, wood door.

“*Sí, señor*,” she said as she slipped into the room. She stood formally, a stenographer’s pad in her hand.

Aarón gestured to one of the plush leather chairs in front of his desk. They were a far cry from the hard, wooden seats that had graced his previous office. Alma sat across from him. The fabric of her black dress crawled up her leg as she settled into the chair exposing the white skin of her knee. She pulled it back down with her right hand.

“We are to have a visitor this afternoon.”

Alma looked at Aarón quizzically. “Who? We’ve just arrived. You need to settle in.”

“Pimental,” Aarón replied.

“That was quick.”

“Yes, but not entirely unexpected.”

“What shall I do?”

“Three things. First, arrange for coffee and some pastries. He likes to eat.”

Alma smiled at Aarón’s remark. “Guava pastry?”

“That would be fine. Second, call Hector Arenas and tell him I need him here immediately. And third, bring me that proposal from Batista’s office about his latest economic plan.”

“The one we received last week?”

“Yes. Can you work through the day, today? I need to present Pimental with something this afternoon at four.”

“Of course.”

Aarón was seated at his desk reviewing the proposal he and Hector scribbled out in less than three hours. Alma typed it in record time. Two pairs of cufflinks sat in the marble ashtray on the corner of Aarón’s desk. They had removed their jackets and rolled up their sleeves against the midday heat. The office was warm despite the breeze that came through the open windows, subtly ruffling the papers on Aarón's desk. The sounds of the street floated in as well. Aarón nodded as he read the brief. "You've phrased this very well, Hector. Better than I could have myself."

"Thank you, sir. I hope this helps."

"Certainly. We must make it clear to Pimental that according to the rules set down in the President's plan and the funding rules set in the law, targets must be met and transparency maintained. If we are ever to help our people, this is the only way."

"Do you think Pimental will go along?"

"I'm trying to leave him no choice, discreetly."

Hector smiled. "You are brave."

The phone rang twice, a signal from Alma that Pimental was on his way. Aarón looked at the clock on his desk, a replica of an old timepiece from a Spanish trading ship. It was reportedly a gift to Martinez from Batista himself. Five minutes to four. Pimental was nothing if not prompt, in a most un-Cuban way. He and Hector rolled down their sleeves, reached for their cufflinks, and donned their jackets just as Alma tapped gently against the glass door. Pimental's large, rotund frame loomed behind her as she entered. She carried a small tray with a plate of guava pastries and tiny cups of espresso.

"Good afternoon, Deputy Minister," Aarón said, reaching for Pimental's hand as he rounded his desk. He gestured to the leather sofa opposite as Alma placed the tray on the ornately carved mahogany coffee table.

"Will you need me to take notes, sir?" Alma asked.

"No, thank you. I'll ring if I need anything…" And to Pimental. "Do you know my assistant?" presenting Hector.

"Yes," Pimental replied, sliding himself into the corner of the couch without offering his hand to Hector. Instead, he reached for one of the tiny pastries and popped it into his mouth. "Nice to see you again, Hector," he mumbled through the pastry, his mouth still full.

"And you too, sir," Hector replied, handing Pimental a copy of the proposal he and Aarón finished reviewing only moments earlier.

Pimental brushed crumbs from his tie. "Not wasting any time, are we," he said, perusing the freshly typed pages.

"Well, it's late in the day, sir," said Aarón. "We don't want to keep you. It was very kind of you to come for a visit with us so quickly. We didn't want to disappoint." Aarón stopped himself. He was aware of how nervous he sounded. He wished he could take back the last two minutes or so.

Pimental focused on the proposal, quiet for a long moment that seemed to stretch into eternity. He turned the page of the proposal and reached for a cup of espresso and a second piece of pastry. "Aren't you going to join me?" he said. "The *cafecitos* are getting cold."

Aarón glanced at Hector. "Of course," Both he and Hector picked up their cups by their dainty handles.

"Very…concise," Pimental said, placing the proposal on the coffee table.

"Is it in accordance with what you anticipate for this program?" Aarón asked.

"For the most part, yes. It reflects the president's position." Pimental smiled. He rummaged through the inside of his jacket. "Hector?"

"Yes, sir."

"It seems I've left my notes on my desk. Could you go up to my office and bring them? Eduardo, my assistant, will help you."

Aarón nodded at Hector. He could have sent Alma but knew this to be a ploy to get Hector out of the room.

"Of course, sir," Hector replied, slipping out quietly.

Pimental waited for the door to close then smiled at Aarón. He reached for the last of the guava pastries and took a bite. This time he chewed and swallowed before speaking. "Aarón, it is so good to see you here…in this office."

"Thank you, sir. As I said, I'm delighted and humbled to be here."

Pimental pushed himself forward a bit on the couch, his stomach protruding, stressing the buttons of his shirt. "I think as a friend I need to offer some words of advice."

"Of course. I welcome any suggestions."

He pointed to the proposal. "This is very, shall we say, patriotic. Your dedication to the growth and welfare of the economy and the nation are both obvious and commendable."

Aarón listened. His legal training taught him that listening was often more important than responding.

"But we have to be…pragmatic."

"Well, of course…"

"Keep in mind how our society works, and how you got here. You'll need friends to stay in this office. You understand how to make friends? And retain them?"

"Yes," Aarón replied. He hadn't expected Pimental to be this direct.

"The President's wish is to help the people. At the same time, we are faced with a growing insurgency in the provinces. We need to be seen as making progress for the people quickly. The most efficient way to do that is through those we trust." Pimental smiled. "The benefits of the President's program as enacted by you will be most effectively executed by our friends."

Aarón felt himself trapped. He should have put Pimental off. "I support the President's policies, completely."

"Then I trust you will consider his proven methods in executing this new program. Both he and I want to see you succeed."

Aarón carried his jacket on his arm as he strolled slowly through the streets on his way home. While his first day as Deputy Director of Economic Development went smoothly, it was much more intense than he expected. He considered what to do about Pimental's suggestions. Were they thinly veiled threats or a strong suggestion for the benefit of Aarón's career? It depended entirely on how one viewed Pimental's own position within the hierarchy.

Aarón spied a flower seller on the next corner. She called out to the passersby aimlessly. Most lacked the money for a modest meal, let alone fresh-cut flowers. They were as poor as she, and she knew that. Rarely did they offer her more than a smile, a nod, and a greeting in the warm evening light. Occasionally, one stopped and handed her a few *centavos* for a single cut bloom of orange birds-of-paradise or a purple gladiola. He reached into his pocket and pulled out several *pesos*.

"*Buenas tardes*," he said.

The flower seller, an old woman, smiled at him. She wore a long, formerly white skirt and a flowered blouse which exposed the weathered skin of her arms. "*Buenas tardes*," she replied, her smile revealing ivory teeth.

Aarón pointed to both the birds-of-paradise and the gladiolas, "mix them for me. My fiancé loves them both."

The flower seller laid out a sheet of newspaper. Batista's likeness graced the page, as it did most days. She deftly picked the fullest blooms and placed them gently on the paper, careful not to damage the delicate petals. The sharp contrast between orange and purple melded into a panoply of color as she wrapped the paper around the stems and fastened them with a small piece of twine. She handed the bouquet to Aarón. He slipped some coins into her hand. She weighed them in her palm, shaking them gently, making a tingling sound. She opened her hand and glanced at them quickly. "*Gracias, señor*, may *el todopoderoso* bless you, *y tu novia*."

Aarón smiled and nodded his head. He continued on, passing a small street that led to the University a few blocks away. He stopped and considered whether Alejandro Martinez would still be at his office. Though he had retired from the bank he retained an office in a building that used to house the law faculty at the University. It was commandeered by Batista's henchmen when the University of Havana closed in 1956, but Martinez, as an official in the government, was able to keep his office. Perhaps, Aarón thought, he should seek his counsel.

He turned quickly to the right and walked down the little street. Children played in the corners in front of the apartment buildings and ground-floor stores. Sound surrounded him in this small, narrow space, the only opening, the sky. Music, laughter, and the calls of mothers to their children, echoed off the buildings. He thought of his own childhood in a small mountain town in central Cuba before they moved to Matanzas when he was ten. His mother's calls to return home late in the afternoon mirrored those he heard now, one mother calling out for her son, also named Aarón, just as his mother had done for him. There was something eternal about Cuba. Something that always comforted and never changed. Something that made him forget the heat of the day and the weight of its poverty. He had risen above it and so could the nation.

As he approached the end of the conduit that was this world, he spotted the stairs that led to the silenced University. He would seek Martinez's counsel.

Alejandro Martinez smiled. "Are those lovely flowers for me?"

Aarón laid them on Martinez's desk and chuckled. "For Beatriz. I'll see her later this evening."

"And how is your lovely fiancé?"

"She is well, very well."

"Have you set a date for your wedding?"

Martinez's question drew Aarón away from more serious thoughts. "Yes," he smiled. We are planning for late March. I hope you will be there."

"I will clear my calendar of all else," Martinez said, checking the leather-bound calendar book on his desk jokingly. "What a pleasant surprise that you stopped by. I wasn't intending to be here tonight. I'm doing some research for my new book. Amalda is having a late dinner party. I won't have time or place to do it at home with guests there."

"My good fortune." Aarón hesitated a moment. "I want to say up front that I hope I'm not putting you in an uncomfortable position by coming to you about this. I know we discussed my independence after your retirement from the bank. I expected this, but not so soon."

Martinez reached for the cigar box on the edge of his expansive desk. He offered one to Aarón.

"No, thank you," Aarón said. "Pimental wasted no

time."

Martinez raised his eyebrow. "No? How did he pose it?"

"He encouraged me to be loyal to the President. To be the conduit of his wishes for the people." Both men laughed.

"Could he be more transparent?" Martinez said. He clipped the end from his cigar and lit it with a gold lighter engraved with his initials

"Unlikely. What would you suggest I do?"

"Nothing, right now. It's too soon. Tell him you will submit a draft of the program and the requirements for applicants that will be to his liking before you make it public."

Aarón looked at Martinez slightly askance. He expected him to suggest that he stay away from Pimental. Martinez took a deep puff on the cigar, its thick, acrid smoke filling the space between them. For Aarón, it was the smell of Cuba, earthy, honest about itself, just the same as its people.

"You're a bit surprised by my suggestion?" Martinez chuckled. "The first thing Pimental will do is turn the draft over to his lackeys, his front men. They will contact you shortly thereafter. They are rough amateurs. You'll know who his allies are and then we can find their weaknesses and duplicities. You'll have the upper hand over Pimental."

Aarón considered Martinez's words. It was the plan of a man with cutthroat political savvy, something necessary in the world of Cuban politics. It was what brought Martinez from the position of the third son of an obscure minor landholder to become a Minister of Economics.

Chapter Four

The night was warm and damp, more so than usual for the time of year. Moises huddled with his co-conspirators under the trees at the edge of the garden of Professor Alarcón's house in San Miguel del Padron. The scratching of crickets broke the silence. Unlike the *barrios* of central Havana, San Miguel, with its *fincas* and walled estates, was the fantasy of tropical life written about in American novels.

"We will split into three groups," Ana Teresa whispered.

She pointed to two uniformed men at the foot of the steps that led to the veranda and the double doors into the house. The usual force of four at the front door and two more at the front gate was cut in half in response to the large demonstration at the University. "Rosario and Maelo, you will take them, quietly." She handed Rosario two rags and a bottle of ether.

"I'd rather they have machetes," said Marcos.

Ana Teresa breathed deeply, glaring at him. Her demeanor changed in the tiniest of moments. The sultry thinker, the philosopher of Cuba's discontent, disappeared. The commander of men arrived and took control. "An act like that would dishonor the Movement," she said. "They are slaves to the system. We are for the people. They are of the people, too."

"We can't take a chance that they will be able to identify us. Any of us."

"We have no choice. Alarcón is too important," Ana Teresa replied, her tone steely. "We've discussed this before. It's a chance we'll have to take. These are our orders." She shifted her gaze from Marcos to Maelo and Rosario, softening her eyes.

Maelo looked at Rosario for confirmation. "We understand, *compañero*," he whispered to Ana Teresa. "We must do whatever is necessary." Rosario nodded, acquiescing.

Ana Teresa's gaze shifted to Moises. At times like this, her determination frightened him. "After Rosario and Maelo drug the guards, you will make your way quietly up to the second floor." She took a pistol from the sack she placed earlier at her feet and handed it to Moises along with a black cloth blindfold, a muslin rag, and lengths of cord. Moises reached for the muzzle of the gun and noted how cold the steel felt in the warm night. He slipped it nervously into the rear of his pants, held close to his body by his belt.

"Clarita, you will follow Moises up the stairs. Stay hidden until he reaches the second floor. There will be one guard at the top of the stairs. Moises, you must pull your revolver and hold him. Clarita, you will come up behind him and bind his hands."

"What if he calls for help?" Clarita asked.

"He may, but the other guard is way in the back in Alarcón's study. Our source at the police station told us they only have four men here tonight. Our propaganda worked. They expect Fidel himself to show up at the demonstration. By the time the guard in the study can get to you, you should have the first guard bound, tied, and gagged. You can use him as a hostage."

Clarita reached out nervously for the small pistol Ana Teresa offered her. "*Por la revolución,*" she mumbled.

The four watched as Rosario and Maelo slipped stealthily away into the inky darkness. The quiet rustle of the bushes caught the ear of one of the guards. He ticked his head to the left, then whispered something to his partner. The partner laughed and sat down on the step to the veranda, pulling a pack of cigarettes from his shirt pocket offering one to his jumpy associate. The nervous guard waved him off, searching the darkness for the presence he felt close by but couldn't see. The sharp scent of tobacco wafted across the lawn in the direction of Moises and his accomplices as they waited for Rosario and Maelo to disarm the men.

Rosario appeared at the edge of the veranda. Maelo stood a half step behind in the shadows. Rosario signaled to Maelo to come in front of him and pointed to the second guard still standing by the step surveying the darkness. With the stealth of panthers and the synchronization of a *pas de deux* they grabbed both simultaneously, covering their mouths with ether-soaked rags stifling any shouts that would alert those inside. With the harmony of experienced dancers, they released the guards' limp bodies onto the wet grass and bound them. They pulled the unconscious men to the edge of the bushes, grabbed their guns, and then crept cautiously to the front gate of the property.

Moises and Clarita emerged from the bushes and took the two steps to the veranda. Moises opened the screened door gently. He entered carefully and light of step, leery of the squeaky, old floorboards. He held the door with two fingers until he felt its resistance lessen as Clarita's tiny hand transferred its weight.

Moises took the stairs slowly, two at a time. He reached for the pistol. Sweat permeated the thin cotton fabric of his shirt under his arms and around his neck. He sensed wetness in his palms as well as he slid his left hand up the polished wood banister. His heart raced. He paused for a moment and turned. Clarita was three steps behind him. She nodded, catching his gaze. She mouthed *pa'lante*, forward. Her silent encouragement filled Moises with purpose. He was capable of more than he thought, more than anyone gave him credit for.

At the top of the stair, he spotted the guard, a middle-aged man in a uniform much too small for him. His stomach protruded, straining the buttons of his shirt. He was asleep in a chair, cap tilted back on his head. This was a welcome, unexpected surprise. A laconic *bolero* played from a radio on a small table, filling the space around him.

Moises took the last step from the stairway onto the second floor. The parlor of the exquisite house—one he had visited many times and knew like his own—lay in front of him. He turned to find Clarita crouched at the last stair. He placed his finger over his lips. She nodded and handed him the gag. He stepped toward the sleeping man, his mouth open, snoring gently.

The sleeping man's eyes opened in terror as he felt Moises's hand settle on his face, the nose of the revolver between his eyes. Moises was surprised at how easy it was. "Don't make any noise and you'll be fine," he whispered. The guard nodded in the affirmative. "Get up," said Moises, emboldened. "Put your hands up over your head."

The guard did as he was instructed. Clarita came forward from behind Moises and bound the cop's hands. She removed his gun from its holster and placed it on the table next to the radio before slipping a black sack over his head. "What good luck that he was sleeping," she said.

"Yes, sometimes fate plays a hand."

Clarita smiled. "Now what would our *compañeros* think if they knew we believed in luck and fate? All events are planned and executed by us, ourselves, aren't they?"

For a very brief moment, Moises thought of his parents' belief in *bashert*, the Jewish concept that sometimes, some things, are meant to be. Who knows? Whether it was luck or the result of human habit—in this case the guard's laziness and disinterest—the cosmos had worked in their favor.

"Well done," came Ana Teresa's voice from the stairs behind them.

"Thank you," Moises replied.

Marcos muscled his way in front of Ana Teresa. He stood in the doorway separating the parlor from the landing and pulled a worn piece of paper from his pocket. Moises recognized it as the floor plan of the house he had drawn for the operation. Marcos examined it, his eyes darting back and forth between the paper and the room, settling on the hallway at the far-left corner. He nodded to Moises and pointed at the paper with his pistol.

"Yes," Moises whispered, "down that hallway."

Marcos nodded back. "You follow me and Ana Teresa," he said in a low, bellicose tone, more commander than *compañero*. He pointed to the guard. "Clarita, you stay here and watch him."

Ana Teresa stepped in front of Moises and drew her pistol. Moises followed her example. The feeling of confidence he'd experienced only a few moments before slipped away, replaced by concern for Alarcón and his own self-doubt. Marcos stepped forward stealthily. Ana Teresa followed him. Moises mimicked her actions.

The time it took to cover the twenty or so feet from the front of the parlor to the rear felt excruciatingly slow.

Marcos nodded as he reached the hallway. Ana Teresa and Moises crouched down a bit. They crept slowly down the hallway past two ornately furnished bedrooms. They knew from their police informant that Alarcón was in his study, the last room in the back overlooking Alarcón's late wife's carefully tended garden. The study, lined with bookcases, was connected to Alarcón's bedroom by French doors, visible from the hallway.

Alarcón was seated in a deep, low, cane chair covered in cushions upholstered in bright-colored, floral-patterned fabric. His legs rested on an ottoman in front of him, a book lay open in his lap. He faced the darkness beyond the veranda that looked out over the garden. The sweet scent of night-blooming jasmine filled the air. They could hear Alarcón's guard on the telephone from where they stood in the hallway but could not see him. He repeated, "*Sí, Capitán*," several times. Marcos held up his hand to signal to Ana Teresa and Moises to hold their positions. At the sound of the guard replacing the phone's handset, Marcos lowered his hand and stepped forward cautiously.

The guard, his back to the hallway entrance, came into view. They watched as he stretched his arms upward and bent back, giving a noisy yawn. "He's a very nervous guy, *mi Capitán*," he said to Alarcón. "That's the third call in under an hour. He doesn't trust me to guard you. He's convinced the students are up to something."

Moises caught Alarcón's eye through the open French doors as the professor turned his head to answer the guard. He didn't betray Moises or his fellow conspirators with even a hint of a facial expression. "I would be nervous if I were him," Alarcón said.

"Why?" the guard asked, his concern for Alarcón's remark evident in the tensing of his back.

"Because regardless of what happens to me, Batista is

never to be trusted. Your captain, or you, could become the next object of his ire, real or imagined, at any moment."

The guard hmphed, his body relaxing. He walked toward the veranda's open doors. "Is that all? That's rubbish. The President knows who is loyal to him."

Marcos took a step forward, then another, moving more rapidly with each additional stride. Ana Teresa followed him, gesturing to Moises to move toward Alarcón, to help him out of the chair and ready his escape. Alarcón, though only in his sixties, was frail and partially disabled. He would need help.

As Marcos—his gun drawn and in front of him—neared Alarcón's desk, the guard turned. His expression clearly betrayed his disbelief at what was happening. He reached for his gun at his right hip, realizing the holster was empty, his gun on Alarcón's desk.

"*Levante sus manos*!" Marcos shouted.

The guard complied, raising his hands above his head.

Ana Teresa came around the desk and behind the guard. She took his wrists, wrapping them tightly in cord. She then took the last of the rags from her black cloth sack and shoved it forcibly into the guard's mouth. "*Maricón*. You betray your people for money," she mumbled before pushing the guard into the chair behind the desk. "Professor, are you all right?" Ana Teresa asked.

"Yes," Alarcón replied, Moises helping him put on his shoes. "Please reach into the desk, top drawer, my other pair of glasses. I won't need anything else. Oh, also my pills. In the same drawer."

As Marcos reached into the drawer the phone rang. He glanced toward Ana Teresa. For a moment it was as if time had stopped. They glanced at each other, no one sure what to do. If they answered it, the police would know something was happening. If they didn't the result would be the same.

Ana Teresa pulled the gag from the guard's mouth. "Be careful," she said. "You can imagine what I'm capable of." The guard nodded, clear that he understood. "Put the phone to his ear," she ordered Marcos.

"*Sí, Capitán*," the guard said into the phone. "No, no, everything is normal, again, as I told you." They strained unsuccessfully to hear the captain's response; his words muffled by the guard's ear on the handset.

"My word. I will call you every fifteen minutes. Yes. Damn these revolutionaries. I believe you are right. They are up to something at the University. Yes, sir. Call you in fifteen minutes." The guard nodded his head. He mumbled, "done," before Marcos shoved the cloth back into his mouth, and before he appeared to replace the handset.

"Moises, go into the professor's room and pack some things for him," Ana Teresa said, as she helped Alarcón into the hallway. "He will need a couple of changes of clothes and some extra shoes. If there's anything else you can think of, bring it. I'll take him down the stairs and out to the street. Esperanza's brother should be here with the car any moment."

Moises moved swiftly. He opened the large, carved teak armoire opposite the bed. The canvas bag he had placed there on his last visit some months ago was still hidden under a pile of small boxes. Moises filled the bag with enough to cover the three days it would take to transport Alarcón to the meeting point near Guantanamo where he would be spirited by boat to the United States to claim political asylum. Batista wouldn't dare challenge his most important ally by demanding Alarcón's return.

On the corner of the nightstand next to Alarcón's bed, Moises spotted the framed photo of Alarcón's wife. He knew how much he missed her; how much he had depended on her. She had treated Moises like a son, as did Alarcón. Moises grabbed the photo and shoved it into the traveling bag.

As he turned to leave, he heard the sirens and shouts from the police. His heart was beating so hard he thought it would jump out of his chest. He thought again of his parents. This would destroy them, to say nothing of how it would affect his father's business. Batista didn't take well to families whose children betrayed his regime.

Moises knew this house as well as his father's. There was a rear staircase leading from the veranda to the first floor next to the kitchen built for both convenience and discretion. He could slip out through the bedroom door to the veranda and down through the garden. He would rendezvous with Ana Teresa, Alarcón, and the car that would slip them into the night at the designated point, if they had not already been caught. If their plan failed, he would escape himself. Better to remain free than to sacrifice himself for Batista's propaganda.

As Moises stole through the door onto the veranda he turned and looked back into the study. The sound of gunshots raged from the direction of the front garden. As he turned, almost as if he were watching from outside his body, he saw Marcos take the guard's gun from the desk. He aimed it at the guard's forehead only inches away and pulled the trigger. The shot rang through the darkness, the guard's head exploding, the blood splattering over everything around it. Marcos saw Moises on the veranda. "He saw our faces," Marcos said, so calmly that his statement seemed an afterthought.

"*Díos mío*," came Clarita's voice from inside the room. "You shot him."

Marcos turned and fired a second time. This time

Clarita's head exploded. With that, Marcos leaped forward and over the veranda's railing, landing on his feet like a cat, quickly sprinting into the bushes. Moises took one long, last look at the carnage in the study before he himself escaped down the back stairs, the sound and shouts of policemen approaching quickly. He looked at the professor's desk. The phone was off its cradle. Marcos never hung it up. The police heard everything.

Chapter Five

Aarón took the nearly empty streets of La Habana Vieja at a moderate pace in the early morning light. He breathed deeply as he approached the stairs leading to the University in anticipation of his sprint upward. The warmth of the sunlight enveloped him as he took them two by two. As he reached the top the nearly empty plaza at the center of the University's campus spread out before him.

He received a message from Moises the previous day. A wisp of a young woman calling herself Luz had shown up at his apartment late in the evening claiming to be a friend. She carried a small, hand-written note signed by Moises asking Aarón to meet him at six-thirty the next morning. Aarón had thought it odd but had written it off as typical of his brother's melodramatic behavior. Moises had his way of doing things. He was always like this. Aarón told Luz he would be there. She was gone before he could offer her a sip of water.

Aarón scanned the large, open space. The neoclassical buildings were imposing in their tropical setting. He breathed heavily, sweat pouring from him, soaking his shirt and shorts. Moises was nowhere to be seen. Aarón shook his head and wiped his brow with his forearm. No matter, he needed the exercise. As he turned to restart his run, Moises appeared like a phantom directly in front of him.

"Thank you for coming." Moises said, his eyes darting from side to side. "Let's go over there." He pointed to a bench under the shade of a broad tree.

Aarón nodded and followed him. "What's all the mystery?" he asked. He looked at Moises more closely as they sat down. Moises was more disheveled than usual. By his smell, Aarón knew Moises hadn't bathed in a few days. He carried a worn sack with him. What appeared to be a change of clothes peeked out of the top.

Moises hesitated a moment. "I need your help," he whispered.

Aarón's alarms went off. He looked around, scanning the open space for anyone who might be associated with the security services, whether in plain clothes or in uniform. "What have you done?" he asked.

"You are aware of what happened at Edgardo Alarcón's villa in San Miguel last week?"

Aarón's stomach tightened. There had been mention in the papers, albeit cursory, of an attempt to free Professor Alarcón from house arrest. Clearly, the government was keeping a lid on the information. Local residents had reported gunshots. The government couldn't ignore it, nor deny it entirely. Cuba loved *chisme*, gossip. If the authorities didn't acknowledge the incident, its size, scope, and success would grow geometrically. So, acknowledge it they did, but very little was made of it officially. The attempt was called unsuccessful. They claimed one revolutionary was killed in the scuffle. No mention of Alarcón's whereabouts was made.

Aarón took a deep breath, as much to calm himself as to give himself a moment to consider what to say. "Yes,

I've heard reports. There was an unsuccessful attempt to kidnap him."

Moises chuckled. "I'm sure we'd describe the operation and its outcome differently."

"What do you mean?"

"It wasn't an attempt, it wasn't a kidnapping, and it wasn't unsuccessful. We released him from unjust political imprisonment."

Terror swept over Aarón. He knew full well what would happen to Moises and anyone he was related to or associated with if he were implicated, or worse, arrested. "And were you involved in this?"

"Yes. We freed Alarcón. He's safe. I can't tell you more than that. Even if I knew, it wouldn't be safe for you to know."

Aarón's chest tightened in anger. "It's not safe for me to know what you've already told me. What else shouldn't I know?"

"A policeman was killed in the attempt."

Aarón looked around again, his paranoia growing. The government was playing a very sly game. They didn't want the people to know revolutionaries had successfully freed a leading figure in their movement. And they certainly didn't want the public to know a policeman had been killed. The police supported the government as part of their job, but any real threat to their lives would likely erode that support. The simple truth was that no one in Cuba cared enough about who occupied the Presidential Palace to give up their life for it.

"Did you kill him?" Aarón asked.

"No."

"But you know who did?"

"Yes."

Aarón's feelings of both resentment and powerlessness

overwhelmed him. “And what do you want me to do?”

“Find out if they are looking for me.”

ക്കൽ

Aarón stopped briefly at Alma’s desk before entering his office. He smiled, wishing her a good morning. Lowering his voice, he added, “Please call Hector and have him come up to see me as soon as possible.”

“Good morning to you as well,” Alma replied, loudly. She pulled several folders from the bottom drawer on the left side of her desk. “Here are those files you requested yesterday.”

“Thank you,” Aarón said, disappearing into his office.

He admired Alma’s sharpness. She knew what to say and how loudly to say it. How to deflect attention from the ever-prying eyes and ears of the clerical staff that circulated continuously around the office. One never knew who might be one of Batista’s minions. He could always depend on her.

Aarón dropped the files on the credenza. He removed his coat and placed it over the back of his chair before grabbing the pile of newspapers on the far end of the desk. Alma saved copies of El Mundo, El Sol, and The Times of Havana for two weeks for easy reference. He had read most but not all of these already, at least in a cursory manner. Now he looked more closely to ferret out any buried details of the attempt to free Alarcón. About halfway through the pile with no useful results, he stopped and rubbed his eyes. A tap on the glass pane of his door broke his concentration. “Come in,” he called out.

Hector stuck his head in. “You needed to see me?”

Aarón gestured to the chair in front of his desk and touched the forefinger of his right hand to his lips. Hector nodded and sat down, waiting for Aarón to begin.

Aarón leaned over the desk and spoke slowly, his tone low and measured. He recounted for Hector what Moises told him earlier that morning. Hector nodded. “How can I help?”

“I need to know if the police are looking for Moises. That will determine what I need to do, who I must call. I can’t make those inquiries myself.”

“I understand,” Hector replied. “Can I bring anyone else into this? We need someone with connections to the Bureau for the Repression of Communist Activities.”

“That depends on how reliable they are.”

Hector smiled. “The Bureau is, shall we say, porous.”

Aarón returned the smile. “As is everything in this country. Just be careful, and quick. I need this information immediately. My position, and by extension yours, may depend on it.”

Aarón had his answer shortly after lunch. When he returned, Hector was seated outside his office. He greeted him warmly, shaking Hector’s hand with both of his and apologizing for his tardiness, making a show of it for the clerical pool. Seated at his desk, he waited for Hector to speak. Instead, Hector handed him a carbon copy of a letter from the deputy head of BRAC, the Bureau to Repress Communist Activities, to Diego Pimental. At the top, the word *SECRETO* was underlined in red. The type, fuzzy from carbon paper, revealed a list of names of those sought in the escape of Professor Edgardo Alarcón. Midway down the list was Moises Cohan.

“Thank you, Hector.”

“There’s no need to thank me.”

“Should I ask how you got this?”

“It’s better if you don’t”

Aarón smiled sardonically. He took the sheet of paper, folded it, and placed it in the top drawer. "I expected you would say that. Perhaps you're correct."

"Good luck," said Hector.

An hour later Aarón was sitting across from Pimental in his office. Pimental lounged in a deep leather club chair gazing out of the window. The deputy minister was always delighted to accommodate his young associate on short notice, he told Alma. "Would you like a *cafecito*?" he asked, waving toward a white porcelain coffee set on the low table in front of him. "Cigar?" Pimental added, reaching into his humidor.

"Yes, and no," replied Aarón. "But you go ahead."

Pimental clipped the end of a Cohiba, lighting it with a silver lighter inlaid with lapis lazuli. "How goes our new economic development program?"

Aarón wasn't surprised by Pimental's question. In fact, he expected it. "Well, thank you. We are beginning to vet the applicants."

"When do you expect to fund the first loans?"

"Immediately after the New Year."

"That's very soon. I applaud your efforts. Much faster than our government has a reputation for. I know there must have been many late nights."

"Thank you, sir. Not so many, really. For Cuba, you know, I'll make any sacrifice."

Pimental hesitated for a moment. He puffed vigorously on his cigar, the smoke filling the room with a green-gray tinge. Aarón didn't dislike the aroma of tobacco. He became used to it living with his father. But today it caused sudden nausea, or perhaps that was the tension he felt over his mission to save Moises—and by extension his whole family—from the wrath of Batista's goons.

"But that's not why you're here," said Pimental, picking up a sheet of paper lying face down on the low table. He handed it to Aarón. It was the original of the copy Hector had given him.

Aarón's nausea increased to an almost overwhelming level. He thought he might vomit. How could his brother have put him, their family, in this position? He struggled to remain calm. He didn't want Pimental to see his fear, his desperation.

"No, sir," he said, examining the letter. But he knew he had a weapon. The government had lied about the raid. The public didn't yet know that Alarcón was free, that the raid was successful. Pimental knew. And Aarón knew. And Pimental knew that Aarón knew. Otherwise, why would Pimental play his cards so quickly?

"This is very serious," said the Minister.

"Yes, it is," replied Aarón. He struggled to keep his composure, to keep his body language neutral. He threw his chips on the table. "For the government, as much as for my brother."

"How did you come to that conclusion?" replied Pimental. He leaned back in his chair and puffed on the Cohiba. "Your brother, if caught, and I believe he will be, will face life in prison, or perhaps worse. The circumstances won't play well for your father either, or sadly, for you."

"Agreed. But the government has lied to the people. The people have little trust in their leaders as it is. They will be embarrassed if the truth comes out. What will they do when Alarcón reappears?"

"He won't reappear."

"You can't guarantee that," said Aarón, surprised by his own boldness.

"Perhaps you can."

"Excuse me?"

"It is clear to me that you know where your brother is. He's contacted you. Otherwise, why would you be here?"

"Go on," Aarón replied.

"Get a message to your brother. Tell him to tell his superiors that Alarcón is to remain hidden. We will not pursue him at this time."

Puzzled, Aarón waited silently for Pimental to continue.

"They will have to sacrifice two or three of the people on this list," said Pimental, tapping the delicate paper with his forefinger. "They can decide. We don't care. We will issue a statement that they were apprehended in their hideout here in the city. We already have a body double replacement for Alarcón at his villa. The compound is heavily guarded. No one goes in, no one goes out. It's impossible for the press to know who's really there."

"What if they ask for an interview?"

Pimental smiled. That same sarcastic, sardonic smile he flashed whenever he knew he was lying and would get away with it. He said nothing more.

"And if they agree to this?"

Pimental pointed at the letter, now face up on the table between them. "This list, or most of it, goes away. For now. A truce of sorts. An acknowledgment that they bested us. They can delight in their victory, but privately."

Aarón questioned the threat and Pimental's statement. The insurgency was well underway and on the verge of victory in parts of the country. Batista and his government relied more on propaganda than astute action. He would go along with Pimental's suggestions at least for now. "Otherwise?"

"We will hunt them all down." The gleam of hate that flashed through Pimental's eyes frightened Aarón. "They can choose prison or death; whichever they believe they are more adept at. It's a good deal. It's one boxer tipping his hat to another. We want to end this chapter quietly. At least for now."

"And that's all? No other terms?"

Pimental smiled. "Of course not. Now, let's discuss the progress of your loan applications. My son-in-law needs some help to grow his export business."

Aarón waited in shadow in a secluded corner of the deserted University campus. He spied Moises approaching. Signaling to him, he receded further into the shadow. He hated the deceit and melodrama involved with what he had been forced into by both his brother and Pimental. Moises, on the other hand, smiled, as if nothing had happened, as if hiding out from the police was his natural existence.

"*Buenas tardes*," Moises said. He reached his hand out to Aarón, met instead by the carbon copy of the damning letter Hector had secured. "What's this?"

"Read it," Aarón replied.

Moises read the letter twice, mumbling to himself. "Is there anything you can do?"

Aarón hesitated for a moment. Though he was angry with himself for the delight he took in the look of terror that crossed Moises's face, he wanted to savor it. What help he would offer was more for his parents than for Moises. His brother's youthful, entitled dalliance with communism was too easily tolerated. Aarón sympathized with the plight of the poor and the corruption of the government. He lived it daily. But he would never jeopardize himself or the family for ideology.

"Yes," Aarón replied. He outlined Pimental's terms.

"You expect me to betray my *compañeros*?" was

Moises's reply.

"I expect your *compañeros*, as you call them, to do whatever they have to do to mollify the government for now, and to help you as their, as you say, *compañero*!" Aarón felt his anger grow as the volume of his voice rose. He calmed himself, not wanting to draw attention, though there was no one nearby enough to hear them. "And that's not all." He puffed out his chest and took a step toward Moises. "I want some answers. First of all, where are you hiding?"

Moises hesitated for a moment. "With one of those on this list."

"Who, and where?"

Moises touched the third name on the list.

"I figured as much. It's always a woman with you." Aarón mumbled. "And who is she in your movement?"

"She is one of our leaders. She's also my lover. I intend to marry her. I love her. You must get her off this list, too. If they catch her, they'll kill her."

Aarón took a deep breath. He held it for a moment contemplating the new information. "Why?"

"She is known to the police, though not under this name."

"What has she done?"

"She has enlightened the people."

"Is that all? I should walk away right now."

"That's your right, brother."

Aarón took a step back. "For the sake of our parents, I won't. But I will demand a payment of sorts." He caught Moises's eyes directly and locked in on them. "You will go to your people and offer them what I have offered you. Come back to me within twenty-four hours. If they cooperate you will give me the names of your *compañeros* who will sacrifice themselves for the cause." Aarón paused a second, relishing his use of their pretentious terminology. "That list will disappear. And you, for your own sake as well as our family's, will disassociate yourself from this woman and from this movement."

"I can never do that," Moises said, his voice rising. He caught himself and glanced in both directions. "You can't tell me what to believe and who to love."

"You will," Aarón demanded, taking a step closer to Moises. "If you love her, and you want to save her, you will offer her a future, but without you. And as for your so-called movement, you will have to consider your family first. Our parents worked like dogs to build a life for themselves and us in this country. You are a spoiled brat. Without *papá's* money and his tolerance of your sophomoric, slavish dedication to the abstractions of politics and economics, you wouldn't have had the opportunity to get yourself caught up in something as dangerous as this."

"You can keep your help," Moises shouted at Aarón, unconcerned now with anyone hearing him. "You cannot tell me what to believe, or who to love!"

Aarón crossed his arms against his chest, puffing it out, widening his stance. "No? I think I can. You came to me for help. If you want that help you will do as I have asked. If not, when you are caught, we will disown you."

"*Papá* and *mamá* would never do that."

Aarón smiled. "I've already spoken with them," he lied. "They told me to tell you we will separate ourselves from you."

"I don't believe you."

"Then ask them yourself."

Moises hesitated. His anger rose into his face. "I will speak to my *compañeros*. Meet me here tomorrow night at 8:30 PM." He walked away quickly, his shoulders up around his ears, his hands in his pockets.

Aarón felt sick. He hated what he he'd just done. He hated lying. He was now caught in a labyrinth of lies so intricate he was unsure he could ever get himself out.

Moises stepped out from the shadows in the same obscure spot where he met Aarón the day before. He looked to Aarón even more disheveled and desperate than he had on their prior two meetings. He handed a sheet of paper to Aarón without so much as hello. Aarón took the paper and tried to read it, but it was too dark. Moises silently took a cigarette lighter from his pocket and held it above the paper, cupping it in his hands so as not to draw attention to them.

Aarón read the note quickly. It was signed by Luis, no last name, followed by Vanguard of the People. The tone of the letter was both condescending and self-aggrandizing. He condemned the Batista regime. Referred to both Aarón and Pimental by name. Called them traitors and cowards and threatened them with punishment when the revolution achieved its final victory. In grand terms, Luis offered himself up as the leader of this mission in response to Pimental's demand for two surrenders. "I alone bear responsibility," Luis wrote in bellicose prose, "for the death of both our *compañeros* and the evil policeman who died in the mission." He would surrender, but he would never betray his *compañeros*, or force them to martyr themselves for his error. They would go on to fight for the revolution and for Cuba.

"Take it or leave it," Moises said.

Aarón looked directly at Moises's face in the semi-darkness. "And you? What have you decided?"

"I will tell you when you bring me your reply."

"Very well. I will speak with Pimental tomorrow and meet you here at this time."

"No," Moises said, "You will go to Pimental and get an answer tonight. I will wait here for three hours. If you don't return with an answer, we are prepared to go to the papers with the truth."

"You're bluffing."

Moises removed a photo from his pocket and lit the lighter again to make it clear to Aarón how serious they were. "That's Alarcón in the middle. And if you take a close look at where they are, it's quite obvious they're not at his villa in San Miguel."

Aarón stared at the photo for a long moment. Three men, Alarcón and two others stood on a jetty stretching into the sea. Alarcón held a copy of *La Prensa* with today's date. San Miguel was miles from any coastline, set in the gently rolling hills that led to the Cordillera that ran down the spine of the island. Aarón was nearly certain this photo was taken along Guantanamo Bay. The rebels were fighting nearby, the government's forces in near retreat.

"I don't think I can get to Pimental tonight."

Moises puffed out his chest. "If you want a deal, you will."

Aarón stopped at his apartment to change into more presentable clothing before arranging a car to take him to Pimental's villa in Miramar. The perks of government service sometimes came in handy. He considered calling Pimental before he went to see him but then thought better of it. He didn't want to give him a chance to say no.

The driver picked him up twenty minutes later and deposited him at the gate of Pimental's villa thirty-five minutes after that. "Wait for me here. I won't be long,"

Aarón instructed. The chauffeur tipped his hat in silent recognition of Aarón's orders.

"Do you have business with the Minister?" the gatehouse guard asked.

"I'm afraid the Minister isn't expecting me," Aarón replied, "but it's an emergency." He handed him his card and waited. The guard signaled to someone inside the compound who quickly took the card and ran to the house. Aarón turned to the chauffeur and indicated to him to return to the car rather than continue to hold the rear door open. This would take more than a few minutes. He checked his watch. More than an hour had passed since he'd left Moises.

A few moments later Pimental appeared at the gate. He signaled for the guard to remove to a more discreet location and opened the gate indicating to Aarón to enter.

"I'm sorry to bother you…"

"No bother," Pimental interrupted. He handed Aarón back the card he'd sent with Pimental's butler to alert him on which Aarón had written urgent on the back. Clearly, Pimental understood. "I apologize for not inviting you in, but we are in the middle of a dinner party, and I thought prudence would be best in this circumstance."

"Yes," Aarón replied. "He pulled the handwritten note from Luis out of his jacket pocket and handed it to Pimental along with the photo. Pimental read it under the light of the guard house. "Tell them we want the woman, too. Otherwise, no deal."

"But sir…"

Pimental stiffened. He dropped the cigarette that balanced itself between his lips as he spoke and crushed it angrily with his shoe against the damp earth. "No buts. If they don't agree, we will begin hunting for them in the morning. We have a good idea where they are, and that photo confirms it. I know that place myself." He chuckled. "You know, Cohan, the Cuban people love only one thing, a winner. They will work with whatever side they think will win, and, of course, will pay them for their support. We know where they are. Tell them that."

"Then why don't you just go in and take them?" Aarón said, surprised at how emboldened his statement was.

"Who says we won't? We want these two alive."

Aarón had the chauffeur drop him off a few blocks from the spot where he'd left Moises. He meandered in and out of the streets to the back of the University. Moises was exactly where he'd left him, a small flashlight focused on a book in his lap. Aarón checked his watch. Nearly four hours had passed since he'd left.

Moises looked up. "What did he say?"

Aarón leaned against a wall. "They want the woman as well."

Moises jumped up. "You're lying. You're saying that just to get her away from me."

Aarón laughed to himself. His younger brother reacted in the same way he always did. It was always about Moises. Even this, a matter of national security, was in his mind a way to control him. "No," replied Aarón. "And if you think that, you're a fool. She must be very high up and very important if they're demanding her."

"She is," replied Moises. "She's a leader. She inspires."

"She's dangerous."

"Yes, true," Moises smiled, pleased with himself. "I won't bring that message back to them. I won't betray her."

Despite himself and his anger, Aarón felt pity for his brother. Moises clearly loved this woman, and not because she was a leader of their movement. He considered for a moment what he would do to protect Beatriz. "She really means something to you. This isn't one of your boyish infatuations?"

"Yes, and no."

Aarón's anger subsided a bit. Despite their differences, Moises was still his brother. "Do you love her enough to save her?"

"Yes," Moises said, his voice falling to a whisper.

"I have an idea."

Aarón knocked gently on Pimental's door at 9:30 the next morning. "Come in," shouted Pimental. He was sitting at his desk in a long sleeve *guayabera* signing papers. "I have to attend a public event celebrating our pastoral heritage this morning," he said without looking up. "What did they say?"

Aarón held out a photograph Hector had provided him early that morning. It was of a dead woman, half of her head blasted off by what could only have been a gunshot. "She's dead, the woman you want."

Pimental looked up. "Let me see that." He reached for the photo and removed his glasses. "How do we know it's her? How did she die? How convenient."

"She killed herself rather than be taken by Batista's men that night in San Miguel. Don't we have a photo of her to compare it to?"

Pimental looked up at him, frustrated and disgusted. "Truthfully, no. She has evaded us for years. She's like a ghost. BRAC never took her seriously enough because she's a woman. They didn't believe that a woman was capable of leadership." Pimental laughed. "Fools."

"What do you want to do?" Aarón asked.

Pimental finished the last of his signatures. "What do I want to do?" It's three days before Christmas. I want to be done with this. Tell them they have a deal. I'll take care of BRAC. I want this Luis brought in tomorrow."

"Yes, sir," replied Aarón, turning to leave.

"And Cohan," Pimental said as Aarón reached for the door handle. "My son needs that loan executed before Christmas. He will call your office today to set up funding for the morning of Christmas Eve."

"Yes, Diego," Aarón said, turning the door handle.

"That's Minister to you."

"Yes, Minister."

"And Cohan, Feliz Navidad."

Chapter Six

Moises peered over the rooftops of old Havana. The sun was setting, casting a golden hue over the colonial buildings. Ana Teresa knelt over the wood-fired stove in the corner of the roof tending to a pot of black beans simmering over it. Moises built a base for the stove recognizing the danger the stove and its wood fire presented to the entire building.

They had been living here on the roof of an apartment building with Ana Teresa's *abuela* in old Havana since a few nights after the incident at San Miguel. In many ways, the setting was both remarkable and unremarkable. Housing was in short supply, landlords wanted to maximize their profit. They didn't let the intended use of a roof stop them from increasing those profits. Why not rent it out? Typical capitalists.

Three families living in huts as they would in the *campo* shared the rooftop. One was Ana Teresa's *abuela*. Though places like this were not unknown to the authorities, it was the last place they would look for two revolutionaries. They were safe here in this mystical world caught somewhere between an urban slum and a *bohio*, the sprawl of Havana spreading before him, the mountains in the distance turning purple as the evening descended.

Moises crossed the roof from his perch at its corner to Ana Teresa. She stirred the beans gently and placed a second pot filled with water and rice next to it. She added a bit of salt and covered the pot. "*Feliz Navidad*," she said, touching Moises's cheek.

He smiled. "I didn't know Christmas was important to you."

Ana Teresa stood up. "It's not, in that way. But it's very important to Abuela. And I have many happy memories of this time of year with her."

She took his hand and led him into the small hut that was the home they shared with Abuela. Abuela sat in the rocking chair Moises had found in the street a few blocks away and repaired for her. He was pleased with himself. He'd learned to do things, no longer the bourgeois his parents had raised him to be. A chill went through him, even in the warm hut. He recalled the night at Professor Alarcón's villa. There were still some things he could never do.

Ana Teresa pulled him to the hammock on which they slept in the corner of the room. For privacy, he hung a sheet in front of it, catty-corner in the recess of the one-room shack. They were quiet when they made love. He wasn't sure if Abuela was deaf, slept like the dead, or simply provided them with the discretion they required.

"Will you go with me to mass tonight?" Abuela asked, mending an old skirt carefully in the dim light.

"Of course," replied Ana Teresa.

Abuela smiled. She'd stopped asking Moises about his faith. He assumed she accepted that his political beliefs eliminated religion.

Ana Teresa pushed Moises back onto the hammock but didn't pull the sheet to close them off from the rest of the room. She laid her head on his chest. "She likes you."

"How do you know that?"

"She doesn't object to your presence."

Moises laughed. He looked around the room. "Perhaps this is the way life is meant to be," he said.

"No," Ana Teresa retorted, her expression changing from content to angry in a flash. "No one, especially an old woman, should live in a hut on a roof.

Moises jumped to his own defense. "Of course not. That's not what I meant."

"Then what?"

"I meant to live simply with your family, happily. Without the pressure of worry. How will you feed them? Will you be thrown out of your home? All those things."

Ana Teresa glanced at Abuela. She had fallen asleep in the rocker, the mending needle and the skirt still in her hands. She kissed Moises gently on the lips. "Hopefully that will change soon. I received a message from Marcos today. We are to meet the day after Christmas."

She handed him a slip of paper she pulled from her pocket. He studied it carefully. The location they were to travel to was near Santa Clara. "That's not an easy place to get to right now. Who delivered this?"

"I didn't recognize her. She came up to me in the market. She addressed me with the password. When I answered, she handed me this slip of paper. We have to be there. She said the time of victory is near."

"How do we know this isn't a trap?"

"You said Aarón had taken care of the police."

Moises swallowed. He may have exaggerated his brother's influence. "I can never be sure." He touched Ana Teresa's cheek. "I can't lose you. We have to be careful."

The journey to Santa Clara was arduous, especially the day after Christmas. Their destination, located far enough outside the city itself, was still accessible despite the fighting. It required several buses, stretching the journey to over six hours though it was little more than one hundred sixty miles. For the final leg, some ten miles to a *finca* outside the town, Marcos had arranged a ride in the back of an old, rickety, pick-up truck. American World War II surplus by the looks of the tires and the faded numbers and lettering on its sides, Moises and Ana Teresa sat in the open back. They watched the little town dissolve into fields of sugarcane as they plowed slowly down the road.

"I was born in a place like this," Ana Teresa said, holding Moises's hand in hers.

"It's very romantic," Moises said.

"Not when you live here," she replied.

Moises thought to ask her why but quickly reconsidered. He recalled her response when he mused about Abuela's rooftop shack. Ana Teresa would have offered an explanation if she wanted to. He knew intrinsically though what she meant. He'd witnessed this kind of poverty since childhood, though he himself had never experienced it. His family lived in the mountains when he was a small boy before moving to Matanzas. He recalled how the children in the village would look into their door when his family sat down to meals. Hunger lingered in their eyes. It lived permanently in their souls. Moises placed his arm around Ana Teresa. She nestled into him. The gentle swaying of the truck lulled them both to sleep. It already felt like a long day and it was barely past noon.

After a while the truck came to a full stop, shaking as the driver turned off the engine, waking them. They found themselves in a clearing in front of an old farmhouse, more shack than permanent structure. A fire smoldered nearby, a pot in the middle, two chickens suspended on a spit over it. The fat from the chickens dripped down into whatever was bubbling in the pot.

Moises helped Ana Teresa down from the lorry. They approached the house. Ana Teresa pushed in the rickety door made of palm fronds. "*Compañeros*," she called out into the semi-darkness.

"*Hola, bienvenidos*," came a woman's voice from inside. The woman soon appeared. It was the same woman who had passed the message along to Ana Teresa in the market a few days earlier. Slight of build and thin, her dark hair was pulled back and tied into a bun. She took Ana Teresa's hand. It's good to meet you, officially. My name is Maria. I've heard so much about you from Marcos."

"Thank you. It's good to meet you as well". Ana Teresa smiled. "This is Moises Cohan."

The woman took Moises hand in both of hers. "A great honor, *compañero*."

"Is Marcos here?" Ana Teresa asked.

"Yes." Maria gestured to the open door at the back of the house and led them through the cluttered shack. On the other side of the door, the sunlight was blinding despite the dense trees that surrounded the cleared area. As their eyes adjusted, they saw Marcos seated on an old, wobbly chair at a rough-hewn table. On the table was a map of some kind, which he studied intently.

"Marcos," Moises called to him.

"*Bienvenidos*," Marcos replied, lifting his head and standing, his hands clasped behind his back. His beard looked more and more like Fidel's though he still looked nothing like him. Where Fidel's features were hard and angular, Marcos's were soft and round. Marcos had also taken to wearing the same kind of military cap favored by *el comandante*. He walked toward them extending his hand to Moises, then embraced Ana Teresa, a bit too long for Moises's taste. "Thank you for coming."

"Of course," replied Ana Teresa. "We were very excited by your message. *¿Llegó la hora?*" she asked. "Has our moment come?"

Marcos stood back, crossed his arms against his chest. "Yes. We are ready. I am waiting for the final orders, date, and time, etc., from Fidel. We are near victory in Santa Clara and Yaguajay. When they fall, we will take Havana."

"You are communicating directly with Fidel?" asked Moises. The clucking of chickens filtered into the clearing.

Marcos straightened his back and smiled. "Yes," he replied, puffing out his chest a little further. "With Luis's surrender, I am now in charge."

Moises shifted his weight nervously from side to side. Ana Teresa was the next in the chain of command in their cell. How had Marcos placed himself in front of her?

"Congratulations, *compañero*," Ana Teresa said, any sense of disappointment she might have well hidden. "Can you tell us though, how it went with Luis? He is a true hero of the people to have sacrificed himself in this way."

Marcos began to pace a bit, appropriating the gestures of a military commander. "Yes, he is a true hero of the people. I hope he doesn't become a martyr of the people. The capitalists are very angry about Alarcón. They are likely to make Luis's stay with them very, shall we say, uncomfortable. Hopefully, he will not be there long."

"Not if our moment has truly arrived," Ana Teresa replied.

"How was the arrest made?" asked Moises.

"Well, I think you know most of that," said Marcos, shifting his gaze directly at Moises. "You arranged it. It was really quite simple. We went to the station as instructed. We dropped him off at the corner. We stayed out of sight. We didn't want to take a chance of them arresting us as well. He walked up to the guards. The exchange was short. We watched it, though we couldn't hear. They took him by his upper arms, not aggressively or roughly mind you, and walked him into the station. That's all we saw. The question now is whether the regime will honor its agreement with us." Marcos looked directly at Moises. "You'd probably know more about that than the rest of us."

Both fear and anger percolated in Moises's gut. He knew full well that his class status made him suspect in the eyes of many of his fellow revolutionaries. At the same time, he felt that he'd proved himself and his commitment more than once and sufficiently. Marcos's innuendo was in reality both an accusation and a threat. If he'd made it now, he might make it again, and in other company.

"Tell us about the plan," Ana Teresa said, breaking the tension.

"Let me show you," he said, leading them to the table. Two maps covered it. One was of Cuba, the other of Havana. "You can see where our forces are now," Marcos said gesturing to the map of Cuba. "Fidel has moved our best forces to Santa Clara and Yaguajay. Other units are stationed outside major towns and cities. We will move on Havana afterward." He pointed to the map of Havana. There were red dots spread over it. "This shows our safe houses in the city. We will mass our forces there over the next few days, so as to be ready when we strike."

Moises and Ana Teresa returned to Havana the following day, but not by bus and not to Abuela's rooftop. They returned instead by car to individual safe houses. Ana Teresa to a house in San Lazaro, and Moises to a penthouse apartment in Vedado. Each had its own risks.

The wood house with the tin roof in San Lazaro was so deep in the *barrio* that the police rarely ventured there. A raid was always possible if someone tipped off the police or Batista's shadowy thugs. For people so poor, with eyes prying every crate and box that came in and out of a neighbor's shack, and ears listening to every overheard word, the meager bounty afforded them by the police for information might well be the difference between a full or empty belly. They were too hungry to recognize the revolution for what it was, their liberation.

Moises faced other challenges. The apartment he was to turn into a safe house was the residence of a wealthy businessman. He, his wife, and younger children were in Miami for the New Year. His two older children, a son, and daughter, were members of the Movement. They had volunteered their parents' apartment. The building though was crawling with servants watching everything that went on, day and night. Gossip was what kept their otherwise struggling lives entertaining.

Moises came up with an idea. That's how the *compañeros* would come and go. They would be disguised as servants and delivery men. The son and daughter of the businessman had already paid off the doormen and concierge. They said they were having a party on New Year's Eve, a costume ball. They didn't want their parents to find out. Revolutionaries would walk right in, guns and bullets in crates that were labeled dishes and glasses. They'd stay put until the moment of revolution had arrived.

Moises stood on the terrace of the apartment. It was high up enough to embrace a panorama of Havana and the Gulf of Mexico to the north as well as the University and the distant mountains in the distance. The sun was warm, the breeze comforting. He thought for a moment of the second-floor terrace of his parents' house. The view and the feeling were similar, though nowhere nearly as dramatic. He missed them. He hadn't seen them since that Sabbath visit a month earlier.

He was uncertain as to how much Aarón had really told them, whether it was a threat, or he had actually told them of Moises's involvement in the incident at San Miguel. He hadn't even tried to call them. It was December 29. The final push would occur within a few days. He considered the possibility that he could be killed. It weighed heavily on him.

He walked back through the apartment to the room in which he was sleeping, the room of the family's youngest child, a girl of eight. Decorated in rose and pink and white, dolls and lace were everywhere. She would never know the hunger of other little girls. Those who lived in the countryside and who by her age were already working in the fields and tiny gardens pulling yuca from the ground. Her photo, sitting on a pony at the family's *finca* in San Miguel, rested on the bureau, which he imagined was filled with her dainty, frilly clothing.

Moises considered visiting his parents. He had today. He knew they would be there. The safe house wouldn't fill until after tomorrow with both guns and revolutionaries. He knew this new government, this new type of government would impact his father. But it was necessary and fair. Though his father was a capitalist, he treated his workers well. But at the same time, what was to come would make the lives of those like his father far less comfortable. The lives of millions though would be made better.

The bus ride to Matanzas was slow and bumpy as always. Moises would arrive at his parents' home at about 2 PM. They would be sitting down to lunch, just before their siesta. It was a Monday. There was no chance of Aarón and Beatriz being there, despite the slow week between Christmas and New Year's.

He had considered and reconsidered what to say during the two-hour ride. He still wasn't sure. He would play it close, depending on what Aarón had or hadn't told them. What still surprised him was that they hadn't tried to contact him in the past few weeks.

The bus bumped to a stop at the end of his parents' street, the mid-day sun hot but not oppressive. If anything, it was pleasing on his skin. He tugged at his *guayabera* as he stepped down, shaking off what perspiration had accumulated under it. The street was quiet. Even the children who normally ran along the pot-holed road were absent. Matanzas was at lunch, the scents of Cuba, garlic frying and pork fat sizzling wafting through the air, followed by muffled conversation.

At his parents' house, Moises tip-toed up the two steps to the screened front door and stealthily pushed it open. He spied them in the dining room, his father's back to him. His mother looked up. She put down her fork and touched his father's arm, pointing. His father turned. Moises smiled. His mother gestured for him to come into the dining room as his father stood up and opened his arms. Moises moved to them and embraced them both.

"Sit down," Esther said as she turned toward the kitchen. "You will eat something, then we can talk."

Moises sopped up the last bits of beef stew with a crusty piece of *pan de agua*. He chuckled to himself. After some thirty years in Cuba, his parents still preferred bread to rice with their meals. The sauce was flavorful and piquant. Despite their preference for bread over rice, his mother had adopted the fuller flavors of Cuba, adding cubanelles to stews and replacing parsley with cilantro. He smiled at them. "No one cooks like you, *mamá*."

Esther touched his hand. "*Gracias, mijo*. We are delighted you are here."

"But where have you been?" Rafael asked. "We were quite worried."

Moises considered his response for a long moment before answering. He wasn't sure how much they knew, what they might not want him to know they knew. "I was away for a couple of weeks. In the *campo*. I should have let you know before I went, but it was very last minute, and I wasn't able to get to a phone.

Moises noted his parents' glance at each other. It was a clear indication that at the very least, they suspected something. His father nodded slowly. "I see." Raphael hesitated a moment before continuing. "Is this about a woman?"

The question didn't necessarily cast any light on what Aarón may or may not have told them. Had Aarón mentioned Moises's romance with Ana Teresa as part of his threat to expose his involvement with the incident at San Miguel to their parents?

"Yes," Moises answered, casting a short line into a dark, deep pool.

Rafael glanced at Esther again. He sat back in his chair. "Well, I suppose that's the better alternative here. We feared much worse."

Moises felt a tug on the imaginary fishing reel. "What do you mean?"

"We were concerned you may have been involved in… something more dangerous…"

"…your politics," Rafael said, completing Esther's thought.

Aarón hadn't told them about San Miguel or Ana Teresa. It was a bluff. Or perhaps they were bluffing? Moises smiled, trying to get his parents to inadvertently confirm what Aarón might have told them. "What do you mean?"

"*Zindle*," Rafael said, switching to the Yiddish diminutive for *mijo*, my son. "We know what your politics are. You've made no secret of it. I don't approve, but I cannot tell you what to believe."

Moises probed further. He knew the oath he'd sworn to the Movement required that he keep his involvement secret, as much to protect his *compañeros* as himself. "Yes, you know my beliefs. Do you think I am involved in the unrest?"

"You've been to demonstrations," Esther said. "You've told us that."

"Everyone who wants a better future attends the demonstrations."

"Is that as far as it's gone?"

"What do you mean, *papá*?"

Rafael leaned forward. His eyes locked on Moises's. "Are you involved with Fidel? Have you joined his forces?"

Moises weighed his answer. How much could he safely say? "I support what he stands for, and more. You know that. But no, I am not a member of the Movement."

The lie both stung and soothed him. Next to Ana Teresa, the revolution was the most important thing in his life. He loved his parents, but they were part of the problem, part of what kept Cuba in poverty. He knew when the time came, the revolution wouldn't consider how benevolent their capitalism had been. He believed that they themselves would come to see how fair and benevolent the new Cuba would be. At the same time, he knew his lie would protect them, should the revolution fail. If he were captured, they could deny knowing anything. This lie and Aarón's position in the government would protect them from Batista's henchmen.

Rafael nodded. "I must say, though I understand your passion for justice for our nation, I also understand the realities of the situation. We may have been here thirty years, but we are still looked upon as guests in this country. *Polacos*, they call us. You have to think of your future. To fight Batista is madness. He is too strong, and the Americans are behind him. Believe what you want but understand that in the end, you will come to work with me. You can be the most benevolent socialist you would like to be with our workers, providing you don't bankrupt us. If you become too visible now you will destroy not only yourself but us as well."

Moises felt his throat tighten. He fought back tears. He understood what his father was telling him. But at the same time, he knew his passion. A life counting beans at the shoe factory was not for him. They had let Aarón follow his own path, why not him? "I understand," he said, hoping to end the conversation entirely.

"Now," his father continued, "as to the subject of the woman. We're not going to ask too many questions. You are a young man, and a young man must, shall we say, find out who he is. This is a different world than the world where I met your mother. We are going to look away from what you are doing. When this has run its course, we are sure you will be ready to find a wife from our community."

Moises knew there was no point in trying to convince them otherwise. His socialism was tolerated, but a non-Jewish daughter-in-law was out of the question. No matter how long his parents and the Jewish community lived in Cuba, they would live essentially separately. They would inhabit the same physical space as their Cuban neighbors but exist in a separate, inaccessible world. Moises nodded his head. There was no point in disagreement at this junction. He rose from the table. "I have to get back to Havana."

"Be careful," his mother whispered as she embraced him.

"I will." He turned to go. As he reached the front door, he turned to them. "I would recommend you stay home for New Year's Eve. Don't go to Havana," he said, regretting the words as they escaped his lips.

Chapter Seven

The garden air was warm and pleasant, calmer and less charged than the atmosphere inside Mar y Arena Cabana Club. On a typical New Year's Eve, the members of Havana's premier Jewish beach club would be both festive and excited, but tonight the air was mixed with a sense of uncertainty. Santa Clara had fallen to Castro's forces three days earlier, and Yaguajay, this very day. Change was in the air, though everyone knew the final result could still go either way. The general feeling was that the community would roll with the wave, whichever way it went. Rumor had it that Che himself was on the outskirts of Havana. The question was what would Batista do now?

Aarón and Beatriz had set a date for their wedding, March 29. It would be at the Patronato. Tonight would serve double duty, both a New Year's Eve celebration and their engagement party. Beatriz's father, Eduardo Resnick, booked six tables at the far corner of the ballroom. Hastily put together, it was an opportunity for their families and friends to get to know each other.

Aarón walked back from the men's room to the main ballroom. He spied Hector at the end of the hall in a small booth on a house phone. Always working, thought Aarón.

Hector was a good friend to have.

The ballroom was decked out in the club's finest. Linen tablecloths, spotless china, gleaming crystal. At the front of the ballroom a fifteen-piece orchestra played mambo, rumba, son, bolero, and American swing.

At eleven o'clock, the dance floor was sparsely populated. Most of the guests were at the appetizer buffet, an interesting mix of Jewish and Cuban favorites. Everything from chopped liver to *bolitas de yuca* and *pastelitos de carne.*

Aarón looked at himself in the mirrored wall, dusting off his cuffs and straightening his tie. He stopped at the bar to pick up another drink. This was a big night for both his impending marriage and his career. He'd invited Alejandro Martinez as well as several contacts from the bank. Men who could become his allies, particularly if Batista fell. But then the President-for-Life was known to have nine lives, the result of his spider-web like network of informants and the threat of punishment for those who betrayed him. He'd survived numerous attempts to dislodge him. The loss of a provincial capital or two to a ragtag band of revolutionaries was by no means in anyone's mind the end of his tenure.

Aarón took his seat next to Beatriz. Martinez sat to his left, Martinez's wife, Amalda next to him. The rest of the table consisted of his parents, Beatriz's parents, and Beatriz's sister and husband. Conspicuously missing was Moises.

Aarón had resisted inviting him, despite his parents' objections. He was still angry with him for the position in which Moises had put him. He didn't want Moises to embarrass him in front of his colleagues. His parents had reluctantly admitted that Moises had shown up at their house two days earlier. They hadn't invited him to tonight's party as per Aarón's wishes, but they had made it clear that they would insist he be invited to the wedding. Aarón said nothing, choosing to deal with that problem when it became necessary.

Aarón's colleagues from the bank and their wives were seated at the next table, Hector at an angle behind Aarón. Hector entered the ballroom directly in Aarón's line of sight. He caught Aarón's eye and nodded discretely, his expression as granite-like as a professional poker player. He crossed the dance floor and the room and retook his seat, reaching his arm out behind his date's chair nonchalantly, passing a note to Aarón's waiting hand.

"What a lovely club this is," Amalda Martinez said, leaning toward Aarón and raising her glass. "Thanks for inviting us. I've always wanted to come here."

"Yes, thanks so much," Alejandro added. "Otherwise, we might have been obligated to a party at the Presidential Palace."

Aarón laughed, signaling to others at the table that it was acceptable to joke about attending a party hosted by Batista. One never knew who was listening. The waiters themselves could be the auricles of *el Presidente*, assigned to this table specifically to keep an ear open for any remark Martinez, or Aarón, or his colleagues or relatives might make that would place them at odds with the President.

"I'm sure that celebration is even more elegant than this," Aarón said.

"Elegant, yes," replied Martinez, "the best of everything. But not nearly as cordial."

"Thank you for coming," Beatriz said. "It's a pleasure to have you with us."

"When is your wedding?" Amalda asked.

"March 29," Beatriz answered.

"Will you have it here?"

"No," said Beatriz, "at the Patronato."

"That's the large synagogue in Vedado," said Eduardo Cohan. "We hope you will be able to attend."

Aarón looked at his watch. Eleven forty-five. He reached into his pocket and felt for the small piece of paper Hector had passed to him. It was still there, folded and waiting. He raised his glass and tapped on it with a spoon to signal a toast. Their corner of the room grew quiet. "A new year is upon us. For Beatriz and me it's the beginning of our life together. Those who are important to us are here with us tonight. May the new year bring all of us happiness and a new start."

Aarón's guests shouted "*salud*" and "*mazel tov*." They tapped on their glasses and drank. The band, fresh from their pre-midnight break, quickly reassembled at the front of the room. The clock read five minutes to midnight. The bandleader took his position in front of the crowd and asked them to stand and raise their glasses. The orchestra began a gentle rumba, some of the guests nearest the dance floor taking to the parquet, champagne flutes in hand. As the second hand neared its inexorable rendezvous with midnight the countdown began, *"diez, nueve, ocho, siete, seis, cinco, cuatro, tres, dos...uno! Feliz Año Nuevo!"* The shout soared in unison from the crowd.

Aarón turned to Beatriz, his arm around her waist. He kissed her gently on the lips. *"Feliz Año Nuevo, mi amor."*

Beatriz smiled. "And to you. You make me so happy. Thank you."

"Thank you." Aarón looked around their tables. Hector caught his eye and nodded his head toward Aarón's pocket. Aarón nodded back. He turned to Beatriz. "I would be nothing without you."

Martinez tapped Aarón's shoulder. He took his hand, pulled him close and whispered in his ear. "Stay vigilant and you will succeed." There were handshakes and embraces all around. Aarón slipped to the side and reached into his pocket. He retrieved Hector's note and opened it. 'I have reliable information," it read. "Batista is fleeing the country tonight."

ᏋᏋ

Moises waited patiently on the terrace overlooking a festive, yet restive city. Revelers filled the street. The new year would arrive in fifteen minutes. Twenty fighters waited nervously throughout the apartment, cleaning their guns, assembling other defenses that would be needed when their forces entered the city.

Moises had been on pins and needles for two days. When he returned from his visit to his parents, Maria was waiting on the corner. She knew better than to create suspicion with the building staff. She handed a note to Moises and slipped away quietly, a phantom in the swirl of busy Havana.

The note from Marcos was handwritten. Their forces were placed strategically around the capital as well as in safe houses like the one Moises maintained, hidden in plain sight. Batista's regime was porous. Moises was to keep his ear to the ground. With their victories this past week, the leaders of the movement believed Batista had only two choices; strike back, making a big show of it in the capital, or flee. Considering who Batista was and the inside intelligence they received about his movements, the movements of his assets, and of his closest advisors, the leadership expected him to flee. General Che was near Havana. He would enter as soon as Batista left, if he did. Otherwise, he would engage the government's forces. In any event, Moises knew what he needed to do.

Gazing into the living room, he watched as the fighters quietly poured rum into cups, readying a toast to the future. Mambo played on the radio, portending a night of celebration and dancing. Cubans loved a good party and New Year's Eve was a perfect excuse for excess. The fighters were calm and restless at the same time, the significance of the moment's potential upon them.

Moises thought of Ana Teresa. He missed her, especially at a moment like this. Perhaps in the future they would share a normal New Year celebration. They would toast to the future and share a passionate kiss. He hadn't seen her since they returned from the *campo*. Though it was only a few days it felt like an eternity. He missed the curve of her body, the scent of her skin, her smile as she tossed back her hair in the breeze.

The shrill ring of the house phone broke his concentration. He looked at his watch. It read five minutes to midnight. A pang of suspicion ran through his body. The fighters in the living room put down their drinks and looked at him. No one was expected.

Moises crossed the living room to the front door and picked up the handset from its cradle on the wall next to the heavy mahogany double entry doors. "*Mandeme*," he said.

"*Señor*," came back the voice from the concierge desk. "You have a visitor."

Moises considered whether to ask for more information. Was it a man? A woman? More than one person? He didn't want to tip off the concierge if it was the police or Batista's goons sent to raid their hideout. "Send him up," he responded.

"Her," corrected the concierge.

Moises felt his body relax. It was a woman. Unlikely a trap. "*Gracias, Juan*," he said, "*y Feliz Año Nuevo*."

A long moment later the elevator opened opposite the apartment doors. Moises watched through the peephole. It was Ana Teresa. His heart beat quickly, both from surprise and desire. He opened the door and pulled her into his arms, kissing her first gently and then deeply with great passion. As their embrace loosened, he heard the fighters in the living room as they finished their countdown, *tres, dos, uno*, and their shouts for the New Year.

"Happy New Year, *mi amor*," Ana Teresa whispered in his ear. She kissed him again. "Our time has come."

Moises's spirits lept even higher. "Then the reports on Radio Rebelde are true."

Aarón made the rounds of the tables wishing everyone a happy and prosperous New Year. The band struck up a mambo and the revelers headed for the dance floor. He excused himself, telling Beatriz he would be right back for their first dance of the new year. He signaled to Hector to follow him at a judicious distance. Once out of the room he ducked into a phone stall at the end of the long, badly lit hallway. Hector arrived a moment later.

"What is this?" he asked Hector, showing him the crumpled note in his palm.

"It's exactly what it says."

"How did you learn of this?"

Hector chuckled. "*Señor* Cohan, that's exactly why you have me as your second. You don't really want to know."

Aarón considered Hector's response. "Perhaps you're right. How reliable is this information and when will this happen?"

"It's one hundred percent reliable and it's imminent."

"How will we know when it happens?"

"There will be an announcement."

Aarón hesitated a moment. "Are you certain?"

"Yes."

"Tell me how?"

Hector hesitated for a moment and took a deep breath. "The informant is leaving with Batista."

Aarón was momentarily speechless. He knew Hector's sources were deep and well placed, but someone that close to the President was much closer than he had ever considered. If that was the case, how committed and close to the regime was Hector himself? "Have you been spying on me all this while?" Aarón asked before he could stop himself. "Will you flee as well?"

Hector reached for Aarón's shoulder. "No, sir. Quite the opposite. I work for a better Cuba for all."

Aarón took Hector at his word. He knew it was too late to question his integrity or his allegiances anyway. He was an ally. At least for now. "What shall we do?"

"Wait and enjoy ourselves, until the news is official," Hector said with a smirk.

Moises couldn't let go of Ana Teresa's hand. They stood on the balcony, their foreheads touching, whispering as their *compañeros* celebrated with shots of rum and cigars courtesy of the owner of the apartment. Ana Teresa had told them of Batista's imminent departure and Che's arrival just past the stroke of midnight. The streets below were full. Moises could only imagine what joy would explode when the people knew they were free.

Ana Teresa had received a note from Marcos early in the day. He was with Che on their way from Santa Clara. They would rendezvous with other troops at a bridge just outside the capital. He instructed her to send her fighters there. They would re-enter with Che's forces. If there was resistance, they would need the manpower. She was to rendezvous with Moises in the city to do what she did best, rally and inspire the people in the streets.

Moises glanced at his watch. "It's one thirty," he whispered, his lips grazing Ana Teresa's. She brushed hers against his and just as quickly pulled away. "It's nearly time. We need to get everyone into the streets. They must be ready when the orders come."

"I thought this will happen without a shot?"

"*Ojalâ*," said Ana Teresa.

She moved quickly into the living room, quieting the young, enthusiastic group, pouring a shot of rum for herself and passing the bottle around. Many other empty bottles, all compliments of their unsuspecting host, littered the floor.

"*Compañeros*," she said, offering a toast, her glass held high in the air, her demeanor changing from lover to leader in a moment, "*Llegó la hora*. The time has come for us to save the nation." Moises watched her, mesmerized as always. "We will take to the streets now. You have been organized in pairs, and each pair has an assigned place." Ana Teresa drew a piece of folded paper from the pocket of her pants. "Take your pistols. Keep them concealed. Blend into the crowd. Celebrate the New Year with our people as it is truly a new beginning this year. Shortly, in about an hour, we will know if our victory is complete or whether we will have to fight for it. When the people learn Batista has fled, their behavior will inform you. If we are to take the capital by force our leaders are in the squares and on the streets. They will call for revolution."

For Aarón the evening proceeded as if in limbo. White gloved waiters served a succession of courses. A salad of hearts of palm in a citrus vinaigrette. *Pescado en coco.* Prime rib with potatoes and vegetables. Aarón ate almost nothing, picking at his food. His mother commented. Beatriz laughed. "He rarely eats anything after nine o'clock."

While that was true, he didn't want anyone to suspect anything, either. He took a big forkful of *pescado en coco*, nearly choking on it.

At two-thirty, the waiters wheeled out an enormous Viennese table, three, ten-foot-long tables covered with desserts of every conceivable kind. The guests swarmed it like locusts. Twenty minutes later the remains littered the tables, half-eaten and picked at. Aarón had a momentary turn of his stomach. So much excess. Perhaps what was coming was needed. Then, suddenly, the band stopped playing.

The maître d' took the microphone. "*Señoras y señores*," he said loudly, quieting both the crowd and the band with both hands. "I have an announcement to make. A very serious announcement." The cacophony in the crowded space lowered to a murmur. "Presidente Fulgencio Batista has left the country."

Aarón observed the room. It seemed to become stuck as if in suspended animation, everyone shocked into silence. This news required a moment to sink in. Then, just as suddenly, there was the sound of a single pair of hands clapping. That pair was then joined by many more, along with joyous shouting reaching a crescendo like an oncoming freight train.

One could clearly see who supported the regime and who did not. Those who welcomed Batista's departure shouted, hugged, and kissed, congratulating each other. Those who did not grabbed their wives. Their wives then grabbed their bags and silk shawls. They ran from the room.

A traffic jam, visible through the window, developed in the parking lot almost immediately. The valets were unable to respond to the onslaught of those wanting to flee. Aarón watched transfixed as men in tuxedoes fought with each other to retrieve the keys to their cars from the valet box. They fought each other as if they needed to get to the airport to claim their seat on Batista's escaping plane. Some might well have.

Beatriz's hand in his, her whisper in his ear, brought Aarón back into the room. He gazed quickly to his left. Hector was gone. He wondered to where and with whom.

"It was inevitable," Professor Martinez pushed himself up from his seat. A quizzical smile crossed his lips. "*Vamos a ver,*" he said with a chuckle. "We shall see what comes next."

Aarón felt Beatriz's hand squeeze his. He turned to her. Her face was a mixture of excitement and fear. "What does this mean?" she said.

"He is gone. I imagine Castro or his forces are near the city. They will fill the void by morning."

"But…the rest of them?"

"I'm sure they're gone as well, Batista's mafia," said Martinez, clapping his hands in delight. "And good riddance."

Beatriz shifted her gaze, a worrying look crossing her face. "Aarón, our parents, the Martinez's" she said. "We have to get them home."

"Yes, of course," he said. The crowd continued to thin. Aarón turned and addressed his remaining guests. "Obviously, it's best to return home. Thank you all for coming." He smiled. "Our lives continue to be interesting."

After handshakes and hugs, Aarón, Beatriz, their parents, and the Martinezes collected their things and headed to the parking lot. Two limousines, both of which Aarón had booked for the evening, stood at the ready. He thanked the drivers for waiting, considering the circumstances.

"Our pleasure, *señor*," they both replied.

Aarón realized he had a logistical problem. He planned on sending his parents home in one car and bringing Beatriz's parents with him and Beatriz to their home for the night. Martinez and his wife would have taken a taxi. That was impossible now. He would have to deliver Martinez and his wife into the center of the city. He didn't want his parents or Beatriz's traveling into Havana. Who knew what was happening there. He turned to them. "Eduardo, Lina, could my parents stay with you tonight? I need to take the second car to bring Professor Martinez and his wife home."

"Of course," Lina replied, even before Aarón finished.

"Thank you." Aarón turned to Beatriz. "You'll go with them."

Beatriz took his hand. "No, I'm going with you."

ఆఆ

Moises's and Ana Teresa's fighters exited two by two, taking the back stairs, and leaving through the servant's entrance at the rear of the building. When the apartment was empty, they summoned the elevator. The cab appeared, the attendant, an old man with a gray goatee greeting them. "*Feliz Año Nuevo*," he said. "*Y tú, igual*," they replied.

As the elevator descended, the attendant—typically very formal, respecting the supposed class differences between himself and his passengers—relaxed and smiled. "We have a future now," he said, as the elevator came to a stop.

"Yes, we do," said Ana Teresa. She stopped and leaned in, kissing him gently on the cheek.

"*Viva la revolución*," said the old man. Ana Teresa smiled. He gestured for her to come closer. "I knew all along who you and your people were. Give us a new world."

"Thank you for protecting us," she said.

Moises took her hand and pulled her through the elegant lobby to the front door. The doormen had abandoned their posts and stood yelping in the streets, their collars open, their stifling red jackets and black bow ties thrown into a corner of the vestibule. Car horns blared. Music played. "Have you heard?" a stranger shouted at them as they left the building. "He's gone! Batista is gone!"

Moises turned to Ana Teresa. He pulled her close and kissed her, hard and deep. She kissed him back. "We have won," she whispered in his ear.

"Let's go back upstairs," he whispered, his voice gravelly.

She pulled back. "Are you crazy? Now? We will have plenty of time for that later. We must go to the University."

She took his hand firmly in hers and forced their way forward through the streets, the sound of revolution deafening in its victory. By the time they made it to the plaza at the University's heart, thousands were cheering. She spotted Luis on a makeshift platform in front of the main administration building. "Look," Ana Teresa shouted, barely audible to Moises over the roar of the crowd, pointing.

"How did he get out of jail?" Moises said.

"Let's find out."

They pushed their way to the front of the crowd by sheer will. The plaza was filled with jubilance. People shouting, crying, singing. Ana Teresa called to Luis. Finally, more by chance than by her efforts, he spotted them. A smile spread across his face. He waved them forward, young men and women wearing the scarlet neckerchiefs of the revolution parting the crowd to make way for them. Luis pulled them up onto the platform. He embraced Ana Teresa, then Moises.

"How did you get out?" she asked, shouting above the roar of the crowds in front of them.

"The police mutinied hours ago. One of them threw his keys into the holding cell. The prisoners released us." He took Ana Teresa's hand in his and raised her arm. "Victory," he shouted into the megaphone. "You don't yet know her, *mi gente*, but you owe much to this woman. She has fought for you from the very beginning. I give you Ana Teresa Colon"

Luis handed the megaphone to Ana Teresa. "*Mi compañeros*," she shouted, "we have waited too long. Many have given their lives. Now is our moment. The moment of our liberation. Tomorrow our leaders will take the reins of government. There will be no more rich and poor. No more hunger. No black or white. No longer will women be relegated to a low position. *Viva Cuba libre*!"

A thunderous cheer rose from the crowd again, this time calling her name, Ana Teresa, over and over. Moises was filled with awe, both by Ana Teresa and the victory over Batista. He looked out over the crowd in the dim light. In its midst some one hundred feet away, he saw something he never expected, not in his wildest dreams. Aarón,

Beatriz at his side, frozen by the sound and fury of the crowd.

Aarón didn't know which image was more shocking to him, the birth of a revolution, or his brother standing on the platform with its leaders. His mind was in chaos. Batista was a cancer on the nation. He himself had fought his influence and corruption any way he could. But this? This was different. This was no ordinary coup. The military hadn't decided they'd had enough of Batista's thieving and pillaging and sent him packing. These were the forces of change, real change.

Yet Aarón was uncertain. Castro had never declared himself to be a communist, but many of those around him had. Perhaps Castro would be the man of the hour? Perhaps he could unite the people and the disparate political elements that had opposed Batista, both openly and secretly, into one united force for the good of the nation. Perhaps he would lift the people out of the never-ending grind of poverty. A part of Aarón was terrified, another part was jubilant. He would give Castro and his people a chance. They deserved that much.

Beatriz gripped his hand like a vise. He never realized her tiny, delicate fingers could have such force. He turned to her and took her in his arms.

"Are you frightened?" he asked.

"Perhaps," she replied. "We are witnessing history. I'm filled with both hope and fear." She kissed him gently on the lips. "We have a new Cuba."

He smiled weakly. "Yes." Nodding discreetly toward the speakers on the platform, he added "Do you see who is there?"

Beatriz squinted in the uneven light, standing on her tiptoes to see over the heads in front of her.

"There, to the left of the woman with the bull horn."

"Moises," she whispered.

"It's not that I didn't expect it. But I didn't think he was high up enough in the Movement to warrant center stage."

"He gave his word to you and your parents that he would leave the Movement."

"Clearly, he didn't," replied Aarón.

It was at that exact moment, as those words escaped Aarón's lips, that Moises's and Aarón's eyes met across the screaming, cheering throng. Aarón couldn't understand how under such circumstances Moises would notice him in the crowd. Perhaps it was a matter of genetics, or sibling telepathy, or serendipity, but it had happened. Moises smiled and nodded. Aarón did the same.

They stood there for some time, unable to leave even if they wanted to. The crowd was too thick. Finally, as the revolution's young leaders finished speaking, it began to disperse. Hours passed. Aarón and Beatriz were exhausted. They walked through the campus in the direction of Aarón's apartment. As they made their way through the dawn, they passed the spot where Aarón met Moises the night after the incident at San Miguel.

"*Hermano*," Aarón heard from his right, the voice unmistakable. He stopped, Beatriz's hand still in his. He pulled her gently back. As she turned, Moises and Ana Teresa stepped out of the shadows.

"*Buenos días*, brother," Aarón said, people jostling by them. They stepped forward to avoid the moving stream of bodies.

"This is Ana Teresa," Moises said.

"Yes, I know," said Aarón. He extended his hand and

tipped his head slightly.

Ana Teresa took his hand firmly. "It's nice to meet you, finally. And this must be…Beatriz?"

"Oh, excuse me," said Aarón, "yes."

"*Mucho gusto*," Ana Teresa offered, extending her hand to Beatriz.

"You were very impressive up there tonight," Beatriz said, taking Ana Teresa's hand in hers. "*Mucho gusto*."

"Thank you. We are living in a new world now. One where women will be equal partners."

Beatriz hesitated for a moment. "That's good, I believe. Though I've always felt like an equal partner, myself."

Ana Teresa smiled. She measured her response. "I'm happy to know that. May all our sisters have that experience as we move forward."

"Yes, all," Aarón said.

A long, awkward moment filled the space between them. "I hope we can put the past behind us now," said Moises.

"I hope so, too.," replied Aarón, the rising sun peaking over the roofs of the buildings, filling the plaza. "We will see what comes next. It's a new day for Cuba, and for us."

Part II
January—November
1959

Chapter Eight

Aarón sat pensively on the veranda sipping a piña colada. He'd been drinking more frequently in the past weeks, though not to the point of drunkenness. It took the edge off his frazzled nerves. When offered a drink, like today, he readily accepted it.

Beatriz sat with her parents in the dining room on the far side of their house, her sister and her two best friends huddled behind her. They discussed plans for their wedding, the intricate details of which Aarón had no interest in. The shades of flowers, the textures of fabrics, the timing between courses, the waiters' gloves. Honestly, he found it all a bit surreal in light of what was going on around them.

A strong breeze blew off the bay through the windows lifting the gauzy curtains behind Beatriz. She would occasionally glance through the house toward the veranda and smile, catching Aarón's eye. Despite his concerns, Aarón was delighted to see her wrapped up in planning their nuptials. It gave them both a respite. Something to focus on during the birth pangs of a new regime.

Aarón, like most everyone he knew, welcomed Castro's arrival. He was, simply, not Batista. That wasn't to say there weren't those he knew who were close to the former regime and had fled shortly thereafter. That coterie included some of his cousins.

One, in particular, left the country piloting his own yacht. He arrived in Miami begging for asylum less than twenty-four hours after Batista's exit. This cousin was well known as an informant. The family joked about it for years. He and his children were no longer invited to family gatherings after the son of another cousin was arrested several days after a Passover Seder they all attended at Aarón's parents' home a few years back.

That cousin, an actor, and also named Aarón Cohan, declared his support for Castro after the assault on the Moncada Barracks at the Seder meal. He was arrested several days later. Obtaining his release cost thousands. He was immediately shipped off to Spain. He returned to Cuba a week after Castro entered Havana. Family gossip suggested that he was rising quickly in the new government.

Aarón pledged to himself to give the new government a chance. Their goals weren't far from his own, though certainly their path to achieving those goals was different from his. As of yet those paths were undefined, at best. Aarón's fantasy ended about two weeks after the triumph of the 26 of July Movement. The real face of Castro's regime showed itself. Batista's henchmen would be put on public trial.

Despite it being a Friday, Aarón found himself out of the office. There wasn't any reason to be there. Until a direction had been chosen by the new government, nothing would happen at the Bank of Cuba's Office of Economic Development. In the meantime, Alma and Hector would stand guard. They would contact him if he was needed.

Sipping his piña colada absentmindedly, Aarón stared anxiously at the television on the airy, sunlit veranda, the loose legs of his linen pants and *guayabera* rustling with the breeze. He'd moved the TV from its perch in the living room to the veranda fiddling with the rabbit-ear antenna until the reception was at least viewable.

Castro's trials of Batista's henchmen began today. Fidel had promised justice. To Aarón it seemed more like revenge. Perhaps it was needed. He had mixed feelings. He understood that this public display—in a stadium filled with 18,000 attendees and broadcast on radio and television to the nation and the world—was much more than that. It was a public display of power and a warning to those who questioned Fidel and his forces. Fidel was both smart and shrewd. He wanted the world to know that.

Aarón's concern was not so much about communism coming to Cuba. While Castro had the support of the left and those who openly argued for a socialist approach to Cuba's future, Fidel himself had not yet committed to communism. His concern was more about Fidel's heavy-handed approach to consolidating power. It was a warning to both his opposition and his allies. He was not to be trifled with. That, in itself, was more alarming than leftist economics. Cuba's history was littered with those who claimed to march in the service of liberty but had quarantined liberty for the sake of what they inevitably referred to as stability. That stability was, in fact, the entrenchment of a new political mafia.

The voice of the prosecutor drifted from the tinny television, recounting the crimes of the accused in great detail. How many men, women, and children had the defendant personally executed in service to the corrupt former Caudillo of Cuba? The frightened men pled innocence, of course.

Aarón questioned himself. As a lawyer, would he have advised the accused to plead innocent? No. There were too many witnesses, and the final judgment of the court was a foregone conclusion. Rather the accused should plead for mercy. His stomach turned. So much for justice. A show trial was a show trial, whether it was Stalin, or Trujillo, or McCarthy in the United States, or Fidel. It was meant to send a message, not to mete out justice. In his head, despite what his heart wanted to see, hear, and believe, Aarón already knew that Fidel was no different from the rest and that what was coming would be terrible.

Beatriz waved at him, gesturing to join them. He smiled and finished off the last of his piña colada, sucking two pieces of ice into his mouth letting them dissolve on his tongue. The vestigial taste of the pineapple faded as he crossed the hallway to the dining room. He walked around the mahogany table covered with tropical-colored cloth swatches and samples of printed place cards and menus. He wrapped his arms around Beatriz's waist.

She smiled and kissed him gently on the lips. "*Como estás, mi amor*," she said. "You seem concerned."

Aarón smiled. "No, not at all. I'm fine. I was watching the trial."

The room fell silent, glances bouncing off each other, then eyes averted. In the past weeks, moments like this had become all too common. No one wanted to talk about what was happening around them. But at the same time, no one stopped thinking about it, not even for a moment.

"Perhaps you should pay less attention," Beatriz's mother, Lina, said. An even longer moment of awkwardness resulted.

"*Mamá*, Aarón's future, our future, is on the line. Where this country goes is where we go." Her voice broke. She turned away for a moment, touching her eyes matter-of-factly, in an effort to hide her tears.

"Everything will be fine, *hermana*," said Roberta,

Beatriz's sister, reaching for her hand.

Beatriz turned. "Yes. I know it will. It's just wedding jitters," she laughed. "Don't all brides get them?" The women laughed. Aarón smiled. Eduardo, Beatriz's father sat stone-faced.

Aarón knew why. Eduardo owned and operated several large food markets in the capital. Some were in the poorest neighborhoods. He was an early and likely target, regardless of where the revolution went. To Fidel, adequate food was a human right. No one had the right to make a profit while children starved.

"Yes, we all get those jitters," said Roberta, embracing Beatriz. "Don't worry, everything will turn out fine. You will be the most beautiful bride.'

Beatriz dabbed her eyes with a small, lace handkerchief. She smiled and reached for two swatches of fabric, one a gauzy lavender, the other pinkish-orange, the color of cantaloupe flesh. "Which do you like better?"

Aarón took the two swatches, rubbing them slightly, the silky smoothness cool against his fingertips. "I have no preference. Which do you like? What are they for?"

"The bridesmaids' dresses and the linens."

"Which would you prefer to wear?" Aarón asked the bridesmaids.

The women laughed. "It's Beatriz's choice," Cecilia, one of Beatriz's friends, replied. "We wear whatever she chooses, whether we like it or not."

"Then, when we get married, we do the same to her!" chimed in Isabel, Beatriz's other friend."

"I see," said Aarón. "Very…democratic," he added, his joke landing flat. He took Beatriz's hand again. "Whatever you prefer."

Beatriz placed the two swatches next to each other. "I think I like them together, like a Bird-of-Paradise blossom."

"And that would be the floral arrangements, Birds-of-Paradise," added Roberta.

"It sounds lovely," said Aarón.

Beatriz smiled and kissed him again, this time quickly on the lips. "We'll pin one right here as well," she said jabbing him playfully on the chest.

"Shall we have lunch?" Lina said.

"Yes," Eduardo replied. "Quickly. My son-in-law looks hungry."

The women cleared the table of the various trappings of wedding planning and moved into the kitchen, leaving Aarón and Eduardo alone. The scratchy, tinny sound of the television drifted in from the veranda.

Eduardo looked directly at Aarón. "What have you learned?" he asked in a hushed tone. "Do my daughters have a future in this country?"

Aarón took in a breath and let it out slowly. He sat down opposite Eduardo and leaned in over the highly polished table. "I've learned nothing, directly. I have no insights. We haven't been given any directives at the bank other than to continue with our 'regular' duties. I have no idea what that means. Clearly, you see how absurd that is."

A muffled cheer came from the television followed by an exhortation from the judge to the crowd to maintain decorum. The trial was moving down its inevitable, inexorable path. The mob would be satiated, one way or another.

"Should we be making…different plans? These so-called liberators are already milling around my stores. They say it's for my own protection against potential looting. Then they saunter through the store and take what they want. They point out that the people have good reason to be angry." Eduardo sighed. "I'm one of the people, too."

Aarón walked to the window and looked outside. The waters of Havana Bay rippled under the midday sun. He considered Eduardo's statement. "I honestly don't know," he said. "You know how these things go. The first few months are always treacherous. I expect things to calm down." He hoped his lie adequately covered his falsely optimistic tone.

Eduardo chortled. "Not this time, I don't think so. I'm thinking the thousands I'm spending on this wedding might be better spent getting us all to Miami, now."

The following Monday Aarón dressed and went to the office as he had every day before the revolution. He decided that the best approach for him, both mentally and professionally, was to resume some semblance of normal activity. He found Alma at her desk as always, dressed more simply than before Castro's victory, but sitting straight backed as always at her desk. She smiled broadly, stood, and offered her hand as Aarón arrived at her desk.

"Good morning, *Señor* Cohan," she said, her usual 'sir,' gone.

"And good morning to you," Aarón replied.

"It's good to see you."

"You, too. Is Hector here?" he asked.

Alma shifted her eyes almost imperceptibly toward the door to Aarón's office. "Yes. He's waiting for you inside."

Aarón took the few steps to his office quickly, turning the knob and entering. Hector sat with his back to the door in front of Aarón's desk. He turned quickly upon hearing Aarón enter. Like Alma, his dress was much less formal than a few weeks ago. Gone was the suit and tie he normally wore, replaced by a simple *guayabera* and slacks. "Good morning," he said.

Aarón dropped his briefcase and suit jacket on the edge of the couch. "And to you. How propitious, I was just asking for you." He took Hector's hand as he rounded his desk. "Do you have mental telepathy?" he joked.

Hector smiled. "Perhaps. I expected you would be in today and I wanted to catch you as soon as you arrived." He looked at his watch. "You are very prompt for a Cuban."

Aarón chuckled. "You already knew that." He leaned over the desk toward Hector's and whispered, "What's going on?"

"There's no need for that," Hector replied. "No one is listening."

Aarón took him at his word. Hector had proved to be a good friend. There was no reason to suspect anything had changed. "Good," he replied, shifting back into the chair.

Hector took two Cohibas from his front pocket and offered one to Aarón. It was an act out of character for Hector, usually so edgy and aware of social position and formality.

Aarón took the cigar with a smile. "Thank you," he said, removing a double-bladed, guillotine cigar cutter and a lighter from the top drawer of his desk. He handed the guillotine to Hector, pushing an ornate crystal ashtray toward him as well. "Please."

Hector clipped the end of his cigar and placed it between his lips. Aarón reached over the desk and lit it, the flame from the lighter dancing as Hector puffed the pungent leaf, handing the clipper back to Aarón. Aarón clipped his own and lit it. "What are we celebrating?" he asked.

"Pimental is gone."

Aarón nodded. "Really?"

"I am to be his replacement here at the bank."

"You have been appointed Deputy Minister of Finance?"

"No," said Hector. "I am to be the representative of the Movement at the bank. A new deputy minister will be appointed in due time."

Aarón held his breath for a brief moment. He wasn't sure what to make of this development. He knew Hector was well connected. He had played both sides. His was a delicate balancing act that had propelled him from a position as a bank teller to one as a lieutenant to a high-ranking official at the bank, namely Aarón. Aarón himself had helped Hector. Though he had trusted him completely, he never knew where Hector's loyalties really lay. Now he questioned his prior actions. Had he placed a viper in his own office? He stood and offered his hand. "Congratulations."

Hector accepted Aarón's good wishes. He held Aarón's hand for a long moment, longer than might have been expected. "There's no need to worry," he said. "I appreciate everything you've done for me. I wouldn't have gotten to where I am without you. I know where your heart lies with respect to Cuba and our people. We will work together for a new and better future."

Spoken like a true revolutionary, Aarón thought. "Thank you. May I ask what happened with Pimental?"

"He's been arrested."

"I see."

"Off the record, we learned he was preparing to flee. We caught him at his estate near Guantanamo. He was there with his children and grandchildren. Their yacht was ready to go. You should have seen the look on his face when I walked in."

Aarón was both surprised by Hector's expression of

satisfaction, and shocked that Hector was present at Pimental's arrest. That fact alone revealed much about how deeply involved and connected to the new government Hector was. Aarón never thought of him as vindictive. "Where is he now?" he asked.

"He's under house arrest. His sons are in Presidio Modelo."

"I see," Aarón replied. He puffed calmly on his Cohiba. The smoked swirled around him, the taste of the tobacco and the sensation of the smoke in his mouth in some way calming. "Hector, may I ask you something?"

"Of course."

"Were you an inside man for Castro here at the bank; before the revolution?"

Hector smiled. He flicked the growing ash off his cigar. "Aarón, we have known each other for a long while. I know you think of me as a friend and a confidant."

"Yes. I wouldn't have trusted anyone else with my brother's life."

"I know that. I'm not your enemy, nor am I here to spy on you."

"But my question…"

"I understand your question. My answer is neither simple nor nuanced. No, I wasn't here as Castro's inside man. But I was connected to the Movement. That much I can tell you. I come from a modest background. You know that. My father was a clerk in the tax office. My mother *es una morena*. I had no real future. No connections, no influence. I began to see that we needed a new direction as a nation, especially after Pimental arrived here at the bank. He was so smug. Those two sons barging in here like they owned the place themselves, their sports cars parked outside while they stole from the people. It maddened me. One day, as I was leaving for lunch and siesta, a friend from my school days was waiting near the entrance. He approached me. He was with the Movement. He asked me to help. I told him, 'I'm not political.' I wanted only a modest, comfortable life. He said, 'everyone had to be political now.' I ran from him."

Hector stopped speaking for a moment. He puffed on his cigar before beginning anew. "I thought about my conversation with him that night. I couldn't sleep. A week later I sought him out through some mutual friends, and I asked what I could do to help. He said, 'keep your eyes open, tell us what you see, what you observe.' Then my involvement grew a bit as I rose in the ranks here. They told me if I had an opportunity to meet people closer to Batista, take it, and report back."

"That's how you came to know the people at BRAC?"

"Yes, exactly."

"May I ask you one question?"

Hector straightened. "Of course."

"Are you a communist?"

"No," he replied without hesitation. "I am a patriot."

Chapter Nine

Moises hurried through the throngs in the market. The presence of their soldiers assured him that now, a month and a half after the revolution, Cuba was securely in their hands. Their work was far from over, he knew that. There was subversion everywhere. With time they would root it out. They would win the hearts and minds of the millions who had welcomed them but had not yet come to believe in the revolution's goals.

At the far end of the market, Moises crossed the street and entered an imposing building fronted with marble columns. Formerly the Ministry of Agriculture, it now served as the home of the Committee for Economic Reform, of which he was a member. No more stifling basements reeking of mold.

While his father had insisted that he study accounting so as to manage and eventually take over the family business, those same skills would now serve the people. Moises was charged with reviewing the accounting practices of privately owned manufacturers, both to root out corruption and cheating and to establish fairness for their workers. An appropriate wage would be required and paid. Equity would be guaranteed.

Two weeks after Che entered Havana, Luis called a

meeting of their group. He was chosen by Che himself to lead the transition of administrative positions for several departments. He placed Moises in this post because he was unique among their group in his knowledge of accounting principles—as bourgeois as they were—and for his family's personal connections to many in the manufacturing and retail sectors in and around La Habana. At first, Moises was both disappointed and a bit angry. He was a political theorist by education and an expert on socialist economic theory by interest. Not a bean counter.

Moises wanted and expected a purely political appointment. One that would provide him with the opportunity to educate and win over those who supported Batista's ouster but had not yet come to understand why their future lay in socialism. Nonetheless, he accepted his assignment with grace in front of his *compañeros* but complained bitterly to Ana Teresa later that evening.

"Luis has taken me out of the vanguard," he said, his back to her. He faced the terrace windows, the lights of Havana twinkling in the distance. They were still living in the same penthouse he used as a safe house when victory came. The owners, already in Miami when the revolution triumphed, requested political asylum in the United States. The son and daughter of the owners, erstwhile revolutionaries, had joined their parents less than two weeks after Batista's fall. Their commitment to the cause was not nearly as deeply ingrained as their feelings of entitlement. Their romance with the revolution faded quickly.

"That's not true," Ana Teresa said, coming up behind him, wrapping her arms around his waist. He felt the warm evenness of her breath against his neck. "Remember, from each according to his abilities."

"I have many abilities," he replied, taking her hands

into his.

"That's true, but few have your abilities in these areas."

Moises turned, still in Ana Teresa's embrace. "I want to be with the people, educate them, win them over to our side. We are at a critical juncture. I'm needed. Bean counting can wait." Moises hesitated for a moment. "I want to be with you, leading the revolution forward."

Ana Teresa smiled that same smile that disarmed Moises every time. "You will be. That's the whole idea. We need you to work on a more personal level, closer to the bourgeoisie, more directly with them. We need to understand each economic unit and how it functions. What its relationship was to the old regime, if any? You have the skills for that."

"We?" Moises said, pulling back a bit, loosening the embrace between them. "I thought Luis made the assignments.

"We made the assignments, Luis, Marcos, and me," said Ana Teresa. "Together, as a committee."

Moises chuckled. "That figures."

"What?"

"Marcos. He gave me this job to get me away from you."

Ana Teresa stepped back. "What are you talking about?"

"I see the way he looks at you."

"You're crazy."

"Maybe a little jealous, not crazy."

Ana Teresa led Moises to the couch and pulled him down next to her. "*Amor*, here is the truth," she said, "I made the decision to give you this job, not the committee. And as to Marcos and how he looks at me, yes, I know. I ignore it. And I'm hurt that you would doubt my feelings and commitment to you. It's not me who stands in the way of our future together."

That last statement, though true, stung sharply. It cut through Moises like a knife. Ana Teresa was right. It wasn't she or Marcos standing in the way of their life together. Despite everything that had happened, he still hadn't found a way to reconcile his love for Ana Teresa and a life with her with the objections of his family to that relationship. "Then marry me," Moises said.

Ana Teresa kissed him deeply and profoundly. Later that afternoon, they were married by a magistrate in the old courthouse in La Habana Vieja.

Moises sat at his desk, a fan whirling gently behind him creating a pleasant breeze. It was warm for February. More than a month since his assignment, he still wasn't comfortable sitting behind the large desk, its wood elegantly carved into leaves and vines climbing its four corners. Sitting at it felt like a betrayal, that somehow the desk would transform him into its previous master, a capitalist. He was so uncomfortable with it that he didn't use its drawers. Rather he piled up papers and folders on two smaller tables on either side.

Moises reached across to the pile of folders on his left. He grabbed the top two. One was thick with the information he had collected on clothing stores and their supply chains. How did they get their inventory? What was the relationship between their suppliers and the former government? What was their own relationship with the former government?

He knew from personal experience that there were many business owners, people like his father, who operated in an opaque environment. They were, for all intents and purposes, apolitical. They didn't want to pay 'commissions,' but had little choice. Their objective was to make a profit. They didn't care who they had to bribe. It was part of the cost of doing business.

The second folder was much thinner. In it were a few slips of paper detailing irregularities Moises had found in several concerns. Sudden changes in store inventory and shipping arrangements, the kinds of things that normally stayed unchanged for years. All the changes had come in the past year. The similarities in the irregularities were unusual, considering the fact that the ownership of the stores and factories involved appeared to be completely unconnected. That was a clear indicator of corruption. The question was why these businesses, and why now?

One of the companies under scrutiny belonged to a longtime friend of his father, Benny Abromo, formerly Abramovitz. Abromo and Moises's father were born in the same small town in eastern Poland. Benny was a few years older than Rafael. He'd come to Cuba two years earlier than Rafael and helped him establish his first shoe factory. He bought Rafael's products and sold them in his stores in the capital. That account itself was enough to nurture Esther Shoes and Handbags through its first few, critical years. The Cohans owed a great debt to Abromo.

Moises considered whether to pay a visit to Benny. It was a double-edged sword. He, like everyone else in Havana's small Jewish community, knew that the son of Rafael Cohan was an influential official in the new government. They assumed that could work for them. What they didn't understand was that Moises couldn't be bought. He wanted the truth, but at the same time didn't want to intimidate his father's friends. He preferred to make allies of them. To bring them to the side of the new government.

Despite Moises's own politics, Castro, while clearly on the left, was not a self-declared communist. If people like his father and his father's friends understood that, they might more easily be persuaded to cooperate with the coming reforms. He reached for a pen and a small white card printed with the name and title of the former occupant of the office. He found them to be pretentious. He scratched out the name and appellation, blotting out the past, and scribbled a quick note to Abromo on its back, addressing him as *tío*.

He chuckled to himself. All of his father's friends were *tío*, though none were really his uncles. He knew almost nothing of his father's siblings. They had died in Hitler's camps, along with his grandparents, never ever talked about. The subject was forbidden. His parents had forged a substitute family here in paradise. He asked Tío Benny if he would be so kind as to meet with him privately, at Benny's home in Miramar. His discretion would be both assumed and appreciated. He signed the note *Moisch*, using the old Yiddish diminutive of his name.

"Luz," he called out.

"Sí," came the pleasant sound of his assistant's voice, followed by her arrival in the doorway a few seconds later.

"I need a favor," he said, slipping the note into a blank envelope and sealing it. He wrote the name and address quickly across its face. "Would you deliver this for me? I could send you in an official car, but I think that would attract unwanted attention."

Luz reached for the envelope and looked at the address. "This will take most of the day."

"Yes. But it's very important to our work."

Luz nodded, still staring at the envelope. "I understand. I will be back as soon as possible."

Moises made his way by bus to Miramar the next afternoon. As expected, Tío Benny accepted Moises's invitation to meet. He invited Moises for lunch. He would send the help home for the afternoon to assure proper discretion.

Moises walked the few blocks from the bus stop to Tío Benny's villa overlooking the water. He looked at the imposing home for a long minute before pushing open the gate that separated it from the street. In a neighborhood of wealth, it stood out. It was a statement to the success of its owner. Moises considered what might become of both it and Tío Benny in the future. He thought of Abuela's shack on a rooftop in Old Havana. The days of such opulence were over.

"*¿Tío, como estás*?" Moises called out.

Benny was seated on the veranda in a wicker chair on deep, plush cushions. He still looked more like a longshoreman, thick and muscular, than a capitalist department store owner. He put down the paper at the sound of Moises's voice. "*Bien, mijo*," he replied, rising from the chair, and taking Moises hand, pulling him in and embracing him. "You look well." He pointed to the ruffled newspaper resting now on the table next to the chair. "But what I read disturbs me."

"Why?"

"I don't like the direction things are going."

"What do you mean?"

Tío Benny sat down. He tapped the paper. "Fidel has named himself Prime Minister."

Moises saw the anger in Benny's eyes. "It's for the good of the nation," he replied.

"It's for the good of Castro. That's who it's good for.

He will replace Urrutia next. Wait, you will see."

Moises held back. He wanted to explain why Fidel's move was for the benefit of Cuba, but it was obvious how much passion and fear Castro's moves were having on those who were critical to the lifeblood of the Cuban economy. He was here for other reasons. He needed Tío Benny to answer his questions. If he pushed him too far about politics, he would stonewall completely. The country was polarized, obsessed with personal considerations and fear. Moises understood how fiercely people like his father and Benny guarded their lives and their property. Benny could see no farther than the gate to his house. The teeming masses of Havana and the squalor of the provinces were not within his purview.

"I understand your concerns," he said. "Fidel is trying to solidify our victory. There are many who would help Batista to return."

"Are you accusing Cardona of complicity with Batista's people?" Tío Benny said, crossing his arms against his puffed-out chest, referring to the ousted Prime Minister. "Cardona was a leader of the resistance against Batista for years. He is also a champion of democracy."

Moises was surprised at the candor Benny displayed, even though it was in private. He hoped Benny knew better than to speak like this in front of others. Moises would never betray him. But others? Benny had much to lose. Those who heard this type of talk had much to gain in an environment that had quickly turned to one of opportunism, especially against the bourgeois class. The recently organized Committee for the Defense of the Revolution was testament to that.

"I would be careful who you say that to. I'm happy to listen to your criticism of the progress of the revolution, but not everyone will be. What is it you are concerned about?"

Benny took in a deep breath, reminding Moises of his father, tough but vulnerable, forever tainted by the experience of the political upheavals of their youth which brought them to Cuba to begin with. "He speaks now of agrarian reform. I've seen and heard that before."

Moises hesitated a moment. Of course there would be land reform. The Cuban people needed it. He wasn't going to explain the politics and economics behind it at this point. Anyway, it would fall on deaf ears. "What concerns you?" he asked.

"Will my business, or your father's, be next? We have built this country and it has built us. We have given back. We have tried to be fair to our workers."

Moises knew this to be true. Nevertheless, it presented an opening for him to begin his questions. "Why do you say that?"

Benny laughed. "Because it's already begun."

"What?"

"The corruption."

Moises said nothing.

"That's why you wanted to see me, yes? You are the last honest man?"

Moises pulled a small pad and pen out of his breast pocket. "Yes, it has. But we will not tolerate corruption. Tell me what happened."

"Can I trust you, *mijo*?" Benny asked.

"You've said more than you should have already. And you know that. Frankly, you knew that when you agreed to see me."

Benny smiled. "Who am I to refuse a meeting with a high ranking official of the new government."

"Who also happens to be your godson. Please Tío, I need your help."

Benny leaned forward in his chair. He reached for a cigar, lit it, and took a long drag. "Alright then, what do you want to know?"

Moises took a single sheet of paper from his pants pocket and unfolded it. "This is a chart that shows us which manufacturers of certain goods supply those goods to retail stores such as yours. In this case we are talking about women's dresses. Specifically, it shows us that certain companies shifted their suppliers in the past year, and others immediately after the revolution. The new contracts are for lesser amounts of money but larger inventory. Yet, the factories are farther away from Havana. Transport costs are higher. I'm not sure how this happens, or why?

Benny chuckled. He looked over Moises's page of figures and graphs. "Your father didn't teach you much."

"He taught me that the goal was to make a profit."

"That's what they did. They lowered cost of goods and increased profit."

"Why would these manufacturers be able to provide the same goods for less from farther away?"

Benny shrugged, playing coy. "Lower labor costs?"

"Perhaps, but I checked on that, too. The prevailing wage was actually higher than that paid by the previous manufacturers."

"All the contracts came from the same factory?"

Moises sat back in his chair. "Several companies, multiple factories."

Benny puffed on his cigar. "You really don't know?"

"I suspect. I want you to confirm my suspicions."

"Off the record."

"Completely."

"Consider where the factories are located. That region has been under the control of your forces for many months now. Also consider who owns the factories, and who was in charge of your people in those areas."

"I have," replied Moises. "And as such, deals were, are, being made?"

"Naturally," said Benny, puffing on his cigar. "By one of yours, obviously. Follow the money. Look at who owns the factory. What family. Look at who is transporting the goods. And remember, the old Cuban saying, *no hay mal, que por bien no venga*."

Moises closed his eyes. Yes, indeed, he thought, something good always comes out of something bad.

⁂

Moises found Ana Teresa in the kitchen of the rambling penthouse when he returned from Benny's house. She was chopping onions. Other ingredients, a coconut, a can of coconut milk, tomatoes, a fragrant bunch of cilantro, sat on the counter. He was always surprised by this juxtaposition of her many sides. Today she was a revolutionary who loved to cook. "What's for dinner?"

"Look in the sink."

Moises crossed the room quickly. A large fish, shiny and smelling faintly of the sea sat on a slab of ice.

He turned and smiled. "*Pescado en coco*?"

"*Sí,*" Ana Teresa replied.

Moises sidled up next to Ana Teresa. "Where did you get that?" he asked. "A bit surprising. Are the fisherman back to work?"

She put down the knife she'd been using to chop the onions. "Yes, they are, but that's not where I got it. Marcos gave it to me."

Moises pulled back a step. "Where did he get it?"

"His cousin brought several in today. He gave them out to a few of the others in the unit as well."

Moises took Ana Teresa's hand. "You know that's completely forbidden. We can't accept anything from anyone. It's corruption."

Ana Teresa turned to him. "Don't you think that's overdoing it a bit? It was a couple of fish from his cousin."

"Did you meet his cousin?"

"No."

"Then how do we know that's the truth?"

Ana Teresa hesitated for a moment. She picked up the knife and began chopping again. "I'm not going to respond to your question. Marcos, like the rest of our *compañeros*, is a man of the people. That fish isn't a bribe. It's a thank you for our sacrifices."

Chapter Ten

Aarón stared at the letter Hector handed him minutes earlier. He drew it closer and read it again. It was signed, simply, Che. "Do you understand what this means?" he said. "What he's asking me to do?"

"Yes. That's why I thought it was best that I deliver it personally."

"Is he aware that my father is among those who would lose their businesses if the leather tanning and shoe manufacturing industries are nationalized?"

"All those affected would receive appropriate compensation."

Aarón laughed in disbelief. "You believe that?"

"Yes."

Aarón looked directly into Hector's face, his new face, the one that appeared after he was appointed as the representative of the revolution at the National Bank of Cuba.

"Do you know that for a fact?" he asked, his voice purposefully modulated now, devoid of the anger he exhibited only seconds earlier.

Hector's face transformed again momentarily. Aarón recognized the old Hector, the one he considered both his protégé and his friend.

"No," Hector replied.

Aarón slumped back into his chair. "I can't do this," he said. "Che is obviously testing me, determining where my loyalties lay. Have other officials here at the bank received similar assignments?"

"Some." Hector softened his tone; less stringent, less official. "You don't have a choice, really. No one says no to Che. For anything. He is Fidel's eyes and ears."

"He is asking me to betray my father."

The new Hector reappeared. "He is asking you to render a legal opinion as to whether an industry, any industry, in this case leather tanning, can be nationalized under our constitution."

"And he knows the answer to that already."

"Tell him the truth. Or find a way for him to do it."

"You believe they're looking for the truth?"

"I believe they're looking for justice. And justice is truth."

Aarón looked directly into Hector's eyes. This was someone he had considered a friend, a confidant. Someone whom he had helped and who had helped him. An ally. Now he wondered. Had that help been merely political? A matter of convenience and self-interest? A way for Hector to improve his position under the former regime? What was his real agenda?

"I asked you a question some weeks ago and I'm going to ask you again. Are you a communist? Do you support these moves?"

"Fidel is not a communist. And what moves exactly are you asking me about?"

Aarón knew he was treading on a minefield. He didn't know for certain what Hector's agenda was, nor apparently his politics, but this request from Che and its delivery by Hector was a clear indication that Hector was securely in their camp. “I asked about you, not Fidel. And Che is an avowed communist. Everyone knows that.”

Hector remained silent.

“Everyone knows that Fidel is developing a plan for agrarian reform,” Aarón continued. “Why not extend that to every part of the economy?” He held up the letter. “And why not start with tanning hides and making *chancletas*? What would satisfy the people more than free sandals?” He regretted his words as he heard himself utter them.

Hector straightened his back. Sat up in the chair, placing his hands on his knees. “I told you, I am not a communist, but Cuba needs a new start. That’s what Fidel promised us.”

“Like those trials in the stadium? Did that wash away Batista and his henchmen? Do we have new henchmen now? Is it the turn now of Batista’s unwitting accomplices, landowners and capitalist factory owners, to bow before the people?”

Hector hesitated, far off for a moment, then nodded. “In some cases, yes. Not all of them were unwitting. There are families who live in fantastical luxury while their farms are worked by people living in squalor, like serfs. Why? Because the Spanish crown awarded land to these families centuries ago. Land that wasn’t theirs to give to begin with.”

“My father didn’t receive anything from the Spanish crown.”

Hector face softened, the old Hector returning once again, if only for a moment. “I know that. I know your father, he’s a good man. But that doesn’t excuse the excesses of those who aren’t.”

“Then you support this?” Aarón replied, tapping his finger on Che’s letter now laying on the table between them.

"I didn't say that. I think there is a middle ground. Perhaps you can show the General that?"

Aarón laughed. "That's why you brought this to me personally? That's the problem we're now facing? A middle ground? You and those like you, desperate to find one? Why? Because you never really looked at Castro, or his movement, what they really stood for. Until it was too late. They were honest. They told us what their intentions were. He told us where he stood by who he surrounded himself with. Those who supported the aims of his fight but didn't agree with his vision simply looked away. Why? Because he wasn't Batista. Anyone but Batista. And what's happening now? He's made himself Prime Minister. What's next? How many have already expressed unhappiness with his direction? How many are backing away? The rats are beginning to jump ship. There are rumors that President Urrutia is on the way out and that General Huber Matos is considering a mutiny."

Hector neither confirmed nor denied the rumors. "Perhaps you should speak with your brother."

"That's the last thing I would do. He's a perfect example of what I'm saying. A convinced communist, and with Fidel from the beginning."

Hector leaned forward a bit. He took a breath. "Aarón, I've told you this before. I'm a friend, not an enemy. I brought the letter myself out of respect, rather than having you summoned to Che's offices, and handed that letter by one of his functionaries. You have to deal with this. Not responding is the worst option. It will mark you. Changes are coming, I agree, not all of them good for everyone." Hector paused for a moment, the tone of his voice changing from sanctimonious to pleading. "It's better at this point to have input into the changes than to object by abstention or inaction. Isn't that what you taught me?"

Aarón studied Hector again, his eyes wishing they had the power to read his mind. Short of that, Aarón searched for any clues that might betray Hector's true thoughts. He wanted to give him the benefit of the doubt, though he knew realistically that the ship was already tossing about in hurricane waters. There might not be a lifeline, even for a friend.

The note Beatriz delivered to Alberto Martinez was disguised as a greeting card. She attached the small envelope to a large bouquet of flowers and showed up at their apartment unexpected. Delighted to see Beatriz, Amalda, Martinez's wife, asked her to wait in the living room while Alberto dressed. The former minister greeted Beatriz in a silk smoking jacket over pajamas, leaning on an ornate carved cane with an ivory handle. He told her he was working hard on recovering from his recent fall, determined to dance at her wedding.

"Their maid didn't leave the living room for a single moment," Beatriz recounted to Aarón in the quiet of her mother's living room.

She kept her own voice down, too low for their own maid to hear. Daily life had become uncomfortable in the ten weeks since the revolution. No one knew who to trust. What to say, what not to say, and in front of whom. Many of their friends and relatives had lost their domestic help. The days of serving the upper classes were over. Servants simply quit.

Aarón sighed. He looked at the small, white card in his hand. Martinez had written his response on the back. "He will see me," Aarón said, both relieved and apprehensive. He suggests we meet at a small café across from the

Malecon near their apartment early this Sunday morning."

"That makes sense," Beatriz said. "Their maid doesn't come in on Sundays anymore. She can't ask where he's going. She can't insist on accompanying him on the ruse of helping him. The café is near enough for him to walk."

"He's made some improvement then?"

"Yes. He and Amalda go out every day." Beatriz smiled. "They are determined to be at our wedding. Amalda whispered to me that she will accompany him as far as the entrance to the café. She'll wait across the Malecon till she sees him come out again."

"He looks well?"

Beatriz vacillated for a moment. She looked away toward the bay through the open window, the sheer curtains fluttering in the breeze.

"Yes, he does, physically. They both do. But one can see how guarded they are in front of the maid."

"She has been with them for years. Do they believe she's spying on them?"

"Likely."

"Why? He never supported Batista. Alejandro was arrested more than once for his statements against him."

"Their son and his family have sought asylum at the American Embassy."

Aarón was taken aback. "When?"

"About a week ago."

"I didn't know."

"No one does." Beatriz pulled a slip of paper from her skirt pocket. "Amalda wrote this note while I was chatting with Alejandro. She slipped it into my bag. I found it when I got home."

Aarón read over the hastily scribbled note written on the back of a shopping list. Their son had been taken into custody, questioned then released. He worked for an

American company. That night in the small, quiet hours, he, his wife, and their two small children crept through Havana's dark alleys to the embassy. They are still there.

Aarón felt a sense of dread build in his chest. "I will see what I can find out before I meet with Alejandro on Sunday."

The next morning Aarón waited outside Hector's office, the one previously occupied by Pimental. The irony of the situation wasn't lost on him. He'd visited Pimental to glean information about his brother's status under the past regime. Now he would seek information about Martinez's son from the new regime in the same place. Power haunted the space, only the masters changed.

Hector showed obvious surprise when he spotted Aarón hurrying down the hallway. "Good to see you. Did I forget that we had an appointment today?"

"No," Aarón replied. "I wanted to chat with you a bit more about our conversation last week." Aarón glanced toward Hector's secretary, sitting some ten feet away. He searched her body language for clues. Was she truly focused on the letter she was typing or was she listening? Beatriz's account of her meeting with the Martinezes and their maid was making him paranoid. BRAC, the Bureau for the Repression of Communist Activities was gone, but now the CDR, the Committee for the Defense of the Revolution was everywhere.

Hector opened his office door and gestured inside. He dropped his bag on his desk and gestured to the couch, an all too familiar and somewhat eerie *déjà vu* for Aarón. Hector joined him, sitting closer than Aarón would have expected.

"Are you making progress on that request?" Hector asked, his voice low.

"Yes," Aarón replied. "But it requires more research. I will need some additional time."

"You came to ask for more time? You could have sent me a note. Take the time you need to get us the answer we need."

Aarón felt his anger rise. Was he nothing more than a tool to contrive a justification for their actions? "That's not why I'm here. I was hoping you could shed some light on something." He kept his voice low and steady.

Hector inched a bit closer. He raised his eyebrow. "What then?"

"Professor Martinez's son."

"What's happened?

"He's under scrutiny."

Hector nodded. "You would like me to do for his son what I did for your brother some months ago?"

"Yes."

"I can tell you this. It would help both Professor Martinez and his son if he was more careful with his comments about the revolution."

"You know him, Hector. He opposed Batista. He supported the revolution. He was very vocal about it."

Hector leaned back, chuckling smugly. "The powers that be are not interested in yesterday, they are interested in tomorrow. We all opposed Batista. The question now is who supports the goals of the revolution?"

Aarón hesitated. "He's an old man. He's not well."

"Yes, I've heard. He had a fall."

"He has one child. It would help to know what his situation is."

Hector nodded. "I understand. I will see what I can find out."

Aarón waited at a corner table in the small café on the Malecon. The air was full of the salty scent of the sea, waves breaking against the promontory. The day was lovely, the skies blue and cloudless. The café was nearly empty. He watched the entrance for Martinez, sipping his *cafecito*. Martinez appeared just as he finished the cup.

Aarón rose from the table and walked quickly to the entrance to help him. He spied Amalda across the street on a bench, the spray from the waves nearly reaching her. Her expression was a mix of preoccupation, fear, and sorrow; her usual smile nowhere to be found.

"*Buenos días*, Minister," Aarón said, reaching out his left hand to Martinez, helping him down the two steps into the café.

"*Igual*," Martinez replied, letting go of Aarón's hand. "I can take it from here. Just point the way. I'm determined to be at your wedding without this," he added, shaking the cane.

Aarón gestured to the corner. He signaled to the waiter to bring two coffees and the plate of palmier pastries he ordered earlier as he followed behind Martinez, ever at the ready if the professor lost his balance. Once seated, Martinez smiled. "See, on the mend."

"Yes. And thank God for that. And how are you doing otherwise?"

Martinez chuckled. "You already know."

Aarón nodded. "Yes. I will tell you that I have made some inquiries. I haven't received any answers yet."

"Thank you. That's not why you wanted to see me."

Aarón pulled Che's letter from his pocket and handed it to Martinez. Martinez placed a pair of rimless glasses on the bridge of his nose. He read the letter several times, touching certain passages with his index finger and re-reading them. Finally, after a few moments, he removed his glasses and looked directly at Aarón. "Before I advise you, what are your thoughts about this?"

"They want to justify an illegal, unconstitutional action."

"Correct. And why do you think they are asking you to do it?"

"They want to know where my sympathies lie."

"Correct. But there's more."

"What?"

"They know who your brother is. You don't know what he may have told them."

Aarón had not considered that.

"This may be a test for him as well. They know your father is in this industry. They want to see what Moises will do if he learns of this, as well as your sympathies. Will he intercede in some way? Have you spoken with him about this?"

"No, of course not."

"Good."

"What should I do?"

"Do you think Moises can be trusted to keep this to himself?"

"I don't know. He's very committed to the revolution."

Martinez laughed. "That's no surprise. The blindness of idealism. Have you seen him since the revolution?"

"Yes, briefly, at my parent's home, twice."

"Has he asked about your work? Your position at the bank?"

"No. If anything, we avoid the subject."

"Judgment tells me he is unaware of this," Martinez said, looking over the letter again. "They may be zealots, but they don't trust each other. Too many factions. You have no choice here, just as you had no choice under Batista. You have to respond. They have asked you for an opinion. That's your job. You are legal counsel to the National Bank of Cuba. It's not about your father as much as it's about our legal system. I suggest you answer them, honestly."

Aarón took a breath. "The truth is, under the present constitution they can't do this, or anything like this."

"That's unfortunate for them. And for you. I would prefer that honesty be a virtue here, but I doubt that. You have a choice. Play ball or fade into the background. But remember, nothing stops the tide of history. We were desperate for change. Now we've got it. The question is can we control it or is it already too late."

Aarón nodded. "I understand."

"How did you receive this letter?"

"What do you mean?"

"Were you summoned to his office?" Martinez said, careful not even to utter that single syllable moniker for fear of who might be listening.

"No. Hector brought it to me."

Martinez hmphed. "Really? I'd be careful around him."

"Why?"

"He's the official who picked up my son at his home and brought him in for questioning."

Chapter Eleven

Moises set up a series of tables in a large, unused, conference room down the hall from his office. The room reflected its nearly imperial past. Conceived as a gathering place for the influential it was gilded in old oil paintings of Spanish colonials on horseback over paneled walls more appropriate to temperate Spain than tropical Cuba. The portraits kept a watchful eye over leather-clad chairs surrounding mahogany tables. Moises kept the door locked. Even Luz didn't have a key.

On the first table, he placed a large map of Cuba tacked down to some old cardboard. He outlined various regions in different color ink, detailing the advance of the Movement's forces at various dates. He stuck pins in the several locations where the factories that manufactured the goods he was tracking were located. He did the same with the stores where the goods were ultimately sold. In dark marker, he noted the truck routes used to deliver the goods, and with a unique set of pins topped with crosses, he noted the locations of the companies that moved the goods.

On the second and third tables, he laid out the reports he received from both the manufacturers and the retailers he was investigating. The papers were divided into ten separate areas, five on each table, each delineated by a thick tape across the table to keep the individual records segregated. He placed a blank pad of accounting paper in each area.

On the fourth table was an accounting calendar for each company with entry spaces for payments and dates. Finally, when he had assembled all the necessary information, he would plot out all the results. The truths of his investigations would appear almost magically. Moises chuckled to himself. The capitalist education his father had paid for would come in handy.

Moises picked up the phone in the corner of the room and dialed. "Could you come to the old conference room, please?" he said into the heavy handset. "Bring your adding machine." A moment later Luz appeared, adding machine in hand. She looked around the room, puzzled.

"We're looking for the answer to a riddle."

"What's the riddle?"

"Why a capitalist would suddenly choose to pay more for the same goods and services than he did in the past."

"I don't understand."

Moises smiled. "Our charge is to root out corruption. No capitalist accepts a reduction in profit…"

"…Unless he's forced to…"

"Exactly." Moises gestured to the tables and explained them to Luz. They would study the financial statements, invoices, receipts, etc., he had collected from these companies and chart the changes. He began by giving her some sheets of accounting paper he had already worked on. "Please tabulate each column and then note the month-to-month difference and indicate a negative change in revenues and/or expenses in red. Keep separate figures for the cost of manufactured goods, transport, and retail sales revenue."

Luz looked at Moises. A smile crept up around her mouth. "You know I have no idea what you're talking about."

Moises stopped himself. He hadn't considered that. He knew instinctively that he could trust Luz. She was reliable and honest, and committed to the cause, but had no knowledge of accounting. Before the revolution, she worked as a stock clerk in a grocery store. The lists of figures and the ruled accounting paper were a mystery to her. "Don't be intimidated," he said, noticing the blush rushing to her face. "I will explain it to you."

Luz hesitated a moment. She put down the adding machine and wrapped her arms around herself. "Perhaps I'm not the best person for this."

"Nonsense," Moises said. "I can trust you. That's more important than accounting skills. I can teach you that." He saw Luz's discomfort, took her by the hand, and led her to the first table. "Let me elucidate."

Moises explained how he had mapped out his suspicions. Someone was extorting both manufacturers and retailers, and the extortion was centered in areas the Movement had controlled for well over a year. That implied the extortionist was in the Movement or at least had extensive connections within it.

He moved with Luz to the second table and briefly explained the basic premise of accounting entries. "The two sides must balance. If you have an entry on one side, you must have a commensurate entry on the other. Where there's a credit, there's a debit."

Luz nodded. She made a quick note on her pad.

"But we have to drill down farther, into the individual entries," Moises explained. "We're looking for changes in variable costs. That's where one can hide things. Rent is fixed. Labor costs for the most part too, but other types of expenses change over time, say transportation costs. What we're doing is called fluctuation analysis. We will look month-over-month and year-over-year."

"How long a period is it necessary to examine?" asked Luz.

Moises smiled. "Good question. Normally, I'd want to look at a year or more, but in this case, we may not have that luxury. We will look at six months at least."

"And then?"

"We will look at the who rather than the what."

"The who?"

"Yes. Which of our people was in the area where we find the probable fraud, and when."

Luz put down her pad and pen. "You really believe one of our people is corrupt?"

Moises leaned against the third table. "Sadly, yes. And it's our job to catch him."

The analysis took the better part of a week. The extortion was not as well hidden as it might have been, which meant that the perpetrator was either not well versed in accounting methods or too brazen to care, or both. The graft was hidden in trucking costs. The factories were all located in provinces under the control of the Movement for at least a year. The bulk of the activity was in and around Santa Clara.

The evidence was well hidden but not well enough. Both the dress manufacturers and the retail operators took a hit. The wholesale cost of the goods dropped, and the retail prices stayed the same, but transportation costs jumped, almost doubling. The overall plan was good enough to keep the untrained eye from detecting the shift of payments from one cost component to another. But a trained eye and a close investigation into the components of bringing a dress to market revealed an inexplicable jump in expenses.

Moises went to see Tío Benny again. This time Benny was less interested in supplying hard information. He did agree to introduce Moises to one of his manufacturers, which is how Moises found himself on a long bus ride to Altagracia, a village just outside Santa Clara. He sat quietly toward the rear of the bus, bouncing about as it hit cracks and holes in the road. He made a note to contact his counterpart in the Department of Public Works. Road repair was an easy and tangible result the Movement could use to build support with the people. It would create jobs and improve conditions.

It took nearly a day to get to Altagracia. Upon arrival, he asked a shirtless old man in sandals sitting under a mango tree next to the bus stop where he would find the dress factory owned by Eugenio Morales. The old man pointed to his right. It was a short walk, he told Moises, just down the road on the right and then set back from the road a bit behind a grove of trees. He would see it. As Moises turned the old man asked him for a few pesos. He was hungry. This is what the revolution was about. No one, especially an old man, should sit in rags begging for a few pesos. Moises reached into his pocket and pulled out some coins and placed them in the old man's bony, outstretched palm. "Things will change soon, *abuelito*," he said.

Moises walked slowly down the dirt road that led to the factory. As he grew closer, he could see it through the trees. When he was nearly upon it, the hum of machinery became evident. The front door was open, as were the few windows. Upon entering the temperature rose dramatically. The presence of so much machinery and so many bodies threw off much heat. He began to sweat.

All the machine operators were women, some of them

clearly too young to be there. Moises himself had written the regulations governing the minimum age for factory work only weeks ago. He made another note, this time mental. More enforcement of new regulations was required. If the revolution was to succeed the people needed to see change, and quickly.

"Can I help you?" said a middle-aged man, approaching him from within the dark space. His voice was difficult to hear. The rattle of sewing machines bounced off both the walls and the low ceiling. "I'm the foreman."

"Yes, thank you," said Moises. He pulled one of the makeshift cards from his pocket. "I'm Moises Cohan. I'm here to see Eugenio Morales. Benny Abromo arranged for him to meet with me."

The man looked at the card, flipping it over more than once. "Of course," he said, "this way." He directed Moises to the left and into the dim interior of the building, the heat and the incessant noise of the sewing machines growing more intense as they receded into its windowless depths. At the rear of the dungeonlike room, they came upon a door. The foreman knocked. "Señor Morales.,"

"*Sí,*" came a voice from within.

"There's someone here to see you."

The door opened a second later. A thin man of about sixty in a white, sweat-stained shirt looked Moises up and down. The foreman gave Moises's card to him. He looked at the card and at Moises again. "Are you from the new government?"

"Yes. But I am here as a friend of Benny Abromo."

"I don't know how you can be both," Morales said. He gestured to Moises to enter and closed the door behind him. "How can I help you," he said, sitting down behind his gray metal desk, without so much as offering Moises a drink of water as a respite from the heat.

"I'm seeking your help."

Morales looked Moises over with a mix of concern and contempt. "Benny told me." Morales hesitated a moment. "Why should I?"

"Because I'm not your enemy. Though you may believe I am,"

Morales laughed. "Okay, of course, continue."

Moises cleared his throat, as much as to give himself a small moment to collect his thoughts and decide where to begin, as to prepare to speak in the heavy air. He believed what he'd said, he wasn't Morales' enemy. "I'm the Director of Industrial Review for garment manufacturing. We are seeking fairness and justice for everyone. As such we seek to root out corruption, at all levels."

Morales smiled. "Yes, corruption hurts us all." He crossed his arms against his chest.

"With that said, we've noticed a change in certain…arrangements."

"And how does that change affect me?"

Moises pulled a folded sheet of paper from inside the book on centralized economic theory he carried with him everywhere. He unfolded it and placed it on Morales's desk, facing him.

"If you will look at the bottom of the page, my notes. Your economic activity for the past twelve months is detailed at the bottom. You are producing the same number of dresses and skirts as you were a year ago. You are selling them to the same shops in Havana as before with only minor changes. Yet your bottom-line profit, as you report it, is lower. How can that be?"

Morales kept his arms wrapped across his chest. "Business is a gamble. Profits can decrease or increase in any given year."

"I know that," Moises replied. "I also know that you

dropped your wholesale price to all six retailers, and you paid more for transport of the goods to the stores." Morales said nothing. "I may be a communist," Moises said, "but I'm also an accountant."

"So, you admit it then, you're communists."

"I said, I'm a communist, not necessarily anyone else."

"Again, *señor*, why should I help you? You'll take what is mine in the end."

Moises paused a moment. He let what Morales said percolate in his mind. They would take what belonged to Morales. Was that true? Did it really belong to Morales? What about those who worked for him? Was their sweat and labor not a major part of what Morales believed to be his? He didn't want to debate that point because he knew that someone like Morales was likely unpersuadable. Their vision ended at the door of what they considered theirs by right, no matter how they had come about acquiring it. What he knew instinctively, and what he knew he had to seek out and extinguish, was the rot that would settle into Cuba's future if the old ways of doing things migrated to the new. Corruption would destroy the future, as it had the past.

"My personal opinions aside," said Moises, "no one is set to take your business from you. My job is to make sure that criminals can no longer continue to prey on you. And if those criminals are hiding behind the Movement, my work is even more urgent."

Morales' expression changed from one of defiance to one of fear. He remained in his seat, silent, for a long moment, then reached behind him into an open shelf. He withdrew two small glasses and a bottle of dark rum. He poured one for himself and one for Moises, placing the one for Moises at the edge of the desk.

"You realize what you are asking of me?"

"I'm asking for the truth. You believe we are here to take your business. We say we are here to improve your life and the life of all Cubans."

Morales downed the shot, poured another, and downed that. Moises left his untouched. Sweat appeared on Morales' forehead. "And how is that?"

"Corruption has ruined this country. That's how we start. Punish those who break the law. Those who use their power for their own benefit."

"And what if they are your own?"

"Then they will be punished in the same way."

Morales downed a third shot. "How did you figure it out?" he asked.

Moises chuckled. "My father, like you, owns a factory. I've been keeping his books since I was sixteen."

Morales looked at Moises for a long moment. "Your father is Rafael Cohan?"

"Yes. You know him?"

"Of course. From your uncle. He's a good man. How does he feel about your involvement with the new government?"

"I can't say he's happy about my politics. He thought it was a phase. In the end, he expected I would come to work for him."

Morales smirked. "I guess he was wrong."

"Yes. But to be honest, I had no intention of ever going to work for him. I just hadn't told him."

Morales leaned forward over the desk. "Before I answer your questions, could I ask you one?"

"Of course."

"What is the intention of your government?"

Moises considered his response before making it. If he told Morales capitalism was doomed in Cuba, he would never cooperate. Capitalism's fate was far from certain anyway. Fidel and the leadership were more focused on freeing Cuba of foreign influence than small businessmen. If he told Morales that nothing would change, he would be lying. He opted for the truth. "Our intention is to move Cuba forward, all of Cuba. That path is still to be determined. But, as I said, we will not tolerate corruption in our midst."

Morales sighed. "I suppose it's better to have a friendly relationship with you than an adversarial one."

Moises smiled to himself. That was the first step. "Yes."

"This province came under the control of your movement about a year before the revolution. At first, we were relieved. Batista's goons were gone. But then we realized we had a problem."

"What was that?"

"Neither your people nor Batista's controlled the roads into the capital. We couldn't get our goods from the factories to the shops.

"Did you contact someone in the Movement to help you?"

"Not exactly. First, we tried to bring the goods in ourselves, by car."

"We?"

"Yes, literally, we. Me, my sons, and other factory owners. Some of us got through. It depended on who was at the checkpoints. Whether they could be, shall we say, induced to let us through?"

Moises nodded in understanding.

"But it wasn't enough. We couldn't afford the gasoline, nor was there enough for so many vehicles. Then out of nowhere, this guy appears."

"When? Who?"

"About a month after your people occupied the

province. He claimed to have connections with the Movement and with Batista's people. He could get his trucks through both checkpoints."

"For a fee?"

"Of course."

Moises took a deep breath. He pulled a pen from his pocket and placed his pad on his lap. "What is his name?"

"Well," chuckled Morales, "that's the interesting part. I don't know his name."

"How can that be?"

"He sent me a note. It was delivered by a young man."

"Why you, as opposed to other factory owners?"

"I am the largest."

"What did the note say?"

Morales reached into his drawer and pulled out an envelope. He handed it to Moises. Moises removed a thin sheet of paper. A handwritten note.

Señor Morales, I think I can be of assistance to you. I have access to Havana. If you are interested, reply in writing. Give the note to my nephew, and I will arrange a meeting with one of my representatives.

"What happened then."

"I wrote him a note. I told him I was interested. The truth is, I was desperate. As were all of the local manufacturers. I handed it to the young man who brought me the note."

"How quickly did you hear from him?"

"The next day. The boy returned. And a day later I met with his so-called representative."

"What was his name?"

"I don't know. I didn't ask and he never told me."

"And you went along with this?"

"Yes, we were desperate. Anyway, I figured why not pay a commission? I always had. I knew he was from your people."

"How?"

"Who else would he be? What was curious was that he could pass through both sides."

"Can you describe him?"

Morales laughed. "Sure. Young, about your age, dark hair, scruffy beard, thin, about two meters. He looked just like Fidel. You all do, generally."

Chapter Twelve

Unlike before the revolution, Hector was no longer at Aarón's beck and call. He now had to submit a request through Hector's secretary for a meeting. Hector responded with a question: Had Aarón completed the brief he requested? Aarón was a bit put off by the response but replied, yes, nonetheless.

He stayed up all night to finish it. Beatriz proofread it that morning. He couldn't trust Alma with something this sensitive anymore. The feeling of suspicion of everyone and everything that now permeated daily life was disconcerting. Like Hector, Alma had been a trusted aide for years, now Aarón couldn't be sure where anyone's loyalties lay.

After two weeks of intensive research in the law library at the recently reopened University of Havana, Aarón had come to a fair and honest decision on Che's question. He reviewed every word in the constitution, every precedent, every decision. He did exactly what Hector asked. He tried to find a way to give Che what he wanted. Impossible. There was no legal basis in the current constitution for the nationalization of private means of production. Not even for the alleged benefit of the people. He then tried to find a middle ground, any ground, on which some reforms could be made to satisfy Che's agenda, but no precedent existed.

The new government would need to draw up a new constitution, and by doing so would have to reveal itself. They would have to take a position for the future. What kind of system would the new Cuba have? Who would be the winners and who the losers? Aarón went with the simple truth in a well-thought-out, logical, approach. The answer was no.

It had become obvious to Aarón that Hector's responsibilities extended past acting as the representative of the Movement at the bank. After he gave his brief to Hector and explained it, he would inquire as to Martinez's son and family.

Hector arrived late. Other matters had run overtime. He took a seat opposite Aarón and placed his briefcase on Aarón's desk.

"You've completed the brief?" Hector was all business.

Aarón reached into his top drawer and pulled out two neatly typed copies and handed one to Hector. "Yes. Feel free to review it. There's a summary in the front. If you have any questions before you give it to the General, I'm happy to answer them."

Hector read the summary and leafed through the document. "Beautifully presented," he said. "Alma did a beautiful job, as always."

Aarón smiled. He didn't tell Hector that Beatriz had typed it. She'd typed it twice, so the second copy didn't have the look of carbon paper. He waited anxiously while Hector read it. Hector closed the document folder. "That's your conclusion?"

"Yes."

"Do you think that's what General Guevara wants to hear?"

Aarón was shocked by the aggressiveness of Hector's question. "I told him the truth."

"Truth?" Hector smiled. "Today the truth can be, shall we say, subjective?"

Aarón sighed. "Hector, I'm sorry, there was just no way to justify his moves constitutionally."

"What about foreign ownership of assets? The Americans are bleeding the country dry. They have been for years. Could we force the nationalization of foreign interests?"

"That's a slightly different question than the one you asked, but I don't believe so. Private property is private property."

"Then what do you suggest?"

"Write and adopt a new constitution. That's what I've told him."

Hector considered Aarón's suggestion for a moment. "That's not an option at this time. The coalition is too large, and too diverse. Fidel knows what he wants, and Che is in charge of getting it."

"Perhaps they should be honest with the people about their ideas and goals?"

"The politics of the moment won't permit it."

Aarón handed the second copy to Hector. "I understand. I hope he takes this analysis in the spirit in which it was written. Honesty. It's not meant to challenge their goals for Cuba. He asked me a specific question. I tried to answer it."

Hector's demeanor softened. "I understand. Though it might go better for you if you had tried to find a way to guide them."

"May we speak about something else?" Aarón said as Hector got up to leave, briefcase in one hand, Aarón's brief in his other."

"What?"

"Please sit down."

"I'm running late."

"Hector, please."

"Fine," Hector replied, retaking his seat. "Quickly."

"It's about Alejandro's son."

"I told you, I don't know anything about that."

Aarón focused on Hector's eyes. "Martinez told me you were the security officer who picked him up for interrogation."

Hector's response registered in his face immediately, a look of anger Aarón had never seen before. "And what difference does that make to you?"

"Are you a member of the security police? Are you observing me? Am I, my family, in danger? Like Alejandro?"

Hector leaned forward across the desk. "Aarón, I have been trying to help you. You don't seem to see that, do you? You have to wake up and see for yourself where things are going. You and your wife come from visible wealth."

"We are far from wealthy. Our parents worked for everything they have. Am I in trouble?"

Hector waved Aarón's brief in the air between them. "This isn't going to help you."

"Should I consider making other arrangements?"

"With your new wife?"

"What does that mean?"

"It means what I said. The two of you should consider your future. You have a honeymoon to Mexico planned. Right?"

Aarón squashed his shock, hoping it hadn't appeared on his face. Hector knew of their plans. He had never discussed them with him. "Are you suggesting we flee?

Our families are here. We are Cubans. We love our country."

Hector hardened. "Have you spoken with your brother?"

"No."

"I suggest you do."

ᘓᘓ

When Aarón asked his parent to invite Moises for lunch on Saturday they were delighted. They had insisted that Moises be included in Aarón's wedding party. Aarón resisted. They took this request as an indication that he had relented. Aarón understood that seeking his parents' help in seeing Moises would mean that he would have to include him, despite his many objections.

Aarón explained to Beatriz why he needed to speak to Moises. He didn't want to but had no choice. He needed guidance from the inside and couldn't find it elsewhere. Hector was no longer a reliable channel.

Of course, Beatriz understood. She knew of Aarón's predicament. It was hers as well. She'd helped him produce the brief he'd given to Hector for Che. As such, she accepted her future in-laws' demand. Moises would be part of the wedding party.

The day was sunny and warm. Aarón borrowed his father-in-law's car to drive to his parents for Saturday's lunch. The house was filled with the scent of picadillo and fried sweet plantains, rice, and black beans.

"*Buenas tardes*," Aarón called from the front door. His parents appeared in the long hallway, his father in a white *guayabera*, his mother in a light yellow, cotton dress covered with an apron.

"*Buenas tardes*," they called back. "*Y un buen*

shabbos."

As Aarón embraced his mother Moises came out of the dining room. To Aarón's surprise, he was dressed in a white shirt and black slacks, a far cry from the well-worn 'revolutionary look' he had sported proudly for the past several years.

"*Buenas tardes, hermano*," Moises said.

Aarón extended his hand. Moises accepted it. After a moment, he pulled Moises to him and embraced him. Hesitantly, Moises embraced him back. "It's good to see you," Aarón said.

"*Igual*," replied Moises.

Aarón caught his mother's smile from the corner of his eye. She was clearly pleased that he had asked for Moises. He knew it was important to both his parents that he and his brother re-establish some kind of relationship. His truth was different from theirs. He and Moises were never close, and now that kind of relationship was even more unlikely. He felt a momentary pang of guilt. He had his own reasons to seek out Moises, and he had manipulated his parents to arrange it.

"Come into the dining room," his father said, taking Beatriz by the hand. "I'm hungry." Rafael kissed Beatriz on the cheek. "And you will sit with me." Rafael pointed to the far side of the table. "Why don't you two sit together, like you did when you were boys." His smile betrayed his happiness. Aarón obliged, as did Moises, taking the seats they'd occupied as children.

Aarón considered the absurdity of the situation. He kept it hidden behind his smile as his mother entered with a large, porcelain soup tureen filled with chicken soup and matzah balls. She placed it in the center of the table and began to serve, Rafael first, followed by Beatriz, then her sons, and finally herself. "*Buen provecho*," she said as she dipped her spoon into the golden liquid.

"Delicious," Beatriz said after a long, silent moment, breaking the awkwardness.

"Yes," said both Aarón and Moises, nearly simultaneously.

"Thank you," Esther replied, the awkward silence returning immediately.

"How goes the revolution?" Aarón said, trying to lighten the mood, immediately realizing his misstep. His brother didn't smile. His father blushed.

"We're trying to move the nation forward," Moises said, putting down his spoon.

"I know that," Aarón replied. "I'm sorry, I didn't mean to mock you."

Moises's body relaxed. "I understand. Sometimes I get a little too serious about these things. We're working very hard to bring change. Quickly."

"What exactly are you doing in your new position?" Aarón said. "If I'm allowed to ask."

"Of course, you're allowed to ask. I'm a liaison with the business community."

"That sounds…interesting," said Aarón.

"Yes, it is. Very. The leadership thought that my family connections to the community and my knowledge of accounting would be an asset in bringing the business community into cooperation with us."

"I see," Aarón said. He couldn't imagine how the business community could be reconciled with a government dedicated to destroying it.

"I understand you've been in touch with Tío Benny," Rafael said.

Moises, surprised by his father's knowledge of his meeting with Benny, fought to cover his emotions. Benny had promised him discretion. Who else knew? He felt the blush rising from his neck. "Yes, as a matter of fact."

"He says you came to him for…information," Rafael continued, sipping at a goblet filled with water.

"I'd use the word advice," Moises countered.

"Call it what you like. What are you looking to learn? Perhaps I could help, as well."

Moises held back for a moment. He considered how much to say. "Thanks, *papá*," he replied. "I will keep that in mind. The truth is we were doing some research into the women's clothing business and so…"

"Of course," Rafael replied. "That is Tío Benny's business."

Aarón considered whether to add something to the conversation or to wait until after lunch when he would ask Moises for some time alone. In light of Che's request about the nationalization of the shoe and leather industries, he believed Moises might be involved with a similar effort in ladies' clothing. He was about to ask Moises about the impending land reform program when his mother entered the room with a platter of picadillo, followed by Beatriz with large bowls of rice and black beans.

"That looks delicious," said Moises.

"It is!" replied Esther.

"Care for a walk?" Aarón asked Moises. Beatriz was helping his mother with the dishes. His father had taken a phone call on the veranda.

"Sure," replied Moises.

They walked down the road in the direction of the small, sandy beach at the street's end. A pleasant breeze blew in from the water lifting the branches of the palm trees. High, full clouds floated in the distance over the sea.

"I guess I should start by asking you if you'd be in my wedding party."

"I didn't think I'd even be invited."

Aarón caught the smile Moises was suppressing. Was it sarcasm or happiness? He stopped and put a hand on Moises's shoulder. "We may see the world very differently, but you're still my brother."

Moises let the smile he'd been suppressing fill his face. "Of course. I'd be happy to. But I should tell you, I'm not alone. I'd like to bring someone."

"The same woman?"

"Yes. Ana Teresa."

Aarón thought for a moment before answering. He'd have to prepare his parents. "Of course." He felt a sense of duplicity. He knew how his parents would react but telling Moises no would end the real conversation he needed to have before it began.

"I'll speak to our parents. Don't concern yourself with that."

"Thanks."

They continued toward the beach past small houses, some made of little more than plywood and palm fronds. Children played in the street, the same way he and Moises had as children. "It's still beautiful here," Aarón said. "May I ask you something?"

"Sure."

"You don't have to answer if you can't."

"I'll try."

"Why did you seek Tío Benny's advice?"

Moises kicked a few stones down the dusty road. He considered his words. "We are trying to build confidence with the business community."

"They believe you will nationalize everything."

"I know. Benny made that clear. But that's not

necessarily true. We just don't want to make the same mistakes that have been made in the past."

"Meaning?"

"We can't and won't let corruption take over."

"And you have reason to believe there are those among you who might be corrupt?"

"Yes."

"And that's why you went to see Benny?"

"Yes. I can't say more."

"I understand."

Silence descended between them for a long moment as they reached the edge of the beach, both more relaxed than either would have expected. Barking dogs, their tails wagging, ran in the dunes, chased by children. The water lapped gently at the sand in the protected cove.

"You mentioned that there wasn't any plan to nationalize small businesses yet."

"Yes, that's what I said."

"May I tell you something in confidence? Off the record?"

"Of course," Moises said without hesitating.

"I was asked to write a brief about the constitutionality of nationalizing the leather tanning and shoe manufacturing industries."

"By whom?"

"Che." Aarón watched as the expression on Moises's face changed from comfortable to serious.

"And what did you tell him?"

"The truth. Under the present constitution, he can't do that."

Moises nodded. "I see."

"Am I in danger here? Our parents? I'm sure they know who our father is…and who my brother is."

Moises put his hand on Aarón's shoulder. "Honestly, I

don't know."

Aarón stood under the *chuppah* in the main sanctuary of the Patronato, his parents at his side. Beatriz entered the room, clinging to her parents. Her beauty transported him from the confusion that had become their lives. She walked down the center aisle of the grand room, evening light twinkling through the stained glass. The overall effect was magical, suspending them in time and place. The chaos of their daily lives gave way to a natural orderliness. This was the way things were meant to be, he and Beatriz together. Now she stood under the *chuppah* next to him. He lifted her veil to make sure she was his intended, a Jewish custom dating back to Jacob. Fooled by his father-in-law Laban, Jacob hadn't looked. He married Leah, the older sister of his beloved Rachel, only to work for Laban for another seven years before he could marry Rachel.

The ceremony went smoothly. But why shouldn't it have? They knew exactly what would occur and when, a far and distant cry from what daily life had become. Aarón didn't feel like everyone was watching him, though in fact, all eyes were on him. He relaxed. When the moment came, he pulled back Beatriz's veil again and they drank together from the wine cup. Shortly after, the rabbi placed a glass under his foot and he stomped down on it, crushing it, as Jewish men had done since the destruction of the second temple. It was a remembrance of both the temple's obliteration and the Jewish people's sorrows, and the unbreakable bond between husband and wife. No one, nothing, could come between them.

"*Mazel tov*," the crowd shouted, jumping to their feet. Aarón kissed Beatriz gently, took her hand, and walked her down the aisle. They greeted their visitors, changed quickly, and headed to their reception at the Hotel Sevilla.

Their wedding was everything Beatriz had wanted. In the end, Eduardo Resnick decided that not even Fidel's revolution would rob his daughter of her day. If they fled their escape wouldn't be paid for with these funds, saved over a lifetime for one express purpose.

Aarón considered telling Eduardo and Rafael about the brief he had written for Che and his meeting with his brother. In the end, he decided it was too dangerous. They might say or do something that would attract the attention of the wrong person. Everyone knew eyes were everywhere. No one could be certain anymore who was listening. Fidel intended to re-make Cuba and no one was going to stop him.

Tío Benny drove them from the Patronato to the hotel in his brand new '59 Buick. He'd had it shipped from the States a month before the revolution. Chauffeured cars were hard to come by these days.

Armed young men clad mostly in army-green uniforms milled about both in front of the hotel and inside. They were more conspicuous in the interior space, their military green uniforms clashing with the red and pink tones of the lobby. He wondered why so many guards were needed at a hotel with virtually no guests.

Tourism nearly vanished in the months since the revolution. Castro closed the casinos a day after Batista fell, only re-opening them to relieve economic stress on the thousands of workers who kept them running and who had become unemployed by his action.

Even their re-opening didn't bring back tourists. Americans were too frightened and angry to come to

Havana. Wedding parties were a rare thing these days too, especially one this size. Aarón had pulled a few strings as an official of the bank to get the necessary permissions.

Armed guards stared at Beatriz and Aarón as they crossed the lobby to the ballroom. Aarón understood instinctively. These young men and women had no idea of the wealth hidden behind the doors of these hotels. Those who might have worked in the hotel's kitchens and cleaning the rooms had some idea, but those thousands who had streamed into the capital from the countryside in support of the revolution were clueless. Many had lived in simple wood huts with thatched palm roofs. Havana's grandeur came as a shock to them, only reinforcing Fidel's message. They were kept in poverty for too long by a fortunate few. Fidel was smart. Their resentment would solidify as support for whatever he chose to do.

Aarón squeezed Beatriz's hand as much to calm his own nerves as hers as they entered the ballroom to the sound of applause. The band struck up a rumba. They danced their first dance together. The orchestra leader invited the guests to join them on the dance floor a long moment after the music began. Aarón looked into Beatriz's eyes. He considered how lucky he was to have met her that day at the Patronato only a few years before.

"Thank you," he said.

"For what?"

"For marrying me. I love you."

Beatriz blushed, the redness in her cheeks and neck emphasized by the bright white of her gown. "Thank you. I love you, too. More than you know," she replied.

Aarón looked toward the door. A group of green-clad soldiers milling about looked in. "We will get through this…disruption," he said.

Beatriz nodded. "Whatever happens, we will be

together." She kissed Aarón gently on the lips, oblivious to their guests. A hand of applause broke out a moment later. As the number ended the orchestra switched to a bolero. Aarón and Beatriz took their seats at the head table. Their parents, Beatriz's sister and her husband Pablo, Moises and Ana Teresa, and Tío Benny and his wife Rosa, rounded out the table.

Eduardo Resnick stood, raised his glass, and tapped on its rim. The room grew quiet. "To my daughter and my new son-in-law. May you have a life full of *nachas*," he said, using the Yiddish term for happiness. The crowded room erupted with applause again. "And may I have a grandchild, quickly," he added, laughter erupting.

"Please!" Rafael Cohan added, standing, and not to be outdone.

The guests tapped their glasses, filled with the only "champagne" Eduardo was able to find, a cheap California sparkling wine stored deep in the Hotel's basement.

"I welcome Beatriz to our family. We are now one family." The guests applauded a third time.

"Now, let's eat!" shouted Tío Benny.

The waiters brought in the first course, a simple salad of hearts of palm and fresh tomatoes over a bed of lettuce. The original first course, foie gras, was impossible to get now.

"How beautiful," Ana Teresa said. She touched the gold-edged rim of the bone-china plate. "Everything. So…opulent."

Esther smiled. "It's a special day."

"Yes," replied Ana Teresa.

"I thought Professor Martinez and his wife would be here," Roberta said, sipping her "champagne" in between bites of her salad.

Beatriz glanced at Aarón before responding. He nodded

almost imperceptibly. “They would have sat with us” she said. “They were…detained.”

“Detained?” Lina said.

“Yes,” Aarón, replied, jumping in, taking control of the conversation. “To be honest, Professor Martinez and his wife were put under house arrest a few days ago.”

Forks dropped around the table. Almost simultaneously eyes shifted to Moises and Ana Teresa. Moises felt the blush rise up under his starched white shirt with its wingtip collar and then up into his face. He glanced at Ana Teresa. The curves of the bustier of her red cocktail dress accentuated her luxurious caramel skin. Moises had never seen her dressed like this before and was even more attracted to her than usual. He’d expected she would object to the formal dress requested. She had surprised him. Where or how she got the dress was more than he cared to know. Ana Teresa straightened her back but remained calm, a defiant smile appearing on her bare lips. A palpable silence followed for an uncomfortably long moment.

“I’m sure they’ll be all right,” said Pablo, Roberta’s husband. “He has always been a champion of the people.”

Moises put his hand over Ana Teresa’s just as she was about to speak. “Yes,” he said. “He has been. Hopefully, he will remain one. I’m sure their confinement is nothing more than protective.”

Glances swung around the table again. Aarón prayed the discussion would end there. “Pablo. How are things going at the power authority?” he asked, steering the conversation back from the rocks that might scuttle it.

“Good. I have to say that I’m impressed with the plans the new administrators have presented to extend the electrical grid. If they can form a working government and get down to business, we have a chance to make some real progress.”

Moises sensed instinctively that Ana Teresa was about to respond. He touched her hand again. “To be fair, Pablo,” he said, “we have been in power for what, only three months? As you suggest, we are trying to do the best for the people. There are political issues that must be resolved first before we begin building roads and extending power lines.”

Pablo leaned into the table. He took a gold cigarette case from the inside pocket of his white dinner jacket, took a cigarette from within and lit it with a mother-of-pearl lighter.

“Moises, I don’t doubt you,” Pablo said, taking a long drag on the cigarette then letting out the smoke, “and this isn’t a criticism, it’s just a statement of fact. I, we, want what is best for Cuba. But we still don’t know where this new government is going.”

There was no holding back Ana Teresa now. Moises didn’t even try.

“I think we all know where we are headed,” she said. “We haven’t been secretive about what we want. This is the people’s government now. Not the playground of the rich.” She settled her gaze on Pablo’s cigarette case and lighter, gleaming on the table. He discreetly slipped it back into his pocket.

“You’re an official in the government as well?” asked Benny.

“Yes,” replied Ana Teresa. “I’m with the Ministry for Public Information.”

A clash of cymbals from the band arrived as if planned to underline Ana Teresa’s response. It was followed by the band leader’s rendition of Babaloo, which nearly drowned out Benny’s reply: “You mean, propaganda.”

Moises reached for Ana Teresa’s hand before she could reply. “Dance with me, amor,” he said, leading her to the dance floor.

"You let him bring that woman here?" Rafael said, his eyes locked on Aarón once Moises was out of earshot.

"Rafael, not now," pleaded Esther.

"Why not?"

"It's their wedding day."

"I did as you wanted," Aarón said.

"How?"

"You wanted him here. We didn't. I fought you on it. I did as you asked. I included him."

"You didn't have to agree to him bringing her. A communist and a *shiksa.*[1]"

"Enough," Eduardo said. "We are a family. We will get through this."

Aarón looked at Beatriz. Tears welled in her eyes.

"It's all right," she said. "He's still your brother."

The wait staff cleared the plates from the appetizer course as the band continued to play. Ana Teresa looked around the room as they arrived back at their seats. There were empty tables at both ends, fully set. The waiters had laid the first course out, regardless of whether anyone was seated at the table or not.

"Did many of your guests cancel?" Ana Teresa asked. Glances darting across the table again.

"There were some," Beatriz offered, finally. "Under the circumstances…" she said, her voice trailing off.

"That's a terrible waste of food," Ana Teresa said.

Eduardo rose. "You're right. Excuse us. I'll tell the staff to remove those plates and not to do the same with the next course."

"No need," Ana Teresa said. She rose and walked with

---

[1] Shiksa, derogatory Yiddish expression for a gentile woman.

authority to the open entrance of the ballroom.

"What is she doing?" Lina asked, looking at Moises.

"*Compañeros,*" Ana Teresa called out from the doorway loud enough for the guests in the room to hear over the music. "Come, join us, there's more than enough for you to enjoy as well."

The assembled guests watched as some fifteen young gendarme in military green, guns slung over their shoulders paraded into the ballroom behind Ana Teresa. They followed her like the Pied Piper. Silence enveloped the room. Ana Teresa led them to two unused tables behind the wedding party.

"*Disfruta, compañeros,*" she called out, then returned to her seat. "There is no reason to waste precious food," she said "No one should go hungry. Ever."

Little conversation occurred after that. Moises kept Ana Teresa on the dance floor as much as possible. He knew well the expression on his father's face, how close to an explosion he was. He agreed with Ana Teresa's actions but asked her to consider the situation and to ratchet down the confrontation with his family.

"Do they know we're married?" she asked, catching him off guard.

Moises continued dancing, turning Ana Teresa to the rhythm of a mambo.

"I see," she said, stopping suddenly. "As I suspected. You are ashamed of me."

"That's not true."

"I think I'll go out for some air." She moved quickly to the door and out into the lobby.

Rafael, seeing her leave, approached Moises. Aarón followed close behind. "Moises," Rafael demanded.

Moises turned to him.

"How dare you."

"How dare I what?" Moises replied, his voice rising.

Hearing their shouts, the bandleader waved his hand at the orchestra to stop playing. Aarón countered, gesturing to raise the volume of the music, pushing both Moises and Rafael toward the door.

"How dare you bring that woman here," Rafael said, once outside the ballroom.

"*Papá*, I invited her," Aarón interjected, hoping to defuse the confrontation.

"She has embarrassed us. She's ruined your brother's wedding. Beatriz deserves your respect and she's stomped on it."

"She lives her beliefs," Moises countered, his voice rising. He spied Ana Teresa leaning against the bar in the lobby.

"She's a girl from the streets and she shows it!" Rafael shouted. "And a communist. They will ruin us!" His voice amplified with each declaration. "You are to end this relationship, immediately."

"End this relationship?" Moises laughed. "She is my wife!"

Rafael reeled as if he had been punched in the stomach. He looked at Moises and then at Aarón, then grabbed his chest. "Your wife?" he said, barely audible now.

"Yes. She is my wife. And you will show her the same respect you show to Beatriz." Moises shocked even himself. He couldn't believe he'd uttered these words. He'd stood up to his father, to all of them, finally. He was the new Cuba. They, the old.

"Respect?" Rafael said, recovering his voice. "For that *shiksa*?" He paused for a moment, took a breath. "I have put up with more from you than I ever should have. Why? For your mother's sake. You, her precious baby boy. I tolerated your politics. I paid for your socialist studies. I kept my mouth shut. I even coddled your infatuation with this *putana*, hoping that if I didn't push too hard you would see the wrongness of it. But no, you went and married her! And never told us! Behind our backs! How long did you think you could hide this?"

Moises opened his mouth. No words came. His father's verbal daggers had hit their mark. But it wasn't Rafael's belittlement of Moises that struck the fatal blow, rather his contempt and scorn for Ana Teresa. To call her a whore. That was too much.

"There was one rule," Rafael said. "No intermarriage. Your politics are yours. I have to accept that. But this, no." The words finally came. "No *shiksa* is welcome in my family."

"Then I'm not your family!" Moises shouted, the words escaping his lips like lava from an exploding volcano. Moises felt a weight lift from him. He looked to his left. Ana Teresa stood with her arms open, a smile on her face. Moises pivoted on his heel and walked towards her. He embraced her and kissed her hard in a way he would never have in public, previously. They walked out of the Sevilla without ever looking back.

Chapter Thirteen

Moises had pep in his walk as he arrived at his office. He was basking in Castro's latest victory. A day earlier agrarian land reform was passed. Cuba's peasants would finally be freed from the semi-feudal serfdom that had crushed them for centuries. Royal Spanish land grants be damned.

This was the beginning of his moment as well. Land reform was the only the first step. Before long, Che would convince Fidel that the only path for Cuba was socialism. Large foreign corporations would be next. American companies would finally be made to pay for their abusive labor practices and their contempt for Cuba and its people. Cubans would take their place managing their own economic lives.

An image of his parents flashed through his mind. Would they lose their business too, as they feared? Moises didn't know. He'd not had any contact with them—nor thought much about them—since Aarón's wedding, some two months earlier.

Aarón had sent him several notes, but he had declined to answer. His future was with Ana Teresa. After the things his father had said, there could be no reconciliation. Once said, these things could not be retracted. His father's attachment to the vestiges of his Jewish identity would not control Moises's own right to love whom he chose.

Moises knew that Aarón considered Rafael a hypocrite. He used his Jewishness as a weapon and a cocoon when it suited him. In making his decision not to respond to his brother's notes though, Moises also considered what Aarón told him about his encounter with Che. As an official in the government, he had to steer clear of anything that gave even the appearance of counter-revolutionary sympathies.

"*Buenas*," said Luz, as Moises approached her desk. He had taken the stairs instead of the elevator, as he did every day. The stairwell was wide and filled with light. The elevator, small and cramped. Without the operator who had manned it for years it would often stop between floors. He'd gotten caught more than once. The stairs were easier and safer.

"And good morning to you," he replied, placing his bag on the corner of Luz's desk. She handed him two envelopes. "These came for you." He looked them over quickly. Both were sealed, with only his name on the front. "*Gracias*." He picked up his bag and headed into his office.

Over the past two months he'd grown used to the decidedly capitalist character of the space. He even began to use the drawers in his desk. With the middle of May, the beginning of the tropical rainy season had arrived. The office was a little warm. Moises clicked on the oscillating fan angled between the large, open windows that overlooked the palm-lined park across the street and his desk. The fan would offer some relief from the intensifying heat.

He reached into the top drawer, retrieving the gold, dagger-like, letter opener he had inherited from the office's prior occupant, slipping it into the corners of both letters, opening them cleanly. So cleanly, in fact, that he gave himself a paper cut when he pulled the contents from the first. He put his bloody index finger into his mouth, smarting from the tiny slice in his flesh. He unfolded the letter clumsily with his other hand to avoid the blood. It was from Luis. It read:

> *"Compañero, we can all rejoice with the passage of land justice for the people. Our leaders have taken the first important step toward redemption of the nation. Please come to my office next Monday, May 25, 1959, at ten o'clock. We will begin planning the next phase of the revolution."*

Moises felt exhilarated. Ana Teresa had promised him that he hadn't been relegated to obscurity through this position. Now that agrarian reform was a reality, his work would figure prominently in the reorganization of the business and manufacturing sectors to come.

He pulled the second letter from its envelope, this time more carefully, his index finger extended so as not to irritate the raw cut or bloody the page. It was from Eugenio Morales.

Morales had reconsidered Moises's request, made some two months earlier, to aid in his investigation of corruption. Moises laughed to himself. Morales wanted to appear friendly to the regime now that land reform was a reality. He was no fool and knew well that he could lose his factory if the plan to reorganize the economy continued down a socialist path. Morales would be in Havana for the week. Could he arrange to meet with Moises? He provided an address to receive a response.

Moises looked at the two letters. He would have a week before his meeting with Luis. He would need to assemble a good amount of information, but nonetheless, this opportunity was unique. Rooting out corruption would be a feather in his cap, especially if he could announce it at that meeting.

The trees in the park across from the Malecon cast long shadows as the sun set into a corner of land, sea, and sky on the horizon. Moises chose a nondescript, open space for his meeting as much to protect himself as Morales. Though he didn't fear it, he was aware of the growing paranoia inside the government. He knew, instinctively, that the coalition was too broad. The days of simply being opposed to Batista were over. Now the battle was for the future. He was completely committed, but nevertheless, wanted to maintain his image as such. Inviting Morales to his office would have tempted scrutiny. While Moises knew himself to be incorruptible, he also knew that virtually anyone working in the ministry might view such a visit as an opportunity to relay suspicion about an important official.

Morales appeared nervous entering the park. Moises, seated on a bench at the far end facing the sea, watched as he walked quickly around the flower beds. Morales extended his hand. Moises nodded and smiled. "Please, join me," he said, gesturing to the seat.

Morales smiled half-heartedly and sat. He left a comfortable distance between them, shooing away the curious pigeons approaching his feet. "Thank you for agreeing to meet," he said.

Moises smiled. "Of course. How can I help?"

Morales became visibly awkward, shifting his posture, unable to find a comfortable position. He avoided direct eye contact with Moises.

Moises was pleased with himself. Morales clearly knew he wasn't the same man he had met with two months ago. Events had changed him, hardened him, and made him confident about who he had become and the path he walked.

"I've thought about what you said for some time now," Morales said.

"What specifically?"

"What you said. About the future of Cuba. About the corruption. About accepting the revolution."

"And?"

"I thought I'd answer your question."

Moises played with Morales. "Which question? I'm not sure I recall."

"Who are we paying…"

Moises nodded, his smile receding from around his lips. "Of course. Now, tell me the real reason you're here."

Morales took in a deep breath, as if he was about to vomit. He looked around the park. The shadows were lengthening, the light receding, casting a pinkish-gold hue across the landscape. The park was nearly empty, save for an old couple, a mother with three small children, one of them in her arms, and the pigeons. "Are you going to nationalize my business?" Morales blurted out, the words fleeing his mouth like thieves.

"Is that what brought you here?"

Morales didn't answer.

"I couldn't possibly tell you that, even if I knew," Moises replied.

"Will it help me if I give you the information you asked for?"

"It will help your conscience, in the end."

Morales regained his composure. He reached into his pocket and took out a small photo. One of the faces in the photo was circled. "This is the carrier. He comes once a month, the first week in the month, to take the payment for the prior month."

"Where did you get this photo? How old is it?"

"It's recent."

Moises searched Morales' face. The fear under his trembling smile was palpable. Moises was surprised, as never in his life had he felt he had inspired fear in anyone. Not even that night in San Miguel. This was a new experience for him. He found in some abstract way that he liked it.

It was obvious to him that Morales was not going to tell him where he obtained the photo. He could live with that for now. He would find out soon enough. "Who calculates the 'commission,'" Moises asked, using the common term for bribery or protection money, or both.

Morales hesitated again, looking off into the distance. He rubbed his right palm with his left thumb. "Whoever the carrier delivers the money to checks it against his own records, how many trips, trucks, etc., were used that month. What the receipts for the goods were. That kind of thing."

"How does he have your monthly accounting figures?"

"He has a man in the factory. Every month when my bookkeeper does the books, this man watches her do the entries. Then he takes the books to his boss, so they know." Morales laughed under his breath. "I wouldn't dare try to short him, anyway. The carrier has a reputation."

"How do you know that?"

"I've known him all his life. He was a tough kid growing up." Morales stopped again, gazing off at the growing darkness. "You know the type. A criminal from childhood." He chuckled, again, nervously. "His father was one of Batista's henchmen. He threw the kid out of the house for petty crime. The kid got involved with Fidel's people in the province. He had nowhere else to go and they needed fighters."

Moises nodded. "I see. What's his name?"

"The boy?"

"Yes."

"Manuel. Manuel Gonzalez."

This time Moises went through "official" channels. He contacted the local leadership in Santa Clara. He asked for a list of young men between the ages of 18 and 25 who might be available to come to Havana for an extended period to do inspections of warehouses. He needed someone who was familiar with women's apparel, explaining that the next step in his research was to do an inventory of goods held by private companies. The request appeared innocuous, and it was signed by a reliable, dedicated official. Moises.

Moises had come to realize in the past few months that he was more well-known and respected than he might have thought. Several of his economic reports had been circulated among provincial leaders to give them a basic education about local industries and owners. His intentions wouldn't be questioned. He received back a response from the provincial leader a few days later. The sealed envelope arrived by hand, carried by a young man with an uncanny resemblance to Manuel Gonzalez, with the addition of a scraggly beard.

"Please, have a seat," Moises said, as he slipped his letter opener into the sealed envelope. The young man, sinewy and tall, relaxed into the carved, wood chair opposite Moises. He looked around at the paneled office in wonderment while Moises read the letter.

> *Compañero Cohan,*
> *I was surprised and delighted to receive your letter. We, as you, are working with the utmost diligence and dedication to bring a new reality to our people. I present Manuel Gonzalez Abreu, the bearer of this letter.*

Moises stopped reading for a moment. Though Abreu was a common name, it was also Marcos's mother's last name. Marcos was from this area. His family still lived there. He'd said as much when they visited him days before the victory. The farmhouse he was hiding in belonged to his uncle. Had Moises struck gold much more quickly than he'd expected? He continued reading.

> *I sent him to you directly, as I believe he is exactly what you are looking for. He is young, energetic, clever, and dedicated to the cause. He is not afraid to 'get his hands dirty,' if you know what I mean. I will also tell you, in the spirit of honesty, that he is my nephew. My wife's sister's son.*
>
> *Please, if I might impose, and no disrespect meant, chat with him. If you think he is who and what you are seeking, feel free to inform him of such and start him immediately. If not, just send him back to us. We have work in the interest of the people for him here as well. There are other*

potential candidates if need be.

Viva, la Revolución,

Fernando Calderon

Moises refolded the letter and placed it back in its envelope. “Welcome, Manuel Gonzalez. Your uncle speaks very highly of you.”

“*Gracias*,” replied Manuel.

“Tell me a little about yourself,” Moises said.

Manuel smiled; a big, toothy smile surrounded by his unkempt beard. “What would you like to know?”

“How old are you?”

“Nineteen.”

“What brought you to the Movement?”

Manuel answered quickly, perhaps too quickly. “I have seen the suffering of my people all my life. I want a better life for myself, my family, our people.”

The answer was either prepared, what Manuel thought Moises wanted to hear, or a little of both. Moises suspected the boy’s uncle had coached him. It couldn’t hurt to have a contact in the Ministry of Economics as close as your own nephew.

“Of course,” Moises replied. “How did you first become involved in the Revolution?”

Manuel grasped the carved wood arms of the chair, holding the claws at the end like one would a parent’s hand. “My father was an official in Batista’s government. I saw what he did, what the government did. I hated it. I hated him for it. One night, I ran away. I knew where the guerillas were. I went to their camp and joined them. I knew my uncle was there. He’s my *padron*.”

His story contradicted what Eugenio Morales told Moises, but Moises remained unfazed. “What did your father say when he found out?"

"He disowned me."

"You are very young. Your uncle says you are reliable."

"*Gracias, ministerio*."

Moises smiled. "No need for that. We are all equal now. Do you know anything about women's garments?"

Manuel smiled and turned his head, avoiding Moises's gaze. "I know how to take them off…" He chuckled then doubled back a moment later. "I apologize. I shouldn't have said that."

Moises laughed. Despite knowing that Manuel was lying, he liked him. There was something entertaining about him. He was clearly intelligent, though easily corruptible. Perhaps, he could be rehabilitated. "No, no, that's fine. I appreciate your joke. But, in the new Cuba, you must remember, we respect women. We don't rule over them. So, do you know anything about women's garments?"

"A little bit."

"How?"

"My grandfather had a small factory. He made dresses there."

"Does he still own that factory?"

"No. When he died, my father sold it to a competitor."

"His name?"

"Eugenio Morales. Do you know him?"

"No," Moises lied.

That truth brought the picture into clearer focus. The age-old personal and family vendettas of Cuba reached down to the most common denominator. There was bad blood between Morales's family and Manuel Gonzalez's for sure. Morales was paying blood money to them now. Of course, Morales had flipped.

"What did you do at your grandfather's factory?"

"I helped keep the warehouse, helped ship the finished product to stores here in the Capital, sometimes." Manuel smiled. He looked down at his feet. "*La verdad, señor*…I mostly swept the floors."

"There's no shame in honest work." Moises said. Manuel looked up. "Would you like an opportunity?" Moises asked.

"Of course, sir."

"*Compañero*."

Manuel smiled. "*Compañero*."

"I need someone to help me with inventory counts. But the work is here in Havana."

"That would be a dream," Manuel replied. "To live in Havana…and to serve the people."

"Welcome to La Habana, *muchacho*." Before long Moises would know the truth. He would befriend the boy, mentor him, and in return the boy would tell him what he wanted to know without ever knowing.

Luis called the meeting to order. There were nearly one hundred people in the room. Many had come from outside Havana, from the provinces. They were Moises's counterparts, economists, and political experts, come to take the next step in the reshaping of Cuba. Seated with Luiz on the dais in the center of the stage at the front of the hall were other leaders of the movement. Most significantly, General Guevara sat to his right.

Moises was awestruck. Perhaps, even more than Fidel, Che was the embodiment of the revolution. He was Fidel's confidant, his advisor. He plotted the path to the future. On the other side of Luis, among the local leaders, sat Ana Teresa and Marcos. Moises felt a tinge of jealousy. He would give anything to sit with Che and discuss his ideas, even for ten minutes.

"Welcome," said Luis, rising from his seat and banging his gavel, bringing the meeting to order. "*¡Viva la Revolución!*" he shouted to ear shattering applause. Luis pointed to Che. "The man who needs no introduction!" The audience rose to its feet, shouting Che's name and applauding even louder.

Guevara smiled and nodded. He rose from his seat and took to the podium. "*Gracias, compañeros*." The room shook with shouts and applause yet again. "We are at a momentous crossroads. That's why we have invited you all here today. Agrarian reform is only the beginning. We seek to reform industry next."

"Down with the *gringos*!" shouted someone toward the back of the auditorium, the applause erupting again.

Che raised his arm, his fist clenched. "*¡Cuba por el pueblo!*" he shouted. "We will send *los Americanos* home!"

He waited for the crowd to quiet, knowing full well how an inspired revolutionary was so much more willing to carry out his plans than one who was unsure.

"As I was saying," Che repeated. "We are at a crossroads. We are developing a plan to provide our workers with the same rights we've given to our farmers. The means of production will be held in their hands."

Sporadic applause erupted around the room, along with some mumbles. The room quieted quickly to the point where a whisper could be heard.

"Thank you for your work and dedication," Che said. "I give you Luis Alvarado, my lieutenant, to present the outline of our plans."

Luis rose to applause, though lighter than for Che. "Thank you general, *viva la Revolución*. May I begin by thanking each and every one of you for your diligence and dedication. As General Guevara said, we are at a crossroads. We are about to embark on a long-awaited journey, from slavery to freedom. Our workers, like our farmers, have been oppressed for centuries. They have lived at the convenience of their employers, exploited, barely able to feed their families, their own sense of worth sublimated to those who cheat them for their labor."

"What will we do about it?" called out one of the conference participants.

Luis smiled and pointed to the questioner. "That's what I'm here to tell you."

Luis spoke for the better part of an hour. He outlined how the leaders of the revolution had decided to remove foreign influence from the nation's economy. How workers would be formed into committees, and how management would have to include those worker committees in planning. The party—this was the first time Moises had heard the term used in an official capacity—would oversee both the worker committees and the companies and their management to ensure the fair treatment and inclusion of workers.

"Would this apply to all firms, or just those with foreign influence?" shouted one of the participants, a woman from the provinces.

"Larger concerns and those with foreign influence to begin," replied Luis. "But eventually all."

A rumble spread through the crowd. This was truly revolutionary. It was clear indication that Fidel himself had given his nod. Cuba was headed toward socialism.

"But," Luis continued, "we must be careful and go slowly. We don't want to frighten the people or provide propaganda for counterrevolutionaries. We will keep our long-term plans to ourselves. You, as economic officers, will continue to collect information. Once we have identified everything we need to know, we will proceed in the most fair and equitable way. I commend you for the work you have done to date, particularly on rooting out corruption. We have identified those who have made themselves rich on the backs of the people, and they are being dealt with appropriately."

"Not all!" Moises shouted, surprising even himself. He was so caught up in the moment, in the energy, that the words escaped his mouth before he could stop them.

Luis looked at him. "Of what do you speak, Moises?"

Moises formulated his thoughts as the eyes in the room turned to him. "I have uncovered what I believe to be a corruption scheme involving the transport of goods from factories in Santa Clara to the Capital."

"Have you identified the source?" asked Luis.

"I believe it's someone inside the Movement."

A hush fell over the room, eyes shifting from Moises to Luis. "There is nothing more contemptible than that. Please come to discuss this with me after we finish here."

Moises was pleased with himself. He looked at the dais. Ana Teresa smiled at him. She mouthed the words, *que bueno,* wonderful. Moises shifted his gaze to Marcos, their eyes meeting, Marcos's eyes on fire, no smile on his face.

ઌ

"Thank you," Luis said, shaking Moises's hand. "You've handled this very well, and your plan to catch the traitor is brilliant. I'm sure this young man, what was his name…"

"Manuel Gonzalez."

"Manuel, yes. I'm sure this will prove fruitful. Keep me posted on your progress."

Moises left feeling elated. What a morning. General Guevara joining them, then a private conversation and alliance with Luis to expose a traitor. He suspected who the traitor was but would bide his time until he had proof to make his accusations stick. Moises had waited for his moment, and it had come.

He continued down the hall to the lobby of the building. Outside the auditorium doors, he spied Ana Teresa. He stopped for a moment to admire her, unnoticed, from afar. How much he loved her. As Moises slipped through the crowd Marcos appeared, walking right up to Ana Teresa. She smiled at him a smile that Moises had previously known only for himself. Marcos moved closer, as if to kiss her but stopped himself. He took Ana Teresa's hand discreetly, intertwining his pinky with hers. He whispered something to her. She dropped his hand. Marcos turned and headed for the doors. A very short moment later Ana Teresa took a breath and smiled. Moises watched as she followed closely behind. He ran down the hallway into the lobby muscling through the crowd and looked out through the doors. Marcos and Ana Teresa walked away, hand in hand. Moises's blood boiled. He knew though, he would have his revenge and his woman.

Chapter Fourteen

Aarón stared out of his office window with little to do other than field calls from American banking and government officials concerned about the direction of Castro's government. Eleven months had passed since Fidel entered Havana. Much had happened. Too much.

Land reform arrived in May, surprising no one. Trujillo's attempted invasion in July however, did. Did the Dominican *Caudillo*, Batista's host-in-refuge, really think he could defeat Fidel's forces? On Cuban soil, no less? Batista couldn't save himself, and he'd had control of Cuba's military.

The government claimed the Americans were behind it. Aarón didn't doubt it. But he'd heard unofficial whispers from many of his contacts in the banking world that the CIA had pulled their backing just before the invasion. Trujillo, chest-puffing dictator that he was, went ahead anyway. His foolishness ended in disaster, uniting many around Fidel's own paranoia.

Growing discord and discontent under Fidel's umbrella erupted in September when Huber Matos attempted an uprising in Camaguey. He was arrested by Camilo Cienfuegos, another long-time supporter of Fidel and the

Movement. Cienfuegos himself disappeared shortly thereafter. The long knives were out, and no one was safe. Cuban politics was downright Shakespearean, factions and characters changing allegiances faster than the audience could follow. The latest drama occurred November 26. Che was made head of the Bank of Cuba. Prior to that, Aarón had observed everything as a concerned citizen. This, however, was different. Che was now his boss. And he was to meet him in fifteen minutes.

The staff of the administration of the National Bank of Cuba lined up in the great hall of the bank's main office. The vaulted ceiling soared above them, held up by arches and surrounded by enormous windows. Tropical light filled the space, warming the tawny marble that lined the walls, floor, and ceiling.

Gone were the days of formal attire. The entire staff dressed in a new uniform. It reflected the viewpoint of the people's liberators. Modest, unpretentious. In truth, it was more pretentious in its unpretentiousness than the suits and silk dresses of a year earlier. This studied look was a nod to the "classless" society—the triumph of the common man and woman that Castro and his followers wished to stamp on the nation.

Aarón stood nervously toward the end of the line. He kept his hands behind his back, almost military at-ease. The first people to meet Che would be the maintenance staff for the building, followed by those who worked on the banking floor. The clerical staff would be next. The bankers, lawyers, and managers, last.

At exactly ten o'clock, Hector entered the cavernous room. The murmuring line quieted itself instantly. Aarón laughed to himself. Here was the change Fidel and his people had brought. Never in his life had he seen Cubans snap to attention for anyone. Nor report on time for anything. Aarón thought of what the Italians used to say about Mussolini. He made the trains run on time.

"*Buenos días*," Hector called out.

"*Buenos días*," replied the assembled.

"I would like to present the new President of the National Bank of Cuba."

Che strolled into the room to thunderous applause and cheers reverberating off the marble walls and floor. He needed no further introduction. He was dressed in his usual green fatigues, black army boots laced nearly to his knees. His cap sat cocked back on his head, smiling through his unkempt beard. His pistol was visible under the waist of his pants.

"*Gracias por sus saludos, compañeros*. I wanted to meet each and every one of you before we begin our momentous work together."

Aarón had tired of the endless superlatives through which Fidel, Che, and their minions addressed the nation. Everything was momentous, history-making, and irreversible. They were the future and would lead the people because it was the people who had put them there. The sacrifices of their leaders were only for them. It was the simplest, most thinly veiled kind of propaganda, fit for children. Yet, "the people" bought it. Aarón understood. They were so traumatized for so long, by so many, who promised so much, that nothing more than the simplest message was needed.

Che approached the first person in the line. The man, bent over with age, should have stopped working years earlier. But, he needed to feed his family. He was dressed in a simple, cream-collared cotton shirt and pants which contrasted with his dark skin. The man took off his straw hat and bowed his head to Che.

Aarón recognized him. He was the building porter. Mostly, he was in charge of collecting and disposing of office garbage, and discarded papers. Prior to the revolution, he was the attendant in the men's restroom on the executive floor, relegated to handing towels to bankers and lawyers after they relieved themselves. He had survived on the paltry coins left for him on a small platter by the door. The main qualification for that job was the ability to forget everything said in that men's room. As the old saying went, men don't lie in restrooms.

Aarón considered that the former bathroom attendant's new job was a negative image of his last. He most likely turned over suspicious documents taken from the garbage to the movement's representative at the bank, Hector. If, in fact, he could read. If not, he likely turned in everything he collected to Hector for someone else to sort through.

With each person in line, Che stopped, smiled, held his cap in his left hand, and offered his right. He held the hand of each subject just a little too long and had a short conversation before bowing oh-so-slightly, smiling broadly, and moving on to the next. Nearly an hour had passed before Che was close enough to Aarón for him to hear bits and pieces of the conversation.

"And what is your position here at the bank?" Che asked one of the accountants. Aarón knew the man, though not well. Jaime Campostela was in his mid-fifties. He'd spent his entire career at the bank, starting as a teller, attending classes at night to become an accountant. He'd moved up through the ranks slowly. He trembled visibly now, slightly stooped yet still taller than Che. Guevara was surprisingly short. Perhaps his notoriety had made Aarón think he was taller than he really was.

"It's my pleasure to meet you, General," Campostela mumbled, barely audible to Aarón, no more than a few feet away.

"Mine, too. What do you do here at the bank?" he asked, for the umpteenth time.

Aarón focused on Che's hair and beard, both not only scruffy and disheveled but greasy, dirty. He noticed an unpleasant odor as well.

Insulting rumors circulated for years about how filthy the revolutionaries were, particularly Che. Aarón realized the odor was coming from Guevara. It grew stronger as Che finished with Campostela and took two steps to his right to the man standing next to Aarón, Roberto Cortez.

Cortez was a business analyst charged with evaluating the financial health and strength of loan applicants before the revolution put a halt to all lending. Cortez was the last man standing in his department. The most important criterion in making most loans was one's relationship with Batista's "associates." The six or seven other men in that department had either fled or been arrested in the first months after the revolution. Cortez had been the least productive, and least corrupted man in his department

Aarón breathed as deeply as he could to calm himself before Guevara stepped in front of him. He cut off his sense of smell as best he could. Though he knew it took only a few moments for Che to interact with Cortez it felt like an eternity before Aarón heard Hector.

"General, may I present Aarón Cohan, resident counsel to the bank."

Aarón extended his hand to meet Che's. It remained outstretched and empty. He felt the flush move from his neck into his face. He lifted his eyes to Che's. The general stood with his hands clasped behind his back, his face expressionless, his chest puffed out, the smile he'd presented to every staff member before Aarón, gone.

"You said no to me," Guevara said, loudly enough for

everyone in the cavernous room to hear. Aarón's head felt like it would explode. His heart pounded as he withdrew his hand. Che took two steps to his right, the smile returning to his face, greeting the next man in line.

Aarón left the bank immediately after Guevara's review of his troops ended. He didn't return to his office to retrieve his briefcase. He slipped his key into the door of their apartment as quietly as possible. He didn't want to alarm Beatriz.

"*Amor*," she called out sweetly, appearing in the hallway. She unconsciously placed her hand gently on her stomach and caressed it. Their child was growing inside her, and it was as if she knew instinctively when the child needed her touch. "What are you doing home so early?" she said. The look of alarm on her face was unavoidable given the constant state of uncertainty and flux since the revolution.

Aarón pulled the bouquet of white mariposa from behind his back. Beatriz's smiled. "I'm just a little early. I slipped out. There was nothing to do."

Beatriz took the flowers and kissed Aarón quickly on his lips. He touched her stomach again, its taut roundness evident under her cotton skirt.

"These are beautiful. I'll put them in water," she said, turning, stepping back into the kitchen.

Aarón followed her. "That smells delicious. What's for lunch?" He lifted the cover from the pot on the stove. A thick, red, mass of shredded beef, peppers, tomatoes, and onions simmered gently. "*Ropa vieja*," he said. "My favorite."

"What's wrong?"

"Nothing."

Beatriz moved closer to Aarón. She took his hand and rested it on her stomach. "I know you. I can tell by your pallor. What's happened?"

Aarón let out a long sigh. "Let's sit down." He led Beatriz the few feet across the kitchen to the small café table where they took most of their meals. The formal dining room across the hall was rarely used. These days he often wondered why they ever needed one to begin with. "Che came to the bank today."

Beatriz placed her hand gently on her chest over her heart. "And?"

Aarón told her everything. How Che had embarrassed him in front of the entire staff. "I should never have given him that brief. I should have given him what he wanted or resigned. They will do whatever they plan anyway. It was a trap."

Beatriz took her hand from her chest and took his in both of hers. "No. You did the right thing."

Aarón looked at her stomach. "We have a child coming in little more than a month. I have obligations to more than my morals now."

Beatriz kissed his hand. "*Te quiero, mi amor*. We will get through this."

Returning to the bank late that afternoon Aarón stopped at his office to pick up his briefcase. Alma barely acknowledged him. He put a few of his personal items into the briefcase and then walked up the two floors to Hector's office.

"Yes?" Hector called out hearing Aarón's tap on the door.

"It's Aarón Cohan," he said. "May I come in?"

A moment later Hector opened the door himself. "I expected you hours ago." He gestured to the sofa. Aarón had a feeling of *déjà vu*. Too many inflection points had been met in the past year on that sofa. "Have a seat."

Hector took the chair opposite him, exactly where Pimental sat a year earlier when Aarón came to him to help Moises. If he never entered this office again, it would be too soon. He pulled an envelope from his pocket and handed it to Hector. "My resignation."

Hector took the envelope and dropped it on the coffee table unopened. "Accepted. Is there anything else I can help you with?"

Aarón hesitated for a long moment. "We were friends."

"Yes, we were."

"I have a child coming in a month."

Hector nodded.

"Is there anything you can do? I need a job. Something, somewhere I can go quietly to earn a living. I accept what's happened." He looked directly into Hector's eyes, tears brimming in his own. "Please Hector, for my wife's sake."

Aarón watched as Hector softened, the old Hector returning for a moment, the one Aarón had treated like a brother, appeared on Hector's face for a fleeting moment. "I will see what I can do."

Aarón heard from Hector four long days later. Hector met him on the street in front of the National Bank and handed Aarón a piece of paper. "Go to see this man tomorrow morning at ten."

Aarón looked at the name and address, both unfamiliar to him.

"He is in charge of assigning magistrate positions in the provinces. He owes me a favor."

"The provinces?" Aarón said. "I have a child coming…"

"You asked for help, this is what I can do," Hector replied, cutting Aarón off. "*Adios* Aarón. *Buena suerte*," he said. "This is the last time we will see each other." Hector pivoted on his heel and walked quickly up the steps and back into the National Bank of Cuba. In fact, Aarón never saw him again.

Part Three
January 1962

Chapter Fifteen

Aarón tossed Miriam playfully in the air on the small terrace of their apartment in Parque Central. She giggled gleefully each time he caught and kissed her. Nearly two years old, Miriam was the center of Aarón's and Beatriz's lives.

Hector proved himself loyal and helpful, if corrupt. The "friend" to whom he sent Aarón did owe Hector a favor. He called it in. Hector's corrupt "friend" assigned Aarón a job as a magistrate traveling the provinces issuing birth, marriage, and death certificates.

Hector's corruption, benign as it might be, was pervasive. It was as if he couldn't stop himself. Once the fixer, always the fixer. Some months after Aarón last saw him, Hector got wind of the fact that the Committee for the Defense of the Revolution was investigating his activities. Aarón learned from Hector's "friend," the one that had arranged the magistrate job for him, that Hector slipped out of Cuba by boat one evening near Guantanamo. The barely seaworthy vessel was moored at the very same slip where Hector nabbed Pimental nearly two years earlier.

Luckily, the seas were calm that night. Hector arrived in Haiti a few hours later. Aarón heard subsequently that Hector received political asylum in the United States. His position in the Movement put him at the head of the line. Now he was a vocal critic of the new Cuba, a leader of the anti-Castro movement.

Aarón found peace and solace traveling the country. In some ways it was eye-opening. He became aware of Cuba's beauty and culture in a way he never knew before. He came to appreciate the simple lives of the people. The villages of the provinces were a far cry from the relentless energy and percolation of Havana. The *campo* represented in some way a simpler, purer, more honest life than the teeming slums of the capital.

Begrudgingly, in an almost abstract way, Aarón understood and admired the intentions and successes of the revolution more clearly through the lens of his travels. It was its philosophy he disagreed with.

On May 1, 1961, Fidel declared Cuba a socialist state. Aarón experienced a profound sadness. Could he reconcile the reality of Cuba's future with his own? The truth was finally out there. No more hiding behind semantics, no more winking and nodding.

While his job kept them housed and fed and his profile low, the weekly separation from Beatriz and Miriam was painful. He lived for those weekend days and worried constantly when he was away.

The leader for the CDR in their building snooped about relentlessly. She came by a couple of times a week to ask Beatriz if she had heard from Aarón. Where was he? Would they be able to attend a building meeting? She would schedule it during the weekend to accommodate him. The questioning was endless and probing, the implication always the same; the CDR knows our class history and they are watching us.

Aarón considered moving. Perhaps out of Havana to a provincial capital. Beatriz changed the subject immediately. She needed what little help and support she got from their parents with Aarón traveling all week, especially now that her sister and brother-in-law had fled.

Pablo, Beatriz's brother-in-law, an engineer with the Cuban Power Authority, was crucial to the continued operation of the electric grid. As such, he was closely watched. He couldn't apply for permission to leave, to go to Miami for a "visit." Nor could Roberta. Too many questions. Who were they visiting? Why did they need to go now? The truth was they didn't know anyone in Miami, or anywhere else in the United States for that matter. The government would figure out quickly what they were up to.

Pablo was uncomfortable with Fidel's government. Initially, he was willing to give them a chance. But the corruption at every level was already evident, especially in his position. The pressure to join the party, and by extension become an informant, proved too much for him. They were spirited out of the country to Jamaica one night on separate boats. They spent months in a refugee center there before they were granted emergency status to enter the United States.

One day, some weeks later, Beatriz's mother received a coded letter from Roberta. The envelope was open when it arrived. Lina and Eduardo understood the code. Roberta and Pablo were still in Miami but would soon go to Brooklyn with the help of HIAS, the Hebrew Immigrant Aid Society.

Aarón settled Miriam into her playpen as Beatriz walked out onto the balcony, a breakfast tray with two cups of espresso and a plate of flaky pastries in her hands. Aarón rose to help her. He took the tray and placed it on the small table between two white cane chairs. The chairs were wedged between the playpen and the door to the living room. Bolero played softly on the radio.

Aarón bit into the small, crescent-shaped pastry. A hidden filling of guava paste oozed out. He savored it and smiled. "These are excellent. You've become quite the baker."

Beatriz touched his hand. "It's better if I bake myself than go to the bakery and buy things others see as frivolous."

Aarón nodded. He sipped at his espresso. "You're probably correct." He chuckled. "Best not to appear too…counterrevolutionary."

They both laughed. Beatriz shushed him. "You never know who's listening."

Miriam, hearing their laughter, stood up, holding the edge of the playpen. She reached up with one hand.

"I'll take her. I miss her all week. How she feels, her scent." Aarón took a sip of his *cafecito*, put down the cup, reached for Miriam. She squealed in delight, grabbing his cheek as he stood her on his knees. "How many times was Josefina here this week?" he asked, his tone shifting.

"*Amor*, let's not discuss that right now. Let's enjoy the day together."

"We need to discuss it. I need to know what's going on when I'm away."

"It's fine, really. I can handle her."

"What did she ask this week?"

Beatriz sighed. There was no point in trying to avoid the conversation. Josefina would stop by before Aarón left for this week's trek to the provinces to check on him. "She wants to know when I'm intending to go to work. Everyone is expected to work."

"Tell her Miriam is too young."

"I did. She insists Miriam will be fine at the neighborhood care center for a few hours a day. She knows

I have secretarial skills. The party needs my skills."

Aarón hesitated a moment. Miriam grabbed his ear. Aarón gently pried it away. "The party? She said that? She said, 'the party?'"

Beatriz nodded.

"And what else did she say?"

"She wanted to know when you, as a government official, intended to join."

Anger filled Aarón's chest. He handed Miriam to Beatriz and covered his eyes with his hands. There was no hiding. He had deceived himself into thinking he could ramble about the country undetected and invisible. Clearly, the building's appointed snoop knew he wasn't a party member. Soon, all the neighbors would know too, if they didn't already. As he was about to curse Fidel, the music on the radio ended abruptly, an announcer interrupting the program. Fidel would address the nation.

Cuban radio was, like Aarón, a servant of the state. A martial crescendo heralded the voice of the leader, more appropriate for Generalissimo Francisco Franco of Spain than Fidel Castro, the liberator of Cuba's workers. Raul, Fidel's brother, introduced him. Fidel launched into yet another of his long-winded diatribes, this time proclaiming himself, officially, a Marxist-Leninist. He had been one, he said, since his university days. It was beyond official now. There really was no turning back, no compromise. Some twenty-three months after it had rolled into Havana, the revolution was complete. As Fidel finished, Aarón looked at Beatriz. "We have to get out of here," he said. "Our daughter has no future in this country."

The secret to successfully leaving Cuba, Aarón

recognized correctly, was silence. No one could know. No one could suspect anything. When visas were obtained, they were for a short trip. Return was expected, at least with a wink and a nod.

What did that really mean? It meant a lifetime of memories—a lifetime of friendships and family—left behind. One's exit had to be stoic, to say the least. Goodbyes were never said, only so-longs, "see-you-next-weeks." No long embraces meant to capture the warmth and feeling of one's mother, father, sister, brother, friend. Just a handshake, a kiss on the cheek, a friendly wave accompanied by an easy smile. There was no time or place for tears. Leaving Cuba was an alternate reality.

According to the government, no one left. The lucky few went on vacation or family business. When they failed to return, they became traitors to the nation. Duplicitous and counterrevolutionary. A stain on their families left behind.

Aarón started with the most innocent of requests. "My sister-in-law is about to give birth," he said, tired after a nearly two hour wait. He stood in front of the desk of an official of the state's visa office in an open room that was once a gymnasium in what was once a private high school.

The setting was both surreal and incomprehensible. He failed to understand why Fidel's government, so set on leveling the playing field between rich and poor, entitled and deprived, would convert a well-equipped school building into government offices.

"My wife's mother is too old to travel and suffers from asthma. Her doctor said it would be too dangerous for her to fly."

The visa official could best be described as disinterested. He picked at his nails with the point of a letter opener as Aarón pled his case.

"Why do you need to go with her?" he asked.

"My wife is afraid to fly alone, and I would like to be there for the birth of the baby."

"But you are a magistrate. You are needed here."

Aarón felt his stomach knot up. "I'm granted two weeks' vacation a year. I've accumulated four weeks over the past two years. My position is very arduous. The travel around the country…"

"…Yet you are asking for more travel" interrupted the visa official, looking up from his nails. "Perhaps, you should take your time to relax, not burden yourself with additional travel." He shuffled through the open file with Aarón's name on it. "Hmmm. It seems your sister-in-law and her husband left Cuba illegally and asked for political asylum in the United States. Your brother-in-law was an engineer with the national power authority. His expertise was needed. He is a traitor."

Aarón calmed himself. The government was clearly keeping tabs. They were efficient at that, if at nothing else. "Yes, I understand your point, *compañero*. But I am not. I, we, will return. I have a responsibility to the people. Our parents are here as well. They are elderly and require help."

"Are you a party member?"

"I have made application."

The words nearly caught in Aarón's throat. It was the first thing he did when he and Beatriz made the decision to flee. He made the application through Josefina, their building's CDR watchdog, hoping it would distract her from sniffing around.

"I see," said the official. He perused Aarón's file. "You are under investigation for class history. Your application is pending." He looked up at Aarón. "I will send your request to the processing office. You should hear something within two weeks."

Aarón nodded and smiled. "*Gracias, compañero. Viva la Revolución.*"

How do you navigate a lifetime of memories? That was the problem now facing Aarón and Beatriz. If their visas were granted, they would have to appear to be leaving with the intent of returning but would, in fact, never see any element of their former lives again. It meant taking nothing but the clothes they would need for a visit.

Though they had been married a mere two years, they had many things they would have liked to keep forever. And then there were the small, sentimental items that both had collected over their lifetimes; everything from a favorite doll to a signed book written by a favorite author, to say nothing of the religious items every Jewish couple received to build a Jewish home. A Passover seder plate, a Chanukah menorah, silver Shabbat candlesticks. Everything would remain, caught in some kind of official, absurd limbo, waiting for their return, a return that would never come.

The most important, most meaningful of these treasures couldn't be easily transferred to their parents or friends either. They couldn't risk telling anyone, overtly or covertly, that they were planning on fleeing. It would endanger their plans and the lives of anyone who knew. While they trusted their parents completely, they didn't want to endanger them later. When they didn't return, the government would come a-calling. What did they know? When did they know it?

Additionally, there was Josefina and her minions. Josefina knew they had applied for visas to visit Beatriz's sister. She knew everything. It was a closed loop. Someone applies for a visa, the visa office notifies the head of the

Committee for the Defense of the Revolution at the building where the applicant lives. Josefina sat on her beach chair, her permanent perch in front of the building, meeting and greeting everyone as they came in and out. She noted whatever they were carrying, inquiring as to where they were taking it, where they got it. Silver candlesticks would be difficult to hide.

"Hand me my granddaughter," Esther said, taking Miriam from Beatriz.

Miriam fussed a bit. She was cranky, just waking from her nap during the car ride from Havana. Aarón and Beatriz had orchestrated this *Shabbos* lunch, coming with Beatriz's parents in Eduardo's car. It was, ostensibly, a celebration of Miriam's second birthday. All four grandparents were therefore necessary. It was the only way they could get their parents together to inform them in carefully coded terms of their intentions. Aarón felt instinctively and with no rational reason, that the covert conversation would be safer at his parent's relatively remote home an hour outside Havana than at his in-laws' place in the city.

Lina followed Esther into the living room. Beatriz was directly behind them, diaper in hand. "Which one of you would like to do the honors?" she asked, waving the cloth over her head.

"We'll do it together," Esther said.

"Our pleasure," Lina added.

Beatriz chuckled. "Be my guest. Here's two more for later."

She turned, stifling the emotion rising in her chest, disappearing quietly into the kitchen. She didn't want to betray their true purpose by falling apart now. Their mothers would be deprived of so much when she and

Aarón took Miriam away. Miriam would grow up without grandparents the way she and her sister, and Aarón and his brother had; a phantom presence lurking in the corner causing one to look for someone that should be there but never was.

"Come, let's relax a bit," Rafael said, gesturing to the veranda. The weather was warm and dry, a light breeze coming from the direction of the sea at the end of the street. January always offered the best weather of the year. Aarón closed his eyes and savored the scent of the sea-salty air. He knew this might well be the last time he experienced that scent and this place, his childhood home. Would the sea have the same scent elsewhere? Would the phantoms of Matanzas remember him?

He and Eduardo followed Rafael onto the veranda behind the house. A bottle of Bacardi *Añejo* sat on a silver tray on the coffee table. Cut crystal glasses and a silver ice bucket accompanied the bottle. "Shall we have a drink before lunch?"

"Of course," Eduardo said.

Rafael picked up a pair of silver tongs inlaid with lapis lazuli and placed ice in each glass. He poured the luscious amber liquid into the glasses and raised his. "To our beautiful Miriam."

"To Miriam," Eduardo and Aarón replied, Aarón struggling to maintain his casual expression.

"Thirteen years until her *quinceañera*," Eduardo said. "May we all be there." He touched his glass to Rafael's."

"*Si Díos quiere*," replied Rafael.

Six adults watched adoringly as Miriam shoved chocolate guava cake—Esther's own creation made to resemble a Cubanized version of Black Forest Cake—into her smiling mouth squealing in delight.

Lunch had gone well. In the privacy of Aarón's parents' home, they could speak honestly with each other about the revolution, but only to a point. It wasn't a matter of who might be listening, but rather what any of them might be asked later. Current and past events were discussable, but future events were not. Gossip, old stories, news of friends and family, most of it sad. Who had lost their business. Who had fled the country. Aarón and Beatriz kept their poker faces, commenting only when necessary. They gauged their parents' comments to gain some understanding of how they would react when they finally exposed their own plan to flee.

Miriam's presence helped. It diverted attention away from reality. Eduardo had lost his grocery stores and Rafael's tanning and shoe factories were in the process of nationalization. Aarón had read over the terms of each conversion. The payment was paltry compared to the true value of the assets. He explained as kindly as possible that there was no room for negotiation. Both his parents and in-laws were best off to take what they were given with the assurance that they could stay in their homes. They begrudgingly agreed.

"She's so beautiful," Esther said, touching Miriam's smooth, soft skin. She turned to Aarón. "Thank you. You have no idea how much an afternoon like this helps."

Lina, nodded. "Your mother is right. It takes my mind off all that's happened."

Aarón glanced at Beatriz. He nodded almost imperceptibly, indicating to her that it was time.

"I've some news," she said. Four sets of eyes settled on her, all with a look of profound terror.

"What's happened?" her father asked.

"We're planning a visit to Roberta in Miami. To be there when her baby comes. So she isn't alone. We've applied for visas. The ministry has given Aarón permission to take a vacation."

Dead silence followed. Eyes darted back and forth. Neither Aarón nor Beatriz needed to explain what the implication of their plan meant. This was the last birthday their parents would spend with Miriam. This last light in the darkness that had become their lives would flicker out as well. Isn't this what they had worked for all their lives? They'd left their parents, siblings, and friends in Poland. They never saw them again, disappeared among the millions murdered. They'd worked hard, saved their money, helped each other, and were helped by each other. They raised families and put down roots. Invested in Cuba. The interest on their hard work was their children's happiness, and the dividend, grandchildren; someone to whom to pass down the accumulated history of their lives before they lay in the warm earth of their adopted land.

The Cohans lost one son to Fidel, and now would lose another because of him. The Resnicks lost one daughter already, another very soon. They would wait alone until perhaps they too could escape. Or would Fidel be toppled as was Batista before him? Such is Latin America. Dictators come and go like hurricanes, devastation in their wake. Silence ensued. Tears streamed down Lina's and Esther's faces. Rafael's and Eduardo's faces gray, drained of the rosiness bestowed by the Caribbean sun.

"You are a wonderful sister," Lina said finally, her cheeks wet, betraying her smile. "How wonderful of both of you. She will be so happy to see you. It's better for her if there's someone there when the baby comes."

"You'll be leaving soon?" Eduardo said, looking directly at Miriam, unable to take his eyes off her. "Roberta is due in less than a month."

"Yes," Beatriz said. "As soon we receive our visas."

"When do you expect that to happen?" Rafael asked, his voice low, cracking.

"Within the week, hopefully. I've scheduled my vacation to begin two weeks from tomorrow."

"I see," said Esther. "We will miss you."

"It's only for a month," Aarón replied, rising from his seat at the dining table. "We'll be back."

He walked around the table and took his mother in his arms. He hugged her like never before and with the thought that he would never again. He felt her legs give out underneath her, holding her up, his arms under hers, slipping her back into her chair. She placed her hands on his cheeks and caressed them. "*Zindele*," the Yiddish term of endearment for a son, was all she could muster.

Aarón embraced his father. Beatriz did the same with her parents. They cried in silence. "*Vaya con Díos, y con muchas bendiciones*," Eduardo whispered in Beatriz's ear. "I know we will see each other again." Beatriz knelt now, in front of her mother. "I'm sorry."

"There's nothing to be sorry about, *mija*. You have been more than I could ever have asked for. I am so proud of you."

Beatriz silently placed a key on the table next to her mother's hand. "Please, water the plants while we're away. I don't want them to die."

This vocalization of the near truth was more than Beatriz or her mother could take. Both broke down weeping, wrapped in each other's arms. The sound of their weeping had the effect on Miriam that crying always has on small children. Miriam's happiness turned quickly to uncertainty. She joined the weeping. Beatriz picked her up, chocolate smeared across her face and hands. She held her between her mother, herself and her mother-in-law in an embrace that would have to sustain them for only God knew how long. The room grew silent, but for the sound of three women and a baby crying.

Chapter Sixteen

Josefina delivered the news that their visas had arrived. Aarón could pick them up that afternoon. They were beginning to worry that the visas wouldn't be issued before Aarón's vacation began. Visas contained an expiration date. If they remained unused, they might not get re-issued. Aarón's vacation could well be canceled. There were too many moving parts. All the wheels had to turn in precise unison.

Aarón thanked Josefina. She stood in the doorway of their apartment forcing the door with the weight of her body. He knew she wanted an invitation to come inside. Then she would expect a *cafecito*, and perhaps a small bit of pastry, and extra to take home. All the while, she would be looking about, snooping with her eyes, calculating everything's worth, waiting for an opportunity to ask to use the bathroom to snoop some more.

"It was very kind of you to let us know," Aarón said.

"You are very fortunate," Josefina replied. "The people trust you."

"Thank you." Aarón gently pressed the door forward. "I must get dressed then. I'll need to pick up the visas before I head to work. I have to go to San Miguel today."

Josefina reluctantly stepped back. "If there is anything

I can do for you while you're away, let me know."

"Yes, we will. Thank you, *vecina*," Aarón said as the door clicked shut. The smile with which he always faced Josefina was gone. He walked quietly to Beatriz, standing in the kitchen. She'd listened to every word, out of sight. They embraced silently, neither knowing whether to laugh or cry. Miriam slept the impenetrable sleep of childhood a few feet away in her playpen. Aarón placed his forehead against Beatriz's and kissed her gently. "It will be all right, you will see."

"What was it we learned as children at the Patronato? The story of Ruth? Whither thou goest, I will go?" She looked up into Aarón's eyes, hers watery, fighting back the tears. "I should be happy…"

"We will be, again. And I promise you, I will do everything I have to do to bring our parents as soon as possible."

The visas were waiting for Aarón at the office in the former school he had visited a few weeks earlier for his interview. There was a long line stretching around the building, but pick-ups were segregated to a separate area. He was in and out quickly this time.

He signed a series of documents that indicated quite clearly that the government was aware of his true intentions. Like everything else in Cuba since the Revolution, it was as if he had fallen through the looking glass. Up was down, down was up. The visas were granted for a one-month visit. Their home would be sealed. If he and Beatriz failed to return, all their possessions would be confiscated, and their passports revoked.

They were permitted two suitcases each, only basic

items, clothing mostly. No valuables could leave the country. The value and use of any jewelry would be considered before they were permitted to board the plane. Currency restrictions were strictly observed. Aarón knew what they were facing. He would comply with every regulation, dotting every "i" and crossing every "t". The goal was to leave.

They would let their parents know they had received their visas by code over the phone before they left, the sullen phrase already memorized by all of them. Lina would come to "water-the-plants" three days after they left. Beatriz left a letter for their parents in the drawer in the kitchen under the silverware tray. She'd told her mother where to find it.

Hopefully, her mother could remove a few of the most important items they left behind; a set of candlesticks, a Seder plate, a menorah, and a photo album from their wedding, if she could successfully evade Josefina. Beatriz explained Josefina's schedule to her mother as best she could figure it. Josefina's delight in her power led her to drink a bit of rum every night. Early in the morning was the best time to slip in and out without being noticed.

"Are you ready?" Aarón asked. Four suitcases sat by the front door.

Beatriz looked around the apartment one last time. She picked up Miriam, caressing her cheek. "Yes." She nodded. "I am."

Aarón pulled a tri-fold leather travel portfolio from his coat jacket. It was a gift from his parents when he graduated from university. He used it only once when he took his first trip to the United States, a trip paid for by his godfather, Tío Benny. He visited Miami, amazed both by what America was and what he believed Cuba could be. He checked their papers one last time, opened the door and walked out on his right foot, an old superstition his father brought with him from Poland. Beatriz walked to the elevator. Aarón brought the suitcases in two trips.

Josefina was waiting for them on the ground floor when they stepped out of the elevator. It was early for her. "I wanted to wish you a good trip. You will see how fortunate we are here in Cuba after visiting the *gringos*."

Both Aarón and Beatriz smiled. "Yes, thank you," Aarón said. "I expect so. Could I ask you to wait here with Beatriz and the baby while I go to find a taxi?"

"Of course," Josefina said.

Aarón disappeared around the corner. Beatriz stood silently, waiting for Josefina to say something, anything. She felt her heart pounding, terrified that she might say or do something that would betray them. Miriam babbled a few words. Beatriz found it a relief, shifting Miriam from one arm to the other.

"She is very beautiful," Josefina said.

"*Gracias*,' Beatriz replied.

"May I hold her?"

Beatriz hesitated. "She's just woken. I don't want to upset her before we get on our way."

Josefina raised an eyebrow. "Upset her?"

"She doesn't know you, really. She's at that age. She's leery of strangers."

"I'm hardly a stranger. I see her almost every day."

Beatriz knew she had no choice. "Well, perhaps you are right." She passed Miriam to Josefina. Miriam reached out and grabbed Josefina's earring, a shiny hoop hanging alongside her cheek. Josefina took her little hand gently away, wincing. "*No, no, no, mi amorcito*," she said. She quickly handed Miriam back to Beatriz. "She has a liking for shiny things."

Like you, Beatriz nearly said. "She's just a baby."

A car drove up before Josefina could comment further.

"Come," Aarón said, jumping out of the back seat.

The driver came around from the other side and opened the trunk.

"Thanks so much for everything, Josefina," he said, ushering Beatriz into the waiting car.

Josefina nodded, slyly. "See you in a month."

The immigration officer, dressed in the unofficially official olive drab uniform and red neckerchief of the revolution reviewed their papers without expression. Aarón and Beatriz waited in silence, smiling. Perspiration began to build under their clothing.

Miriam squirmed happily in Beatriz's arms. She kissed Beatriz on her cheek, causing Beatriz to replace her artificial smile with a real one, kissing Miriam back. She made a small, playful, swishing sound with her lips against Miriam's cheek.

Even this spontaneous display of motherly affection didn't elicit a smile from the immigration officer. Her face remained stony. She picked up the in-house phone on her desk, turned her back to Aarón and Beatriz, and covered her mouth as she spoke quickly in a hushed, nearly inaudible tone.

Aarón knew instinctively that the scrutinization the young woman in the uniform bestowed on their papers was not a good thing. Her call to whoever was on the other end of the line was even worse. It indicated both a problem and a lack of initiative in decision making to solve that problem. Or more accurately, a choice to defer decision-making to a superior to avoid possible future consequences for that decision, a method shared by functionaries of all top-down, authoritarian governments. Pass the buck upward and you might move up the ladder when your superior fell off for a judgment not made in line with the policy of the moment.

The immigration officer turned back to them. A smirk finally broke her stonelike appearance. “There are only two visas here.”

“What do you mean?” Aarón replied.

Miriam wriggled in Beatriz’s arms. She turned and waved with her tiny hand to the immigration officer.

“You are three.”

Aarón was shocked. “Three?” he said.

“Yes, you, your wife, and your daughter.”

Aarón took a half step closer to the desk. “She is two years old. She doesn’t need a visa.”

“She is a Cuban citizen. It says so right here on her birth certificate.” She tapped the sheet of white paper in her left hand. “All citizens need a visa to leave the country.”

“That’s absurd.”

“That’s the law.”

Aarón glanced over his shoulder at Beatriz. Terror filled her eyes. He shook his head from side to side. He prayed she would recognize his thought. Stay calm.

“I am a lawyer, and a magistrate, I think I know our laws. This is ludicrous. She is our minor child. We are legally responsible for her. We would have to grant permission for her to leave the country. We are here. We are standing in front of you. We grant permission.”

“I have consulted with my superiors…” The immigration agent looked at Aarón’s passport quickly, “…Señor Cohan. My superiors have instructed me that the regulations are very clear. All Cuban citizens leaving the country must have a valid visa with a required re-entry date and a valid Cuban passport. You have three passports but only two visas, and I might add that we are making an exception for you already. Your wife's passport will expire before your return." She tapped on the date. "You should have renewed her passport before leaving. You did not. The two of you are free to leave for Miami, but the child stays."

Aarón closed his eyes to calm himself. His heart beat so rapidly that he thought his chest might explode. He had to think of something, and quickly. He never considered a scenario like this. Had this all been a trap set by the government? His request for vacation was granted without question. His visas were granted in record time, and with only passing acknowledgment to the fact that he was a government magistrate while not a party member. How had he overlooked the expiration date on Beatriz's passport?

"May I speak to my wife privately?" he asked, regaining his composure, at least for the moment. The official pointed to the corner of the room and stepped away from her desk, disappearing behind a partition, unseen but not necessarily gone.

Aarón placed his hand on Beatriz's shoulder and tipped his head toward the corner of the room. All color had drained from her face. She looked terrified. Miriam laid her head on Beatriz's shoulder and yawned as they walked across the room.

"We have a problem," Aarón said, realizing how ludicrous his statement sounded as it came out of his mouth. He placed his hands on Miriam to take her from Beatriz. Beatriz wrapped her arms even more tightly around Miriam, falling asleep in her arms, thumb in her mouth.

Beatriz took a step back, away from Aarón. "Problem?" she said, responding as if Aarón wasn't speaking Spanish.

Aarón sighed, as much to calm himself as to keep Beatriz from imploding. "More than one," he said.

Beatriz began to hyperventilate.

Aarón looked behind him at the desk. He spied the immigration officer at the edge of the partition peering into the otherwise empty space. "Please, *mi amor, mi vida,* you have to remain calm. Our futures depend on it."

Beatriz took a deep breath, followed by two short ones then another deep. She wiped the tears pooling in her eyes with her free hand. "*Sí, sí*, I understand. *Tranquila*, calm." Miriam shifted in her arms. "*Dime*, and the truth, quickly."

"I'm sorry…"

"No sorries, just tell me what we are going to do…"

Aarón nodded. "Okay. Here's the situation. We only have two visas. They won't let Miriam leave with us."

Beatriz's breath caught in her throat. Her face became red, as if she were about to faint. She leaned into the corner of the wall, clutching Miriam so tightly she began to wake. "I can't leave her. I will stay. You go."

"*No, mi amor*," Aarón said, shaking his head. "That won't work. I made an error, a terrible error. Your passport is expiring in less than a month. They will never renew it if I leave. You will both be stuck here. You go. I will stay with her." Those last words stuck in his throat, the thought of losing Beatriz so overwhelming he couldn't breathe.

A look of horror crossed Beatriz's face. "*No, nunca jamas*, never," she said, shaking her head vigorously, sinking deeper into the corner to escape Aarón's words. She placed her hand on the back of Miriam's head as she'd done when Miriam was an infant. She held her as if she could melt her back into her own body, disappearing inside. "I will never leave her."

Aarón turned again. The immigration agent had returned to her perch on the far side of her desk. "Beatriz, we have no choice. You must listen to me. I promise you. I will get us out. But you must go, now. If you don't, none of us will leave, ever. They will find a way to punish me. This was all a set-up. It was too easy. I promise you. Please."

Beatriz sank into the corner of the wall, her legs barely able to support her. She wept quietly, the pangs of her sorrow wracking her body, her face covered with tears. Miriam was fully awake now and clearly confused, on the verge of a breakdown herself, puzzled both by her surroundings and her parents' near hysteria. She reached for Aarón. He took her with one arm while holding Beatriz up with the other, all the while fighting desperately to keep his own composure, his own knees from buckling.

"Beatriz, *mi amor*, please you have to calm down, to listen to me."

Beatriz forced herself up. She saw the immigration officer over Aarón's shoulder, smug and smiling behind her desk. What was it about these women who followed Fidel? Why were they so hateful? What was it they thought she had done that had affected them so negatively? She was simply a young mother and wife, a young, Cuban woman. She had the same dreams as they. She had never begrudged anyone anything, never taken anything from anyone.

"*Sí, sí*. I'm listening," she said, steadying herself with both hands and her back against the wall behind her. "Tell me." She took several uneven breaths. "What must I do."

"You have to go now. I will take Miriam to your parents. I will do whatever I have to do to get another visa. I promise you we will join you, soon."

"I can't do that."

"You have to"

"I can't."

Aarón looked over his shoulder again. The immigration officer stood now with her head and shoulders back, her arms clasped across her chest, a defiant look in her eyes. "Give us a small moment, please. My wife will be leaving. I will stay with the child." He turned back to Beatriz. "Think about this differently. If you go to Miami now, you can ask for asylum. Then you can bring Miriam, even without me."

"I can't live my life without her, or you."

"If only for now…"

Beatriz broke down again, the sobs convulsing her body. "How can you ask me to choose between you and our child? Trade your freedom for mine?"

Aarón could no longer control his own desperation. "Please," he begged, tears streaming down his face. "For me, for us. You have to go. I promise. I…we…will join you soon. You have to trust me."

Beatriz nodded her head in submission. "I understand." She reached out for Miriam one last time. Took her in her arms, hugged her, placed a million little kisses on her face and forehead. She breathed in her scent so as to remember it when her heart ached the most. She lifted her head and wiped her eyes, pushing her shoulders back. As she approached the immigration officer, hate filled her. How could these people take everything from her, her child, her husband, her parents, her home, her country? Why?

Beatriz took her stamped passport and papers from the sullen woman on the other side of the desk, picked up her suitcases, took a step forward. She stopped, put down the suitcases, and walked back to Aarón and Miriam one last time. She put her hand on Miriam's head and caressed it.

"*Te quiero mija, te amo por siempre*," she said. She turned her head to Aarón and kissed him deeply. "*Te quiero, mi amor, te amo por siempre*" she repeated. I will love you forever. "*En mis suenos, te busco.* I'll search for you in my dreams."

Aarón watched as Beatriz picked up her suitcases and walked through the gate. She disappeared behind the partition that separated them from their future. He had promised Beatriz he would do everything to get himself and Miriam out. He wasn't sure what connections he still had that might help him. Nearly all of them were already on the other side of that partition.

Chapter Seventeen

"What are you doing here?" Lina asked, reacting as if in a dream. She looked around and behind Aarón. A moment later she screamed. "Where is my daughter? Where is Beatriz?"

Eduardo came up behind her, pulling her out of the doorway. He gestured to Aarón to come in, putting his finger over his mouth. "Shhh, shhh," he mumbled to Lina, guiding her into the living room. Aarón followed them, Miriam in his arms. Eduardo seated Lina on the sofa, her mouth open in disbelief, her eyes fixed on Aarón.

"What's happened?" Eduardo said.

Aarón handed Miriam to Eduardo. He sat next to Lina and took her hand. "I'm sorry to have frightened you. I will explain. Give me a moment to collect myself. Calm yourself as well. Please, let's keep our voices down." Aarón took several deep breaths. "Beatriz is fine. Hopefully, she is on her way to Miami by now."

Eduardo put Miriam down on the floor. She grabbed for one of her dolls, hidden under the couch. "I don't understand."

"We only had two visas."

Aarón recounted their nightmare at the airport. By the time he finished, he was up and pacing, Eduardo now sitting next to Lina, his arm around her shoulders. Lina cried silently, dabbing at her eyes with a small, white, lace handkerchief.

"What do you plan to do?"

Aarón stopped pacing. He picked up Miriam and sat down in the deep club chair opposite the sofa. "I'm not sure. One possibility is to leave illegally." He stroked Miriam's hair. "I don't think that's safe with the baby."

"No, no, definitely not," said Lina, her first words since Aarón began his tale.

"Perhaps…your brother?" Eduardo suggested.

"I thought about that, but I don't think it's a good idea. We haven't had any communication since our wedding. I've tried to contact him several times. He hasn't responded. He's clearly not interested in any rapprochement. He's chosen his life. I don't want to complicate it for him by asking for help. That may not be viewed well by his so-called associates for either of us."

Eduardo nodded. "I agree. What about your cousin? The one with the same name as you. The actor."

Aarón chuckled. "I heard he's fallen out of favor with the regime."

"Already?"

Apparently. He mocked Fidel or Raul at some performance he was in. They were unhappy. He's supposedly in hiding, but who knows if he hasn't already left the country or is perhaps in prison?"

"They have very thin skins."

"True." Aarón chuckled to himself. This whole experience would seem comic if he wasn't living it. How could a society descend into an alternate reality so quickly? "May I ask a favor of you?"

"Of course."

"Would you take Miriam until I can figure out a plan?"

"Of course," said Lina. "Whatever you need."

"And also, please go see my parents. Don't phone them. Visit them. Tell them what's happened. Let them see Miriam."

Aarón debated whether to return to his apartment or to seek a place to stay. In the end, he realized Josefina was no longer a threat. In all likelihood, not only did she already know he hadn't left, but she also likely knew what they would face at the airport. The CDR was everywhere. The best place for Aarón to hide was out in the open. Sure enough, when Aarón arrived Josefina was waiting on her perch at the front door.

"What happened?" she barked, a half-smirk on her face.

Aarón threw caution to the wind. "I think you know." He pulled open the heavy door to the lobby and entered, walking quickly to the elevator. A few long moments later he was standing in front of the police tape already strung in front of his door. He tore it down, placed the key in the lock and turned.

Upon entering he experienced a strange feeling, something like *déjà vu* but not exactly. This hadn't happened to him before but rather was something he thought would never happen. He'd returned to a place he never expected to see again.

Everything was as they left it that morning. The CDR hadn't ransacked the apartment yet, typical behavior after someone "betrayed" Cuba. Perhaps they intended to save that until Aarón and Beatriz hadn't returned. To make a show of it. Aarón imagined their things in the courtyard of the building, Josefina holding up their wedding photos and calling them traitors. Or perhaps, as he suspected, they knew he would be back that evening.

Aarón took a shower and made himself a *cafecito*. The apartment felt strange without Beatriz and Miriam. The hum of family life was missing. No one talking, no one singing along with the radio. No fresh flowers on the windowsill, nor the scents of Beatriz's cooking, or sounds of Miriam's chattering. He had to develop a plan.

What was his father's lifelong creed? The truth is the best lie. Leaving Cuba, especially with Miriam, had to be done legally. He couldn't risk her life, or his. He promised Beatriz he would get them out. He would keep that promise. Had he made a critical mistake? Or had he been misled? It didn't really matter now. He simply needed another visa, one specifically for Miriam. As a lawyer, it was his job to know the law, and his rights, even in this version of Cuba.

After two days at the law library, and certain of his argument, Aarón arrived at the visa appeals office at nine o'clock sharp. The line was around the block. At twelve, an armed guard came around. At one o'clock the office would close for two hours for lunch, then re-open to process those who had already received a number. The rest could return tomorrow.

The next morning Aarón arrived at six o'clock. He was near the entrance to the building when the same guard came out again at noon and made the same announcement as the day before. The third night he arrived at three o'clock in the morning. He brought a thermos of coffee and a sandwich. He was in sight of the front doors.

Aarón watched the light change as dawn broke over Havana. The deserted streets sprang to life. It was almost as if people appeared from nowhere suddenly, hurrying along to their secret destinations. Hawkers called out from their stalls. Children, dressed in uniforms, skipped their way to school. The scent of Havana, heavy with garlic frying in oil, wafted through the air. The sound of *son* and *bolero* springing from a thousand radios mixed in the air, competing for attention. Aarón was at once embraced by his senses and aware that he would never feel so at home again. This was the true Cuba, the Cuba of the streets and of the *campo*, full of the five senses. And he was a true *Cubano*, at home in it all.

At nine o'clock exactly the door to the building opened. Cuba was perpetually late, except for official purposes. He would gain entrance today, he knew it. He felt it. He had donned his nicest *guayabera* and a fedora. His briefcase held not only the necessary papers and proof but two thin binders of opinions relevant to his case.

The law was clear. A child under the age of five did not require a visa to leave the country. But, if that was not the position of the current government, he would make an application for Miriam's. He would assume sole responsibility for his error and her safety. He would plead *mea culpa*. He was Miriam's sole guardian in Cuba and could act on her behalf.

Two hours later, just after eleven o'clock, Aarón entered the building. He walked across the marble lobby to the elevator and took it to the third floor.

A young woman sat at a desk just outside the elevator. She was dressed simply in a white shirt, her hair pulled back. "May I help you," she said without a smile.

"I would like to apply for a visa for a minor child," Aarón said.

"You are at the wrong office. You need to go to the visa office. This is the visa appeals office."

Aarón maintained his composure. Dealing with the bureaucracy hadn't changed under Fidel. "They sent me here," he lied.

"Is the child your child?"

"Yes."

"Is she under five?"

"Yes."

The young woman pointed to the right. "The forms are there, on those shelves. *¿Sigue…?*" she said, pointing to the woman behind Aarón.

"No," Aarón interrupted. "I need to see someone. Now!"

"The forms are over there," the young woman repeated, chewing each syllable, beckoning with her hand to the woman behind him again.

Aarón stood his ground. "I am a lawyer, and this is an urgent matter."

The young woman stood up. "Wait here," she scowled, glancing at the guard at the door. She disappeared behind a glass and wood partition. Aarón waited, rubbing his hands together nervously, the people in line behind him mumbling. "You're holding us up," one said, loud enough for him to hear.

The young woman returned a few minutes later. "Why do you need to see someone today?" she demanded, glaring at him.

"Because I have a visa for myself that will expire in a few days, and I need to take my daughter with me."

She stared at Aarón then disappeared again behind the opaque glass. The grumbling behind him increased. The tension in his stomach rose into his chest. This was his chance. He wouldn't lose it. A long moment later the door opened again. A man around his age with a beard and a cigar appeared in the doorway. His shirt was crumpled and his hair disorderly. "Are you the citizen seeking a visa for a child?" he said, looking directly at Aarón.

"Yes," Aarón replied. He grasped his briefcase so tightly the knuckles of his right hand hurt.

"Follow me."

Aarón tacked behind the man through the outer office into a smaller interior one. It was dark and cluttered and looked out onto an interior courtyard behind the building.

"Have a seat," the official said. "My name is Marcos Abreu. I am in charge of approving emergency visas. How can I help you?"

Aarón opened his briefcase. He handed him his card. Abreu perused it, raising an eyebrow. "A magistrate?"

"Yes."

"Why would you be leaving the country?"

"Vacation."

"We have many beautiful spots for vacation here in Cuba, why would you need to go abroad?"

"My sister-in-law is about to give birth. We are going so as to be with her for the birth."

"We?"

"My wife, myself, our daughter."

Abreu looked over the card again. "Aarón Cohan. That's not a common name." Abreu puffed on his cigar. He paced in front of Aarón for what felt like an eternity. "We are looking for an Aarón Cohan. You aren't him, though. He is an accomplished actor."

Aarón felt himself flush a bit. "No. He is my cousin."

"Do you have any idea where we might find him?"

Aarón tensed again. "No. We're not in contact. I haven't seen him in years."

"I see," said Abreu. "If you are Aarón Cohan's cousin, you must be Moises Cohan's…brother?

Aarón thought his head would explode. There was little

Fidel's thugs didn't know. He considered whether to answer yes or no to Abreu's question. His father's voice echoed in his head again. The truth is always the best lie. "Yes," he mumbled

"Interesting," said Abreu. "Now, what is your emergency?"

Aarón explained what had transpired at the airport. "I apologize. It was entirely my fault." He reveled in his humility, hoping it would sway Abreu. "I should have applied for a separate visa for my daughter." He pointed to the notes in his open briefcase, "technically, as she is under five, and the law has not been changed, I didn't need to. There are new internal regulations. I didn't know about them but should have, and as such didn't apply for a separate visa for her."

"Yes, magistrate. You should have known." Abreu smirked. He picked up his cigar from a glass ashtray and leaned on the desk's edge. He nodded. "I see. Very astute from a legal point of view, but I'm afraid we make the rules, now. Tell me this, magistrate, why does the whole family need to go north to the *gringos* for the birth of this child? As you've told me, it's your wife's sister who is about to give birth and your wife is already there. Why do you need to be there as well? You're a lawyer, not a doctor, and they have plenty of those in Miami."

Aarón straightened his back, puffing out his chest a bit. He had to maintain the appearance of strength, as he would defending a client in court. He transformed from a man begging for help into the lawyer necessary for this trial. He gambled that Abreu would have little knowledge of Jewish practices.

"We are Jews," he said.

Abreu nodded. "Go on."

"We are to be the child's godparents. We both must be

there. It is a very big honor in our culture. In addition, I am of the priestly class and must perform a special ceremony for their first child if it's a boy."

Abreu tapped the ash off the end of his cigar, the gray-green smoke swirling and dissipating into the room. Its heavy odor was beginning to weigh on Aarón. "What is your sister-in-law's name? And her husband?"

"Roberta and Pablo Goldman," Aarón replied, their names nearly catching in his throat. He knew what was coming next.

Abreu picked up a heavy file of papers tied together with a cord through holes. He dropped it with a thud in front of Aarón on the edge of the desk. "This is a list of our countrymen who have fled and have requested asylum in the United States. If I look there—and that could take a while, it's not alphabetized—would I find their names?"

Aarón felt himself waver. The truth was the best lie, he repeated silently to himself. "Yes. I believe you would," he said in a low voice, his eyes directed away from Abreu. He realized he may have just put a knife in his own best chance of escape.

"Your sister-in-law and her husband are traitors."

"I wouldn't call them that. They love this country."

"As do you, I suspect," Abreu retorted, without missing a beat. "Yet, they fled."

"I do, and they do," Aarón replied.

Abreu leafed through the heavy file, now in his hands. "Leave your documents with me. I will consider your request. That doesn't mean I am inclined to grant it. When does your visa expire?"

"In about three weeks."

"And that would give you enough time to do what your customs require and to return to Havana?"

"Yes."

Abreu chuckled. "You know, Fidel has a soft spot for your people. Come back Monday afternoon after three o'clock. You won't have to wait. Here is my card. Show this to the guard at the door and he will let you in."

Chapter Eighteen

Come back Monday. It felt like an eternity. And it was only Thursday evening. Aarón sat alone in the living room. The remains of his breakfast continued to live on a plate on the coffee table. Lina sent him home with enough food to last for weeks. He couldn't eat dinner. He considered taking a run.

It had been years since he was able to run regularly. His job traveling the island as a magistrate made it difficult to run regularly during the week. Initially, Aarón had tried running early in the morning wherever he was but found that the condition of the roads, or the lack thereof altogether, made running difficult, in some cases, downright dangerous. He couldn't take a chance of an injury, especially outside Havana. Weekends presented another roadblock, his own. He coveted his time with his wife and daughter. He wasn't willing to give up any of it, for any reason.

Aarón stretched. He had to get out of the apartment. He walked into the bedroom and opened the large mahogany armoire that held his clothes, his whole life really. Some air would do him good. He needed to think, and a good run always helped. His running shoes were buried in the corner at the bottom of the armoire. He dusted them off and found a pair of shorts and a T-shirt. Dressed, he stretched his legs, his hamstrings tight. He would start with a brisk walk, work up to a jog, and if he felt good and loose, he would sprint as well.

Opening the door, he looked out in both directions. He didn't want to encounter any of his neighbors. He pushed the call button for the elevator then thought better of it and took the five flights down. Arriving at the lobby, he spotted Josefina at her perch by the front door interrogating one of his neighbors. He slipped down the hall to the rear courtyard of the building. An alley behind the building was accessible to the street behind, over a low wall. In a few moments he was free of both Josefina and the weight of the puzzle he needed to solve to get out of Cuba, at least for a little while.

Aarón looked for change as he transversed the streets of Havana. It had been more than three years since the revolution, but Cuba, Havana, was ostensibly the same. The streets were still full of people. They rushed to their lives, nearly oblivious to the crowds of which they were a part, until, almost on cue, someone might stop at the sound of their name or a familiar voice. "*Pana, socio, hermano*," rang out regularly, interspersed with the calls from peddlers, many of whom were now plying their trade illegally. The government tolerated it, at least for now. A government of the people couldn't alienate the people.

Aarón smiled and tipped his head to a flower seller he had known for years. She was too old to stand now. She sat on a rickety wooden chair next to her table. A young girl of perhaps six or seven assisted her, probably her granddaughter. She smiled back, enough teeth still in her mouth for her to eat.

Aarón took a deep breath as he came to the familiar steps that led to the plaza of the University of Havana. He considered a sprint up the steps. Tightness in his left calf warned him, don't push it. He stopped briefly and stretched, then took the steps, two at a time, the majesty of the University's neo-classical buildings appearing over the horizon at the top of the stairs. Arriving at the top, he surveyed the large plaza, now filled with students. Re-opening the University of Havana was one of Fidel's first acts. It earned him high marks with the young who brought him to power.

Aarón proceeded across the quad at a jog, carefully avoiding the many young students seated on the grass. His meeting with Moises, the night he learned of his brother's involvement in the incident at San Miguel, flashed through his mind. He did what a brother should do. He helped Moises. There were many times when he questioned whether he should have. Perhaps Moises might have seen things differently had he been arrested and gone to prison. In the end, a mere few weeks later, Che and Fidel captured the capital and the nation. Aarón knew whatever short incarceration Moises might have experienced would have been meaningless after their victory.

Aarón stopped at a water fountain at the edge of the plaza. He took a moment and glanced back at the scene, Moises still in his head. The situation was reversed now. He needed help. He asked himself for the thousandth time, should he contact Moises? Could he ask Moises to help him to get out of Cuba? Aarón shook his head. Moises didn't even know Miriam existed.

Nonetheless, Aarón realized, as he stood there remembering a world that looked exactly like this one but no longer existed that he needed a Plan B. What would he do if Abreu didn't grant him a visa for Miriam?

A part of him imagined Miriam grown up and attending this university, sitting among her friends on the grass laughing, discussing how to solve the problems of the world as young people do. As these young people sitting around him were doing now. That was when he heard his name. At first, he didn't think anyone was calling him. No one he knew would be in this place at this time. Then he heard his last name as well.

Alma appeared changed. Her hair was shorter. The formal clothes she wore as Aarón's secretary were replaced by a pleated skirt and a simple, white top. The heels that tapped across the terrazzo floors of the executive offices of the bank were gone. Simple, comfortable flats cushioned her feet. Her makeup was still impeccable.

They sat on a bench in a small park just outside the University, sipping *cafecitos* from a small stand at the entrance. Children hurried by with their mothers and siblings on their way home. The sun lost strength and the air cooled, the shadows cast by the buildings surrounding them lengthening as the sun set behind them.

Aarón, happy to see a friendly face, was reticent, nonetheless. He recalled how Alma's attitude toward him changed after the revolution, becoming more distant, more measured. She was still at the bank when he left. Clearly, she wasn't with them any longer.

"I left shortly after Hector fled. Did you know about that?" she asked.

"I heard," he replied, careful not to reveal too much information. "What are you doing now?"

"I'm working at a school for orphaned children."

Aarón smiled. "That's to be admired. God's work," he said, recalling how religious Alma was.

Alma smiled. "Yes, but we don't mention God."

Aarón smiled back and nodded. There was nothing more to say on the subject.

"And I got married." Alma lifted her left hand to show Aarón the simple, thin gold ring she wore. The fading sunlight gave it a pinkish hue. "We live in La Habana Vieja. Not far from the school. And you?"

Aarón considered how much to tell her. "I'm a…magistrate."

"Yes. I heard. From Hector. Shortly after you left the bank." She reached out her hand to his. "I'm sorry for what happened to you. And I'm sorry for the way I behaved. You didn't deserve it. You were always a friend to me. There were forces working against you from more than one direction." Alma's eyes welled up. She touched a tiny paper napkin to them. "I should have warned you."

Aarón was caught completely off guard. He had rerun his conversations with Hector in his head thousands of times to try to determine what it was that had really happened. Had he been targeted? If so, why? The assignment from Che was a thinly veiled attack from the beginning. The General knew what Aarón's answer would be. The question was, why?

"I'm sorry," Alma said, drying her eyes. "I hope you can forgive me."

"There's nothing to forgive," he said, his words sounding a bit hollow, even to him. Alma, like everyone else, stood by, unwilling to defend him. "How did you know?"

"Hector told me. An official from the Movement came to see him shortly after the revolution. He was high up in the new government. He came to discuss the political aims for the bank but asked a lot of questions, specifically about you."

"Did you see him? Meet him?"

"No," Alma said, shaking her head.

Aarón touched her hand. "No apologies needed," he said. "We live in challenging times."

Alma nodded. "Yes, we do." She looked away and then directly at him, a broad smile on her face now. "How is Beatriz? I remember she was pregnant when you left the bank. Do you have a son or a daughter?"

"A daughter," Aarón said, smiling. "Her name is Miriam."

Alma took both Aarón's hands in hers. "That's wonderful. How old is she?"

"Two. Earlier this month."

"And Beatriz? How is she? Where are you living? Nearby?" Again, Aarón considered how much to say. He hesitated. Alma leaned into him and whispered, "you can trust me."

Though his doubts lingered, Aarón chose the truth, though only the basic facts. "Beatriz is in Miami. She left earlier this week."

Alma tightened her hold on Aarón's hands. "Is Miriam with her?"

"No." He felt a lump form in his throat, his heart beating rapidly.

Alma's expression changed. The color drained from her face. "Can you tell me?"

Aarón outlined the events of the past few days. At moments during their conversation he thought he would break down. The reality of his situation finally hit him sitting in a tiny park in the heart of Havana with his former secretary. He didn't know if his family would ever be whole again. "I don't know what I'm going to do if I don't get a visa for Miriam."

Alma released Aarón's hand and looked around. She inched closer to him and whispered. "I can help you. I am working with a Catholic organization. We bring children out of Cuba to the United States. It's done under the guise of adoption. The veracity of the children's personal history is rarely checked. Enough hard currency will make almost anyone blind."

Aarón felt elated and terrified at the same time. At least there might be some hope of getting Miriam to Beatriz safely if a visa wasn't granted. "Thank you," he said. "How does this happen?"

Late Saturday Aarón met Alma at a church tucked into a small street in La Habana Vieja. She pointed toward the confessional at the far end of the apse. Though never particularly religious, Aarón felt incredibly uncomfortable. He had been inside churches, but never inside the dark, closet-like recesses where the faithful went to repent. It was completely alien to him, but if it would lead to a way out for Miriam, he would enter. He'd spent a sleepless Friday night, the window open, distant sounds of mambo and cha-cha-cha filtering through the filmy curtains, weighing his alternatives. The one thing he was certain of was that if Miriam wasn't granted a visa they would be stuck here forever.

Once inside the dark confessional Aarón sat on the hard, wooden bench built into one side. A hassock for kneeling faced the partition open to the priest on the other side. He slid open the shutter revealing a latticed screen.

"I seek your guidance, father," he said, as Alma instructed.

"Tell me of your tribulation," came back the expected response.

"I have a child who must leave the country," Aarón

said, his voice cracking when he came to the word, child.

"What are the circumstances?" the voice on the other side of the lattice asked.

"My child is in danger," Aarón said, recounting his story again.

"You are not of our faith?"

"No."

The priest hesitated, his breathing heavy. "You are…Hebrew?"

"Yes."

Aarón tensed. Though he had never in his life experienced anti-Semitism, Aarón suddenly become concerned that their identity as Jews would disqualify Miriam.

"I see," said the priest.

"Is that a problem?" Aarón asked, his voice rising above the whisper he'd been told to maintain.

"Not for me," said the priest. "But some of what we may need to do may be a problem for you."

"If it will save my daughter, bring her to her mother, it's not a problem. Please, tell me more."

"We are a clandestine organization," the priest explained. "The new government is clearly, if not yet openly, anti-religion, particularly anti-Catholic. They are opposed to teaching our children our faith. We are securing visas for orphans to be sent to Italy and Spain for adoption. The first stop on the route is Miami. I suppose it goes without saying that the children never go any further than the United States. Refugee families and relatives already there are caring for them until their parents can escape."

"I thought these children were orphans."

"We make it seem that way. It's easier to convince the government to issue immigration papers for orphans. They no longer have to absorb the cost of caring for these children once they leave Cuba. Even in a socialist country, everything boils down to money."

Aarón laughed to himself. He knew the priest's statement to be true.

"We will create an identity for your daughter. That could take some time. She would come to live with us at one of our orphanages for a few months. You will be separated from her."

Aarón's heart raced as hard as if he had just run a sprint up the steps at the University. "I understand," he said. "Forgive me father. I appreciate and thank you for your time and your confidence. I have to think about this. I have to speak with my parents and my wife's…"

"No, no," the priest said, his fingers wrapping around and through the latticed partition. "You may not speak to anyone about this. It could compromise everything."

Tears fell from Aarón's eyes. He'd never felt so alone in his life. "Of course," he said. "Forgive me. I will get back to you in a day or two."

Aarón left the confessional and looked around the church for Alma. She was gone. He sat in a pew at the rear of the church and stared at the image of Jesus on his cross, a mass of fresh flowers on the altar before him. He realized how alone Jesus must have felt at the moment of his crucifixion.

That Sunday Aarón went to his in-laws' home. They'd visited with his parents a few days earlier with Miriam, as he asked. Lina told him his mother nearly fainted when she saw them. They explained everything. His parents would be at the Resnicks as well.

He took a series of buses by an indirect route to make

sure he wasn't being followed. He didn't want his parents or in-laws implicated in anything later, whether he got out of Cuba or not. The normally thirty-minute trip took nearly two hours.

Miriam screeched when she saw him then jumped into his arms. She wouldn't leave him. He wasn't surprised, though his feelings of guilt at leaving her were multiplied. He held her close and kissed her repeatedly as she played in his lap.

"We spoke with Beatriz," his father-in-law reported. "The conversation was superficial, at best."

"To be expected," replied Aarón. "Did she mention me or Miriam?"

"She said you were out. That you were visiting with Tío Benny. We knew that meant you were in Cuba, as Benny is in *Presidio Modelo*."

"Did she say when she expected me?"

"No," said Eduardo. "She said she didn't know when you would be back."

"She's frightened," Aarón said, the guilt weighing more and more heavily on him.

"Yes," said Eduardo. "She's terrified."

An eerie quiet filled the room. His parents and in-laws looked at each other repeatedly, none of them wanting to ask the inevitable question. Finally, Aarón offered an answer. "I have a plan if I don't get a visa for Miriam."

He outlined his meeting with the priest the day before, breaking the priest's confidence. He left out crucial details to protect the clandestine operation. He couldn't decide this alone. He needed their input. When he finished, he looked at his father. "What do you think?"

"Over my dead body."

"Excuse me," Aarón replied, incredulous that his father didn't seem to understand the impossibility of their situation.

"I won't permit you to turn my granddaughter over to *goyim*. To raise her in a Catholic environment. What if they can't get papers for her? What if she never leaves Cuba? What will we do? Once they have her, they will never give her back. Shall we lose her forever? No. I'd rather you fled alone and left her with us. The four of us will care for her and raise her as a Jew until you can get her out of here."

Aarón put Miriam down on the floor. She walked off toward the pile of toys in the corner of the room. "You never learn do you?" he said. "What is this obsession you have with this Jewish thing? You were never particularly observant to begin with." He shifted his gaze from one to the other. "And that goes for all of you."

He settled his gaze back on his father. "You've already lost one son to this. We've had no contact with Moises since that scene you perpetrated at our wedding. So what if the girl wasn't Jewish? The fact that they were communists? You could tolerate that? But a *shiksa*, never." Aarón glared at all of them again, so angry he thought he would explode.

"*Papá*, I have never defied you. Any of you. But this time it's my daughter who is at stake. I won't let her grow up in this country. She'll have no future. This stand-off with the United States will only get worse. I'd rather see her take communion than stay here. They said they will bring her to Beatriz, and I trust them to do that. Even if I never leave, even if I never see either of them again."

With that Aarón collapsed into the club chair. This time the sobs that he'd held back since the moment Beatriz disappeared behind the partition in the airport wracked his body.

"Perhaps you should try to contact Moises," his father-in-law mumbled.

"He refuses to speak with us," Esther said. "I've tried to reach him."

Rafael looked at her, his eyes wild with anger. "You've contacted him?"

"I've tried," Esther said, through her own tears.

"I've forbidden it! He betrayed us!" Rafael bellowed.

"He's still my son!" Esther shouted back.

Aarón stood. He calmed himself. "We shall see. After Monday." He picked up Miriam, climbing the stairs to the bedrooms on the second floor. He needed to be alone with his child. Who knew how much more time he would have with her?

Chapter Nineteen

Sunday morning Aarón went to the little church in Habana Vieja and looked for Alma at the end of the mass. They walked through the nearby market together.

"I've thought about it," he said.

"And?"

"If I don't get Miriam's visa tomorrow, I will take you up on your offer."

Alma nodded. "It's my honor to help you, and her. I will guard her as if she were my own. Return to the church this afternoon at five o'clock. The confessional line should be finished by then. If not, wait in the back till the last parishioner leaves. Father Ignacio will be waiting for you in the confessional. He will work out the details. And you? What are your plans?"

Aarón shook his head. "I don't know. That's a work in progress."

A few minutes after five the last parishioner hurried away from the confessional. Father Ignacio spied Aarón in the pews and turned back to the booth. Aarón hurried across the church and looked in both directions before entering the confessional. He sat down on the bench and slipped back the partition. “Good afternoon, father,” he whispered.

“Good afternoon.”

“I’ve made my decision,” Aarón said, questioning himself even as he heard his own words. “If I don’t get a visa for my daughter, I want to pursue your option. But I’d like to understand better how this would work, what would happen.”

Father Ignacio cleared his throat. “I see. I can tell you only so much. I hope you understand that it’s for your protection as well as ours.”

“Of course.”

“To begin, you will turn the child over to us. We will place her in the care of one of our orphanages in the provinces. We’ve found there are fewer eyes on us outside the capital.”

“Will I be able to visit her?”

“No. I’m sorry.”

Aarón’s heart pounded. He felt his face flush. He considered running from the church. How could he do this? Beatriz would never forgive him, he would never forgive himself, if they lost Miriam. “I understand,” he said, finally. “Then what?”

“We will match her to an identity. We keep records of children who died and who were baptized. We create a new identity for her. We pay off the clerks in the local records offices to remove the record of the death of these children until the children we are substituting for them are safely out of the country.”

A chill rushed up Aarón’s spine. He’d spent two years in provincial records offices. He knew how easily the clerks could be bought. Corruption was in their genes. No political movement could change that. The plan was workable. A logical idea. But nonetheless, it terrified him as much for its morbid nature as for what it said about his country.

"How long does this take, this process? When would she leave the country?"

Father Ignacio ruminated for a long moment. "Anywhere from six months to a year."

Aarón hesitated for a moment. "Would you have to baptize her?"

"No," Father Ignacio said, reassuringly. "That's not necessary. The certificate is enough. Things are difficult, *señor*, but this isn't Nazi Germany."

Aarón appreciated the priest's words. They were, in some way calming, reassuring. He then considered the effect the separation would have on a two-year-old's sense of self and family. Miriam might forget them completely.

"Is there any way to speed that up?"

"Unlikely. And it's expensive. We would need the equivalent in pesos of $500 US."

"That's a huge amount of money."

"We will work with you as best we can."

Abreu's card was a magic pass. Upon seeing it, the armed guard ushered Aarón past the security desk directly to the elevator. The stone-faced woman who had proven so difficult on Aarón's prior visit passed him through without so much as a look. For a moment he felt important, then the reality of his notoriety occurred to him. Anonymity was the key to survival in a system where surveillance was the norm. He was anything but anonymous in this place.

Abreu's door was open. He sat with his feet on his desk, lazily smoking his cigar. It seemed to Aarón that Abreu's cigar was omnipresent, and by its scent, not cheap. But wasn't that the prerogative of the victors? The spoils of war?

"Come in," Abreu said. He pointed his cigar to the chair in front of the desk. Aarón turned to close the door behind him. "No, leave it open," Abreu said. "It's a bit warm today."

Aarón did as he was instructed. He sat opposite Abreu, his briefcase in his lap, his hands clasped on top. He waited for Abreu to speak.

"Do you have any questions?" Abreu said, finally.

Aarón was confused by Abreu's statement. "What kind of question would I have?" he replied.

"We could start with whether or not I have a visa for your daughter."

Aarón played along. "Do you have a visa for my daughter?"

"Do you believe she should receive one?"

Aarón began to sweat. In fact, while the room was warm, his increasing fear did the rest. "Please," he said. "May I have the visa? Again, I'm sorry to have caused this problem. I should have been more diligent in my application."

"Yes, you should have," Abreu said, the fire in his eyes growing, the volume of his voice rising. "We are concerned that you won't return. There are too many like you. You are a servant of the people, Magistrate. You have a responsibility."

Aarón felt eyes on his back. He wanted to turn to see if his audience with Abreu had developed an audience of its own.

"We will return, I give you my word."

"What good is your word?"

"I am a loyal citizen, as is my wife. Our parents are

here. They need us. We would never leave them."

"Will you sign an affidavit testifying to such?"

Aarón's heart skipped several beats. Would he sign an affidavit? As a lawyer, he knew the answer to that. It depended on what it said. He realized at that moment that Fidel's government, his brother's government, was threatening his parents with his daughter. He would have to make a choice between them. If he agreed, signed, and didn't return, they would be constantly surveilled, likely threatened, and most certainly marked for official discrimination. He felt his stomach rumble and was thankful he hadn't eaten since the early morning.

"I will sign," he mumbled, his eyes cast down at the floor.

Abreu laughed. "Good. To be honest, I have not made my decision yet as to the visa. I will tell you that I don't trust you. You are a bourgeois pig. My decision could go in any of several ways. I may give you a visa for your daughter and take yours away, or I may give you a new one and keep her here as a ward of the state until you return with your wife. Or, if I can convince myself that you are not a traitor and that it serves the spirit of the revolution, I may let you both go. Come back tomorrow at this time."

Aarón looked at Abreu. He had no words, no voice. He turned to see the small crowd that had gathered in front of Abreu's door, all of them smiling, sufficiently entertained. He walked out with what little dignity he could muster.

By the time Aarón arrived home, he'd calmed himself enough to command himself to think clearly. He'd heard stories of how cruel Fidel's men could be. He'd heard the same about Batista's. Yet, he never expected to find himself the object of that cruelty.

The reality that he and Miriam might not get out together, or at all, hit him like a thunderbolt. Father Ignacio's offer might be his only option. Five hundred American dollars was a lot of money. The simple truth was that it was the equivalent of what some might save in a lifetime. It was nearly what he and Beatriz had accumulated over the last few years through savings and their wedding gifts.

When Batista fell, he used his position at the bank to clear his accounts and convert his money to cash, American dollars. He put himself at the head of the line before other depositors. Was that a privilege of his position? Yes. Did that make him a counterrevolutionary? No. He didn't turn against Fidel until it became clear that Fidel and his cohorts had turned against him. He'd been marked an enemy of the working class, that was clear.

Aarón opened one of the still-packed suitcases he'd left in the bedroom when he returned from the airport a week earlier. Inside, was his *tallis*[2] bag. He was prepared to explain what it was to the police inspectors at the airport if asked. He needed it for the ceremony he would perform for his new nephew if the baby was a boy. A *pidyon-ha-ben*, an ancient custom of buying back a first-born son from the priesthood, the *Cohanim*, that dated back to the time of the first temple in Jerusalem.

Aarón knew the power that religion and superstition had on most Cubans. They would be enthralled by the story. They would never think to check the bag for contraband cash. Inside that bag, hidden between the velvet exterior and the interior satin lining was a little over $800. It was all they had in the world and was meant to

---

[2] Tallis, a shawl used by Jewish men during prayer.

give them a new start in America. If that was the price of Miriam's freedom, so be it. If he ended up in *Presidio Modelo* with Tío Benny, so be it.

As he entered the ministry, Aarón checked nervously to see if the five twenty-dollar bills he'd slipped into his pocket before leaving his apartment were still there. Of course, they were. He might have laughed at his own silliness if he wasn't so terrified.

He entered without incident and made his way to the third floor by elevator. He was directed without a word through the door behind the woman attendant into the inner sanctum of visas. Abreu waved to him. He left the door open this time.

"Close the door," Abreu said after Aarón sat down.

Aarón jumped up and did as he was instructed quietly, unsure whether this was a positive or negative indication of Abreu's intentions.

"Do you have any questions?" Abreu asked again as he did the day before, the question still odd, still out of place.

"May I have my visas?" Aarón responded, taking the most direct approach. If Abreu was intent on playing him, he wanted to get it over with as quickly as possible.

"Not so fast." Abreu placed a document in front of Aarón on the edge of the desk. "Please sign this."

"May I read it?"

"If you'd like," Abreu said, reaching for a new cigar, cutting its end, and lighting it.

Aarón took a moment to read the affidavit. He must swear that he is a loyal citizen of the Cuban Republic. He is obligated to return to Cuba at the end of his visa. He took a deep breath. That meant his visa was still valid. He continued reading.

He, Aarón Cohan, is permitted to take his daughter Miriam with him. The affidavit further declared that though she was a minor, the government considered her to be an individual and unique citizen. If Cohan failed to return and the government desired, they could demand her return without her parents. Aarón considered this clause preposterous. The Cuban government wouldn't make an international issue out of one child.

The document continued with several other absurd and nonsensical clauses. It was clearly not written by an attorney. Aarón took a breath. "Give me a pen."

"Not so fast," Abreu said. "I think you might want to see these as well."

Aarón took two pieces of paper from Abreu's outstretched hand. He perused them quickly. His breath caught in his throat when he looked at the bottom of each. One contained the signatures of his parents, the other of his in-laws. He read the identical documents quickly. Both his parents and his in-laws objected to his removing their granddaughter from Cuba. The affidavits further stated that in the event he and the child's mother, Beatriz Resnick Goldstein de Cohan, did not return by the appointed date, they would request that the government of Cuba take all due actions to have the child returned. If their son/daughter did not seek to return to Cuba at all, they, the child's grandparents, would serve as her guardians.

Aarón's mind was in disarray. He knew both his parents and in-laws had been pressured to sign. He knew how they felt about Castro and his government. Somehow he always knew it would come to this, a choice between Miriam's freedom and endangering their parents. But what choice did he have?

"I told you," Aarón said, summoning his most calm, serene demeanor "we will return, all of us. Now, please, give me a pen."

Abreu picked up a pen and held it out to Aarón, but only as far as his arm would reach across his desk without moving his body forward. Aarón reached and took it. Abreu held on to it just long enough to make his point: he owned Aarón. Aarón scribbled his signature across the bottom of the affidavit, then handed it to Abreu. "May I have my visas now?"

Abreu reached into his desk and pulled out the visas. He handed them to Aarón. Despite Aarón's desire to flee from Abreu as quickly as possible, he reviewed the visas to make sure they were correct and valid.

"Thank you," he said, the words bitter in his mouth. He placed the visas in his briefcase and turned to leave. He stopped a moment later and reached into his pocket turning back toward Abreu; the unique green and white of American currency peeking above the line of Aarón's pocket.

Abreu laughed. "That won't be necessary, Magistrate. And I'm surprised at you. Do you think I would fall into that trap? Besides, I've already received my payment for this transaction."

Aarón had no idea what Abreu meant. Nor did he care. He just wanted to get out of this office, and Cuba.

The next day Aarón went to the government travel agency and purchased two tickets to Miami. He went back to his apartment and repacked his suitcases. He slipped out in the evening from the back of the building to avoid Josefina. He didn't know how much she might know, and he didn't want to find out. Down at the far corner of the street behind the building he found a young man polishing the fenders of his Chevrolet. The Americans had left, but their cars hadn't. He flashed some pesos at the boy. "I need a ride, quietly."

The young man looked him over and smiled. "*Por supuesto*," he said. Of course. He helped Aarón put the two suitcases in the trunk. "Where to?"

First stop is the Church of the Annunciation in La Habana Vieja.

The young man smiled. "Looks like you're going on a trip. You need to be blessed first?"

Aarón laughed. "I like a man with a sense of humor." Then his expression changed completely in the smallest of moments. He pointed to his pocket. "What's in here is your business, not where I'm going. Got it?"

"Got it," the young man said.

The trip to the church took about thirty minutes. Aarón could have walked it faster, but for his bags. "Wait here," he said to the young man, handing him two, five-dollar bills. Both the young man and Aarón knew the value of American currency on the black market.

"Of course, sir." The young man took his polishing rag from the glove compartment and resumed his work on the rear chrome bumper.

Aarón entered the church and looked around in the soft light. He spotted Father Ignacio to the left of the alter arranging the cups and communion wafers. Ignacio saw him and gestured with his head to the confessional. Aarón walked quickly across the cavernous room, the scent of incense tickling his nose. He entered the confessional, sliding the partition open quickly. "Thank you, father," he said.

"You are trusting us with your daughter, then?"

"No. By some miracle, they gave me visas. I'm leaving in the morning."

"Thank God. I prayed for you both."

Aarón smiled to himself. Did God, anyone's God, really have anything to do with this? He doubted it. "Thank you for that."

"Godspeed," the priest said. He put his hand on the lattice to touch Aarón's.

"Father, I have something for you. A thank you for what you offered to do for my daughter." Aarón slipped a roll of twenty-dollar bills, $100 US, through the lattice. "Save another child. Please." With that, he turned and exited the confessional and the church.

"Take me to this address," he said to the young man, repeating his in-law's address twice. He handed him more bills, a combination of pesos and dollars. Aarón realized this was probably more money than the young man had ever seen at one time in his life. The young man started the car and made his way out of the crowded street. He worked his way out of the old town.

"What's your name?" Aarón asked.

"Ernesto."

"Ernesto, honest. I hope you live up to that name. My life and the life of my daughter may depend on it."

Aarón arrived at his in-law's house about an hour later. He handed Ernesto another twenty-dollar bill. The young man's eyes widened impossibly. "Do I have your word? We never met?"

"Yes," Ernesto said. "And good luck to you."

"Thank you, and to you as well."

As the big Chevy pulled away, Aarón walked up the front door of the house. His father-in-law, having heard a car engine, was already there.

"Let me help you with that," Eduardo said, taking one

of the suitcases.

"Thank you," Aarón replied.

Entering the house, Aarón heard Miriam chattering in the kitchen. When he entered the room, she shrieked in joy. Aarón looked at Lina. It was obvious she knew what was about to happen, the sadness already on her face, as it would be eternally until she saw her family again.

"We're sorry," Eduardo said. "You must forgive us, and your parents. We had no choice. They threatened to take our homes."

Aarón turned. He pulled Eduardo to him. "There's nothing to forgive you for. I understand." Lina came to him. He did the same, enveloping her tiny frame in his arms. "I, we, will miss you. You must do something for me, though."

"Anything."

"I won't be able to see my parents. You must tell them I'm not angry. Tell them I love them." Aarón began to cry. "Tell them I will do whatever I have to do to get all of you out of here." He took the remaining bills from his pocket. He counted out one hundred dollars twice. "It's not much, but it will help you. Give half to my parents."

Lina took the money. She tucked it into the pocket of her apron. "May God bless you and grant you peace. You've been a son to us, the son we never had."

The next morning Aarón bade farewell to Lina. He hugged her so tightly he thought he might break her ribs. "No more tears," he said, more for himself than for her.

"No more tears," she said. She took Miriam in her arms one last time and kissed her gently on the forehead. "*Recuérdame mi tesoro*," she whispered in her ear. "Remember me, my treasure. And be a good girl."

Eduardo drove them to the airport. He dropped them at

the entrance and left quickly. Aarón struggled with the bags and Miriam. A porter offered help. Aarón walked up to the desk, presented his tickets, and proceeded with the help of the porter to immigration.

There were several groups in line ahead of him. The same official who had declined to let them leave previously was on duty. He felt the perspiration begin to form under his collar. He held Miriam tightly, kissing her on the cheek intermittently. She remained amazingly calm.

Finally, after what felt like hours, the woman waved at them to come to her desk. “Papers please,” she said, no indication that she recognized him from their earlier encounter.

Aarón handed his portfolio to the woman, her face still expressionless. She checked the dates and signatures on the documents and stamped them. “Through there,” she said, oblivious to Aarón, waving to the next passenger to approach her desk.

Aarón asked the guard for some help with his bags.

“Of course,” the guard said, smiling at Miriam. At the next desk, Aarón checked his bags without so much as having to open them. An hour later he was settled into his seat on the plane, Miriam in the seat next to him.

He felt his heartbeat quicken as the plane taxied out to the runway. The sound of the propellers whirring intensified as the plane picked up speed. Aarón sensed the nose lift and the plane soar. His heart soared with it yet sank at the same time. He looked out the window at Cuba receding behind him, the palm trees growing smaller as the plane climbed higher. Paradise lost.

Now the tears came. They came for so many reasons. He’d succeeded. He and Miriam had escaped. He would be reunited with Beatriz in a matter of hours. But the tragedy of a refugee awaited him. Torn from his home, his country, his culture, his parents. Miriam reached up and touched his cheek.

"*Lagrimas*," she said, her tiny fingers wet with his tears."

"*Sí, lagrimas*," Aarón replied, caressing her cheek. "Tears of happiness…for your happiness."

Part IV
September 2001

Chapter Twenty

Though the day was warm, the light was the same as that January day some forty years earlier when Aarón and Beatriz arrived in New York City. Stark, grey-white-cold, like a cemetery. Far from the colors of Cuba, deep and alive. Vibrant green, lipstick red, azure like the tropical sea. Burnt orange, turquoise, and lemon yellow. There the air was filled with palpitating music, the sounds of children laughing and mothers calling. Havana tickled the nose with the scent of garlic sizzling in fragrant olive oil. One's skin tingled with the momentary rush of raindrops caressing as through a gauzy veil. Havana was a kaleidoscope, always moving, changing. New York, a black and white photo, even in summer, inured to the senses.

Aarón stood at the edge of the boarding area, waiting. His legs were spread to the width of his shoulders, his hands clasped behind his back. He stood ramrod straight, the whiteness of his *guayabera* resplendent, a statement against the grayness of the carpet and the black pleather seating. The New York skyline, dominated by the twin towers of the World Trade Center, stood in the distance.

Chin held high, Aarón waited for the security door to open. His chest and shoulders rose rhythmically with his slow, deep breathing. He waited for the unknown. He truly didn't know what to expect when those doors opened. It had been too long, another lifetime.

Too much happened and too much remained unsaid. With the passing of time, there wasn't any reason to try to fill those holes, to say what perhaps should have been said. Yet now, faced with the reality that living, breathing flesh would soon fill the void in which only the imagined existed before he considered what to say. The workings of his mind rebelled against the stiffness of his body and stance. Like the runner he once was he waited at the starting line ready to dash off. Now that starting line was its own finish line, the place where their paths would finally reconverge.

As the gate door opened, Aarón leaned ever so slightly forward, waiting for the starting pistol's signal. Faces passed through the portal, some with small handbags, others with children, some checking their cellphones, holding them up for a signal. They exited the ramp nonchalantly oblivious to this moment in his life. He had imagined it for forty years. At the same time, he never thought it would ever happen.

A face appeared in the doorway. Both Aarón's throat and stomach tightened. It wasn't the face he'd expected, but rather, another face, a different face, though one familiar to him. It was his father's face, not his brother's. In the smallest of moments, he recognized it as his face as well. He laughed. They were always too much alike in too many ways.

Aarón straightened and took that first step forward. He nearly stopped, his foot feeling like it was nailed to the floor. At that moment that face, his face, looked directly at him. A smile came up around the corners of its mouth, exactly as it had so many years ago, always really.

In a fraction of a moment, Aarón was transported. He

wasn't at John F. Kennedy International Airport in eastern Queens, New York City, in 2001. He was in Havana in 1958, at the plaza of the University waiting for Moises, the December breeze on his skin. Then, as now, Moises raised his arm and waved.

"*Hermano*," Moises called out, as if forty years had never passed, as if nothing had ever happened. Before Aarón knew it, he was in the embrace of his brother, the warm, familiar feeling of a world forgotten suddenly overtaking him.

Aarón stepped back. He took a good, long look at Moises. Sadness passed through him despite his happiness. A life wasted, he thought. He smiled, hiding his melancholy. "I'm so glad you're here," he said, embracing Moises again.

"*Igual*," Moises whispered in Aarón's ear.

Moises was both pleased and surprised by the warmth of Aarón's embrace. To be truthful, he hadn't expected it. They hadn't seen each other in what amounted to a lifetime and had only begun speaking to each other by phone some years earlier. The calls were often uncomfortable and contentious, old angers reigniting. He hoped some of that contention would be resolved by this visit.

Moises had considered and reconsidered the visit many times. It wasn't just that he wanted to re-establish some real connection with his brother all these years later—he would have liked to come while his parents, or at least his mother, was still alive. As an official in the Cuban government it was inappropriate for him to visit the United States while the *gringos* continued their embargo. Things appeared to be changing though. The long, glacial freeze that hovered around Cuban American relations seemed to be receding, if only by centimeters. His superiors at his job and in the party blessed his trip. "We need to look forward, not back" they said, to the last.

"This is Luz, my wife," said Moises.

Aarón extended his hand. A moment of recognition followed. Her face looked familiar, but how could it? And what had happened to Ana Teresa? He would have to wait for the right moment to ask. "It's a pleasure to meet you," he said, taking her hand in his.

Beatriz came up from behind. "Welcome, *cuñado*," she said.

Moises stepped forward, took her hand, and after a moment's hesitation, pulled Beatriz to him. "I always liked you better," he said. They all laughed.

"I'm so glad you finally came." Beatriz took a step and reached for Luz's hands taking them in hers. She kissed both Luz's cheeks. "And you are Luz. *Bienvenida cuñada*. So good to finally meet."

"Let's get your bags and go home," Aarón said, the intense stress of the anticipation of this reunion receding. Perhaps, after all these years, it was time.

The ride to Brooklyn was slow. It was Sunday of Labor Day weekend. Those who hadn't left the city prior to the weekend were traveling around it. The weather was clear and beautiful. Over the years, Aarón and Beatriz had grown accustomed to the change in seasons. The clear blue, cloudless sky and seventy-degree temperatures were an early harbinger of autumn's crispness.

Moises and Luz sat in the back seat of Aarón's Ford, huddled together. Aarón could see his brother's eyes in the rear-view mirror peering out of the window at the passing landscape.

The expression on Moises's face did not betray his thoughts. Rather, he looked like the economics expert he was, surveying the results of someone else's project, listing its accomplishments and failures in a ledger in his mind. Not judgment but rather evaluation, balancing how well an idea could be executed in the real world.

"Are you cold?" Aarón asked. "I could turn down the air conditioning."

"Yes," Moises answered. "That would be good. It is a bit cold in here."

Aarón adjusted the temperature. He recalled those first few months in 1962 when he arrived with Miriam. He, Beatriz, and Miriam were moved to Brooklyn by HIAS. Despite what they'd been told and the heavy winter clothes they were provided, he couldn't have imagined how the cold felt on his skin. The howling wind made it difficult, nearly impossible, to breathe. That first apartment. A tiny one-bedroom with a Pullman kitchen on the fourth floor of a walk-up in Midwood. The windows were older than he was. They rattled each time the wind passed through them into the room. He thought he'd never be warm again.

"I thought we would go home and get you settled. Give you some time to get acclimated. Tomorrow, we're going to Miriam's house on Long Island for a BBQ. You'll meet our children and grandchildren."

Moises hesitated for a moment before responding. He thought of his own children, none of them living nearby enough for him and Luz to see them with any regularity. He considered how fortunate Aarón was to have his family close by.

Moises was happy. Especially, to meet Miriam. She had taken to writing to him. Her Spanish was better than he'd expected, but then it was her first language. They'd developed something of a relationship through these letters. He was thankful for that, and to know her, and now, finally, to meet her.

"We're both looking forward to meeting your children."

"Thank you," said Beatriz. "She is very excited that you're here. So is Leah."

"Leah is your younger daughter?" said Luz.

"Yes," Beatriz replied.

"Does she speak Spanish like Miriam?" Moises asked.

Both Aarón and Beatriz laughed. "Not much. She was born here," said Beatriz. "She has some understanding but little ability to speak. If we speak to her in Spanish, she will reply in English."

"A real American," said Aarón, as he pulled off the Belt Parkway at King's Highway.

Later that evening Moises looked around the living room of the small, tidy, red-brick house on the corner of King's Highway and East 34th Street. It was well appointed and inviting, walls lined with photos, a cabinet filled with books and mementos. He touched the frame of a photo of his parents. They sat next to each other on the porch of this house on a sunny day, much older than how he remembered them. His father was in a wheelchair, his legs covered by a blanket.

"Moises," Luz called out from the kitchen. "Come in, Beatriz has prepared *una comida* for us."

He felt a hand on his shoulder. It was Aarón. "You must be hungry. Come, let's eat something."

"Of course," Moises said, his finger brushing against the top of the picture frame as he turned and followed Aarón into the kitchen.

The table was set simply but elegantly. Platters of rice, black beans, *ropa vieja*, and salad graced the table. The dishes and platters, were a matched set.

"Please, sit down. You must be very hungry," Beatriz said. She brought out a wicker basket, its contents wrapped in a napkin, and placed it in the middle of the table. "*Pan de ajo*?"

"Yes, please," said Luz. She took a slice, tasting it quickly. "*Rico,*" she said. "Thank you for all this."

"There's no need to thank us," Aarón said. "It's long overdue. Please pass me your plate."

Moises looked around. He realized Aarón had no idea how this table set for four with enough food for twelve appeared to him. It wasn't abundance, but rather excess. Fidel made food a priority from the start, but even now it remained hard to get. That was mostly a result of the American embargo. Forty years later rationing continued.

"Thank you, that's more than enough," Moises said before Aarón could pile on more braised beef. It was one of his favorites when he was a boy. It reminded him of his mother.

"Are you sure? There's plenty," said Aarón.

Moises smiled. "Thanks, but no. That's fine."

Moises's eyes continued to dart around the walls as they made strained small talk. Most of the photos were of the family. Weddings, religious ceremonies. He assumed the photos of his nieces as teenagers in formal dresses were from their Bat Mitzvahs. In one, a baby boy was wearing a tiny *yarmulke*. Two books with Hebrew lettering on their spine sat on the small cart behind Aarón. Forty years was a long time for small talk. Moises chose to be direct.

"When did you become religious?" he asked, taking a forkful of rice and beans.

Aarón looked at him for a moment before answering. "That's a bit complicated. We're not really religious, but certainly more observant than we were in Cuba. We aren't strictly observant of the Shabbat, but we do keep the house kosher."

"So, no more pork?" Moises said, sitting back a bit, a smile creeping up around his lips.

"Nope," Aarón said, deciding to make light of Moises's comment. Aarón's resentment about Moises's intense disregard for their heritage and all aspects of Judaism went all the way back to their childhood. It nudged its way into his thoughts. "And I don't miss it," he added

"Life is different here than it was in Cuba in the old days," Beatriz said. "First of all, everyone we met when we arrived was Jewish. There, in Havana, we had a small community. Here the community is very large, in the millions just in New York. We couldn't get kosher meat easily back home. Here, there are kosher butchers and shops everywhere. It was a Jewish organization, HIAS, that settled us here in Brooklyn."

"HIAS?"

"The Hebrew Immigrant Aid Society," Beatriz explained. "That was how we met people, how we came into a community. From other Jews. They helped us. The U.S government didn't help us integrate into America." She sighed. "Honestly, it wasn't easy."

"I'm sure," said Luz. She reached for Beatriz's hand. "It's good there was someone, something, to help you."

"Yes. I don't know how we would have done it without them."

"Were you under pressure to become more… observant?" Moises asked.

Aarón looked at Beatriz before answering. She nodded her head.

"No, there wasn't pressure, not from those who helped us. It was more a matter of circumstance," Aarón explained. "When Miriam was in the first grade there was a teachers' strike."

"A strike?" said Moises. "I didn't think your government tolerated such things."

Aarón smiled, disguising his irritation with Moises's comment. He considered it for a moment. Was Moises mocking America or did he truly, after forty years under his own government's propaganda, believe that the working class in the United States was deprived of a basic civil right? He would give him the benefit of the doubt this time.

"American workers have unions and the right to strike. They are protected under the law. Anyway, I, we, were concerned about Miriam's education. I wasn't entirely comfortable with the public schools to begin with." Aarón waited a moment, expecting another remark from Moises. Moises simply nodded. "We began looking at private schools, but the cost was prohibitive, even though some offered reduced tuition. It was still too much."

"And most were in Manhattan," added Beatriz. "Getting her there and picking her up would involve an entire day's travel."

"I went to HIAS again for help, for direction. They suggested Solomon Schechter, a Jewish Day School. Not very observant, nonetheless religious enough that we needed to make some changes to how we lived."

"And so…" Moises gestured around the room to the various religious objects and photos.

"Yes," said Beatriz. "That's how we became more observant. We've never looked back. All the children Miriam and Leah went to school with came from homes more observant than ours. If they were to have their friends here to our house, the food had to be kosher. We needed to observe the sabbath as well, at least to some extent."

"I had to learn, or should I say relearn things as well.

How to read Hebrew. The service. Certain customs," said Aarón.

"And now?" said Moises. "It has meaning for you?"

Aarón smiled. "Surprisingly, yes."

Moises thought of his son, Raul. He answered the same question the same way.

"Are you and Luz comfortable?" Aarón asked, hovering in the doorway of the bathroom.

"Yes, very much so," Moises said. He picked up his toothbrush and towel. Aarón stepped aside. Moises brushed past him and stopped. "Thank you," he said.

"For what?"

"For inviting us."

"I wish I could have done it so many years ago. But…"

"Let's not split hairs over who or what caused the problem."

"Yes," Aarón replied. "Let's not. *Buenas noches*."

"*Buenas noches*." Moises turned, his hand reaching for the knob to the bedroom door.

"Moises," Aarón said.

"*Sí*?"

"May I ask you something?"

"Of course."

"Luz. She was the young woman who delivered your note to me after San Miguel, wasn't she?

"Yes," Moises smiled. "You have a good memory for faces."

"Hers has hardly changed."

"*Verdad*. She has been my strength and my rock all these years."

Aarón hesitated for a moment. “I’m not prying, but may I ask what happened between you and Ana Teresa?”

“Of course. I know you’re not prying. It’s only normal that you would ask. It’s just, I don’t much like talking about it.”

“You don’t have to tell me.”

“Suffice to say she didn’t like being a wife and mother. The revolution was her child.”

“I understand,” Aarón said. He suspected as much. Aarón always believed Moises was as blinded by her public persona as her private, perhaps even more.

“Good night,” Moises said, stepping into the bedroom and closing the door.

Luz was already asleep. Moises turned off the light and slipped under the sheet. He touched Luz gently on the shoulder and kissed her. She smiled and pulled his arm to her breast. After a short moment Moises sensed her even breathing. She had fallen back to sleep. He slipped his arm out from under hers and turned onto his back. Aarón’s question about Ana Teresa was one he preferred not to think about, especially just before bed. Now it was stuck in his mind…

Havana
December 1961

Patricia wrapped her tiny hand around Moises’s finger. She took her first tentative steps across the living room. Moises fought the urge to help her. Ana Teresa told him, let her take the initiative. Don’t help her too much, also don’t discourage her. Ana Teresa’s methods were so different from what he had watched in his extended family growing up. Less fearful, more encouraging.

The fact that they now had this child, this angel nearing one year old, was in itself nearly a miracle. After spying Ana Teresa with Marcos hand in hand that day at the planning meeting, Moises disappeared for about a week.

Luis had suggested he continue his investigation into corruption in Santa Clara. He used Luis' suggestion as a cover to get out of Havana and clear his head before he confronted Ana Teresa. Now he had all the evidence he needed about the corruption scheme and who was behind it. He hadn't decided yet when to present it to Luis. Information was power, and he had the information. He told Luz to tell anyone who was looking for him that he'd taken some time out to travel to the *campo* to experience the life of the people, to know and understand their needs better. That was a good cover.

He went quietly to Santa Clara, to Eugenio Morales's factory. He desired the dignity of labor, and in the dignity of labor, he found his own dignity. After a few days, he knew what he would say to Ana Teresa. He was a man, and he loved her, but he would not be cuckolded. Moises didn't tell her he was leaving. She showed no surprise when he returned a week later.

"What did you learn from your time in Santa Clara?" Ana Teresa asked as he entered their apartment, smaller and noticeably less elegant than the penthouse they had lived in just after the revolution. Though in a less desirable neighborhood, it was nearer to his office. And, it was still spacious enough for Abuela to live with them. The scent of her cooking drifted in from the kitchen.

Moises was surprised, though not shocked, by Ana Teresa's question. Not so much that Ana Teresa knew where he had gone—there were eyes everywhere—but that she let him know she knew before he had taken off his cap. She wore the same seductive smile she slew him with the first time he saw her. And she exuded the same confidence.

"It was quite enlightening. Good for the soul." Moises wouldn't give her the satisfaction of asking how she knew where he had gone. "And you? How are you? How goes your work?"

Ana Teresa sat up from her reclining position on the low couch that dominated the living room. Her flowered blouse and red slacks accentuated her figure and contrasted against the green fabric of the sofa.

"Enlightening is good," she said. "Abuela, Moises has returned."

Abuela appeared a moment later with a tall glass of juice. She stood on her tippy toes and handed it to him, his hat still on his head.

He kissed her forehead. "I missed you, Abuelita."

"*Igual*," she said, returning quickly to the kitchen to tend whatever she had left on the stove.

Finally, Moises removed his hat. He took the chair opposite Ana Teresa. He was aware that he smelled like he hadn't bathed in a week. He hadn't.

"We need to talk," he said.

"Certainly, what about?"

Moises took a breath. He'd rehearsed this conversation dozens of times in his head but now it was real, as was his pounding heart. He couldn't deny that he loved Ana Teresa, but, despite her view of marriage in this new world they had fought so hard together to bring about, he wouldn't share her.

"I know about Marcos."

"What about Marcos?" she replied.

"About you and Marcos."

Ana Teresa drew her legs up under her. A sardonic smile crept up the right side of her mouth. She chuckled and took a sip from the cup beside her on the low table. "I see. And what is it you think you know about me and Marcos?" Her tone was superior, the same tone she used when conducting a party meeting.

"I saw you, at the conference. You nearly kissed him in the lobby. You left with him, holding hands."

Ana Teresa said nothing.

"I understand your beliefs about marriage. That it's a bourgeois construct. A way to control women."

"That's correct."

"I respect your beliefs. But I won't share you."

Ana Teresa rose from the couch. She walked slowly, seductively around the low coffee table to the chair and sat down in Moises's lap. She caressed him.

"You're right. I did something that hurt you, and I apologize. I was wrong. I should have respected you and your commitment to me." She kissed him deeply, profoundly. "I know that's why you disappeared. It's over. I've ended it. Can you forgive me?"

Moises was stunned. He had fully expected his life with Ana Teresa to come to its natural end today. He kissed her back, deeply, with passion.

"I do," he said. "I do forgive you."

Moises felt both relieved and triumphant. He accepted his victory without question. The truth was he had no idea how he would have gone on without her. For Moises, there was no him without her.

They rose silently, together. Ana Teresa took Moises's hand. They slipped into their bedroom, Abuela singing loudly with the radio in the kitchen.

Ana Teresa cast the same spell over him she had since the first time they were together. Truthfully, since the first time he saw her. He knew this instinctively yet buried it in the fantasy that he had triumphed over Marcos. She was still his. She would remain his. While he felt vindicated, he would never completely trust Ana Teresa, or Marcos, again.

ᏅᏅ

Several weeks later Moises found Ana Teresa alone in the kitchen when he arrived from work. She was preparing an herbal tea for Abuela. "You're home early," he said. "I thought you had a meeting with the neighborhood committee this evening?"

"I did. Señora Gomez from down the hall sent her grandson to fetch me. Abuela wasn't feeling well. She was dizzy. I didn't want to leave her alone, so I postponed the meeting till later this evening." Ana Teresa poured the odd-smelling concoction through a strainer into a large porcelain cup. "Now that you're here, I can go."

Ana Teresa placed the cup on a small tray next to a plate with some plain wafers. She disappeared through the kitchen door and down the hall to the bedrooms.

When she returned, Moises was seated at the table. She was gone long enough for him to consider what she told him, and to question it.

"Could we speak for a moment?" he said.

Ana Teresa looked at the clock on the wall. "Could it

wait till later? I'm very late."

Moises hesitated.

"What is it? I can see something is bothering you."

"Are you really going to a neighborhood committee meeting?"

Ana Teresa stiffened. "Where else would I be going?"

"To see Marcos."

Ana Teresa's body and eyes told Moises how angry she was. "That was settled weeks ago."

"I need to be sure."

"You can believe me, or not," Ana Teresa replied, modulating the level of her voice. She didn't want Abuela disturbed by their argument. She moved toward the door.

Moises blocked her path. He considered taking her arm, then thought better of it. That would escalate things too much, and it wasn't who he was.

"Let me pass," Ana Teresa said, calmly.

Moises stood where he was. "I accept what you've said, and I apologize. I just...

"Just what?"

"I...can't lose you."

The tone of Ana Teresa's voice changed. She spoke now to Moises as a superior speaks to an inferior. "You haven't. Continue like this and you will."

A switch flipped inside him. The parental character of her tone might work on their minions, but not on him. Not anymore.

"Sit down," he commanded.

"I'm late."

"Sit down," he repeated, his tone as superior as hers.

"Fine," Ana Teresa said, pulling a chair out from under the table, turning it, and placing herself opposite Moises.

"I believe what you said, and I apologize again. There's something I haven't told you though and it's something I think you should know."

"Yes..."

"When I went to Santa Clara it wasn't just to clear my head. I went under Luis's instructions. There was a corruption scheme. Bribery. Protection money for transporting goods from factories to stores in Havana and elsewhere."

Ana Teresa remained silent, her eyes plastered to his.

"Would you like to know who was behind it?"

"Certainly."

Moises smiled and waited a moment to savor it. "Marcos Abreu."

Ana Teresa was unreadable. Moises had no idea if she knew about this or not.

"And how do you know this?" she asked.

Moises recounted the rudimentary details of how Marcos had recruited his sister's family to gain control of the transport of goods from factories in and around Santa Clara to Havana and other parts of the country. A portion of the payola was passed through to Marcos

"Have you told Luis?" Ana Teresa asked.

"Not everything."

"What have you left out?"

"The connection to Marcos."

"Why?"

Moises crossed his arms over his chest. He felt both triumphant and sickened by what he was about to do. He wasn't a vengeful, controlling person. He also couldn't continue to live with the idea that Ana Teresa wasn't being truthful with him. He didn't know exactly why he didn't trust her, but he'd come to realize he didn't and never would again.

"If you ever leave me for him I will tell Luis everything."

Ana Teresa nodded, her face still unreadable. "I'm late, I have to go." She turned to the door and stopped, a whimper came from her, her body shaking slightly. Her response shocked Moises. He had never seen her lose composure.

Moises jumped up from his chair. He put his hands on Ana Teresa's shoulders. "I'm sorry, *mi amor,*" he said, close to tears himself. "I shouldn't have said what I did. I should trust you."

Ana Teresa turned. "Yes, you should." Her eyes were aflame. "I'm pregnant. And I assure you, it's yours. I was going to tell you tonight. Now you've ruined it."

Moises took Ana Teresa in his arms. Her embrace wasn't forthcoming. He broke down himself. "Can you forgive me," he said.

"I have to go," she mumbled, drying her face with a paper napkin from the table. "We can discuss this later."

Chapter Twenty-One

Aarón, heard the floorboards squeak in the living room as he prepared the morning coffee in the kitchen. It was Moises. They smiled awkwardly at each other.

"It's been a long, long time since we've had breakfast together," Moises said.

Aarón laughed. "A lifetime. Would you like a coffee?"

"Yes."

"*Americano o Cubano*?"

"*Cubano*, if it's not too much trouble."

"It's not. I prefer it too. Beatriz prefers American coffee in the morning. I'll make both."

Moises took a seat at the table. He reached for the copy of *La Prensa*, delivered daily to Aarón's doorstep. Back home, he went out in the morning to fetch the paper while Luz prepared their coffee, always ready when he returned.

He perused the paper, counting the negative references to Cuba and Castro. Forty years later the exiles were still angry. If only they could see what had been accomplished. Despite the embargo, no one starved. Children learned to read. Crime was minimal, and the people had their pride and the respect of other nations around the world. They were no longer subject to the whims and dictates of

American puppets, sucking them dry. He was proud of what they'd accomplished, despite the deprivation and occasional disappointments.

"*Por favor*," Aarón said, placing the tiny demitasse cup in front of Moises. He set a plate of Goya Maria cookies between them.

"*Gracias*," Moises said. He took a sip of his coffee and a small bite of a cookie.

Aarón reached for the top drawer of the small hutch to the left of the table. He pulled out a plain envelope, yellowed with age, and placed it between them. Moises recognized it immediately.

Aarón pointed to the postmark. Moises read it silently, *Marzo 1975, Ciudad de Mexico.* "Why did this take thirteen years?"

Moises said nothing. He averted his gaze from Aarón. He recalled the moment he sent the letter, writing it earlier the same day as the postmark. It had been so long since he'd received any word from Aarón. He made his request short and sweet.

> *"I have a son. He has juvenile diabetes. Please send money, insulin, or both."*

Moises recalled how he felt the moment he asked his brother for help. As if he had failed, because the system he championed failed him.

Havana
1975

Moises stood in the doorway of their apartment. The

arched entrance led his eye through their home to the kitchen where Luz moved about. The apartment was spacious. A two-bedroom cut up from a much larger apartment in a building with an elevator, when it worked. The original apartment had five bedrooms and four baths. His cut-up had two of each. The former dining room was their living room, and thankfully they had the original kitchen and the small terrace that looked out over the garden in the building's courtyard. The garden was wild but maintained enough by Moises and his neighbors to provide a quiet, charming respite.

Patricia sat at the table, focused on her books. Her long, jet-black hair nearly covered her face as she took notes while reading. She was a diligent student, as he was, and a fierce defender of the revolution, as her mother, Ana Teresa, was. He couldn't be prouder of her.

Luz placed a plate of *fufu de platano* next to Patricia's book, stroked her hair, and kissed her tenderly on the top of her head. Patricia put down her pencil. Moises read her lips from where he stood silently observing them. "*Gracias, mamá.*" She picked up a fork and tasted the mashed green plantains and fried egg. "*Rico, gracias*" she added.

"*De nada, mija,*" Luz replied.

It touched Moises that Luz always addressed Patricia as her daughter and Patricia addressed Luz as her mother. Patricia was barely three years old when he and Luz began their lives together.

"*Buenos,*" Moises called out, entering the kitchen. He leaned over Patricia and kissed her head.

"*Buenos, papá,*" Patricia replied, pecking him quickly on the cheek.

"Buenos, Moises," Luz said, placing a *cafecito* in front of him. "Would you like some *fufu*?"

Moises pulled a small gray paper bag from behind his back along with a copy of *Hoy,* which he read religiously.

Luz smiled. "What is this?"

Moises held the bag out to her. "Look."

She opened the bag and took out two *pastelitos de guayaba*.

"Happy anniversary," Moises said. He came around the table and kissed Luz tenderly.

"And to you," She laughed. "To tell you the truth, I forgot!" She placed a portion of *fufu* in a bowl with two slices of salami and handed it to Moises.

"That's all right, *mi amor,* I still love you."

"I don't want that," Nestor said, standing in the entrance of the kitchen in pajama bottoms, rubbing his eyes. His seven-year-old body was so thin his ribs were its most prominent feature.

"You need to eat something," Luz said. "Look at you, nothing but skin and bones."

Nestor sat on Moises's lap, pouting. "I won't eat it."

"Do you want one of these?" Luz said, holding out the plate on which she had placed the *pastelitos*.

"Yes," Nestor said, smiling now.

"Then you have to eat some of this first." She placed a small bowl with a couple of spoons of *fufu* and an egg in front of Nestor. She handed him a spoon, the frown returning to his face.

"Okay," Nestor said, "but only half, then I get one of those."

"We'll see," Moises said, shifting Nestor to the chair next to him. "Where is your brother?"

"I don't know," Nestor replied, now digging into the *fufu* with gusto.

Patricia touched Moises's hand. "I'll go wake him, *papá*."

"Thanks," Moises said.

Patricia disappeared down the hallway reappearing a moment later. "*Papá,* I think you should come. Quickly. I can't wake him."

Both Moises and Luz hurried down the hall. Raul lay on the bed, one leg thrown over the other, his mouth open and drooling. Moises shook him gently. "Raul, wake up."

No response. Luz pulled back the top sheet covering him. The fan in the window blew gently, dissipating the smell of urine coming from the bed. The sheets and Raul's pajama bottoms were soaked.

Moises tried to wake him again. "We've got to get him to a hospital. Patricia, go downstairs to Señora Sanz, and tell her what's happened. I need to borrow her car."

Señora Sanz's twenty-five-year-old Chevy was kept in top shape by her seventy-five-year-old boyfriend. It got them to the hospital quickly.

Moises and Luz sat in the waiting room holding hands. The worn, sea-foam green walls appeared dirty, but the spotless floors attested to the cleanliness of the place. The ancient, time-warp look of the hallways and visitor areas concealed the modern, cutting-edge equipment and medical practices Cuba had achieved in the sixteen years since the revolution.

Moises hadn't let go of Luz's hand since the nurse led them to the waiting room and sat them under a window. He could feel her steady heartbeat through her palm and fingers, its rapid pace matching his. Few words passed between them.

When they arrived, the emergency room doctor did a quick appraisal and some blood tests. They injected something into Raul's arm that brought him minimally back to consciousness a few moments later. He was moaning and confused.

"Has this happened before?" the doctor asked.

"No," Luz said.

"Has he been acting strangely? Any behavior different than normal?"

"None," Luz replied.

"Is he a bed wetter?"

"No," Luz snapped back, almost before the doctor finished his sentence. She was lost in thought for a moment, then interrupted the doctor's continuing examination. "But he has been urinating a lot."

The doctor straightened up and looked directly at Luz. "Go on."

"I asked him if he felt okay and if he had been drinking more than usual."

"What did he reply?"

"No."

The doctor nodded. "Let us do some quick tests and continue our evaluation. The nurse will take you to the parents' waiting area. I'll be there shortly."

That was some ninety minutes earlier.

Moises spied the nurse coming down the hall toward the waiting area. She veered off to the left, out-of-sight for a long moment before reappearing. Now she walked directly toward them. Her face was unreadable, neither positive nor negative. Moises felt Luz's fingers tighten in his palm.

"Señor *y* Señora Cohan," the nurse said.

"Yes. How is our son?"

"Awake, and communicating," the nurse said, her face still neutral. "The doctor will be here momentarily to speak with you."

At this, Luz broke down. Moises put his arm around her, fighting back his own tears.

"That's good, he's awake," he said, his own voice cracking. About to let himself go, Moises saw the doctor coming down the hall toward them. He took a deep breath and steadied himself, wiping the vestiges of his tears from his cheeks.

"Señor *y* Señora Cohan," the doctor called out.

Moises and Luz started to get up from their seats.

"No, no," the doctor called out again, gesturing downward with his hands, now nearly upon them. He took the seat next to Luz.

"What's wrong with our son?" Luz asked. "Will he be all right?"

"We know what's wrong, and it's manageable. He's diabetic."

Moises was caught off guard. Diabetic? "That's a disease of the aged. He's a child. How could he be diabetic?"

The doctor took Luz's hand. "I know. We think of it as a disease of the old. It is, but it's not. There is more than one kind. He has juvenile diabetes."

"I don't understand," Luz said.

"Let me explain," the doctor continued. "In older people, diabetes, the presence of sugar in the blood, is related to what they eat, how much they sit around, and other related factors. In children, the disease is caused by a malfunction in the pancreas. It stops working, stops producing insulin."

"What caused this?" Luz asked.

"We don't know."

"Can it happen again?" she asked, the tension in her shoulders obvious to Moises. Sadly, he already knew the answer.

"I'm afraid it's permanent. I'm sorry."

Luz began to shake. "*Díos,*" she said. "Will he die?"

The doctor stroked Luz's hand. "We can treat him. With insulin. He will have to take insulin every day, several times a day."

Luz turned her head to Moises.

"He'll be all right," he reassured her. "We will learn how to help him."

At first, the problem wasn't insulin, in and of itself. The doctor and the hospital showed them how to administer it. They taught them to recognize the highs and lows of Raul's blood sugar by his behavior. The problem was Raul. It was hard to control him. He was a little boy. He behaved like a little boy. More than once, Luz received a call from Raul's school via Señora Sanchez, the only person in their building with a still operating phone line.

Raul had nearly fainted on the sports field during recess. They'd forced juice into him. He'd come around. A couple of times he was taken to the hospital. Raul admitted that he hadn't eaten his lunch before sports. He was too excited to play baseball to eat. He wasn't hungry. He'd given his sandwich to fat Mauro.

The low blood sugars were the worst. When he was too high there was always another shot of insulin, as inexact as the treatment was, but when it dropped too low, well, he could die. His sleepiness after dinner often prompted Luz to give him an extra shot. That first experience when he was diagnosed haunted her. The ups and downs of his blood sugar were unpredictable at best. The result: their supply rarely lasted the month.

And that was what led to the second problem. They received a fixed amount of insulin each month. It was based on what the doctor calculated was needed for a typical child of Raul's age and size. No more, no less. There was an embargo. The Americans were still determined to bring down Castro.

What supplies they had came mostly from the Soviet Union, their eastern European allies, and friendly governments in Latin America. None of these were leaders in medical treatment and pharmaceutical development. If anything, Cuba itself was making greater strides in these fields than their so-called brothers in communist solidarity. Nevertheless, there was still a shortage.

Moises waited patiently in the office of the director of the formulary at the hospital where Raul was diagnosed. His request to meet with the director was turned down several times before he appealed to Luis to intervene. There was still resistance. Why did he need to meet with the director? The director was very busy. He didn't meet with patients or their families. All contact was through their doctor. Finally, the hospital relented, but only because Moises was a Hero of the Revolution. Despite that, the written reply clearly stated that no change in the dispensary could or would be made.

Gustavo Garcia, a tall, graying man sporting a goatee and wearing a white medical tunic walked into the empty waiting area approximately thirty minutes after Moises's scheduled appointment. He carried a clipboard in his right hand. "Señor Cohan?" he called out without so much as looking up.

"*Sí,*" Moises said, rising from the chair. He extended his hand. Garcia gripped it limply. "Follow me."

Moises followed Garcia down a long hallway to a small office. He gestured to a chair opposite his desk and closed the door. Behind Garcia's chair was a window that faced a quiet, somewhat overgrown garden. Sunlight filtered into the room through the trees and the Venetian blinds.

"How can I help you?" Garcia said, finally making eye contact.

Moises cleared his throat. "Thank you for seeing me." Garcia nodded, still non-committal. "I wanted to speak to you about my son. He's diabetic. Juvenile diabetes."

Garcia pointed to the clipboard. "I see that."

Moises took a deep breath. "I understand full well the extent of our nation's problems. I am an economist and an official in the government. The embargo has a stranglehold on us. But at the same time, we, my family, can't make it to the end of each month on the insulin we are allotted for our son. He's a small boy, active, hungry, you understand, difficult to control. We need more."

Garcia sat stone-faced. "Señor Cohan, you have used very important and high-level connections to convince me to meet with you. Are you suggesting in some way that because of your connections and because of your own position you are entitled to more than your fair share of our very limited resources?"

Moises stiffened. A charge like that could put him in prison. Who knew better than him that corruption was not tolerated? And who knew better than him that Garcia could use this scenario to improve his own position? Reporting a government official for attempted influence could result in public disgrace or worse. He'd prosecuted corruption himself. It was treated very seriously.

"Señor Garcia, that was never my intention," he said.

"Then what is your intention?"

"To appeal to you to take a slightly different view of my son's needs and to perhaps provide us more insulin on a monthly basis to meet his specific needs more effectively."

"Señor Cohan, I don't know how to do that. We have limited supplies. We distribute them fairly, as equitably as we can. Perhaps you need to consider other ways to control your son. He has to understand his condition."

Moises sighed. "He's a small boy."

"I understand," Garcia said, stonelike. His gaze returned to his clipboard. "I'm sorry I can't be of more help.

"Gracias," Moises said, getting up from the chair and turning to leave. His disgust for the Americans and their blockade tore at him as he reached for the door. Their hate for Castro, and their evil desire to control Cuba and its people was in fact destroying the life of his son.

"Cohan," Garcia said as Moises turned the doorknob. "Close the door."

"Why?"

"I will suggest two things to you. But if you ever tell anyone I said either I will deny it and accuse you of trying to bribe me."

Moises turned. "Understood," he said, retaking his seat.

"I understand your situation. There are two possibilities. First, there are aid organizations in Canada that funnel money and drugs from the United States to us here. It's very quiet and the government closes its eyes. I don't have to tell you why. If you have relatives in the U.S. they can help you. Second, if they can send you cash, and that's difficult, you can buy insulin on the black market here. I will even tell you where and how, though I will deny it, as I told you before."

"Thank you. I will consider that." Moises hesitated. "Why did you wait till I was leaving to tell me?

"I wanted to be sure that you weren't here to trap me."

Luz was sitting in the kitchen, her hand propping up her head, eyes closed. Moises knew how tired she was. The constant worry about Raul and keeping his sugar under control on top of everything else she had to do meant she slept little. When she did sleep, it was restless. Her eyes opened as Moises entered the room. She conveyed her question without words, simply by the anxious, worried, look on her face.

"The answer is no, and yes."

Luz straightened in the chair, crossing her arms against her chest. "What does that mean?"

Moises recounted his meeting with Garcia. "What bothers me most is this is exactly what we fought to change. There can't be more access for those with connections or money."

Luz slid her hand over Moises's. She chuckled. "Clearly,

that's what the pharmacist thought, that you were using your position for privilege. If only he understood who you are."

Moises smiled. "Thank you, *mi amor*. One honest man. I said that to Aarón and my father once, long ago, just before the revolution. He received a promotion at the bank. They made him the head of a new economic development plan. I asked him if the people would ever benefit. He said, 'yes.' I quoted the bible."

Luz laughed.

"A story about the angels, Abraham, and Sodom and Gomorrah. I asked him if he was that one honest man."

Moises too began to laugh now. "Imagine, in my parent's dining room. A lifetime ago." Moises locked his eyes on Luz's. "*Te amo*," he said. "You make my life so much better, and easier. No matter the circumstance."

Luz smile. She shifted her gaze toward the window. "And what the administrator said, what do you think?"

"What do you mean?"

"About asking for help. From outside."

Moises hesitated. "I can't."

"We have to." She withdrew her hand from Moises's and looked directly at him, desperation in her eyes. "Raul's life may depend upon it."

"I'm an official in the government. Contacting Aarón, asking for help from outside, that would be viewed as an act of betrayal."

"How would they know?"

Moises lifted an eyebrow. It wasn't necessary for him to answer.

"Please," Luz whispered. "For Raul, and for me. I don't know how much more I can take and there's no more I can do." Tears fell from her eyes.

"We've had no contact in fifteen years. Besides..."

"Besides, what? Other than your pride."

That struck Moises. It wasn't something he would ever expect to hear or feel from Luz. She was the most kind, most supportive person he'd ever known. He saw her pain on her face. This was about her child, their child.

"Let me consider it. There would be repercussions. I have to determine how to do it without any eyes."

"The hospital, the government, provided us with insulin and supplies." Moises gave Aarón the most basic details. "There was a shortage of insulin. We never had quite enough to get through the month. We rationed it, but he was a child, and it was difficult to control him. What he ate, how much he ran around. I'm sure you understand."

Aarón nodded.

Moises hesitated for a moment. "There were shortages of everything." He wanted to continue, to say what was in his heart, that there were shortages of everything because of the U.S. embargo. He reconsidered and kept his counsel.

"I'm sorry," Aarón said. "I wish I had known sooner. I wish I could have helped sooner. That's what I'm asking, why didn't we hear from you until 1975?" Aarón pointed to the postmark on the letter again. "Even before Raul became diabetic. I wrote to you many times, especially just after we left, and then when I brought our parents here, but I never heard from you. Not until this letter."

Moises pursed his lips and nodded. "That's why I sent this letter from Mexico. I was on a government mission with the Ministry of International Trade. I'd sent two letters to you about Raul before this. I never heard back from you. I wasn't sure."

"You weren't sure about what?"

"If you didn't want any contact with me, or if the censors had intercepted my letters. I suspected the censors were preventing our correspondence. Your response to this letter confirmed my fears."

"Censors?" Aarón said. "Cuban censors?"

"American." Moises hesitated. "Or both."

Aarón stopped himself. The U.S. government didn't censor or intercept mail from private citizens. He didn't respond. There was no benefit to confronting Moises with that fact.

Chapter Twenty-Two

Moises noted the gradual change of the cityscape as they traveled to Miriam's house in the suburbs of New York. A place called Woodmere. Aarón explained that it was in New York State, but not in New York City. The slow transition from city to something not city was completely different than in Cuba. In Cuba, leaving the city was abrupt. The change to the countryside came quickly. This seemingly endless land of small houses and manicured lawns was new to Moises.

They arrived at Miriam's home in less than an hour. Moises squeezed Luz's hand as they parked in the driveway. A large banner hung from the second story windows with the words, *Bienvenidos, Tío y Tía*.

Brick and stone mimicking an English-looking style, the house reminded Moises of some of the homes the rich had built in San Miguel. Hemingway had made the town famous. Other ex-pats, along with wealthy Cubans, flocked to the area to be near him. Moises had seen him once at a gathering at the home of Professor Alarcón. He recalled him as bombastic and insouciant.

That critical moment in the study the night they liberated Alarcón flooded back into Moises's mind, Marcos firing the shot that killed the policeman and then another that killed Clarita. Now, decades later, Moises was sorry he hadn't turned in Marcos to Batista's men. How much easier his life might have been if he had. But for the revolution's sake he'd remained silent. But then, if he had, he might never have come to know Luz and to love her. Such was fate.

"*Bienvenidos*," called out a young woman with dark hair in blue jeans and a red and white top. Moises recognized her from the photos she'd sent. She waved, walking toward the car.

"Welcome to my home, Tío, and to America," she said in Spanish, embracing him tightly. She moved around the car to Luz and did the same. Luz's tiny frame nearly disappeared in her arms. "I'm so glad you're both here."

"As are we," said Luz.

Miriam took them by the hand and led them to the front door. "Normally, I would just walk you around the house to the backyard," she said, pointing to a path paved with gray slate slabs. "But I want you to see my home. *Porque, mi casa es tu casa*," she said, all of them laughing.

Moises was delighted that Miriam had retained her Spanish. She was Cuban at heart. He could feel it emanate from her. Entering her house he noticed the mezuzah on the doorpost. It reminded him of his parents' home so long ago. Aarón and Beatriz had explained to them that she had married an observant boy. She kept a kosher home, as they did.

"This is our living room," Miriam said gesturing to the left from the center hall. To the right was a dining room, behind that a kitchen.

Over the couch was a wall of family photos. One caught his attention immediately. It was of Aarón, their parents, and him, on the day of Aarón's Bar Mitzvah. He learned later that Aarón hid it in his suitcase the day he left Cuba.

Moises's consciousness drifted back. The Cuba of his childhood flooded into his mind. How simple things were then.

Tío Benny took that picture. A heavy sadness settled on Moises for a moment. Tío Benny was gone. Moises had tried to get him out of *Presidio Modelo*, but the old man just wouldn't give in to new realities. He died there. Moises was never sure of what or how. The official record listed pneumonia. Or it might have been something worse which Benny would have invited upon himself by his obstinance.

"You can leave your bag there," Miriam said, her voice grabbing Moises's attention, bringing him back to the present. "Let me show you the rest of the house, and then come meet my family."

Moises admired the comfortable, somehow familiar feel of Miriam's home. It reflected who she was, securely grounded in Jewish, American, and Cuban influences. He was surprised to find several more old photos around the house—photos he thought were long lost—of his grandparents whom he'd never met, of his parents on their wedding day, even one of him as an infant.

"How did you get these?" he asked, as they walked down the stairs and out through the kitchen to the backyard.

"Abuela brought them with her," Miriam replied. "Is that unusual? I never really thought about it."

Moises considered his reply, making a quick decision. There was no need to revisit some of the more draconian policies of that time. Mistakes were made, recognized, corrected, and better forgotten.

"Let me introduce you to my children," Miriam said.

The bright sunlight blinded Moises as they left the house, Luz just behind him. Miriam led them across the yard to a semi-circle of chairs near a low table. Three children, all under ten, gathered around.

“This is David, our oldest,” Miriam said, in Spanish.

“*Bienvenidos, tío y tía,*” the boy said, his accent as *gringo* as any Moises had ever heard, but his effort touching.

“And these are my twins, Elise and Alice.”

With a moment’s hesitation, the twins repeated the same Spanish greeting. “*Bienvenidos, tío y tía.*”

“*Gracias,*” Moises said.

“Nice to meet you,” Luz added, reaching out and touching the twins gently on their heads.

“You speak English!” one of them said.

“Yust a little,” Luz replied. “I studied in school, more than fifty years ago,” she added in Spanish, turning back to Miriam.

A tall, thin, dark-haired, man around Miriam’s age approached. “And this is my husband, Saul,” Miriam said.

“So glad you’re here with us.”

“And clearly, he hasn’t learned one word of Spanish,” Miriam said to Moises and Luz in Spanish. “Go, cook some burgers for my aunt and uncle.” Miriam sat with Moises and Luz. “We are all so delighted you’re finally here.”

“We are too,” Luz said. “It took too many years.”

“Yes. I hope I’ll be able to come to Cuba to visit at some point. The government makes it very difficult.”

Moises nodded. “The embargo. You would think it’s time…”

Luz put her hand over his. “Yes, yes, that would be nice,” he said, smiling. “To see where you were born.”

“And to meet my cousins.”

“That, too,” Moises replied, “but only Patricia. Nestor is in Spain now.”

"Yes. You wrote to me about that. And how is Raul doing in Israel?"

Moises felt the same tug at his heart he felt a little earlier when he saw the old photo of himself with Aarón and his parents. Those he loved so far from him or gone altogether.

"He's doing well, or so he tells us in his letters. Phone calls are difficult…"

Havana
late 1990

Moises sat deep in thought at his desk. As vice deputy for international trade, Moises's office reflected his position, a "once-upon-a-time" suite on the top floor of the former Hotel Esperanza. Chipping paint and stained carpet betrayed the fading elegance. He even had a small terrace.

Though converted to offices long ago, the space still looked like a 1950s hotel room. French-style moldings on the plaster walls, crystal chandeliers, and an expansive, four-piece bathroom, though the toilet no longer emptied without the aid of a bucket of water.

The Ministries of Trade and Agriculture shared the building. Moises's position straddled both. The ghosts of American tourists still lingered in the corners and shadows. The swimming pool, once one of the most sought after social scenes in Havana, was visible from Moises's terrace, though it hadn't seen a drop of water in thirty years.

The stats Moises was reviewing were troubling at best,

disastrous at worst. Sugar prices had dropped through the floor. The Soviet Union, Cuba's biggest trading partner, was disintegrating. Events affecting Cuba's position in the world since the fall of the Berlin Wall were gaining momentum. The Eastern Block was collapsing. Moises had to find new trading partners, and quickly. Otherwise, this year's sugar crop, sitting in aging warehouse facilities subject to heat and rain, would be lost entirely. The government had about as much ability to maintain those storage facilities as they had to convert the Esperanza to modern offices. And then there was the never-ending theft.

In the nearly forty years since Moises first become a socialist, he would never have considered that the liberated republics of Eastern Europe would opt out. They claimed they wanted to pursue socialism in their own way. He saw that as an equivocation. Agents of the United States had subverted the people and the communist movement there in the same way they sought to subvert Cuba and its revolution.

The difference? Cubans were stalwart. They didn't suffer from the stasis of physical proximity to Moscow. When they made a mistake, they corrected it. Fidel was pragmatic. The people loved him and were grateful for the many benefits the revolution brought them. Illiteracy was gone, medical care was available to all, and no one slept in the street or lived on rooftops. They had come far but still had a long way to go. Now, a major bump appeared on the horizon.

Moises dialed his secretary's extension. "Adina, please contact both the Minister of Trade and the Minister of Agriculture and find out when they are available for a joint meeting. And tell them it's urgent."

"Of course," she said, hanging up quickly.

Moises took a small bottle of soda from inside the miniature refrigerator in what was once the suite's kitchenette. The refrigerator was a minor miracle. Nearly fifty years old, it still chilled his beverages. He popped the top with an old bottle opener, the Hotel Esperanza's insignia etched into it.

Moises walked a few feet to the terrace and looked out over the rooftops of Havana. Sadly, the city hadn't aged well. It was crumbling, like a living ruin. He blamed the embargo as he did for just about everything. As a trade official, he knew how difficult it was for Cuba to navigate the persistent, never-abating anger of the Americans. They wanted to strangle the island nation as punishment for its David-standing-up-to-Goliath audacity. Soviet support kept them afloat, allowed some level of economic stability, and until recently, growth. He feared that path would end now.

"Come in," Moises called out at the knock on the door. Why hadn't Adina just buzzed him to confirm the appointment?

Raul stood in the doorway. Now twenty-five, Raul had drifted away from them. Moises attributed it to his age and his desire to become an adult. He was confounded by circumstances to do so.

He still lived with them. There was no other choice. Housing was scarce and single men fell at the bottom of the list. Moises and Luz gave him their living room to provide him with as much privacy as possible. He disappeared behind its curtained entrance when he came home, rarely venturing out for more than a few minutes to eat something in the late evening. Some nights he didn't come home at all. Moises didn't question him. He was surprised by Raul's visit and delighted to have some time alone with him. "Welcome, *mijo*. I'm happy to see you. What a surprise! What brings you here?"

Raul embraced Moises and held him for a long moment. "I wanted to speak to you about something. Alone. There's nowhere at home to have a private conversation."

Moises led Raul to the terrace. Raul took the chair farthest from the door, an old, art deco lounger. The green paint on the arms was chipped, revealing the dull metal underneath.

"Is something wrong?"

Raul hesitated for a moment. "It's not that something is wrong, *papá*. It's that, to the contrary, perhaps, something is finally right."

"I don't understand," Moises replied. "That sounds like a riddle."

"Well, I'm not really sure where to start," Raul said.

"How about the beginning?"

Raul nodded. "I'm very appreciative of how much you've helped me; a spot at the University, a job..."

"No need to thank me. You earned that all yourself."

Raul smiled. "That remains to be seen."

Moises avoided glancing at his watch, though he felt compelled to. He wanted Raul to feel he was available to him though he was preoccupied with the problems on his desk.

Raul gazed out over the city. He relaxed a bit. "Considering the situation here, and what's happening in the world...I don't think I have a future here. I want to leave Cuba."

Moises's heart skipped a beat. "What are you talking about?"

"*Papá*, communism, this way of life, it's over." Raul leaned back into the lounger. "And I don't believe in it. I find it hard to fathom you still do." He looked out over the cityscape and gestured. "Look at Havana. It's crumbling. With what's happening in Europe and the Soviet Union, I'd say we're in for very difficult times. This system hasn't worked."

Moises took Raul's declaration like a dagger. "That's a rather broad statement." He too gestured defensively toward the city sprawled out before them. "We can build socialism here, without the Russians. We are unique." Moises felt his heart racing. Raul's expression—a youthful disregard for Moises's position—told him more than any words could. He reverted to a more practical argument. "And where do you plan to go? The embargo limits your options."

"Israel," Raul replied, without missing a beat.

Moises was stunned, too caught off guard to respond before Raul spoke again.

"I've been thinking about who I am, who we are."

Moises's voice rose, despite his efforts to control it. "What are you talking about?"

"Our name, it's not very Cuban." Raul's smile infuriated Moises even more.

"There's nothing about us that isn't Cuban. People came here from all over the world. We're Cubans. Your mother and I are veterans of the revolution."

"That's all true," Raul conceded, "but it's a Jewish name. And not just any Jewish name. It means we come from the priestly class."

Raul's anger grew exponentially. "Where did you learn that? Who has been filling your head with this nonsense?"

Raul stiffened, his smile gone. "I went to the Patronato. I was curious. I wanted to know more about who I am, where we came from. I knew I couldn't ask you."

"You can ask me anything" Moises snapped. "I've never lied to you." His mind flipped back a decade and a half, sitting in a hospital room explaining to Raul how he would have to live his life, a hypodermic in one hand and a vial of insulin in the other. Not an easy thing for a parent to do.

Raul took another stab at Moises's heart. "I had to find out for myself, without your filters."

Moises pushed himself up from his chair. He turned away from Raul.

"I'm sorry, I shouldn't have said that."

Moises calmed himself. He knew anger wouldn't serve his argument. "And what did you find at the Patronato."

"I met an old man there. His name is Avraham Silverstein. He knew your father, my grandfather."

Tío Avi. Moises smiled. He remembered him fondly. He'd swiped an old printing machine from Tío Avi's junkpile just before the revolution. Moises didn't know Avi was still alive and in Havana. He thought he'd fled with the other ninety percent of Cuba's pre-revolution Jewish community.

"And what did he tell you?"

"He said my grandfather was a good man who got a bad deal."

A vision of his parents materialized in Moises's mind's

eye. He remembered them as they were when he was a boy; young. He'd loved them both very deeply. That love exploded, disappeared into thin air that day at Aarón and Beatriz's wedding, his father forcing him to choose between them and the woman he loved. What parent does that? What kind of parent does that?

"And what exactly do you think that means?" Moises demanded.

"Fidel took everything from them." Raul hesitated for a moment. He leaned forward. He took a velvet bag from the cloth knapsack he carried with him and laid it on the rusting table between them. "Couldn't you have helped them? Why didn't we ever see them? Why do you never speak of them? This was your father's," he said, pushing the bag a bit farther across the table. "He left it at the Patronato. He wasn't able to retrieve it before they left for the United States."

Moises felt as if he'd been hit by a wrecking ball. The sight of his father's tallis bag and the prayer shawl he knew was within was more than he could possibly digest after what Raul had already said.

"It's not quite all that simple." Moises took a deep breath to quiet himself, wanting to avoid a shouting match. "I did help them. As much as I could. I softened the blows as much as possible. If not for my intervention, they would have lost their home when their factory was nationalized. I interceded. They were permitted to stay there until they died. Instead, a few years later, they chose to leave. As to contact with them? When they left you were only two years old. I hadn't spoken to them since my brother's wedding, some eight years earlier."

"Why?"

"For exactly the reason you came here to speak to me today." Moises puffed out his chest defensively. "They placed their religion above their own son, me. They cut me off for marrying a gentile woman."

"Patricia's mother?"

"Yes," Moises said, the anguish of that moment still as raw as a fresh wound. "So, when you tell me you have rediscovered this most divisive of identities, please don't expect me to be happy about it."

Raul looked out over the city, silent.

"And what will you tell your mother?"

"The truth."

The truth, thought Moises, is sometimes a matter of interpretation.

Luz sat quietly at the kitchen table digesting what Raul told them. Moises sat next to her, her tiny hand in his, this singular act of intimacy the hallmark of their relationship. He loved to hold her hand, regardless of the circumstances. Good times or bad. It made him feel connected and supported in a way he never felt otherwise.

Moises waited till he heard the front door to their apartment close. Raul told them everything, more than he had admitted to Moises earlier that day. He'd wondered about his grandparents for years. When he decided to learn more, he visited the National Library. Cohan was an unusual name. Yet, Raul had found it in too many articles and too many records. He had an uncle. He wanted to know more about him. Now he had even more questions. He went to the *Patronato* to learn what he could before he asked his parents.

At the *Patronato* he learned about the community. He felt a connection he'd never had to anything before, deeper and more compelling than the slogans and red kerchiefs of his communist youth league. He began to pray regularly. The grip of the *tefillin*[3] wrapped around his arm brought him a quiet calmness he'd never before known. He talked to God. He learned the Hebrew alphabet.

"When did this start?" Luz asked him.

Raul sighed. "Four years ago, when I was still at university. I met another student. She wore an unusual pendant on a leather string. A *hamsa*, an ancient Jewish good luck symbol. Protection against evil."

"Nonsense," Moises mumbled, his arms crossed against his chest. "Superstition."

"No, *papá*," Raul replied, "She wore it because it was innocuous, not easily identified as religious. It was safe, as opposed to a Jewish star, yet still an object with religious significance. It connected her to her people without making her a target."

"We were never targets in this country," Moises snapped. "Fidel has an excellent relationship with the community, those who stayed!"

"That's true," Raul acknowledged, "but nevertheless, outward expressions of religious belief are frowned upon. Regardless of which religion. As I said, that amulet served her well."

---

[3] *Tefillin—known in English as phylacteries, a set of boxes containing biblical verses attached to the arm and forehead during morning prayer.*

"What is this young woman's name?" Moises said.

"Rachel Pinto. She's a medical student."

"A Sephardi," Moises said.

Luz looked at him quizzically.

"I'll explain later."

"She took me to the Patronato the first time," Raul said. "They welcomed me. After that it was simple."

"And how will going to Israel help you?" Luz asked. "You don't speak the language. You won't have a job or any family..."

Raul reached for his mother's hand. "I know. But it is who I am. And they will help me to learn the language and become part of society. And I won't be alone. Rachel plans to go with me. We plan to marry. Her family has given their blessing."

"You plan to marry?" Moises said. He recalled his first few months with Ana Teresa, how he kept her a secret from his family. "We haven't even met her."

"You will."

"And you will have to serve in their military," Moises added.

"Gladly," Raul replied.

"If you leave, you can never come back," Moises muttered. Luz shook her head in response to Moises. Raul remained silent.

"We were young once," Luz said. "We saw the world around us and didn't like it. That's normal. Mistakes have been made here. Fidel himself admits that. You can make a difference here."

"I don't feel like I belong here," Raul said. "We have been here for a little over sixty years..."

"...Israel is only a little over forty..." Moises interjected.

"But our history goes back thousands of years. I feel it inside me...deep inside."

"Rubbish!" Moises shouted.

Luz reached out for Moises, to calm him. He pulled his hand away.

"You have a fire in your soul," Luz said. "As we did. I understand. The question is how? How do you intend to do this?"

"I don't know. But I was hoping for your blessing, or at least your support. And perhaps your help."

With Raul gone, Moises waited for Luz to speak. He saw the kindness with which she treated Raul earlier. He knew he himself was incapable of such kindness. There were many things he could tolerate, but not this. Luz, his children, and the revolution were the only constants in his life. They were the fabric that held everything together. He couldn't survive without them.

"You must contact Aarón," Luz said finally.

Moises felt his heart sink. He knew she would say this. "No, not again."

"We have no other choice."

"You're willing to let our child leave? You don't think we should convince him this is a mistake? We will never see him again."

"Did you listen when your father tried to convince you that you were making a mistake?"

Moises knew Luz wasn't referring to his politics. "That was different."

Luz took both his hands in hers. "How?"

"He was a bigot and a hypocrite. He claimed his Jewishness was more important than...me." Tears filled

Moises's eyes. The pain never lessened.

"And it will be the same with Raul," said Luz. "We have two choices. We can help him, and perhaps he won't cut himself off from us, or we can reject him as your father did you, and we will lose him, completely, whether he is here, or there."

Contacting Aarón was dangerous. A subject as potentially damaging as asking for help to leave Cuba, particularly from a party member and government official, couldn't be underestimated. A plan was necessary, and it took some time to develop it. Nothing could be done on the phone or through the limited mail service that now ran from Cuba to the United States and back. One couldn't say much on the phone as the calls were heavily monitored. Conversation was usually reduced to discussions about the weather, ludicrous in the winter months. "Yes, it's cold here. How nice, it's 85 degrees there."

This time, in the winter of 1992 when Aarón received a letter postmarked Mexico City, he knew who it was from and that its contents were serious. In the years since Moises's first letter posted in Mexico, he and Moises had re-established some cordial if shallow level of contact. They communicated primarily by letter through émigré organizations based in Canada. When letters were sent outside that route, the recipient had to be mindful of their contents.

Aarón was reticent about opening the envelope. He placed it on the kitchen table and went into the bedroom to change out of his suit to something more comfortable. He looked at the clock. Beatriz would be home shortly.

Perhaps he'd wait to open the letter until she arrived.

Walking back into the kitchen for a snack—something best eaten before Beatriz arrived—curiosity got the better of him. He reached for the letter opener on the cart next to the table and slid the point into the corner of the envelope. It opened in one clean slice. Inside was a letter of several pages, a surprise, as Moises was generally tight lipped and exact in his remarks, requests, and comments. He was a man of few words and even less introspection.

Aarón read the three-page letter twice. He was more shocked by Moises's honesty than by his request. Raul needed Aarón's help. He'd re-discovered his Judaism, or, as Moises phrased it, he'd "discovered" it, as he never had it to begin with. He wanted to "make *Aliyah*[4]." Raul used the term in a clearly derogatory manner, mocking Raul for referring to leaving Cuba and moving to Israel in that way, as if somehow Israel existed on a higher level than the rest of the world. Several paragraphs were dedicated to Moises's views on whether socialism or Zionism, though related, represented a higher level of human societal organization.

No diplomatic relations existed between the Cuban and Israeli governments and hadn't for the two decades following the Six-Day War. Raul would need a contact in the United States to arrange his move through the appropriate Jewish agencies and organizations. Of course

---

[4] *Aliyah—In Hebrew emigration TO Israel is referred to as Aliyah, which literally means, "going up." The Land of Israel is considered to be on a higher metaphysical plane than the rest of the earth. Conversely, leaving the Land of Israel is referred to as Yerida, to go down.*

he would also need financial assistance to make all this happen, including, Moises supposed, a plane ticket and help to enter the United States. He didn't have the money to buy the ticket, nor could he do so as a member of the party and an official in the government. He would have to distance himself from his son. Aarón wasn't sure from the letter if Moises was expressing anger or anguish.

The rest of the letter was even more remarkable. In an about-face from his unhappiness about Raul's decision, the letter served as an explanation, brother to brother, of why he would support Raul's desire to leave Cuba. He wanted to be a better father than theirs was, even if he never saw his son again. He didn't want Raul to live his life in anger, the way he himself had done. He never forgave their father for what he did and said at Aarón's wedding. He never would, despite the fact that his relationship with Ana Teresa ended in divorce. He noted that he was certain his current marriage would have been received in the same manner, despite what a wonderful person, wife, and mother Luz is. He wrote honestly of how he never stopped loving their father but never stopped hating him either.

"What are you reading?" Beatriz asked, her coat still on, standing in the doorway.

"Let me take that," Aarón said, reaching for the grocery bag Beatriz held in her arms and handing her the letter. "It's from Moises."

Beatriz perused the first page of the letter. "*Díos mío*," she said, sitting down on the edge of the chair at the head of the table, her coat still on. "How? What are you going to tell him?"

"One short sentence. Whatever you need, I will do it."

ഗ്ദ

Moises sipped his *cafecito* as he looked around the backyard. His brother was fortunate. His children were near him. He was happy for him. Aarón had made his choices, as had Moises. One truth nibbled at the back of Moises's head. In the end you really only have your family. He waved to Miriam and called her name. "Could you and Leah come over here for a moment."

"*Por supuesto*," Miriam called back, tapping Leah on her shoulder. They sat down on either side of Moises. Moises picked up the paper bag he'd brought with him. He took two small boxes from inside and handed one to Miriam and one to Leah. "I brought you something, one for each of you. These belonged to your grandmother. We thought you should have them."

Miriam and Leah opened the small boxes simultaneously. Inside one was a pair of pearl earrings, in the other a pearl brooch. "Where, I mean how…?" Miriam asked.

Moises smiled. "I had my ways."

Chapter Twenty-Three

The trip to Mt. Sinai cemetery took less than an hour. "We were very lucky," Aarón commented, as they pulled into the long drive, a large Star-of-David prominently displayed over the arched gates at the entrance. "With traffic, this trip could have taken twice as long."

Moises considered what Aarón said. Traffic. It wasn't a concept he could easily absorb. There weren't enough cars in Havana to create traffic. The American embargo and the cost of vehicles left Cuba a mostly pedestrian society. Long distance travel was done by train, bus, or lorry. The closest memory Moises had to streets clogged with cars was La Habana Vieja as a young man. Those jams were more likely caused by narrow lanes clogged with vendors and pedestrians holding up the few cars than by the number of cars themselves, their incessant honking demanding movement.

As they drove slowly through the cemetery Moises was overwhelmed by the sheer number of graves laid out in orderly fashion. Even the headstones seemed uniform, a far cry from a cemetery in Cuba, Jewish or otherwise.

It occurred to him that there were more Jews buried at Mt. Sinai Cemetery than had lived in Cuba before the revolution. A sea of dead Jews stretched out before him, each memorialized by an engraved Star of David, a seven-armed menorah, or some other symbol of the faith carved into stone. The scene gave the impression of a vast flotilla of small boats awaiting their flagship.

Aarón pulled over. He pointed to the right. "The graves are there. Just about halfway in." He handed Moises a *yarmulke*.

Moises hesitated.

"You have to. It's a holy place."

Moises relented without a fight. He followed Aarón, Luz and Beatriz behind them, past a concrete post that read, '*Chevra Kaddisha, Asociación de Israelitos Cubanos de Nueva York.*'

Aarón stopped a few graves down. Moises looked at the headstone. It read Cohan—Resnick, emblazoned with a Star of David above, a rendering of a pair of open-palmed hands expressing the priestly blessing of the Cohanim beneath the names.

At the foot of each grave was a smaller stone, angled slightly upward like an open volume on a bookstand. The name of the dear departed was chiseled in both Latin and Hebrew alphabets on each footstone with their dates of birth and death. Moises could barely remember the Hebrew letters let alone the words of the prayer Aarón now recited.

Luz came up from behind Moises and took his hand. He felt calm, instantly.

"I wish I had known them," she whispered in his ear.

"You would have liked my mother," he said.

"You know," said Aarón, "Your name was the last word she uttered in this life."

Moises felt his throat tighten.

"It's true," Beatriz said. "I took care of her that last year after your father died. She asked for you constantly."

Moises took a handkerchief from his pocket and wiped away his brimming tears. "I loved her very much."

"The truth is, you were her favorite," said Aarón.

"How would you know that?"

"I could always tell."

They all laughed.

"And *Papá*?" Moises said, taking a step to the left, standing in front of his father's grave. He placed a pebble on the footstone.

"You know, you never really gave him a chance..."

"That's not true," said Moises, responding more like the twelve-year-old boy that his father always made him feel like than the sixty-five-year-old man he was. "He never gave me a chance."

"He tolerated your politics. That was a pretty big thing."

"He thought it was a phase. He fully expected me to go to work in the business."

"We never know what's down the road," Beatriz said, brushing some lichen off her mother's stone. "If anyone told my parents they would lay for eternity in the cold earth of New York they would have laughed. They owned plots in the Patronato*'s* cemetery. They expected to spend eternity in the warmth of the tropics."

"Moises," Aarón said, haltingly. "May I ask you something? And it's not meant to pry."

"Of course."

"Did you ever see them again after our wedding?"

Moises hesitated a moment. "I saw *mamá*. Yes. Regularly, in fact. *Papá* never knew."

"How?"

Moises shifted his gaze to Beatriz. "Your parents helped us. We would see each other at their house. Your father would come to get *mamá* on the ruse that she was playing canasta with your mother and their friends for the day. I'd come to see her there."

"Do you think *papá* knew?"

"I don't know. If he did, he kept it to himself"

Aarón recalled the chaos in his in-laws living room after his first attempt to leave Cuba. His mother had as much as admitted she was trying to reestablish contact with Moises.

"I never realized how much I would miss her until they left to come here."

Havana
1968

Luz waited for the children to leave the dinner table before she told Moises what she'd learned earlier that day. She took his hand. "I have something to share with you."

Moises didn't like the sound of it. That was the way bad news was delivered. "Go ahead. I hope you're not telling me you're leaving me." He smiled, trying to break the unexpected tension.

"Do you remember Claudia Santos?"

"Yes, she worked with you at the trade ministry."

"She's at the immigration office now."

"And?"

"She was filing some applications and she found this."

Moises looked at the carbon copy of a visa application Luz handed him. It was for Rafael and Esther Cohan. They sought permission to leave the country to visit their son in the United States.

"So? If Aarón can afford to bring them to New York for a visit that's fine. He is their son."

Luz looked at Moises. "You know that's not what's happening here. They're never coming back. This is just part of the charade."

Moises looked away. "Then, so be it."

"You should make peace with your father before they go."

Moises's anger surfaced quickly. "I don't think so. I'm dead to him. How laughable, considering that Ana Teresa and I are divorced. But then, he'd be no more willing to accept you."

"Please, for your own sake, speak to your mother about it the next time you see her."

Moises found Esther waiting for him on the rear veranda of the Resnick's house on the second Wednesday of the month, as he always did. He felt a pang of sorrow when he saw her there with Lina, embroidering together and chatting quietly. This was the image he would keep of her. A quiet, gentle woman dedicated to her family.

"*Mamá*," he called out, the door closing behind him.

Esther turned her head and smiled, putting down her embroidery and pushing herself up from the deep chair. He embraced her and kissed her on both cheeks. "So good to see you, both of you." He kissed Lina as well.

"I'll leave you two to talk," said Lina. "I'll finish preparing lunch." She turned to Moises before leaving the veranda. "I'm afraid there isn't anything special today, just some picadillo with rice. I couldn't get enough beef, so I had to combine it with pork. There's very little in the market. Shortages."

Moises knew these comments were for his benefit. Perhaps Lina thought by telling him, the information would filter up the line directly to Fidel himself.

He took his mother's hand, as they sat down on the soft pillows of the low couch.

"How are you, *mamá*?"

"Good, *mijo*. Fine."

Moises could sense that something was wrong, confirming Luz's information. He decided not to avoid the conversation. "*Mamá*. I have to ask you something,"

Esther's expression was a clear indication that she knew what he'd learned.

"Why didn't you tell me that you and *papá* were planning on visiting Aarón?"

Esther hesitated. "How did you find out?"

"That's not important. Why didn't you tell me?"

"Because we thought it might cause trouble for you." She took a handkerchief from her pocket and wiped her eyes.

"Why are you crying?"

"You know why."

Moises felt a deep sense of sadness come over him. Luz was right, as usual. She saw things for what they were, without rancor or judgment. No one went for a quick trip from Havana to New York and returned.

The charade had been the same for years. Those with a few connections, a little money to buy a ticket or a benefactor to supply the ticket, and family outside the country would apply for permission to leave and return, but never return. The government, with a little lubrication, would issue visas. A wink and a nod. When the visa expired and the holder didn't return, they would be declared counter-revolutionary traitors. Their possession would be confiscated. Their remaining family forever marked by their treacherous behavior.

"When are you leaving?"

"In a few weeks. As soon as the visas are issued."

Moises fortified himself. "I would like to see *papá* before you leave."

Esther pulled Moises to her. Her tears turned to weeping. "*Gracias, mijo*. And I'm sorry."

Luz handed Moises the note Lina sent earlier that day in a small, sealed envelope.

"The Resnick's neighbor dropped it off on his way to work."

Moises opened it, knowing full well what was inside. *Meet me at Lina's on Wednesday as usual.* It made no mention of his father or when they would leave.

The next day, Moises took the bus to the Resnicks. He laughed to himself. Neither his parents nor the Resnicks knew that he had intervened on their behalf when their businesses were nationalized. The government planned to take their homes as well and move them to small apartments more appropriate in their opinion to the needs of the elderly. Old people didn't need large houses, young families did.

He'd gone to Luis and pled with him. After much deliberation, Luis relented. He said it was in recognition of all that Moises had done for the Movement and the Revolution. It would have to be kept quiet though. Who, Moises asked, would he tell? He never even told his parents or the Resnicks that he intervened on their behalf. He didn't do it for a thank you.

Esther was in the living room when he arrived. She was alone. He was nervous enough about the prospect of seeing his father for the first time in years but now was disappointed that the chance to make peace with him had evaporated into thin air. He was angry all over again, as angry as that night at Aarón's wedding. His father was obstinate. Let it be on him.

"Hello, *mamá*," he said, embracing her tightly, her small frame already quivering. "No, please, don't cry. Let's not let this be how we spend our last visit together."

With that Esther broke down. She willed herself to regain her composure moments later.

"I asked him," she trembled. "I begged him."

"It's all right," Moises said, comforting her.

Esther took a deep breath, shuddering as she exhaled. "He was so angry that I defied him. That we see each other."

Moises's anger hardened. Could his father be this selfish? Not only to him but to his wife? "It's on him," Moises said. "Let's enjoy our visit."

Esther took Moises's hand and kissed it. "I will miss you, *mijo*. But I will never stop loving you or thinking of you."

"And that was the last time I saw her," Moises said. "She handed me a plain brown bag when I left. Inside were three pieces of jewelry, a matching set. Pearl earrings, a pearl brooch, and a pearl necklace."

"That's how you got the pieces you gave to Miriam and

Leah yesterday," Beatriz said.

"Yes. I gave the necklace to Patricia before we left."

"*Papá* bought those for *mamá* for their twentieth anniversary," Aarón said. "Tío Benny knew a guy…"

They all laughed.

"Tío Benny always knew a guy," said Moises. "Funny, I was never sure if she gave me those pieces because she hoped I would pass them to my daughter or because she thought I could sell them for some emergency money. No one could have worn them in public until recently. It would have invited too much scrutiny."

"Yes," Aarón said, concealing his disgust at what he saw as communism's haughtiness. "Too counter-revolutionary."

Chapter Twenty-Four

"This was my stop when I started my first job in New York," Aarón said as they climbed out of the Fulton Street station in Lower Manhattan. The Twin Towers of the World Trade Center soared above them. "It looked very different then. The Towers didn't open till early in the 1970s."

The foursome walked quickly through the streets to the marina on the other side of the Towers. They passed through a large hall known as the Palm Court. It was nearly empty, a few tourists taking their morning coffees at the tables under the soaring palms, some couples in tux and gowns posing for what could only be wedding photos. Aarón led them out into an open plaza to a line in front of a sailing yacht, its sheets still unfurled.

"This is my surprise," he said, a broad smile lighting up his face. "The boat will take us on a tour of the harbor. You can see everything from the water! When we're done, I thought we could walk over to Chinatown for lunch."

Luz squeezed Moises's hand. "*Gracias*," she said, "*que bello*."

"I wanted you to see New York from a different perspective," Aarón said.

They took seats on the starboard side of the boat as it

started to move. By the time they motored out into the Hudson a breeze picked up and the crew unfurled the mainsail.

"It looks a lot different from here. More friendly," Aarón said, pointing to lower Manhattan. "I was overwhelmed by it when I started my first job."

"May I ask you something?" Moises said.

"Why not? You're my brother," Aarón replied, surprising himself with his response. Though they were brothers, he'd always approached his relationship with Moises more as one of an obligation by virtue of birth than brotherhood.

"Why didn't you go back to the law?"

Aarón lingered in his memory for a moment. "I thought about it," he said. "There was the language. There were the differences in the two legal systems. Re-education. It was daunting. The truth is, I took my first job with that in mind. But as time went on I realized I didn't have the faith in law, or should I say the law, that I did as a younger man."

Moises smiled. "Circumstances."

"Yes. I guess. The revolution changed me."

"It changed everyone."

"I was lucky," Aarón said.

"How so?"

"I was working as a messenger for a law firm." He laughed. "I thought I could learn their legal system by reading their documents. I would take their documents home with me at night and study them with two dictionaries by my side, one for English translation and one for legal terms."

Moises laughed. "Admirable but ineffective?"

"Very," said Beatriz. "I would find him sleeping on his books in the middle of the night."

"One of the partners in the firm caught wind of what I

was doing. He looked into my background. He learned that I was a lawyer back in Cuba. His wife worked for Jewish Family Services. She was aiding Cuban refugees. They needed Spanish speaking counselors. They hired me. Then sent me to school. That's how I became a social worker. Look!" Aarón pointed to the Statue of Liberty as they approached it.

"How beautiful," Luz said.

"The first time we saw her was from the air. When we flew here from Miami. It was the middle of the winter," said Beatriz. "After what had happened to us it gave us hope." Beatriz caught Aarón's eye. "I'm sorry Moises, Luz, I didn't mean it to sound that way. We made our choices."

Moises smiled again. "Yes," he said. "We all made our choices. And it is beautiful. Majestic. Like liberty, itself."

Havana
1998

Moises read Luis's note a second time. He was perplexed as well as irritated. He was a senior official. Why would Luis ask him to escort an American couple through customs? It was a job for the most minor of officials.

Moises considered asking Luis to assign someone else. He had more pressing work. The economy was just beginning to wake from the coma into which it descended during what was now euphemistically referred to as the "special period;" the economic chaos that resulted from the collapse of the Soviet Union. He knew full well what Luis would say. That's exactly why he had chosen Moises.

Because Moises understood the importance of demonstrating to certain guests that Cuba was ready to re-engage the world.

The "special period" brought the nation to near ruin. People were so desperate they attempted to eat plastic as a substitute for cheese. The housing stock had deteriorated so badly that not only did Havana look like a crumbling ruin from the outside, it was also a crumbling ruin on the inside. Pipes and electrical wiring that ceased to work a decade ago were never repaired or replaced. Once elegant homes were now slums. What were once slums were now nearly uninhabitable.

That same period brought personal disintegration to Moises's family. Raul emigrated to Israel some six years earlier. Nestor was considering leaving as well. He was seeking a visa to live in Spain. Moises and Luz were trying to convince him to stay. Things would improve, he and Luz assured Nestor. He, like so many of his generation, didn't believe it.

The discord in his family situation wasn't complimentary for Moises. The party was watching, and his sons weren't loyal. Only Patricia was committed. She worked for the party and the nation tirelessly. Though Ana Teresa hadn't raised her, Patricia had her mother's fire for the revolution. That was why Moises couldn't question Luis's request.

Luis provided Moises with photos of Mr. and Mrs. Everett Newman. He was a successful gallery owner in Carmel, California. Newman had met the Chilean artist, Dolores Garcia—a friend and confidant of Fidel—in Mexico in 1995. Garcia was well known for her murals and her leftist politics. Her husband was a general under the deposed Marxist, Salvador Allende. She invited Newman and his wife to Cuba in reciprocation for a gallery show they held for Garcia in Carmel in 1996. Moises was to escort Newman and his wife to a villa in San Miguel where Garcia was staying.

With little knowledge of or interest in art, Moises was unaware—until Luis informed him—that Garcia was Fidel's guest. She was creating a series of murals all over Havana to the glory of the revolution for the celebration of its fortieth anniversary in January. It was at that precise moment that he realized Garcia was staying in one of Fidel's private lodgings.

Fidel's perks as the Father of the Revolution and the nation were well known but rarely spoken of. He maintained the myth of his spartan existence. Moises was not happy to become privy to the luxuries Fidel and his closest coterie enjoyed while the people starved their way through the so-called, "special period." He would deposit the *gringos* at their destination and hurry back to his desk.

The arrival of their flight from Mexico City was announced over the airport's public address system. Moises pulled his party credentials and the special pass given to him by the DGI, the *Dirección General de Inteligensia*, and presented them to the guard at the gate to the customs and immigration area. The guard nodded, ushering Moises through. Moises laughed to himself. In situations like this, he often felt like his biblical namesake opening the Red Sea.

He proceeded to the area in front of the arrival gate, photo in hand. Some minutes later, Señor Newman and his wife entered the area from debarkation. He waved and called out their names. They smiled and waved back.

"*Bienvenidos a Cuba*," he said, extending his hand to both. "Do you speak Spanish?" he asked in broken English.

"*Sí*," said Newman. "*Yo puedo, un poco*."

"*Bueno*," Moises replied, adding in Spanish, "May I have your passports and your luggage tags?"

Newman handed him his documents.

"Follow me," Moises said. He would shepherd them through customs, pick up their luggage, and deposit them at their destination. His job done, he could return to his office and his life.

Merely showing his badge and pass was enough to clear customs. Not even a look at their passports. Their luggage was waiting outside the customs area protected by two armed guards. The Gucci bags were as conspicuous as they were numerous, all eight of them. Moises wondered for how long they had come. Americans visited occasionally, anonymously of course, but their visits were typically short. Rarely more than a week. Eight bags, Moises considered, was a lot of luggage for two people for a week.

Moises spotted Luis waiting at a car outside the doors of the terminal. He was surprised to see him here. Standing next to Luis was an attractive, well-dressed woman of about fifty.

Luis waved and called out, "Moises."

Moises waved back. "This way, please," he said to his charges gesturing at the same time. An armed security officer pushed a cart with their luggage behind them.

"This is Dolores Garcia," Luis said, as Moises arrived with the Newmans.

Garcia nodded and reached out for the Americans. “Everett, Loretta!” she shouted, pulling them in close. “I’m so glad you’re here. I have so much to show you in our marvelous country.”

Luis pulled Moises aside. “Thank you.”

“Nothing to thank me for.”

“There will be.”

“What do you mean?”

“I will need you to set the next two weeks aside. You will be escorting our guests around Havana...”

“I can’t. I have too much to attend to...”

Luis placed his hand on Moises’s upper arm. “You don’t understand. These instructions are from Fidel himself.”

Moises didn’t say another word.

“I think you understand. They are to see only what we want them to see. We need someone we can trust.”

Moises nodded. He didn’t want this assignment.

“And needless to say, we need discretion.”

The ride to San Miguel was quick. The Newmans chattered with Dolores Garcia in the rear of the limousine in English. Moises picked up very little of it. English was never something that much interested him. As such, his study of the language was rudimentary going all the way back to high school and university.

A security car followed closely behind. When they passed the barely paved road that led off to what was previously Professor Alarcón’s home Moises replayed that fateful night in his mind again, this time on fast forward. So much, too much, of his life pivoted on those few critical moments. He didn’t believe in fate. But he couldn’t shake the feeling any time he thought about it that something, some kind of cosmic force, had come into play that night and had carried his life forward ever since.

The limousine pulled off the winding, forested road onto a gravel drive that wound up into the hills behind San Miguel. The driver switched to a lower gear. Ahead of them in a small clearing was a high steel gate, attached on both sides to a barely disguised, electrified fence.

The driver pulled out a walkie-talkie and offered a code to the listener. A moment later the gate swung open slowly revealing a manicured lawn leading up to an elegant hacienda. The limo and the security car behind them pulled in slowly and up to the house. Moises noticed the security guards patrolling. He opened the car door and stopped dead in his tracks. Coming out of the house was Raul Castro. Moises had seen him at many party meetings and official government events, but never this close. Raul walked past him, his hand outstretched.

"*Bienvenidos*," Castro said, taking Mr. Newman's hand. He did the same with Mrs. Newman, kissing her on both cheeks as well, then embraced Dolores Garcia.

"We are delighted to be here," Newman replied in Spanish.

"Please, come in, let's get settled," Castro said, again in Spanish, Garcia translating for Mrs. Newman.

Moises stood in amazement, almost unable to move. Now he understood why Luis insisted he needed him here. This was very sensitive, more so than Moises would have imagined. But who were these people? Why were they so important?

"*Permiso*," the driver said.

"*Sí*," Moises replied. "I'm sorry sir, but could I ask you to give us a hand with the bags?"

Moises looked around at the platoon of security men walking the property offering no assistance. “Of course.” He grabbed two of the bags and followed the driver into the house.

“You can leave them in the bedroom in the guesthouse behind the pool,” Garcia called out to them.

Moises followed the driver again, this time through the living room then out a door to a large terrace. Steps led down to a pool circled by a tiled patio. The water in the pool was crystal clear, the bottom of the pool tiled with the same intricate geometric pattern as the patio. Beyond the pool was a small, single-story house.

“You can drop the bags in there,” called out a well-dressed, silver-haired, middle-aged man carrying a drink and walking toward them from the little house.

Moises and the driver walked carefully down the steps and around the pool to the guest house. The door was open. They left the bags in the front room, a casually decorated salon with wicker couches covered in soft pillows upholstered in bright, tropical colors. Several half-finished canvasses lined one wall. Off to the left was a kitchen and a large dining table and to the right a shallow hallway to a bedroom. Moises peered in. It was cool and clean looking, mosquito netting hanging over the bed. Just off the hallway was a bathroom. Moises considered using it but thought better of it.

Luz brought two plates to the table, placed one in front of Moises, and sat down. Before she picked up her fork she touched Moises’s hand. “Why so quiet?”

Moises wasn’t sure how much he could or should tell her. He picked up his fork and took a taste of the omelet

Luz had prepared for them. Eggs were hard to get, yet somehow, she found a way. It was prepared exactly as he liked, a bit runny and with some cheese and ham. Just enough.

"I had a very odd experience today," he said, finally.

Luz smiled. She tore off a piece from the end of one of the two small rolls she brought to the table along with the eggs.

"Would you like to tell me?"

Moises put down his fork. "I've never held anything back from you. I'm not sure how much I can tell you about this."

Luz leaned back in her chair, her expression one of concern.

"Luis contacted me yesterday with a special assignment."

"That's not unusual," Luz said.

"This is."

Moises recounted his day with the Newmans. He spared no detail about the compound in San Miguel. "If was the first time in my life I have ever been made to feel like a servant."

Luz hesitated a moment before responding. "You can't tell anyone about this."

"I know. I was leery of telling you."

Luz nodded. "You know who that compound belongs to?"

"Yes."

"There are many rumors. There have been for years."

"But he's the leader of the nation. We have to have places where important guests and dignitaries can stay."

"I agree."

Moises sighed. "Yet, I was so…I don't know what the word should be. I think I would say, disappointed. We, all of Cuba, have suffered so much, especially these last few years…"

"Sí."

"There's nothing to say, really. Perhaps I'd feel differently if I hadn't been treated in such a way…"

"Perhaps." Luz patted Moises's hand again. "Finish your dinner. It was difficult for me to get these eggs."

Moises smiled. Luz was, as always, a comfort to him. He cut off a small piece of the omelet. It hung in the air on his fork. "I bet one thing for certain."

"What's that?"

"The flush works on the toilet in that guesthouse. They don't have to pour water into the bowl to force the waste down."

Luz laughed so hard she nearly fell off her chair.

The following morning the driver picked up Moises at his building at seven o'clock. They made a stop at a warehouse on the way to San Miguel on the outskirts of Havana. The driver quickly packed four large cartons into the trunk and back seat of the car. He was silent the rest of the way to the compound.

"Do you need some help with those?" asked Moises as they arrived.

"Thanks, if you wouldn't mind, the security guys never help."

"Do you come here a lot?" Moises asked as they removed the cartons.

The driver nodded. He moved closer to Moises. "You understand whose *casita* this is?" he asked.

"Yes."

"I bring these deliveries regularly. I've been bringing them almost every day since the artist and her husband arrived."

"How long have they been here?"

"Almost four months."

"What's in them?"

The driver hesitated. "Let's say provisions. Follow me."

Moises took one box and placed it on his shoulder. He followed the driver around the house to the kitchen entrance. They put the boxes down on a long work counter and made a second trip for the remaining two.

"*Gracias*," the cook said.

She opened the first carton and removed six lobsters, and bags of fresh shrimp and squid, along with a blue tin marked caviar. In the second was produce, but not of the kind one would find in Havana's markets these past few years. This was fresh and of the highest quality. The third carton held meat. Steaks, also of the highest quality. More beef than Moises had seen perhaps since before the revolution, nearly forty years earlier. He turned his back and left the kitchen before she opened the fourth.

The driver stepped out of the kitchen behind him. He pulled a pack of cigarettes from his shirt pocket. He offered one to Moises.

"No, thank you," Moises replied.

The driver stood next to Moises, lit the cigarette, taking a long drag, holding it for a moment before exhaling. "I know. That's pretty shocking the first time you see it. After a while you just accept it."

Moises nodded. He nearly replied, ready to express his dismay but stopped himself. He didn't know the driver well enough.

"To each according to his needs," he said. He plastered a smile on his face. "Will you be driving us into the city today?"

"Yes."

"Good, let's discuss our itinerary."

Moises walked the Newmans around old Havana all morning pointing out the sites and explaining their significance particularly with regard to the Revolution. History is told by the victors, as they say. Dolores Garcia translated. He wanted them to get a feel for both Cuban culture and the fight the nation made over forty years against the American embargo.

Mrs. Newman seemed the more receptive of the two. Dressed in a light floral outfit with a matching hat and shoes no Cuban could afford, she smiled continuously, often stopping to pat the head of a child or touching the hand of an old woman. She was the picture of a *gringa.* Her unintentional condescension was offensive to Moises, but forgivable. She was clearly well-meaning if ignorant of both history and class struggle.

Moises noted how his fellow Cubans reacted to her. More with curiosity than anything else. It wasn't the Cuban way to be rude, especially to strangers. Yet it was obvious by their expressions that they hid little kindness behind their smiles. He believed they saw in her what he saw, a person of privilege whose government's actions deprived them of a better life. They still had their dignity.

Mrs. Newman dabbed at her forehead with a cloth

handkerchief that matched her dress.

"It does get quite warm," she said.

Garcia translated.

"Yes," replied Moises. "Did you want to take a break?"

This time Señor Newman translated. He said something else to his wife in English and then turned to Moises. "My wife has a request," he said in Spanish.

Though he appreciated Newman's attempts to communicate in Spanish, his accent was so severe and his usage so poor it was an assault on the ears. In addition, while Moises had led foreign delegations on tours of both the city and the country many times before, those efforts were in an official capacity. This was simply demeaning. And sadly, if tourism was to return on a large scale Moises realized, this was their future. Cubans would act as babysitters for those who could afford the luxury of travel.

"*Por supuesto*," Moises replied.

"She would like to have lunch at that place Hemingway frequented."

"Which?"

"*La Bodeguita del Medio*," Mrs. Newman said, over pronouncing each syllable.

Moises nodded and smiled. "Of course."

Moises led them the few blocks to the restaurant. It was reasonably crowded. He pulled the *maître d'* to the side and discreetly flashed his DGI credentials. A table for four was set immediately in a far corner. Moises directed Mrs. Newman to the chair in the corner with the best view of the room.

"How beautiful," she said sliding the folds of her dress under her as she sat. "And to think, Hemingway himself frequented this place. So exciting."

Moises laughed to himself. Hemingway haunted La Floridita, not this place. As a matter of fact, this place was too left-wing for him. This was where Salvador Allende, Gabriel Garcia Marquez, and Pablo Neruda among others, spent their nights eating, drinking, and arguing. Dolores Garcia must know that, he thought, as her husband was one of Allende's deposed colonels. Yet she said nothing, preferring to go along with whatever Señora Newman chose to believe in her own Cuban fantasy.

In the end, Hemingway, the great American hero of the Spanish Civil War, left Cuba. He and his wife fled in 1960 after hearing that Castro intended to nationalize property owned by foreigners. He never returned. Rather he sent his wife to negotiate the final disposition of his farm in San Miguel and the repatriation of his books and artwork in exchange for the donation of Finca Vigia to the Cuban people. So much for the "man's man."

The *maître d'* approached the table. He spoke in Spanish. Garcia translated. He proposed a typical Cuban meal. A fresh salad, *croquettas de camarones, churrasco,* rice and beans, and of course, *platanos maduros*. And mojitos to drink, pitchers of them, as this was the birthplace of the drink, a fact as disputed as Hemingway's presence here. The first round was already there on a tray held by a young woman standing at attention behind him.

"This is the real Cuba," Mrs. Newman said, sipping at her mojito. Garcia translated for Moises's benefit.

He smiled. *"Sí, señora,"* he replied out of politeness, hoping that would end her observations.

She looked at her watch. "This must be the lunch crowd." She turned to Moises, Garcia translating again. "I understand you eat your large meal at lunch and then take a nap."

Moises looked around the room. Ordinary Cubans couldn't afford to eat here, and government officials didn't take their lunch in restaurants. They brought them to work with them from home. As to *siesta*, well, that was mostly a thing of the past. Wages were so low and rationing so extreme that most worked more than one job in the gray market to make a little extra to buy what they needed on the black market.

These diners were mostly tourists. Cuba had become a popular destination for wealthy Latin Americans over the past couple of years. The government promoted tourism to prop up the economy after the collapse of the Soviet Union. No more guaranteed market for Cuba's goods.

"*Sí,*" Moises said again, politely.

Mrs. Newman turned to her husband. "See, they are just like us."

Moises struggled to untangle the English words.

"My wife says, Cubans are just like us," Newman translated. This time Moises could do little more than smile. That couldn't be farther from the truth.

Luz set out a light dinner in the living room.

Moises thought of the cartons of food he and the driver had carried into the kitchen at Castro's compound in San Miguel that morning. They feasted while the people skimped by. The thought made him both physically sick and angry.

"You're not eating," Luz said.

"I can't."

"Why? You love *pastelitos*."

Moises took a deep breath. He felt he was about to explode. He understood intellectually why he'd seen what he'd seen and why he was chosen to see it. Forever the good soldier, he could be trusted. He looked at Luz, his food still untouched. "I understand why Nestor wants to leave, and why Raul left," he blurted out.

Luz was so shocked she nearly choked on her last bite. "What are you talking about?"

Moises told her about his day. About the cartons of food, things no Cuban would ever see, let alone eat. About the ignorance of the *gringa*. Why, he questioned, would these people be invited to Havana? And who was this woman? This artist? Had Fidel lost his mind? Especially after the last few years. What the nation needed was a rebirth of revolutionary sentiment, a recommitment to building socialism and equity. Instead, Fidel invited an artist to paint murals.

"Shhhh," cautioned Luz, touching Moises's hand. "Quiet, you don't know who might hear you. Lower your voice."

"I no longer care."

"You have to. For my sake."

Moises took both Luz's hands in his. "Forgive me, *mi amor.* I never doubted my commitment for a moment, not in all these years. Not through all the difficulties, the disappointments, and the changes in direction. You know that. I put the people and the party before everything." He hesitated for a moment. "Even our family." A tear came to his eyes. Perhaps his sons would be with them still if he had behaved differently.

"Until today. Today I question what we fought for. I have been reduced to a tour guide for a frivolous, silly woman and her wealthy husband. I, we, have come full circle in forty years. What did we fight for?"

"We fought for our beliefs," Luz said. She moved next to him and took him in her arms. "We fought for our honor and the dignity of our people."

"*Gracias, amor,*" Moises said, his head on Luz's shoulder. "But after today. I'm not sure I still believe."

Chapter Twenty-Five

Aarón took the daily papers from the delivery box next to the door. It was a beautiful day, one of those early September days, crisp air, blue sky, not a cloud. While he still hated the northern winters, he'd come to appreciate certain other times of the year, particularly September, which in some way reminded him of January in Havana, the best time of year.

Moises and Luz would be leaving on Thursday. He considered their visit. It had gone better than he could possibly have imagined. They spent nine days together without incident. He wasn't sure he and Moises had ever spent nine days together without a fight of some kind. But then they were children, teenagers, young men. The passions of that age and time were long gone, blown away by events both large and small, personal and global. He couldn't say he felt close to his brother in the way some might hope, but his feelings of resentment and anger were gone. He could at least consider Moises a friend.

Aarón picked up the remote and turned on the small television on top of the utility cart in the corner of the kitchen. The clock above it read, eight-forty. Matt Lauer and Katie Couric chattered away as he prepared the coffee and put plates on the table. He thought he'd take Moises and Luz to Coney Island today for a walk down the boardwalk and lunch. If they liked, they could take in the rides at Astroland. They could brave the Cyclone. Brighton Beach featured Russian restaurants. Moises had visited Moscow once as part of an official delegation. He might enjoy it.

Katie Couric's normally chipper tones transformed into sudden alarm. Aarón took a step into the dinette to look at the TV. An image of the Twin Towers of the World Trade Center filled the screen. Smoke billowed from the north tower.

"It appears a plane has crashed into the World Trade Center," Lauer said, incredulous. Aarón stared at the TV in disbelief. It was a perfect, clear day. How could that happen?

Couric added, "we are awaiting more details," as Beatriz entered the kitchen. Aarón pointed to the screen.

"What's happening?" she asked, sitting down. She watched and listened as the latest details rolled in. "How?" was all Beatriz could muster.

"It's impossible," Aarón said, both of them now at the table.

"A terrible accident," Couric said, Lauer agreeing and mumbling something.

The alarm on the coffee machine brought Aarón back from the tragedy unfolding live on the TV. Though they all preferred Cuban-style *cafecitos*, each would have to be made individually, so he opted for American coffee this morning to save time. He took the few steps back into the kitchen quickly and laid out the fresh pastries he picked up earlier at the bakery a few blocks down King's Highway.

"*Díos mío!*" Beatriz screamed.

Aarón turned, pastries in hand. "What happened?"

"Another plane!" Beatriz shouted, pointing at the

screen. Aarón walked back into the dinette. There was a huge gaping hole, black smoke and flames billowing from the south tower.

"Another plane? Impossible."

Luz stood in the archway between the dinette and the living room. "Is everything all right?" Moises followed a moment later.

"Two planes hit the World Trade Center," said Beatriz. "They are calling it a terrorist attack."

"Where we visited on Sunday?" Luz said, easing into a chair at the end of the table.

"Yes," Aarón said.

"Moises," Luz said, "sit down," shifting over one seat to make room.

"What are they saying?" Moises asked, unable to understand a word as Couric and Lauer continued their updates.

"Sorry, sorry," Aarón said. "Forgive me. I wasn't thinking." He began to translate simultaneously. "They've grounded all flights. Wait, let me listen. They're saying they've received messages from a third plane, passengers saying their plane has been hijacked. It appears this is a terrorist attack." Aarón's heart pounded against his chest. He hadn't felt this kind of fear in decades. "Now they say a plane has crashed into the Pentagon."

"What's the Pentagon?" Luz asked.

"Where the U.S. Military is based," Moises said. "It's near Washington D.C., their capital."

The four stared at the scene unfolding on the small screen in silence. Both towers of the World Trade Center burned. The sight of office workers jumping from the windows rather than being consumed by flames was inconceivable. Both Luz and Beatriz covered their eyes. Couric and Lauer continued to supply details. Police and fire units arrived at the buildings. Workers were being evacuated. The subways were halted. Thousands fled, many with ash covered faces, tissues or just their hands over their noses. The Brooklyn Bridge was swamped with those escaping.

At one minute to ten, the screen was filled with gray smoke and debris. Aarón stood, now speechless. As the collapse became evident and was confirmed by Couric and Lauer, Aarón placed a hand on the table to steady himself. The image on the screen cleared enough to make the impossible real. "I thought perhaps the windows had blown out," he said. "The whole building is gone." He lowered himself into a chair, his hands on the sides of his head.

They sat speechless for nearly a half hour. At ten twenty-eight, the north tower collapsed as well, providing a moment of *déjà vu* only a half-hour old.

"May God rest their souls," Beatriz said, taking Aarón's hand.

They spent the day watching the aftermath of the attacks. Perhaps thousands were dead in New York, at the Pentagon, in a field in Pennsylvania. The unthinkable had occurred. They ate little and said less. What was there to say, really?

By the middle of the afternoon, it was confirmed that the attacks were carried out by an Islamist group called Al Qaeda. Aarón had never heard of them. Moises had. He didn't elaborate. By dinnertime, the parameters of the attack began to solidify. "How could they hate us so?" Aarón asked, almost rhetorically, as they began dinner.

"Why does that surprise you?" Moises replied, almost as rhetorically.

Aarón was speechless. Had he just heard that? He gave Moises a moment to correct himself, to withdraw what he said. Instead, Moises went about eating his dinner.

Aarón put down his knife and fork. “Did I hear you correctly?”

Moises stopped eating. “Yes.”

In his mind’s eye, Aarón was transported back to their parents’ house. Moises was defending the Movement, blaming the Americans for every problem in Cuba. It never occurred to him that Cubans were responsible for their own failures.

“We are to blame for an attack on our country?”

Moises straightened his back and took a deep breath. “It has always been like this. Your government can’t stop meddling in other peoples’ lives, the lives of other nations. You manipulate the weak to serve your interests. This is no different than what happened in Cuba. All over Latin America. You *gringos* viewed Latin America as your playground. You’ve done the same in the Middle East. This is the result. You reap what you sow. It was inevitable.” With that, Moises picked up his knife and fork and continued eating.

Aarón stood. “How dare you. In my house. You are a guest in my house.”

“How dare I?” Moises said, dropping his cutlery. “Things haven’t changed, and clearly, things haven’t changed between us, either. I speak the truth!”

Moises stood now as well. “You never want to face the truth. What happened in Cuba? What happened in Vietnam? What’s happened now? You and your government think you can control the world, others’ wealth and resources, forever. And what’s worse, America thinks it’s special, entitled, exceptional!” Moises screamed. “Let me tell you, you’re not. And if your government and this country don’t learn that, this won’t be the last time!”

"Communist!" Aarón shouted, pushing the table to one side, his fists clenched.

"Aarón!" shouted Beatriz. "Stop, that's enough!"

"*¿Basta?*" Aarón screamed. "Enough? He's exactly as he always was. A fool! I'll show you who's special, who's entitled, who is exceptional!"

With that Aarón moved quickly around the table, lithe and agile in a way he hadn't in decades.

"This country," he said as he pulled back his arm to propel his fist, "has given me everything I have, after you and your friends took away everything I had. It gave your parents a place of refuge from their persecutors. And what's worse? You were one of them!"

Aarón launched his fist at Moises's face. Luz pulled Moises away. Aarón lunged over the table, crashing into the breakfront on its far side, shattering the glass panes. Moises fell to the other side, the chair behind him breaking his fall.

Aarón forced himself up. "You disgust me," he said, wrapping his bleeding hand in a dishtowel. "I knew this reunion was a mistake," he growled then left the room.

Moises found Aarón on the porch some hours later, his hand bandaged.

"May I join you?" he asked.

Aarón gestured with his head to the lawn chair on the other side of the front door. Moises sat down, painfully. Though Aarón's fist had missed him, his resulting fall bruised him badly.

"I would like to apologize for what I said earlier. This is your home. I had no right."

Aarón remained silent.

"I'd like to clear the air."

"Go ahead."

"You believe I was selfish, that I put myself, my beliefs, before the family. You and our parents."

Aarón chuckled.

"I would like you to know the truth."

"About what?"

"About what I did and didn't do, and what really happened. You asked me about Ana Teresa. Let's start there. I didn't tell you the whole truth."

"What is the whole truth? I wish you would tell me."

"I knew you were in trouble when you tried to leave."

Aarón tensed. "When we tried to leave Cuba?"

"Yes."

"Continue."

"I received a handwritten note from Marcos Abreu."

The name awoke anger in Aarón. Though he hadn't heard the name or thought of it in years it was a name he would never forget. "How did you know him?"

Moises hesitated for a moment. "I knew him for years. Before the revolution. He was my nemesis."

Aarón sensed how uncomfortable Moises was. "You don't have to continue."

"I promised you the truth. Here it is. Marcos and Ana Teresa were lovers."

Aarón was caught completely off guard. "I'm sorry," he said, embarrassed for them both. "Some things are too personal to speak of."

"No, there's no need to be sorry. It was a long time ago. In many ways, another lifetime. I want you to understand."

Aarón nodded. He couldn't imagine what being on the other side of this conversation would be like. If Beatriz had betrayed him he would never be able to share it with anyone.

"At first, she denied it, then later, when I confronted her, she admitted it. Of course, she said it meant nothing.

It did to me and I told her so. I told her I wouldn't share her. In the end she came back to me. She was pregnant with Patricia when I confronted her."

Aarón was uncomfortable. He was about to tell Moises that he understood his pain in the hope that would stop Moises when Moises began again.

"I know what you're thinking: Is Patricia really mine? She likely is, but does it really matter? I raised her. Luz and I raised her. We're the only parents she knows." Moises chuckled, catching Aarón off guard.

"Abreu was a revolutionary, but too full of the old Cuban macho to let another man raise his child. Anyway, I was at my office when I received a letter from him. He asked me to meet him at the abandoned offices of our old student revolutionary group. When I arrived Marcos was sitting on top of an old metal desk. The basement was musty and damp."

Aarón watched Moises. His expression was lost in memory. Aarón knew that while Moises was sitting across from him on his porch in Brooklyn, he was really in Havana forty years earlier. After a long moment, Moises continued.

"Abreu had gained weight since I'd last seen him. His hair and beard were as unkempt as ever. 'What an odd place for a meeting,' I said, in place of a greeting. He asked me how I'd been, as if nothing had happened, as if no time had passed at all." Moises broke free of his memories for a moment. "I remember our conversation as if it happened yesterday. I told him I was fine, busy. Then he asked after Ana Teresa."

"Moises," Aarón said, "You don't have to continue. I'm sorry about what happened between us. Today and back then. I'm not angry."

"I told him Ana Teresa is well." Moises continued

without missing a beat. "And that we have a daughter."

Aarón realized there was no stopping Moises now. He was too deep in his memory. He needed to tell Aarón everything. Aarón felt that he was seeing his brother exposed in a way that was embarrassing for both of them.

"Marcos smiled," Moises continued, almost as if Aarón was not there. "Can you imagine? He smiled at me. Then he stood up and reached for his back pocket, taking some papers from it. He handed them to me. 'I've had a very interesting visitor,' he said, that smirk growing on his face.

"I unfolded them. *SOLICITUD de VISA* was printed at the top of both pages. I looked farther down the page. There was your name. I looked at the other. It was for Miriam, two years of age. I had a niece. That broke my heart. I didn't know she existed. Patricia had a cousin. I looked at her birthdate. They were nearly the same age."

Aarón did everything he could to control himself but the tears came, nonetheless. He stifled his weeping, ashamed of the resentment he held for Moises.

"'Your brother wants to leave the country,' Abreu said to me. I realized something was amiss. 'Where is one for Beatriz, his wife,' I asked. He told me she was already in Miami. That's when he told me that you'd attempted to leave the country with the child but only had two visas."

That memory was too painful for Aarón. He wept openly now. He sensed what was coming. "Please, Moises, stop. I understand. You don't have to say anything more."

Moises smiled. "No, *hermano*, you need to know. Everything will be clear when you do. To be honest, I was confused about what was happening. Miriam was only two. I didn't think she needed a separate visa. Abreu told me that no longer mattered. He said, 'we make the rules now. We won't sentence a child to life in a capitalist hell.' He was so arrogant. 'Your brother wants me to issue a visa for the child, and a new one for him,' he said. I asked Abreu, why he brought me into this? I'd had no contact with you in years. He said, 'because I have something your brother wants, and you have something I want.' 'What,' I asked. 'Ana Teresa,' he said."

Aarón's heart nearly stopped.

"'Let her go, and I will let them go,' he said. My mind was on fire. I was so confused by what was happening. "Your relationship with Ana Teresa is over. She told me so." I said to Abreu. He laughed. 'That remains to be seen,' he sniped."

Aarón thought he might vomit. This confession, on the heels of a terrorist attack, was overwhelming. "What are you saying? You traded Ana Teresa for our freedom?"

"Yes," replied Moises, his voice almost inaudible.

"Did you still love her?"

"Yes. At that very moment, yes. I looked Abreu in the eye and asked him if she still loved him. 'A passion like ours,' he said, 'even as a sleeping love, doesn't die.'"

"I shouted at him that I didn't believe him. 'Ask her yourself,' he said. With that, she stepped out of the shadows. '*Hola*, Moises,' she said, a smile on her face. 'I'm sorry it had to come to this.'"

Aarón calmed himself. He dried his eyes and wiped the tears from his face. Despite everything that had happened between them, he realized that Moises had made the ultimate sacrifice for him. He regretted the rancor with which he had regarded him over the past four decades.

"We have a daughter…I love you…," I said. She responded with the same reply I gave to you when you asked me about her and what happened between us; that the revolution will always be her first child. I knew then that Patricia needed me. That I had to put my love into her, to give her the best life I could."

Moises felt the tears form in the corners of his eyes, as they did whenever he thought of that awful moment. He leaned forward. In the dim light he sought out Aarón's eyes.

"You would rather be with this liar, this fraud, than me and your daughter?" I asked Ana Teresa. Marcos laughed at me, his guffaws bouncing off the musty walls. 'Liar? Fraud?' he said, mimicking me. 'What are you talking about?' I felt renewed and strengthened as I confronted him. "Let me tell you who he is," I said to Ana Teresa. You remember that night at San Miguel? The cop who was shot. It wasn't a suicide as was reported. The cop didn't kill himself for fear of what Batista's men would do to him for losing Professor Alarcón. Marcos shot him with his own gun. In cold blood. Then he shot Clarita because she walked in on him as he pulled the trigger. I saw it. Your lover is a murderer."

"What did she say?" Aarón asked, almost involuntarily. He felt now as if he had to hear the rest, despite how much he wanted the story to end.

Moises's body relaxed a bit. He sat back in the beach chair before he continued. "She wrapped her arm around Marcos's waist. She laughed at me. 'Really?' she said. 'Who cares about one fascist cop and a confused girl, long dead? Marcos fought for the revolution. Like you did,' she added, just to taunt me."

"Murder isn't enough for you," I shouted at her. I was furious. Was she so devoid of empathy, this woman I thought I loved? 'He's corrupt, as well,' I shouted even louder. 'You know that. I told you that night in our kitchen. The night you told me you were pregnant with Patricia.'

I focused my eyes on Marcos. "I uncovered your scheme," I said. 'What scheme would that be?' he snarled back, playing with me. "You extorted money from dress manufacturers near Santa Clara. I know all about you and Manuel, your nephew."

"Marcos laughed at me. 'That was a long time ago,' he said. 'Those factories are in the hands of the workers now. Those owners deserved it. They took food out of the mouths of their workers' children.'

"And you put it into your pocket," I screamed. Marcos smirked again. "Perhaps I'll go to Luis. Tell him what I know. 'Luis?' Marcos said, both he and Ana Teresa laughing. 'Who do you think was behind the whole scheme?'"

"I looked at them together, entwined in each other's arms. They appeared like a serpent. I turned and walked out of the dark, musty basement into the tropical sunlight. I didn't even say goodbye. I realized Ana Teresa was gone from my life for good, as was Marcos…and you."

"I'm sorry," Aarón said. "I had no idea."

"How could you?"

"You should have told me."

"I wasn't looking for a thank you. I had Patricia. Then Luz and I found each other. She saved me. That was worth everything. She saved me in my sadness. I should have known. She was always there. She, not Ana Teresa, was the great love and rock of my life. I have no regrets."

Aarón looked off into the darkness for a long moment. There were sirens in the distance, as there had been all day. A few cars passed, their headlights illuminating King's Highway. He wasn't sure what to say. What Moises just told him was more intimate than anything they had ever shared in their entire lives. His brother had sacrificed for him. He wanted Moises to keep his dignity.

"It all goes back to that night at San Miguel," Aarón said, finally. "That was the inflection point of our lives."

"It seems that way."

They were silent for a long while.

"Would you like a drink?" Aarón asked, finally. "I have some nice rum."

"I could use one."

"Beatriz," Aarón called out. "Please bring me that bottle of *Añejo* I've been saving. And two glasses."

A moment later, Beatriz pushed open the screen door. "I've brought you some ice, as well."

"Thank you, *amor*."

He poured two drinks and handed one to Moises. "*Salud, hermano*," he said. "And, I'm sorry."

"*Igual*," Moises replied. They reached across the porch and touched their glasses. They never spoke of it again.

THE END

Acknowledgments

When I wrote my debut novel, Forgiving Máximo Rothman, my wife suggested I send it to the Jewish Book Council for a review. Jewish Book Council assigned that review to Miriam Bradman Abrahams, who, it turned out, was a friend of a friend, Sue Kass. Thanks goes out first and foremost to Sue for introducing me to Miriam. It's Miriam's family story that is the basis for this book.

Incident at San Miguel, as my other works, seeks to examine the question of how ordinary people react to extraordinary circumstances. In the case of Juan and Pola Bradman, that extraordinary circumstance was the Cuban Revolution of 1958-59, which brought Fidel Castro to power.

Juan and Pola, educated, middle-class, in their 20's, and on the eve of marriage, were swept up by one of the most important and consequential events of the twentieth century. Cuba, a small island nation located in the heart of the geopolitically important Caribbean, would assume a new level of importance as a result of the Cold War far larger than its size. The Cuban Missile Crisis, which brought the world to the brink of nuclear Armageddon, was a direct result of decisions taken by both Fidel Castro as Cuba's new leader, and the United States, his antagonist to the north.

Juan and Pola were members of Cuba's small but prosperous Jewish community. Their parents immigrated to Cuba in the late 1920s after open immigration policies ended in the United States. Many who went to Cuba went with the intention of eventually continuing on to the United States. Some did. Others fell in love with this tropical paradise and stayed. They opened businesses, synagogues, and schools, and built lives.

Juan and his brother Salomon came from this very experience. Juan became an attorney and a Magistrate. Salomon supported Castro and his revolution. They found themselves at opposing ends of the political hurricane enveloping Cuba. I had the pleasure of meeting, interviewing, and getting to know Juan and Pola. Unfortunately, Salomon passed away many years ago. This is their story based on interviews with Juan, Pola, and many other refugees from Castro's revolution, and re-imagined by me.

In addition to Juan and Pola, I would like to thank, Barry Sharpe, Lillian Brosnick, and Ana Fitter for sharing their experiences as 'Jew-bans,' as well as many other Cubans in the United States, both Jewish and not, too numerous to name here. Also thanks to my cousin, Fred Miller, who proofreads my work and compensates for my inability to use a comma correctly. To Robin West for sharing her experience visiting Cuba. To my cousin, Professor David Pion-Berlin, for sharing his knowledge of Latin America, its politics, and its history. To Ben Sternberg, my son Jake's childhood friend from Jewish summer camp, for teaching me the basics of forensic accounting. To my dear friend, Reverend Dr. Nigel Pearce for his recommendation on a quote to represent what this story is all about.

To Jeffrey Markowitz, Albert Tucher, and Victoria Weisfeld, my friends and fellow authors for reading this manuscript and giving me honest and helpful feedback. And to Patricia King for her never ending encouragement and advice. To my son Jake, who I can always depend on to tell me what's working and what's not, and who reads multiple drafts to make sure I get it right. To my wife

Hope, who puts up with my endless, multi-year, writing projects.

Most importantly, my eternal thanks to Juan and Pola Bradman and to Miriam Bradman Abrahams for sharing this story with me. It's a story that needs to be told. While the protagonist and antagonist are Jewish, their experience in Cuba is in no way unique to Cuban Jews. It is, rather, the common experience unique to Cuban refugees, many of whom continue coming to our shores today. More broadly, it is the experience of immigration through the lens of economic persecution, a phenomenon still plaguing us today.

To Juan and Pola may I add:

Muchas gracias por su hospitalidad y su confianza y permitiendome a conocer su historia. A conocerte es un privilegio. Me recibieron como un miembro de la familia. Y por esto, siempre estaré agradecido.

To those who read this book, I urge you to consider what reading historical fiction does for readers and why it's important in understanding our world and its history. There is much value in well reported history, biography, and memoir. Yet, only a work of fiction, a work of the imagination, has the ability to place the reader in the head of the character to experience the emotions of that character as events are happening. That experience is the closest we can get to being there.

A. J. Sidransky
New York
October 2022

About the Author

A. J. Sidransky writes about ordinary people faced with extraordinary situations and events. His work has been well received by both readers and reviewers. Genres include mystery, thriller, and historical fiction. His work has been described as a mystery wrapped in history and tied in a bow with a little romance. His works include **Forgiving Máximo Rothman**, **Forgiving Stephen Redmond, Forgiving Mariela Camacho, and The Interpreter**. **Incident at San Miguel**, a thriller set during the Cuban Revolution is his newest work.

His short stories have appeared in anthologies, magazines, and e-zines. ***La Libreta, (The Notebook)*** appeared in Small Axe Salon (on-line) and was the winner of the Institute of Caribbean Studies short story contest 2014. ***Mother Knows Best,*** appeared in Noir Nation 5, an anthology. ***The Glint of Metal*** appeared in Crime Café Short Story Anthology, and Fictional Café Anthology. ***El Ladron*** *(The Thief)* was published by Rock and a Hard Place Magazine. ***The Just Men of Bennett Avenue*** was released in August 2022 in **Jewish Noir II,** an anthology of stories examining the intersection of noir and the Jewish experience.

A. J. Sidransky lives in upper Manhattan with his wife.

Made in the USA
Middletown, DE
25 October 2023

41367814R00205